Michelle Douglas has been writing for Mills & Boon since 2007, and believes she has the best job in the world. She lives in a leafy suburb of Newcastle, on Australia's east coast, with her own romantic hero, a house full of dust and books and an eclectic collection of sixties and seventies vinyl. She loves to hear from readers and can be contacted via her website: michelle-douglas.com.

Rosanna Battigelli loved Mills & Boon Romances as a teenager, and dreamed of being a romance writer. For a family trip to Italy when she was fifteen, she packed enough Mills & Boons to last the month! Rosanna's passion for reading and her love of children resulted in a stellar teaching career, with four Best Practice Awards, and she also pursued another passion: writing. She has been published in over a dozen anthologies, and since retiring her dream of being a Mills & Boon writer has come true!

BILLIONAIRE'S ROAD TRIP TO FOREVER

MICHELLE DOUGLAS

FALLING FOR THE SARDINIAN BARON

ROSANNA BATTIGELLI

MILLS & BOON

First Published in Great Britain 2021
by Mills & Boon, an imprint of HarperCollins*Publishers* Ltd,
1 London Bridge Street, London, SE1 9GF

www.harpercollins.co.uk

HarperCollins*Publishers*
1st Floor, Watermarque Building,
Ringsend Road, Dublin 4, Ireland

Billionaire's Road Trip to Forever © 2021 Michelle Douglas

Falling for the Sardinian Baron © 2021 Rosanna Battigelli

ISBN: 978-0-263-29985-4

07/21

MIX
Paper from
responsible sources
FSC™ C007454

This book is produced from independently certified FSC™ paper
to ensure responsible forest management.
For more information visit www.harpercollins.co.uk/green.

Printed and bound in Spain
by CPI, Barcelona

BILLIONAIRE'S ROAD TRIP TO FOREVER

MICHELLE DOUGLAS

MILLS & BOON

To Greg, the best lockdown companion in the world!

Thanks for the jigsaws, for always being able to make me laugh, and for managing to keep us in essentials.

There's no one I'd rather be in lockdown with.

CHAPTER ONE

THEY WERE THROUGH the 'dearly beloveds' and on to the 'if any person can show just cause why they may not be lawfully joined together' part of the marriage service, and just for a moment Bree's heart beat a little harder and faster in the hushed silence of Brisbane's Anglican cathedral. Well, as hushed as the crowded pews for the society wedding of the year would allow.

Noah might be about to make a mistake of monolithic proportions in marrying Courtney Fraser, but it was a little late to be standing up and pointing that out.

Could you imagine everyone's faces if she did, though?

She barely managed to suppress a shudder at the thought, but she couldn't suppress a sigh. Not that she had any real reason to object to the marriage, just gut instinct. And she doubted the Anglican minister officiating would consider that as 'just cause'.

Deep breaths, Bree. Paste on a smile.

It was just…seeing Noah about to make such a huge mistake had everything inside her protesting. She'd known Noah since she was a bratty eight-year-old. He was her twin brothers' best friend. She no more wanted to see him make such a mistake than she would them.

She glared at Blake's and Ryder's backs now. They were Noah's groomsmen—they had responsibilities! Why hadn't they taken Noah aside and talked sense into him…or at least grilled him to make sure this was what he really wanted?

She blew out a silent breath when nobody stood up to make a *Jane Eyre*-esque pronouncement to call a halt to the wedding. She pressed her hands together and hauled in a breath. Given the current divorce statistics, this marriage wouldn't be an irreversible mistake.

Oh, but what a wealth of pain and upheaval a divorce would cause all concerned. She wanted to weep at the thought of it.

'Stop fidgeting,' her mother murmured. 'You're making me nervous.'

Enough, she berated herself. It was time to stop being Miss Doom-and-Gloom, time to stop thinking such ugly thoughts. It wasn't as if she were a relationship expert or anything. Maybe Noah and Courtney would have a gloriously long and happy marriage and bless the day they'd met forever. She hoped so. Noah deserved to be happy.

Bree lifted her gaze from the *happy couple* to the stained-glass window and zoned out. In roughly five hours, as soon as she could politely and legitimately absent herself from the afternoon reception, she'd be on the first leg of her road trip—a road trip that was going to utterly change her entire life.

Her fingers started to ache and she glanced down to find them clenched in her lap. She flexed them, and swallowed. It was *normal* to find change a bit intimidating, right?

What about downright terrifying?

She dragged her attention back to the service in time to see the bride—an utter vision in white—push back her veil. 'I need to speak to you—' she pointed to the minister and then the bridal party '—in the vestry. *Now.*'

Bree blinked. *Say what?* Courtney had kept her voice low, but it still carried to the second pew where Bree sat.

The minister hesitated for two beats before silently gesturing for the bride to precede him to the small room off to the right. The rest of the bridal party followed with varying expressions of bewilderment and concern. Bree couldn't see Noah's face, but the tight set of his shoulders and uncompromising line of his back made her wince.

A murmur that all too quickly became a quiet roar went around the church. Bree exchanged glances with her parents, but they each remained silent. Nearly five minutes passed before a stern-faced Ryder stalked out and…

Dear God. Her brother was making directly for her.

'Bree, you're needed.' His eyes burned into hers trying to send her some secret message. 'Can you…?'

She rose and followed only because she couldn't think of an excuse to refuse. Not for the first time, she wished she hadn't come to the wedding, wished she'd made her excuses. Except this was Noah. She couldn't *not* attend Noah's wedding.

It felt as if every eye in the church—and there must've been over two hundred sets of them—was on her as she made what felt like the mile-long journey to the vestry. She supposed it would be awfully poor form to bolt out through the side door and get an early start on her road trip. Change might be scary, but *this*? Ooh, she had a feeling *this* was going to be truly awful.

Or not. Maybe this was just a minor hiccup.

The tension in the vestry squeezed her chest tight. Noah's pallor and the way he clenched his jaw had her own jaw aching in sympathy. As soon as Ryder closed the door behind them, Courtney swung to her. '*You* don't think I ought to marry Noah, do you?'

Whoa. Wait! *What?*

'That's why you refused to be my bridesmaid.'

Courtney was going to dump Noah. *At the altar?* It took what felt like a full minute to find her voice. 'I politely declined your request to be bridesmaid because nobody wants to be paired in a bridal party with one of their brothers. But more importantly,' she added when Courtney snorted—it was the oddest thing to hear such an inelegant sound emerge from an archetypal vision of bridal loveliness. 'More importantly,' she forced herself to continue, 'I'm Noah's friend, not yours.'

'I mean, I'm sure we could be friends,' she added with unholy haste. In another dimension, perhaps. Or in a galaxy far, far away. 'But I'm of the firm belief that, on the wedding day, the bridesmaids should be there for the bride and only the bride, not as some kind of support or sop to the groom.'

For the entire time she spoke, Bree could feel the force and weight of Noah's gaze—as if by sheer force of will he could compel her to make things right. She didn't want to let him down. But she couldn't make things right until she knew what on earth was wrong.

'Why didn't you tell me that in the first place, then, instead of blathering on that you weren't sure you'd have the time or if you were even going to be in town for the wedding?'

She lifted a reluctant shoulder. 'I thought it sounded politer than the truth,' she mumbled. 'Besides, I had a feeling you only asked me to make Noah happy and, excuse me, but I'm always going to pass on playing the role of the pity bridesmaid.'

Courtney inclined her head as if acknowledging a hit. 'You still haven't answered my original question, though. You don't think I should marry Noah, do you?'

It was Bree's turn to snort, and she made sure it was

twice as inelegant as Courtney's. 'No way am I weighing in on that. No one can make that decision except you and Noah.'

What was Courtney trying to do—turn Bree into the bad guy here? She'd pass on that role too, thank you very much.

'Why the hell are you having second thoughts *now*?' Noah ground out, his eyes blazing in the pallor of his face.

Bree winced. His every muscle was clenched so tight he shook. It made him look angry, belligerent, but she knew better. All of that mad tension hid panic…and probably a world of pain.

The finger he pointed at Courtney shook. 'I asked you to marry me *over a year ago*. You said yes *over a year ago*. You've had *over a year* to change your mind.'

He dragged a hand down his face and Bree's heart throbbed. Courtney couldn't do this to him. She just couldn't.

With what looked like a superhuman effort, he lifted his head. 'Look, wedding jitters are normal but…'

Courtney folded her arms over her tightly laced bodice. 'But?'

'But this is crazy. And don't you think it's a bit…overdramatic?'

He spread his hands as he spoke, but something inside Bree froze as she stared into his face. Her stomach tightened, and she backed up until she was out of the circle. She scrutinised his face and then Courtney's and slowly lowered herself to a chair.

Courtney's laugh held a note of hysteria. 'What if we're making a mistake? Doesn't that worry you?'

Bree's heart caught. Was she the only one who could see the sudden vulnerability in those china-blue eyes? Or was everyone else blinded by the vision of picture-perfect bridal perfection?

'We can talk about this later,' Noah hissed. 'We have over two hundred guests out there who are waiting to see us get married.' His hands clenched. 'Not to mention the press. The wedding reception is booked and a veritable feast awaiting, not to mention the plan for the honeymoon. I don't know what else you want me to do. I've agreed to *everything* you wanted.'

It was only because she knew him so well that Bree recognised how he bit back the expletive chafing through him. Silently she said it for him, *Courtney, he's agreed to every* damn *thing you wanted.*

He went on to name all the manifold delights they had waiting to share with their guests at the wedding reception, and the secret European location they'd chosen for their honeymoon and had so been looking forward to. He listed the myriad things they had to look forward to in their shared life when they returned home from their honeymoon. A shared life full of potential, purpose and privilege.

He spoke of holiday houses in Palm Springs and an apartment in Sydney, named the best grammar schools for the three children they planned to have, mentioned the awards and accolades they'd win in their glittering and magnificent careers. 'Courtney, sweetheart—' he spread his hands, his expression bewildered '—this is dream-come-true stuff.'

Bree swallowed the sigh welling through her. He made it sound amazing.

'We've talked and talked about this,' he continued, 'planned everything down to the smallest detail. I have every intention of doing all I can to make every single one of your dreams come true. Why have second thoughts now?'

It sounded like the most amazing dream.

Except for one thing.

He spread his arms wide. 'What have I missed? What else do you want?'

'Oh, yes! *You're* giving *me* so much.' Courtney threw up her arms. 'And what do *you* get in return?'

He stared. 'I get to marry you. I get the life I just described. What more *could* I want?'

Bree leaned forward on her chair, suddenly and achingly hyperaware. Say it, she urged silently. *Say it.*

'I get to be married to the smartest, most beautiful woman I know. A woman I never in a million years imagined would ever marry me.'

'I'm not some damn trophy you get to hold aloft, Noah!'

His mouth opened and closed but not a single word emerged.

Bree waited, her heart thumping. But still he didn't say it. For the briefest of moments her and Courtney's gazes collided. Courtney kinked an eyebrow and Bree found herself slumping.

Noah *didn't* love Courtney.

And Courtney had only just realised that.

Bree couldn't blame the other woman for running as fast from Noah as she could. But why the heck couldn't she have come to this decision last week? Or even yesterday?

Courtney pressed her fingers to her temples. 'Noah, let's postpone the wedding so we can talk…work through a few things.' She dragged in a breath so shaky it made Bree think she was only holding it together by a thread.

The expression on Noah's face told them all what he thought about that idea.

Courtney's throat bobbed as she swallowed, her hands tightly clenched at her waist. 'It's just a delay. If you really love me…?'

Two beats of silence passed.

'Or, how's this for a plan?' Noah widened his stance. 'We get married right now.' He pointed back the way they'd come. 'We have a church full of guests, the caterers are booked, and everything is in place for your whole damn dream wedding.'

Courtney's eyes flashed. 'But it's not your whole damn dream wedding.'

'I don't care about the wedding. I just want to marry you!'

'Fine, marry me in a month, then!'

A terrifying smile stole across Noah's lips then and Bree's heart clenched at the self-loathing she recognised in his eyes, though she wondered if anyone else recognised it as such.

'If *you* loved *me*…' His lips twisted into a bitter smile. 'Here are the options, Courtney. Marry me now…'

'Or?'

'Don't marry me at all.'

Bree closed her eyes. A man in love didn't give those kinds of ultimatums.

Courtney's lips twisted. 'My dream wedding perhaps, but not my dream groom. I'm sorry, Noah, but I can't marry you.'

He'd gone so pale it made Bree's stomach churn. He could fix this so easily.

All he had to do was tell Courtney he loved her!

But the fact that saying the words didn't even occur to him spoke volumes. She wanted to drop her head to her hands. What a God-awful mess.

To Noah's credit, he didn't beg. He kept his chin high and his eyes hard. 'You're certain about this?'

'A hundred per cent.'

'And let me guess—' his nostrils flared '—you're going to walk out and leave me to clean up the mess?'

Courtney hesitated, before turning to the minister. 'Are any of the wedding party required to go out there and explain that the wedding has been cancelled?'

'Absolutely not. In fact, I can do it with far less fuss and uproar than anyone else. And to be frank, I'd rather my church not be turned into a circus.'

Noah's lips twisted. 'The press are going to have a field day with this.'

'Then I'm leaving through the side door now.' Courtney picked up her skirts. 'I'm sorry to do this to you, Noah, but it really is for the best.'

'Wait.' Bree found herself on her feet. 'I have a bit of a plan. We all know the two of you are going to be pursued by the media.' Not just pursued, but probably hounded. 'Why don't the two of you leave—?'

'Separately,' Courtney snapped.

'That message has been received loud and clear,' Noah bit out through white lips.

Bree swallowed and started again. 'While you two slip away, separately, the rest of the bridal party can assemble back out there—' she hitched her head in the direction of the church '—as if the wedding is going to go ahead. It'll buy you both a little time to leave the church unhindered.'

Noah drew himself up to his full height of six feet one inch and the coldness in his eyes sent a shiver down Bree's spine. 'I'm not a coward, Bree. Courtney might be happy to make her little announcement and dash away, but I'm more than capable of going out there and facing the music, even if she isn't.'

Ooh, really bad idea. Especially when he was this angry. One look at his face and nobody in the church would blame Courtney for bolting. The press would go to town on him.

If Noah chose to annihilate Courtney's character in public, Bree wanted him to make the decision with a clear head, not this *fury*. She moistened her lips. 'It's not about being capable, Noah. It's about not feeding a media frenzy.'

'She's right, dude,' Ryder said. 'The two of you either go out there to make the announcement together or not at all.'

Courtney's eyes widened. '*I'm* not going out there.'

Ryder's lips twisted. 'Which is exactly what I'd expect of you...*now*.'

'Back off, hotshot!'

Hallelujah. The maid of honour could actually speak. Bree felt as if the only one doing any talking besides the bride and groom had been her.

'Why should it be your face that's splashed across the newspapers in the morning or on the TV this evening?' Bree said over the rising tide of voices. 'Let them drag out an old picture of the two of you and speculate to their hearts' content. You don't owe them anything.'

'And who'll cancel everything that needs cancelling?' Noah demanded.

'Goldilocks here and I will take care of all that.' Ryder gestured towards the maid of honour. 'You don't have to worry about a thing.'

She saw the exact moment Noah registered that whatever he did in the next few minutes would have repercussions on the company he and Ryder had built from the ground up. He could wilfully destroy his own reputation— and the company's—or he could go into damage control.

'I agree with your friends,' the minister said. 'This is the wisest course of action.'

Noah swore, making them all flinch.

'Do you have your car keys?' Ryder shot at Bree.

She nodded, blessing the fact she'd brought her clutch purse with her to the vestry and hadn't left it on the seat beside her mother.

'Take him straight to Mum and Dad's.'

Her? Why her?

'Whatever you do, don't take him to his apartment. The press will be swarming all over the place in an hour.'

Well, *doh*. But—

'Blake and I will try and delay them for as long as we can.'

Damn. Her brothers still had a role to play in all of this. One glance at Noah's pinched lips and the dangerous glitter in his eyes and she knew she couldn't let him go off by himself. Heaven only knew what he'd do.

'Go now,' Ryder whispered in her ear, pushing her in the direction of the door.

Refusing to give herself any time to think, she grabbed Noah's arm and towed him through the side entrance. Beneath the material of his tux, his arm was rock-solid muscle. Unbidden, a little shiver shook through her. Did Courtney know what she was doing, what she was giving up?

The woman was an idiot on so many levels. And yet Bree couldn't blame her for refusing to marry a man who didn't love her.

'Are you pleased with yourself?' Noah snarled as she drove her hatchback away from the church.

Uh-huh. Male logic at its best, no doubt. She understood his need to lash out, though. And as she was the only one currently available…

'Ecstatic,' she murmured, doing her best to keep her attention on the road rather than the bristling hulk of masculinity beside her. They said a woman scorned was a scary proposition, but perhaps they'd never seen a jilted groom. Bree would put them on a par.

'You had it in your power to convince Courtney to marry me and yet you refused to do it. Why would you serve me such a bad turn?' His brow pleated. 'Hell, Bree, I thought we were friends.'

His words cut her to her marrow, and she ran an orange light. 'Of course we're friends.'

'Then why would you destroy all my chances of happiness? You knew marrying Courtney is the only thing I've ever wanted.'

Her hands tightened on the steering wheel. 'I know you're feeling bad at the moment, Noah—hurt, angry, betrayed. But I refuse to take the blame for this. If you couldn't convince her to marry you, I don't see what hope you think I had.'

'All you had to say was that you thought we were well suited!' His voice rose. 'All you had to do was tell her we should *get married*!'

'You wanted me to lie?' They weren't the words she meant to say, but they were the ones that burst from her mouth.

'This is what it looks like at your apartment complex at the moment.'

Ryder handed Noah his phone and Noah grimaced. Talk about a media circus.

He closed his eyes. Everything ached. His temples pounded. His jaw throbbed. His throat burned with the effort of holding back all the ugly words he wanted to spew forth. His hands and shoulders ached at how tightly he clenched the one and braced the other.

And inside his chest an ugly gaping darkness lay in wait to claim him.

'Believe me, you don't want to go back there at the moment.'

'What's it like at yours?' he asked, handing back the phone. Ryder was his business partner and best man. His friend would be considered fair game—guilty by association—and Noah hated to have brought this furore to his friend's door as well.

'It's being staked out by a few hacks but nothing on this scale.'

But if Noah showed his face there... He shook his head. He wasn't bringing the slathering hordes to Ryder's doorstep.

'You can couch surf at mine,' Blake offered.

Blake shared the ultimate bachelor pad with two of the firefighters he worked with—but there was no room there, there'd be no privacy...and he couldn't face all the false jollification they'd rally for his benefit.

He understood it. He appreciated it. But he couldn't face it.

'Nonsense,' Janice Allenby said. 'You're staying here with us, Noah. We have plenty of room and we'd love to have you.'

A little gentle non-intrusive mothering from Mrs A would certainly help soothe the savage beast, but neither she nor her husband, Colin, needed the hassle of the media camped outside their front door. Janice was a high-profile public servant while Colin was a well-respected ophthalmologist. They were busy, hardworking people and he wasn't repaying their unremitting kindness with that.

It would kill him if they ever came to regret taking him under their wings. They'd all but adopted him when he'd moved to the area as an eleven-year-old—had even had brief custodial stints when his parents had been...otherwise occupied.

'Or,' Bree put in and then stopped.

They hadn't spoken since their harsh words in the car. He owed her an apology. And maybe she owed him one as well. He frowned. He wasn't sure about that, though. Maybe she'd had every right to say what she'd said.

Whatever the rights and wrongs of the case were, she'd brought him inside, rustled him up a pair of jeans and long-sleeved T, before sitting him at the kitchen table and handing him a beer. She'd sat on the other side of the table sipping a soda. It had been weirdly soothing—a bubble of quiet—before the rest of the Allenbys had raced in and the bubble had burst.

He dragged a hand down his face, suddenly feeling a hundred years old. When had everything become so complicated? When had it all gone to hell in a hand basket? How the hell had he not seen what had happened today coming?

He'd not had a single inkling that anything was wrong. Courtney's pronouncement had totally blindsided him. Just when he'd thought he was about to get everything he'd ever wanted.

When he pulled his hand back to his side and glanced up, something in Bree's eyes—the same colour as the milk chocolate she loved—gentled. 'Or,' she repeated, glancing at her watch, 'I'm leaving on my road trip in two hours.'

Very slowly, he straightened. What was she saying?

She dragged in a breath as if to bolster her resolve. 'You're welcome to tag along if you want.'

She shook her head and then rolled her eyes towards the ceiling as if she couldn't believe she'd just made the offer.

He frowned. 'Thanks, Bree, but I don't think—'

'Hold on a moment! *Think* about it.' Ryder swung to Noah, punching a fist into his hand. 'It could be the perfect solution. It's the last thing anyone would expect and, therefore, the last place anyone would think to look for you.'

Her father wrapped an arm around Bree's shoulders. 'Nice thinking, sweetie.'

It touched him the way the Allenby family wanted to protect him from the fallout of today's debacle. He couldn't avoid it forever, they all knew that—eventually he and Courtney would have to make some kind of public statement—but they'd do all they could to buy him some breathing space first.

And they were right. He needed a time out. His brain had shut down and he couldn't make sense of anything. God only knew what he'd say if cornered by the press at the moment.

And for the sake of his and Ryder's company, Fitness Ark, he couldn't afford to make a statement before thinking through what he was going to say very carefully first.

'It'd ease my mind to know Bree wasn't travelling alone,' Janice said.

'Mum.' Bree rolled her eyes again.

Blake shrugged. 'At least it'll give you someone to share the driving with.'

'As I'm not driving longer than six hours on any given day, that won't make much difference.'

'Ah, but with the two of you, you'll be able to go further faster,' Ryder said.

'I don't want to go further faster. I want to take my time.' She glared at Noah as if he'd just agreed with her brother. 'And I'm not changing my mind about that.'

This trip of hers—a road trip to Tasmania—was mighty mysterious. Not to mention out of character. Sure, Bree had flown to Hobart several times over the last few years to visit her best friend, Tina. But that had only been for the odd long weekend.

Why drive when she could fly? Why would someone who was always on the move suddenly decide she needed to slow down?

Whenever questioned Bree just said the road trip was the break she needed before knuckling back down to work and thinking about the next phase of her life.

Due to The Plan, they all knew the next phase of Bree's life consisted of starting up her own physiotherapy practice. She'd been working hard towards that goal for the last seven years.

Still, a month-long road trip to Tasmania seemed too... random.

Why hadn't she chosen two weeks on a beach in Barbados? Or a month in Italy and France? She was up to something—and he knew he was using it as a displacement activity to take his mind off what had happened earlier in the day—but tagging along would help him solve that particular mystery.

And it would get him out of town. While he had zero enthusiasm for a road trip, it was better than the alternative—staying put and hiding from the press. 'I'm happy to take things slow, Bree,' he found himself saying.

A bad taste filled his mouth then. He had no right to invade her privacy or to spy on her or force a confidence she wasn't ready to share. 'Are you sure about this?' He searched her face. 'It's a really kind offer and one I don't deserve after what I said to you in the car on the way over here. I owe you an apology for that.'

She dismissed that with a wave of her hand. 'It's forgotten already. You were upset. Understandably so.'

Bree had always had a big heart. The three of them—he, Ryder and Blake—had teased her mercilessly when they'd been growing up. But whenever they'd been down, it had always been Bree that they'd turned to.

'I need to warn you there's going to be a lot of singing to ABBA. I have multiple playlists at the ready.'

That made him smile. Ever since the *Mamma Mia!* movies she'd been ABBA-mad. 'Can I negotiate for a little Creedence Clearwater Revival?'

It was one of their ongoing jokes and an oblique reference to the *Die Hard* franchise. *Mamma Mia!* was all well and good, but it had nothing on *Die Hard 4*.

She laughed and for no reason at all some of the weight that pressed him flat lifted. 'I'm sure I can manage some Creedence, but no thrash metal.'

He was long past his thrash-metal days.

'Noah,' she said softly.

He glanced up.

'If you decide to come along, I want you to know you can jump ship at any time. You don't have to go all the way to Hobart.'

That was true. 'I could probably lose myself in Sydney for a few days. No one will be expecting to see me there.' It would give him a breather and mean he'd only be cramping Bree's style for part of her journey.

He hauled in a breath and nodded. 'Thanks, Bree. If you're sure I won't be cramping your style, then I'd like to accept your very kind offer and tag along.'

'Right, well…' She glanced at her brothers and then at him. 'All we need now is to pack you a suitcase.'

Damn it. He couldn't go back to his apartment. 'I'll have to buy something on the road.'

'Not necessary,' Ryder said. 'I grabbed the suitcase you'd packed for your honeymoon before that monster of a maid of honour tore off in the bridal car.'

His honeymoon… He should be getting ready—

'Also,' Bree said in her bossy tone, 'you don't get to drive at all today.'

His head came up. 'I'm perfectly capable of driving. I've been jilted, not crippled, and—'

She pointed at the beer he held. 'That's your third and it's not even lunchtime yet.'

Damn! She was right. He couldn't remember when he'd last had a beer this early in the day. 'Fine, whatever. What time did you want to set off?' He did his best to keep the scowl out of his voice.

She consulted her watch again. 'In an hour and a half.'

Why couldn't they leave now? He wanted away from this scene of defeat and humiliation as fast as possible. He opened his mouth, but shut it again when he recognised the stubborn light in her eyes. She wouldn't budge.

'We're having lunch before we leave, and you're putting something in your stomach besides beer, that's non-negotiable.'

He ground back a sigh. She was setting the ground rules—going on as she meant to continue. She was the boss and he was merely a passenger. He scowled at her. He couldn't help it. But then his scowls had never had the slightest impact on her. He swung to Colin. 'Do you mind if I jump on your treadmill for half an hour?'

'Knock yourself out, son.'

He was barely out through the door, only partway down the hallway that led downstairs to Colin's home gym, before Bree's entire family jumped on her with varying bits of advice.

Folding his arms, he leaned against the wall and listened. It was probably beneath him to eavesdrop, but today he simply didn't have the strength to fight his baser instincts. Today he couldn't cope with any more surprises.

'You need to keep a close eye on him.'

'Don't let him get too morose.'

'And don't let him jump ship—at least not for the next two days.'

'I want daily updates.'

'And, darling, please make sure he eats something every day. We don't want him getting sick on top of everything else.'

This wasn't fair. All this pressure they were putting on her. He appreciated their support, but he couldn't ruin her holiday. She hadn't had a proper holiday in six or seven years, and while he might be throwing himself a big pity party, he had no right to drag Bree into the middle of that. She had big plans—they all knew that—and he'd be the lowest of the low if he inadvertently derailed them. He'd never forgive himself.

'But get him rolling drunk tonight. If he passes out he won't have to think about what happened today and—'

'Enough!' Bree's voice cut through the directives and general mayhem. 'I know what happened today was awful. I know it has to be a terrible blow for Noah. But he's a grown-up. And he's *not* an idiot. None of you have the right or any reason whatsoever to believe he'll do something stupid.'

Noah's head came up.

'I am not a nursemaid and I'm not going to order Noah around like he's a child. We're going to head south, put some distance between us and Brisbane's tabloid press, and sing loudly to whatever takes our fancy. We'll stop when we want to stop, and eat when we want to eat.'

Sounded like a brilliant plan to him.

'Also, I am *not* drinking beer and bourbon. But I'll sip a glass of Shiraz while Noah does *if* he decides he wants to drink beer and bourbon.'

Drinking beer and bourbon sounded like a hell of a good plan too.

'No more,' she said when everyone started talking at one another again.

Noah shot downstairs to the home gym before someone caught him listening. Bree had it all under control.

Blake and Ryder cornered him in the foyer after lunch where he was waiting for Bree so they could finally leave this mess of a day behind them.

'You sure you're okay with this plan, buddy?' Ryder asked. 'If you'd rather hunker down here at Mum and Dad's…?'

He shook his head. 'That would send me stir crazy and you know it. At least driving will give me the illusion of doing something.' And heading somewhere. Even if it was a lie and his life was stuck fast in a deep rut and he was spinning his wheels in the same spot.

Ryder grimaced.

Noah's gut clenched. 'What?' Was there more bad news?

'I know this isn't wholly within your power, but I'd appreciate it if you could keep Bree's name out of the papers for as long as the two of you travel together.'

'Hell, Ryder, it's not my plan that Bree be named in any fashion at all—before, after or in between.'

His friend raised his hands. 'I know. I know. Just thought I'd mention it.'

Hell, if the press linked them together… His gut churned. He could just imagine the salacious headlines. 'You have my word.'

'You know, mate…' Blake leaned against the wall '…it'd be great if you could get a heads-up on what this trip of Bree's is about. She's been as closed as a clam.'

Bree appeared at the end of the corridor, but her brothers had their backs to her and didn't see her. He met her eyes briefly, though he couldn't make out their expression. He recalled what she'd said about him earlier. Her words hadn't made him feel like a victim. They'd made him feel strong. 'In case you guys haven't noticed, Bree's a grown-up now. I'm not prying into her private business. If she wants you to know what she's up to, she'll tell you.'

When he met her gaze again, she was smiling.

CHAPTER TWO

THEY DIDN'T SAY much about anything until Bree had cleared the city and turned the car onto the highway heading south. She darted a glance across at Noah. He didn't have his eyes shut, wasn't pretending to be asleep in an attempt to avoid conversation. For the first time—or at least the first time in a long, long time—she noticed what a beautiful profile he had: square jaw, straight nose…firm, inviting lips.

'Eyes on the road, please, Bree,' he said without turning his head.

She reefed her gaze back to the front. He was right. She should give her full attention to the driving. Except a tiny part of her mind refused to obey her. If he wasn't pretending to be asleep… Did that mean he wanted to talk?

If he wanted to talk, she'd listen, sympathise, and cast all the aspersions he wanted on faithless Courtney's character. In short, she'd treat him like one of her girlfriends when they'd been dumped by some thoughtless, good-for-nothing louse.

She risked another quick glance at him. Except, for some reason, it was coming home to her now with a ferocity she couldn't ignore that Noah was about as opposite to one of her girlfriends as it was possible to get. He was a potent mix of half-bristling, half-slumbering masculinity.

It threw her because she'd never thought of him in that way before. Not really.

Her hands tightened about the steering wheel. And she wasn't going to start thinking about him in that way now either! Lord, talk about asking for an avalanche of trouble to land on your head.

She forced her hands to unclench. She was a woman. She could see the guy was hot. But even if she actually found herself truly attracted to Noah there was no way on God's green earth that she'd ever get involved with a guy on the rebound. Especially at this point in her life. She was about to turn her entire world on its head. She didn't have the time for a man—*any* man.

But in the coming year she was going to need her family *and* her friends. And as Noah was practically family *and* one of her very best friends…

A tremble shivered through the very centre of her. Was she really going to do this? *Could* she do it? What about The Plan? If she went through with this she'd be smashing it to smithereens, and The Plan had been her safety net for the last seven years.

Gah, don't think about it now!

She gnawed on her bottom lip. She'd have time enough to go through it all once she'd left Noah behind in Sydney. She had days and days yet on the road to sort through it all. She and Tina would work it all out.

For the moment she needed to focus on Noah.

Blowing out a long breath, she kept her gaze trained ahead. She could at least ask the question. 'Did you want to talk?'

She wouldn't push. Pushing him would bring him to full-bristling masculine life and she had a feeling she should be doing all she could to lull the beast into full slumber.

'Not unless it's about why you're heading to Tassie.'

She recalled his words to her brothers—*'It's Bree's private business…she's a grown-up.'* Those words had wrapped her in a golden glow, warming her to the soles of her feet. But even as her lips curved upwards, she shook her head. 'Like I keep telling everyone, I haven't had a holiday in over six years.'

She wasn't ready to talk about the real reason.

'If you want to see Tasmania it'd be quicker to fly and hire a car once you got there.'

'Ah, but it's not about the destination. It's about the journey.'

He gave a low laugh that had all the fine hairs on her arms lifting in a delicious little shiver. 'Fine, keep your secrets and your inspirational platitudes to yourself for the time being, Busy Bree.'

It was the nickname he'd given her when she was eight. She hadn't heard him use it in *forever*.

'But be warned, I'll ask again.'

'Naturally. You're as nosy as Blake and Ryder.'

Eventually she'd have to tell everyone. But she wasn't ready to do that just yet. As soon as she said the words it would make them real.

'They love you, Bree. They worry. It's natural. It comes with the territory of being the youngest.'

'Perhaps, but, as you pointed out to them, I'm all grown up now.'

'But—'

'And their constant vigilance—which you call concern— makes me feel like a screw-up.' It reminded her of how badly she'd messed up in the past. Maybe she was being paranoid, but she now felt as if they were constantly keeping tabs on her.

'Nobody thinks you're a screw-up.'

It made her think they were simply waiting for her to mess up again.

He turned in his seat to face her more fully, but she refused to send him so much as the briefest of glances. It took a concerted effort to ease her foot off the accelerator and not speed.

'Bree, *nobody* thinks you're a screw-up. Everyone, your entire family, is proud of you. We're all proud of how hard you've been working and all you've achieved.'

'It doesn't change the fact that their constant vigilance, their constant worry, makes me *feel* like a screw-up.'

From the corner of her eye she saw him open his mouth, but he shut it again and settled back in his seat. 'Fair enough,' he finally said.

Unlike her brothers, Noah had always heard what she said—he acknowledged her feelings without the need to impress his own version of the truth on her. She'd always loved that about him. 'Thank you,' she murmured softly.

'Do *you* think you're a screw-up?'

She bit her lip. 'No.'

But she knew he'd heard her hesitation. While she'd had The Plan—and had stuck to it—she'd been confident all would be well. But now she was turning The Plan on its head, she felt rudderless.

She swallowed and ignored the panicked pounding of her pulse. All she had to do was come up with a new plan, that was all. She was on holiday…lots of wide, open spaces and long stretches of road…plenty of time to work on Plan B.

That was the real reason she'd opted to drive to Hobart rather than fly—the open road, the wind in her hair, and all the time in the world to consider her options and find a way to make it all…work. It had seemed the perfect strategy.

Except now she had a giant-sized distraction in the shape of Noah.

But it was only a temporary one. They'd stay at Coffs Harbour tonight and would be in Sydney tomorrow afternoon. With Noah remaining behind in Sydney, there'd still be oodles of time to think and plan…to come to terms with her new future.

'Music?' she asked, because she didn't want to pursue this conversation any further.

He heaved a mock sigh. 'Fine. Hit me with ABBA.'

Grinning, she hit play on her carefully curated playlist, created after lunch to remove all slow, sad and lovelorn ballads as well as any songs that mentioned 'I do' or weddings in any fashion whatsoever.

He laughed when he discovered she'd alternated ABBA with Creedence Clearwater Revival. For the next hour they both belted out the lyrics to the songs, woefully torturing the high notes and taking alternate parts in the duets. On the surface they were having more fun than it had seemed possible earlier in the day, but all the while she was aware of the storm simmering inside the man beside her.

When a song came to an end, he checked his watch. 'I'd like to listen to the news.'

She wanted to talk him out of it, but one glance at his face and she turned off the music and gestured to the console for him to choose whichever radio station he wanted.

The cancelled wedding made the breaking headlines: *Shock Halt to Society Wedding!* The full story claimed that Courtney Fraser had called a shock halt to the wedding just after the service had started, with neither bride nor groom reappearing after a short conference and neither available for comment now. 'Sources close to the couple quote irreconcilable differences as the reason the wedding did not go ahead as planned. The father of the bride says he supports his daughter's decision. It's believed the bride has fled to the family's private island retreat in the Mediterranean while the groom is holed up at his friend and business partner Ryder Allenby's inner-city condominium.'

With a savage stab of his finger, Noah turned the radio back off.

'I'm sorry,' she said quietly.

'They made me sound pathetic.'

'No, they didn't!'

'I should've given a statement.'

'And come across as angry instead? That would've been ten times worse and you know it. They'd have made it sound like she was in her right mind to cancel the wedding. Or,' she added when he opened his mouth, 'you'd have looked and sounded so utterly shell-shocked, as if the rug had been literally pulled out from under you. And while that's absolutely natural and an understandable reaction, the press would've had a feeding frenzy with it. You'd have been portrayed as a hapless victim, which *would've* been pathetic, while Courtney would've been made out as the villain of the piece.'

'She is the villain of the piece!'

She swallowed. 'I'm still glad you didn't feed her to the wolves.'

With a muttered oath he dragged a hand down his face. 'I just hate feeling like I ran away.'

'You didn't run away.'

'That's what it *feels* like,' he shot back, raising an eyebrow full of pregnant meaning.

He was right. He'd treated her feelings with respect. She should show him the same courtesy. She nodded. 'I'm sorry you feel that way. I know you're not a coward. And you can make a statement whenever you damn well please, but the simple fact is you owe the press nothing.'

'Where's that line, though? Ryder and I are more than happy to exploit the press when we want the publicity for Fitness Ark.'

Fitness Ark was the name of their highly successful gym franchise and the name of the brand of fitness machines Noah had patented.

'You and Ryder didn't sign a contract to bare your souls in exchange for said publicity. What would you expect from Ryder in the same situation?'

He was quiet for so long she'd started to think she'd come up with an argument that had finally held some weight with him.

'Ryder would never find himself in that situation,' he said quietly. 'He's too smart for that.'

'Rubbish!'

He stiffened at her rudeness but she didn't care.

She glared. 'I hope you were touching wood when you said that. That's exactly the kind of challenge one should never put out in the universe.'

'Why the hell didn't you think me and Courtney well suited?' he flung at her.

She wondered how long he'd been holding the question back. She'd been expecting an outburst since they'd left Brisbane, but the shock of it now still made her heart hammer in her chest. She had to tread carefully. There were so many reasons but to detail them all would be like kicking a man when he was down.

Why on earth had he wanted to marry a woman he didn't love anyhow? She sent him a sidelong glance. Short answer—maybe he'd thought himself in love with her.

'I want an answer, Bree.'

'Even if it hurts your feelings or you find my answer confronting?'

'Even then,' he bit out.

'You know this is just my opinion, right? There's every chance I'm wrong?'

'Absolutely.'

He wholly and totally believed she'd be wrong. She thrust her jaw out. She *wasn't* wrong. 'Courtney tried to change you.'

He swung to face her, his knee banging against the centre console. *'What?'*

To her right a sugar-cane crop stretched for as far as the eye could see. To her left the blue sliver of a river snaking through the landscape glinted and flashed. She let the serenity of the landscape filter into her soul before opening her mouth again. 'It seems to me that if people are well suited then they accept each other as they are and don't try to change each other. You didn't try to change her.'

'She was perfect the way she was.'

Bree snorted. 'So not true. She just wants everyone to think she is.' Which meant calling off this morning's wedding had to have taken a lot of courage, because appearances mattered something fierce to Courtney.

'She's not exactly what I'd call warm and pally either.' She'd never once made Bree feel welcome at any of her soirées or made any real gesture of friendship.

'You just have to get to know her better.'

She didn't want to know Courtney better. They had zero in common. 'Before you met Courtney, what did you like to do?' She didn't wait for him to answer. 'You used to like hiking and camping, jet skiing and water sports, playing indoor cricket and hockey. You'd try a new sport—rock climbing or white-water rafting—just for fun. When was the last time you did any of that?'

'I needed to make time for Courtney.'

'You didn't have to give *all* of it up.'

'That was my decisions, not hers.'

'You sure about that?'

'Of course I am.'

'She manipulated you,' Bree continued. 'Instead of doing any of the things you wanted to do, you did all the things she wanted to do—the theatre appreciation society, the wine club…society dinners. On and on and on until you no longer had time for even your weekly one-hour indoor cricket game on a Wednesday night.'

And even then Courtney hadn't been happy. Noah deserved so much better.

Noah blinked as the truth of Bree's words burrowed into the hard grey matter of his brain and stuck there with barbs that refused to let go.

'I enjoyed doing those things with Courtney.'

But had he?

Or had he simply told himself that he *should* enjoy them?

His jaw started to ache. The right kind of man, the kind of man who could win a woman like Courtney—the kind of man he wanted to be—would appreciate wine societies and foreign film clubs and mixing with Brisbane's elite.

In his heart of hearts, though, he still preferred a game of indoor cricket.

Which just went to prove what a failure he was. His bride had seen through his façade. She'd seen beneath the money and success to the rough and ready kid from the wrong side of the tracks—and it had appalled her so much she'd fled. *On their wedding day.*

His hands clenched. Courtney Fraser had been his ideal, the perfect woman, and everything he aspired to be worthy of. She was polished, sophisticated…charming, and she came from a good family—all the things he wasn't and didn't.

She knew about art history, how to host a dinner party for a foreign diplomat and who to be seen with, along with a corresponding knowledge of who to avoid. For God's sake, she knew when to use who or whom in a sentence!

What did he know? He knew how to engineer fitness machines; he knew how to calibrate them to create the perfect workout experience for every single level from raw beginner to advanced athlete. He knew how to broker business partnerships and drive a hard bargain. And he knew how to duck a punch. He sure as hell didn't know how to grease the wheels of social intercourse, and his grammar was second-rate at best.

Being married to Courtney would've given him access to the things he lacked. She'd completed him. As he said—his ideal.

Except his perfect woman *didn't* jilt him at the altar. A scowl built through him. Obviously he hadn't completed her. She didn't need a guy from the wrong side of the tracks made good. Seriously, what did a guy like him have to bring to the table to tempt a woman like her?

Money? said a cynical voice in his head.

He shook that thought off. Courtney's family came from old money. She'd joined her father's law firm as a divorce lawyer and would make partner by the time she was thirty-five. Courtney Fraser was beautiful, driven, ambitious, and too damn intelligent to hitch her wagon to a guy like him. And who could blame her?

She'd always been out of his league. He'd just been a fool for not realising sooner.

'Out of your league?'

Bree snorted, and he realised he'd spoken those last words out loud.

'What a load of superannuated, noxious old garbage with prawn shells that have been sitting out in the burning sun for over a week!' Bree's nose wrinkled and then she rolled her eyes. 'I take it we're up to the pity-party phase of proceedings?'

He had to bite back what felt like an entirely inappropriate grin. Bree could never just say *garbage*. She had to add a ton of qualifiers so the listener wouldn't mistake her meaning. To an outsider she'd sound unsympathetic, insensitive, but he knew her too well. She'd do everything she could to prevent him from descending into a cycle of despondency and shame...to stop him from wallowing in today's humiliation.

He sobered. Except the events of the day were more than just an average case of the blues or a minor setback. This kicked a guy's legs out from under him, gutted him, and left him bleeding and scarred for life.

'You were plenty good enough for Princess Courtney, but the only person who couldn't see it was you.'

'You never liked her, so excuse me if I consider your comments a little biased.'

'I didn't know her well enough to either like or dislike her.'

But when she glanced at him, he raised an eyebrow and she reefed her gaze back to the road again and blew out a breath.

'Okay, I was leaning more on the side of dislike,' she muttered. 'I'll admit that much. But I hadn't given up hope that I was wrong about her and that at some indeterminate time in the future we'd become friends.'

'Why the dislike?' A lot of women didn't like Courtney, but he'd noticed that those same women also felt intimidated by her achievements, her intelligence and her effortless polish. He'd have not placed Bree among their number, though, and the thought started a low burn in his gut.

As if she could read his thoughts, and she probably

could, she said, 'I can forgive her for her model-style figure, that perfect face and a complexion to die for. I can even forgive her the university medal she won for academic excellence, not to mention the Premier's Award for her charity work.'

Something inside him started to lighten. He should've known better. Bree wasn't the kind of woman to feel jealous of other women. 'What couldn't you forgive?'

She was quiet for several long moments. 'She stopped you from coming to Sunday night dinners.'

Sunday night dinner was an Allenby family tradition, started back before he knew them. Of course now, with all the kids grown up, absences were common. But whenever possible the entire family would gather at Janice and Colin's for a roast dinner and family catch-up. He'd had a longstanding invitation from the age of eleven onwards.

'That was my doing, not hers.' His mind started to race. But was it? 'Besides, I didn't stop coming. I just didn't make it quite so often.'

'You went four months without showing your face on a Sunday night. Mum missed you.'

A bad taste filled his mouth. How could he have been so insensitive? 'My fault,' he repeated.

'Courtney had a standing invitation. Everyone made sure she knew she was welcome. But how often did she come?'

He could count them all on the fingers of one hand. She'd only accompanied him to the Allenbys' four times, and the last had to have been over seven months ago. He'd thought each evening had gone well, everyone had got along just fine and there'd been lots of laughter. Courtney had told him on each occasion that she'd really enjoyed herself, and yet…in two years she'd only accompanied him four times.

Why the hell hadn't that fact bothered him more before today?

Because yesterday he'd been too busy seeing her as perfect?

He dragged a hand down his face, starting to see the flimsiness of the excuses he'd made on her behalf in his own mind. They'd been easy to make, though. After all, she was a busy woman with a lot of demands on her time. Her excuses whenever he'd extended the family night invitation had seemed genuinely plausible...understandable.

But actions spoke louder than words. She'd known how much the Allenbys meant to him and yet she still hadn't found the time, not once in seven months, to join him there for another family dinner.

'So there you have it, Noah.' She flexed her hands on the wheel. 'That's why I didn't like her. I felt she was stealing you away—that we were losing you rather than gaining her. She was always perfectly polite and pleasant, but it was clear she didn't want...'

'Didn't want?'

Bree lifted one shoulder. 'Didn't want to be part of us.' She continued to stare doggedly out of the window at the road ahead, and he found himself aching for her to turn and look at him, however briefly. 'Which is fair enough, I suppose.'

No, it damn well wasn't! He'd given Courtney everything she'd asked for. Why couldn't she have done this one thing for him?

For the first time since he and Courtney had started dating, he saw a significant crack in their relationship and it made him suck in a breath. If he had married her, would she have forced him to choose between her and the Allenbys? The thought sent icy fingers creeping across his skull.

'She played on your insecurities too, and I found that hard to forgive.'

He stiffened, and then immediately made himself relax and laugh. 'Insecurities? What insecurities?'

She threw her head back and laughed—a deep warm sound so full of genuine humour and affection that he blinked. It should've jarred his nerves. Instead a strange warmth stirred in his blood. 'You, Blake and Ryder are all so alike. It's hilarious! Me, macho and indestructible.' She beat on her chest Tarzan fashion.

She laughed again and he started, realising he'd been staring at her chest, his gaze drawn there when she beat on it. He gulped. When had Bree developed curves like that?

'Everyone has insecurities, tough guy.'

He dragged his gaze away, forced himself to focus on her words rather than the pounding of his pulse.

Did Bree have insecurities? He'd never really thought about it. She always seemed so together and driven—knew what she wanted and how to go about getting it. 'Fine, Ms Sigmund Freud, what are my insecurities?'

She glanced at him, eyes wide as if his question had startled her, but the expression in them gentled. 'Oh, Noah.'

Something in her tone made him swallow. Her knuckles whitened about the steering wheel and he wanted to call the question back but he couldn't. Because he was macho and a tough guy and he didn't want to lose face. He'd lost enough face for one day. 'Well?'

'You said it yourself—you never felt worthy of Courtney. You always felt she was out of your league.'

His every muscle tensed and cramped.

'You don't know how wrong you are. Though I know you won't believe me, you're worth a hundred Courtneys.' Her knuckles turned white again. 'Courtney knew you felt that way too—knew your background bugged you.'

He folded his arms to hide the way his insides shrivelled at her words. 'Courtney finally realised I wouldn't fit into her perfectly polished world. And with that came the realisation she couldn't go through with the wedding. Damn pity she didn't come to that conclusion prior to the wedding ceremony with two hundred guests in attendance, though.'

Bree glanced at him. 'You're wrong, you know? She never considered you not worthy or herself somehow above you. I might not have liked her very much but I'll give credit where it's due. She led a privileged life, but I don't think she was a snob.'

'Like you said, you didn't know her.' He knew he was being unfair, but who would blame him after what Courtney had done today?

'I'm not a trophy you get to hold aloft,' Bree said quietly.

He shifted, the car seat suddenly hard beneath his backside. 'I never thought of her as a trophy.' *He hadn't.* But a sense of unease wormed into the centre of his soul all the same.

'She obviously thought you did.'

She glanced at him as if expecting him to say something, but he had nothing to say. He'd given Courtney everything. He'd given her his full attention, his total support…not to mention his time. Whatever she'd wanted to do, he'd always been on board with. He'd given her free rein with the wedding, and had left the choice of where they'd live once their married life had started up to her. It still hadn't been enough. *He* hadn't been enough.

He wanted to say good riddance and be done with her. He wanted to feel as if he'd dodged a bullet. But all he felt was small and cheap—the way his parents had made him feel as a child. The way he'd been fighting against for thirty years. He wanted to crawl into some dark hidden hole, the way he'd used to crawl under the house as a little kid to avoid his father's abuse and his mother's backhands.

He'd worked hard over the past ten years—had achieved more than he'd ever dreamed possible. And yet here he was feeling like crap again, despite all of that. This was what happened when you gave someone that kind of power over you.

Well, no more. Never again. He hadn't had any choice as a child, but he had the choice now as a grown man.

'Let's have some music,' Bree finally said.

Inane pop immediately filled the car and while Bree hummed along, he couldn't join in. He knew her casual attitude was simply a show of bravado, the glances she sent him when she didn't think he was looking confirmed it, but he didn't have the energy to ease her mind. The events of the day had finally caught up with him, and he was starting to see the impossibility of the dreams he'd once dared to dream. What an idiot he'd been.

He stared out of the window, not seeing the rich farmland, green after recent rains, or the signposts for popular beachside holiday destinations—Yamba, Caloundra, Byron Bay—all of it darkened by the grimness of his thoughts.

Family life, a wife and kids, were not meant for the likes of him. A howl started up at the centre of him, but he resolutely ignored it. He was a ridiculously successful businessman, the Allenbys were his surrogate family, and he had a circle of friends he'd die for. It was enough. He refused to want more.

If Courtney had given him an ultimatum, had asked him outright to choose between her and the Allenbys, he'd have sent her packing. There were no two ways about it. But she hadn't—not in so many words. Now that he started to see what Bree had seen, though, the scales were falling from his eyes.

Courtney's tactics had been far less direct, but more insidious for all of that. How long would it have taken him to work it out on his own—her weaning him away from them inch by careful inch? Once he'd worked it out, he'd have not stood for it. And if Courtney hadn't given way it would've driven a wedge between them.

Was that why she'd called a halt to the wedding? Had she realised she'd never be able to wholly steal him away from the Allenbys? Why the hell would she want to anyway?

Things inside him went hard and cold. Courtney had wanted to make him over, mould him, into something more appropriate. And he'd wanted her to! He'd yearned for the polish and sophistication, the ease and composure, to navigate a world so far removed from the one that he'd grown up in.

Only he hadn't seen where it might lead—the less than favourable consequences associated with such an overhaul.

Like he'd said, *What an idiot*.

They reached Coffs Harbour just before seven o'clock. He laughed at the spartan motel rooms Bree had booked. 'I see you're going all out here, Bree, and really treating yourself.'

'Coffs Harbour was always just a layover. As I'm going to be spending two or three nights in Sydney, I'm planning to stay somewhere nicer there. This...' she gestured around '...was just a convenient place to get some shut-eye. So...did you want to do anything? I was just going to grab takeaway unless you want to eat out.'

'God, no.'

She nodded as if she'd figured that was what he'd say. 'What would you like?'

'Beer and bourbon.' He fished out his wallet and held

his credit card towards her. 'And grab a bottle of Shiraz for yourself.'

She ignored the card. 'How about a side order of pizza to go with that?'

'Whatever you want.' He wasn't the slightest bit hungry.

With that, she left and it was only once he was alone that Noah realised how grounding Bree's presence had been all day.

He'd been left at the altar. His bride had jilted him. The life he'd mapped out—the life he'd hungered for with every atom inside him—was gone.

He'd failed.

He was a failure.

He paced the room. 'C'mon, Bree, hurry up.' He wanted to get good and drunk before his thoughts ate him alive.

CHAPTER THREE

'DON'T LET THE pizza go cold.' Bree swiped the can of beer Noah had grabbed from the little bar fridge in her room and set it back inside before pushing the pizza box into his arms instead. 'Have one slice at least. Please?'

She planted herself in front of the fridge and folded her arms. Noah had already drunk two beers in quick succession, and while she knew that he and her brothers could drink a lot when they put their minds to it, that didn't mean they'd not wake up with sore heads the next day.

She didn't kid herself—Noah was going to have a hangover tomorrow, probably one of mammoth proportions. She wasn't even going to try and stop him from drowning his sorrows. But she'd do all she could to mitigate the damage.

He could pick her up and set her aside easily enough, and grab what was left of the six-pack. She fancied she saw that notion momentarily flash through his mind, but he eventually just shrugged and flashed her a grin. *That* grin. The grin she'd seen fell more women over the years than she could count.

'I'll have two pieces if it'll make you feel better, Breanna.'

Dear God. The way he said her name in that lazy, husky-as-sin voice, enunciating each syllable as if her name were a delectable dish worth savouring. It made her aware that they were alone together in a hotel room. Her heart pitter-pattered to a faster beat while warmth gathered beneath her breastbone and rose to flood her cheeks.

Ooh, no, no, no. She wasn't going to have those kinds of thoughts about Noah. She wasn't going to become one of Noah's Nymphettes.

Noah's Nymphettes and the Twinses' Minxes were what she'd dubbed the multitude of girls that had hovered in the three boys' orbits from the time they'd hit puberty.

And once Bree had reached puberty, Bree's Bad Boys had been added to the mix.

The last thought came out of nowhere, making her flinch.

'Hell, Bree, I'll stop drinking altogether if it bugs you that much.'

He'd taken the pizza box across to the bed and settled on one side with the pillows at his back, and while he looked relaxed and at ease she sensed the keenness behind the warm hazel of his eyes. She realised then that he'd thought *he'd* made her flinch.

She shook her head. 'I don't mind you drinking, Noah, but I am going to make you eat something first.'

She dropped a bag of salt and vinegar crisps to the bed—his favourite—along with a couple of bars of fruit and nut chocolate—her favourite—before settling on the other side of the bed and helping herself to a piece of pizza. 'And a little later on I'm going to make you drink big glasses of water and you're going to promise to drink them.'

'Cross my heart.' He pressed a hand to his chest before reaching for another slice of pizza. 'No pineapple?'

She was pro pineapple on pizza. He wasn't. 'I wasn't giving you any reason to refuse to eat it.'

He was quiet for several long seconds and just stared at her. 'You're a hell of a friend, you know that?'

'Absolutely.' She turned the compliment off lightly, but it warmed her to the soles of her feet.

'Today's been a bitch of a day, but—'

The golden highlights in his hazel eyes caught the light, making them spark. His eyes looked as deep and soulful as a galaxy. Her breath stuttered. 'But?' she choked out.

'But that hasn't stopped me from enjoying hanging out with you.'

Slowly she nodded. 'I know what you mean. It's the weirdest thing, right?' It should've been an unrelentingly bad day.

Not that it hadn't been bad. The morning had been appalling...atrocious...gob-smackingly awful. But there'd been pockets of time during the drive when things had been...*nice*. It seemed an insipid word to use, but that didn't make it any less appropriate. Parts of today, hanging out with Noah, had been nice.

Obviously neither of them had expected that. Perhaps it was testament to the resilience of the human spirit? Or simply the comfort that could be found in old friends? Whatever, she was grateful for it.

She reached for the remote. 'There has to be a game on. If memory serves me correct the women's soccer team play an international friendly tonight and—'

'I think I should feel more gutted than I am.'

Whoa!

She tossed the remote to the bedside table with a clatter and swung back to him. He'd leapt up to grab another beer. She shook her head when he gestured at the bottle of wine she'd bought. She'd only bought it to look sociable. She had no intention of drinking it. At least, not tonight.

Instinct told her to stay alert. Not to dull them...not to

let her guard down and let the wildness inside her win. It had been trying to break free ever since she'd agreed to Tina's plan, but she *would* keep a rein on it. Besides, tonight was for Noah. She needed to keep her wits sharp and do all she could to be the friend he needed.

'You've had your heart broken, Bree.' The bed dipped as he settled back down beside her. 'Is this normal?'

Nobody in her circle ever mentioned Otis or the heartbreak she'd suffered at his hands, not even obliquely.

He shrugged. 'I know nobody talks about it, and I hope you don't mind, but...'

'I don't mind,' she said slowly. She knew everyone only avoided the topic out of respect for her, for fear of upsetting her. At the time she'd just wanted to bury the experience and forget it had ever happened. She wondered now if that had been the best strategy.

She glanced at Noah. 'You looked pretty gutted to me earlier.'

He grimaced.

'I don't know if heartbreak is the same for everyone, but in my experience the grief comes in waves. One moment you're feeling down and out as if nothing good or bright can ever happen again, and then something dumb will catch your attention and take you out of yourself for a bit.'

'Dumb...like what?'

'The football scores might flash up on the telly and you'll see your team has had a huge win in a derby match and you'll jump out of your chair and do a victory dance. Or a catchy tune comes on the radio and without noticing you'll find yourself singing along. Or you hear a funny story and find yourself laughing out loud.'

She met his gaze and shrugged. 'So in the midst of the awfulness you have these moments where you forget the awfulness and feel…almost normal, almost happy. I found it a bit confronting at first.'

Her eyes burned as she remembered how she'd let down everyone she'd loved. She'd let them down so badly. She still hated that. It was why she was so worried about throwing out The Plan now.

In changing the direction her life was about to take… Dear God, what guarantee did she have that she wouldn't fail again? She couldn't afford to fail. Not at this. Not when so many people were relying on her. She had to find a way to make sure she wouldn't go off the rails again, to stay on track.

'Bree?'

She shook herself, forced her mind back to the present conversation, sent Noah what she hoped was a smile. 'When the Otis situation exploded, it felt as if my whole world had been turned upside down.'

His hand closed around hers. 'I know.'

The pain in his eyes made her suck in a breath. That pain… Her heart started to pound. Had she read the situation between him and Courtney wrong? Had he truly loved the other woman and she'd just been too blind to see it?

She swallowed and forced herself to answer his question as fully and frankly as she could. 'So it felt wrong, disorienting, to find that I still enjoyed some of the things I had prior to the heartbreak.'

If Noah truly did love Courtney, then she had to help him fix things.

'Waves,' he mused. 'That sounds like a good way to describe it.'

'It happens the other way too. You'll be happily going along feeling fine—thinking you're doing fine—when a memory slams into you out of nowhere and hurtles you back into a black pit of depression.'

'What kind of memories?'

That old heaviness settled over her. 'Odd things—like the foot massage he gave you after the particularly awful day you'd had and how good it felt—not just the massage but the fact he understood how bad your day had been and wanted to make it better. Or the time you went to the cinema to see a horror film together and he held your hand all the way through it, even though he was also juggling popcorn and a drink, and he let you hide your face in his shoulder… and never ever teased you about it, not once, because you begged him not to. Or the night you went out on the town and it was freezing on the way home and he put his jacket around your shoulders and it was warm and it smelled like him…' she'd always loved Otis's scent '…and it was a still night and the stars were all out and then he kissed you and told you he loved you and you thought there would never be a more perfect moment in your entire life.'

They were the memories she'd tried to forget. Some things, though, refused to be forgotten. The memory of what it was like to feel loved and wanted, for one…or how—

Noah swore and she crashed back into the present with a thump.

He seized another beer, and she realised he'd finished the previous one in record time. She opened the crisps and held them out to him. 'Salt and vinegar,' she said somewhat unnecessarily.

He took a handful, scowling at her. 'And has there?'

'Has there what?'

'Has there ever been a more perfect moment in your life, Bree?'

He enunciated every syllable with a savage accuracy that made her throat ache. What memory had she just resurrected for him that was burned into his brain for all eternity? She wanted to tell him she was sorry for bringing it to roaring life, except she knew he'd scorn her apology.

'I take it that's a no, then?'

He lifted the beer and drank it down too hard and fast. She bit into a crisp with a savage crunch. 'I have high expectations that it'll be eclipsed in the future.'

He lowered the beer to stare at her. She shrugged at him. 'The thing about broken hearts, Noah, is that they do eventually mend.'

'Your heart isn't broken any more?'

Why on earth was she wasting calories on crisps? She reached for a chocolate bar. 'It's not broken any more. I'm glad I'm no longer with Otis.'

She hadn't spoken about any of this in any detail with anyone, but now that she'd started she couldn't seem to stop. 'For a long time I bounced. One day I was ready to forgive Otis for every wrong he'd ever done me, making every excuse for him that I could—and, believe me, there was no excuse too small. I ached for things to go back the way they were before everything exploded. I'd make deals with the universe—if the universe gave him back to me, I'd make sure he never took drugs again.'

Noah groaned and rubbed a hand over his face.

She nodded. 'I know. It was sobering to realise there were days when I didn't have an ounce of pride. But then there were other days when I'd be burning with anger and outrage at what he'd done to me, how much he'd betrayed me, and I'd swear that nothing would ever prevail upon me to take him back. Eventually I started having more of those days than I did the others.' Thank God.

She pointed the bar of fruit and nut at him. 'One of the good things, once you've gained a little distance, is you remember all the annoying things about them and you start to see all the reasons you weren't suited.'

Narrowed eyes raked her face. 'Like what?'

She could practically see the thought in his mind—it was like a flashing neon sign above his head—*Courtney is perfect*. No, she darn well wasn't!

She bit into her chocolate bar, letting the sweetness coat her tongue. 'Not having to put up with his sulking fits when he didn't get his own way—he could brood over something for days. I didn't like his taste in comedians either. I like smart, good-natured comedy, not smut or mean humour. So now I never have to watch another comedy show like that for as long as I live.'

She crunched another crisp because the crunch was too satisfying. 'Oh!' She tapped her head as if she'd forgotten something important. 'There's the small fact that the entire the time we were together he was doing drugs. So, yeah, there's that.'

'Bree—'

'Now it's your turn.'

'What? I—'

'Three things that annoyed you about Courtney.'

'There's nothing—'

'How long did it take her to get ready for a night out?' She had two brothers. She was well versed in the peccadillos of the female population.

He straightened. 'It'd take her two hours minimum! What the hell is that all about? And she'd never leave the house without a full face of make-up—even if she was only going to the gym.' He shook his head as if the vagaries of womankind made no sense at all.

'I bet she really appreciated it when you belched too.'

That made him snort. 'I learned early on to leave the room if I was going to belch. God forbid I do anything so uncouth in her presence. Which, of course, means a guy can never relax for a minute whenever she's around, not even in his own house.'

'Well, there you go. You can now belch to your heart's content.'

'And I'll never have to watch another one of those dark, bleak foreign films she's so crazy about. Or feel guilty for watching a footy game on TV rather than doing something to improve my mind.'

Indignation swelled in her chest. 'She wanted you to improve your mind?'

He spread his hands. 'I know.'

Bree started to giggle. 'I hope you told her one couldn't improve upon perfection.'

His mouth dropped open to form a perfect O and then he threw his head back with a roar of laughter, and the shaking of the bed made Bree laugh harder until they were both laughing so hard it almost hurt.

The release in the tension that had bound them up tight all day was welcome, but left her feeling spent when it had finally subsided.

Noah swore and reached for the bottle of bourbon. 'I thought I was going to get it all, Bree. I thought I was going to live the life I'd always dreamed. I thought Courtney was my perfect woman—the ying to my yang. You know the spiel—*You complete me...yada-yada-yada.*'

Her heart clenched at the bitterness lacing his words.

He took a long pull on the bottle, not even bothering with a glass. 'I didn't expect life to always be rosy and perfect, because nobody's ever is. But I still thought we'd achieve the really important things—children, family, supporting each other, making a difference in the community. Children,' he repeated on a harsh laugh. 'Hell, I thought we'd grow old together!'

The rawness in his voice, the bleakness in his eyes, made hers burn.

'I don't know how the hell I'm supposed to go forward from here.'

She reached across and gripped his hand. 'You don't have to work that out all at once. You sure as hell don't have to work it out tonight. And you don't work it out on your own. You take it one day at a time. And what you do is you rely on your friends, because we'll all help you through it. And you will get through it, Noah, because you're strong and you're smart.'

He stared at her, and just for a moment it looked as if he'd stopped drowning—as if her words had provided him with a lifeline. But then he glanced away and she knew it was only a front. 'I know it's not the same, Noah, but we're all here for you—we're all in your corner.'

He was quiet for a moment, but then he nodded. 'It does help, Bree, knowing you guys have my back. It helps a lot.'

But his heart had been broken. And she knew from experience how long and hard the journey back from that took. How could she have misjudged his feelings for Courtney so badly? 'Noah—'

'No more, Bree, let's just watch the game.'

He took another swig from his bottle and she knew it would be for the best to let the subject drop for now. She grabbed him a big glass of water and insisted he drink it before turning on the TV to watch the replay of the women's soccer match.

Noah finally flaked out a bit after two a.m. On her bed. She'd chosen her room as the 'let's hang out in here' room, as she'd thought it might keep Noah in check more…that he'd simply leave when he'd had enough and wanted to be morose on his own.

She tucked his room key into her back pocket. Fine,

she'd take his room instead. 'You're going to have a hell of a head when you wake up, Noah Fitzgerald,' she said, pulling off his shoes. He was lying on top of the covers so she covered him with the throw rug from the foot of the bed and placed a glass of water on the bedside table, making sure the pathway to the bathroom was clear. She left the lamp beside the door on, but dimmed it low.

She glanced down at his sleeping form, her gut clenching tight. Courtney had broken his heart. And now his dreams were dust.

Her hands fisted. She'd been so certain he wasn't in love with the other woman. She'd been so sure he'd been in love with an ideal rather than the reality. But what the hell did she know? She'd been in love with a drug dealer who, when busted, had told the police he'd been working for her. She knew nothing!

On impulse, she smoothed the dark hair from his brow and bent down to press a kiss to his forehead. 'Goodnight, Noah.'

When she eased away, dark smoky eyes flecked with gold stared into hers as if plumbing the depths of her soul. For a moment it hadn't been Noah's eyes she'd stared into but a stranger's. A beguiling stranger that made her blood heat and had the wind roaring in her ears.

Noah had never looked at her like that before.

With a mouth that had gone strangely dry, she stumbled backwards. 'Sleep tight,' she managed in a strangled tone before turning and fleeing the room.

Noah cracked one eye open at the sound of the door to his room opening. He winced when one of the curtains at the front window was partially pushed to one side to let in some light. He winced even though the light didn't strike any part of his face, as if the opener of the curtain had been careful to shield him from the ill effects of blinding sunlight on oversensitive eyes.

His temples pounded, and his mouth tasted of a rank mixture of bourbon and salt and vinegar crisps. He ran his tongue around disgustingly furry teeth as his stomach burned acid. He remained *very* still to counter the nausea circling at the edges of everything, waiting to claim him.

How much had he drunk last night? He didn't dare reach out to pat the floor and find the bourbon bottle to check how much was left, in case it overset his current steady-ish equilibrium.

A zip opened and closed—a suitcase, he guessed—and then a rustling as someone moved towards the bed. A hand came into view as it placed a package on the bedside table.

'Bree?' he croaked, and then wished he hadn't as an electrical storm started flashing and thundering through his head.

'You're awake?'

She kept her voice low and if he could've moved without throwing up, he'd have hugged her. 'Not for long if I have any say in the matter,' he muttered.

'If it's any consolation, you can stay there all day. I've booked us in for another night.'

He stiffened. *Damn.* Her road trip!

He groaned. *Don't move.*

'We've switched rooms too, by the way. Your suitcase is just inside the door.'

He'd flaked out in her room? On her bed? Bad form. Really bad form.

'There are headache tablets and water on the bedside table if you want either.'

She was a saint. 'Thank you.'

He wanted to tell her she was a man among men—

that should probably be a woman among women—but he couldn't concentrate on anything but battling nausea.

What on earth was she going to do all day? He should haul his sorry bones out of bed. He was wrecking her plans. This wasn't the holiday she'd signed up for.

'I'm spending the day at the beach, and it's going to be lovely,' she added as if she could read his mind. 'I'll see you later, Noah.'

He managed to croak out a 'Bye' before the door closed behind her.

It wasn't until she left that he suddenly realised she hadn't once met his eyes—not directly. He dragged himself upright, breathing hard, heart pounding. Sure, he'd been bleary eyed—and said eyes were probably bloodshot and hanging out of his head, so he wouldn't blame her for not wanting to look at them—but…that wasn't Bree's style. In fact, the more he thought about it, the more he realised she'd actively avoided making eye contact with him.

What the hell had he done last night?

He reached for the water, took two headache tablets.

Right… There'd been the beer, pizza, bourbon and crisps. They'd talked about heartbreak. He remembered that.

He scowled, a ferocious wave of something black and ugly making his hands clench. What he wouldn't give to rip Otis apart with his bare hands for having so utterly betrayed Bree. She hadn't deserved that. Nobody deserved that, but for some reason it seemed especially contemptible that Bree had been the victim of such a snake.

He ran a hand over his face. Although Courtney had left him at the altar, she hadn't gutted him the way Otis had Bree.

Well, of course not! The jerk had tried to make her his

fall guy. She'd been arrested, for God's sake. Talk about a brutal wake-up call.

That didn't stem his growing unease. The fact remained, he couldn't relate to the heartbreak Bree had described. If he'd loved Courtney...

He pushed the thought away. Shock, he was still in shock. Eventually it would wear off and no doubt he'd then experience in full Technicolor glory all that Bree had recounted. For the moment, though, he needed to focus on what mattered right now—Bree...and last night.

There'd been the game on the TV. He remembered Bree cheering a couple of times, but after that...?

His mind blanked. He'd obviously drunk himself into a stupor and passed out *on her bed*. He'd have not—

His mind flashed to a startlingly clear image of Bree leaning over him. He touched his fingers to his brow and fancied he could feel tingling warmth from the spot where she'd pressed her lips. She'd smelled so good—sweet like chocolate and fresh like night jasmine. He'd stared into those warm brown eyes, and had noticed the full promise of her plump bottom lip. In that precise moment, all he'd wanted to do was kiss her. He'd always thought her eyes extraordinary, but when the hell had he started noticing her lips?

His chest clenched. He'd wanted to kiss her, the need still burned through him and—

Hell! He hadn't...?

He lurched off the bed, just making it to the bathroom before losing the contents of his stomach.

Flushing the toilet and lowering the lid, he sat on it, head in hands. He hadn't kissed Bree, had he? He'd never cross that boundary. No matter how drunk he was. Not with Bree.

But he had been *very* drunk.

If he hadn't kissed her—and he really didn't want to believe he'd kissed her—maybe he'd done something ridiculous like told her he wanted to kiss her. Because alcohol, as they all knew, was a truth serum.

He groaned out loud. Still, it would be the lesser of two evils. 'Never. Drinking. Again.'

Even if he hadn't behaved badly, last night couldn't have been fun for her. He needed to make that up to her somehow. First a shower, then some food, and then he'd make a plan.

Noah glanced across at Bree in the driver's seat. She'd insisted on driving the first leg of their journey to Sydney—a six-hour drive from Coffs Harbour. He'd barely seen her yesterday. Once she'd returned from her day at the beach, she'd excused herself to have an early night—had said she'd stayed up too late the previous night, and that all the sun, surf and fresh air had worn her out.

She hadn't looked worn out. She'd glowed from a day spent in the fresh air. A fact he'd done his very best not to notice. He told himself that the awareness he was starting to feel for her had to be some kind of weird hangover from being jilted at the altar.

It was probably some stupid male ego thing—his masculine pride wanting to reassert itself and prove he was still attractive and virile. To prove he was still worth something. As if pulling a girl proved anything.

As if taking advantage of a friend proved anything other than the fact he was worthless scum.

'I want to thank you, Bree.'

She started as if she'd been lost in her thoughts. She glanced at him briefly, eyebrows raised. 'What for?'

'You could've seriously punished me yesterday morning. You could've thrown the curtains open wide, turned the radio on loud and banged about the room. But you didn't. You brought me painkillers, which was way more than I deserved. And you've not given me any grief over it since.'

'Why on earth would I want to punish you? And why would I give you grief?'

Please God, don't let him have given her any reason for either of those things.

'I don't think I know another woman who'd have acted the same way. Who'd have been so understanding.'

Her brows drew together. 'I had a pretty good idea what Saturday night was going to look like for you. After the day you'd had, nobody was going to blame you for drowning your sorrows, least of all me.'

'I stole your room.'

That made her laugh. 'What's a motel room between friends?'

He turned more fully towards her, careful not to knock the centre console with his knee. 'I know you just said you had no reason to have hard feelings, but I've got to ask— did I…behave badly towards you?'

'Whoa! Wait, *what*?' Her eyes went wide and a tiny bit panicked.

'Did I do something really stupid? Like, um…try to drunkenly kiss you?'

'I…*no*!' She shot him a wild-eyed glare before turning back to the road.

His nose curled at her…horror? Or was it repugnance? Did the idea of him kissing her revolt her that much?

'Hell, Noah, why would you even think such a thing?'

'Because you've been really quiet. I can't help thinking something's on your mind. And I get the feeling you're trying to avoid me.'

Stricken eyes met his. He swallowed. Was she lying to

protect him? He had to have done something seriously bad to bring that expression to her eyes.

His gut churned but he kept his tone gentle. 'And I don't know if you've noticed or not, but we're in a car together. So avoiding me isn't going to work.'

She straightened, her knuckles white on the steering wheel. 'Lunch. It's lunchtime. I'm not having this conversation while I'm driving.'

They grabbed burgers, fries and shakes from the drive-thru of a fast-food chain and ate them at an all but deserted rest stop, where Noah hopefully wouldn't be recognised by anyone. They were closer to Sydney than Brisbane now and hopefully the cancelled wedding was of less interest the further south they went.

Bree bit into her burger and then closed her eyes and sipped her shake. He couldn't help feeling she was using the food as a way to keep avoiding him.

Catching his eyes, she shrugged. 'For the duration of the holiday I'm off the diet.'

His eyebrows shot up. 'In your normal day-to-day life you diet?'

'Not really.' She popped a couple of fries into her mouth. 'But I try to be mindful of what I eat. Still, holidays are for indulgences, right?'

He stared down at his food. He didn't want to think about indulgence. Not when Bree sat across from him with her plump bottom lip calling to him and the sun turning her hair the most delicious shade of ash blonde.

From the corner of his eye he saw her shrug. 'Still, I'll have to stop eating so much fast food, no matter how much I love it. Too many pizzas, burgers and chocolate bars will make me feel like crap, and there's still a long stretch of road between me and Hobart.'

'Then how about we indulge in some fine food rather

than the fast variety when we're in Sydney?' It could be part of his make-it-up-to-her plan.

'Excellent idea.'

Her lips closed around her straw again and she darted a glance at him. He forced himself to not stare at her lips.

'Why did you ask if you'd kissed me?' she finally asked.

His gut churned. 'I can't remember if it was a real moment or whether I dreamed it, but I seem to recall a moment when I…uh, wanted to kiss you.'

He wasn't wearing a collared shirt, but a collar felt as if it were strangling him all the same. To Bree's credit, she didn't flinch or look the least bit appalled.

'Hand on my heart, Noah. You didn't try to kiss me, you didn't say anything inappropriate, you didn't do anything inappropriate.'

He sagged. Thank God for that. He picked up his burger again, suddenly hungry. 'So you want to tell me why you've been avoiding me?'

She coughed as if food had gone down the wrong way. Setting his burger down, he gave her his full attention.

She dabbed her lips with a paper napkin—*those lips*—and then nodded as if coming to a decision. 'You were honest with me so…'

He'd been uncomfortably honest with her. And she looked just as uncomfortable now.

Her lips twisted. 'I suspect I'm about to raise an upsetting topic and I apologise in advance for that, but I think we better talk about it or I'll never be able to look you in the eye again.'

Hell!

'The thing is, Noah, I never for one moment thought you were really in love with Courtney.'

Things inside him stiffened, objected, protested and… agreed. His mouth dried.

'So on Saturday morning when we were all in the vestry and Courtney asked me what she did—whether I thought she should marry you or not—in my heart the answer was no.'

He could feel all the blood drain from his face as the truth descended on him with all the unpalatable weight of a T-Rex, which was what he felt like—an obsolete, out-dated dinosaur.

'But after the things you said on Saturday night, I realise I was wrong—that you did love her. And rather than being bruised, your heart is in fact broken.

What on earth had he said on Saturday night to make her change her mind? He'd have asked except his throat had closed over.

Had he seriously been about to marry a woman he didn't love? He rubbed a hand over his face. He'd *thought* he'd been in love with Courtney, but now...

A wave of nausea rolled through him. Had he been so desperate to create his vision of the perfect life, the perfect family, he'd been prepared to marry a woman he didn't love?

Had he been that desperate to prove himself? So desperate he'd not only deceived her, but himself as well?

Except Courtney had seen through him. And so had Bree.

She pressed her hands together, her gaze pleading into his. 'Noah, I'm truly sorry for any assumptions I made, but I can fix this. If you want to win Courtney back, I can tell you exactly how to do it.'

CHAPTER FOUR

BREE STARED OUT of the passenger side window as they sped down the motorway, national park forest stretching on either side for as far as the eye could see, Noah's capable hands on the steering wheel and his forbidding *'No'* still ringing in her ears. That had been an hour and a half ago. In another hour they'd reach Sydney.

He hadn't explained why he'd said no—why he didn't want to win Courtney back. She couldn't work out if he loved the other woman or not. But if he did…

She twisted her hands together. If he did, she had to make him see that all wasn't lost.

If he didn't… The weight pressing down on her momentarily lifted. She *really* hoped he didn't.

One thing was becoming increasingly clear. She had to do something to cheer him up. Just a little. It would be impossible to entirely lift the darkness smothering him, but she could let in a chink of light, couldn't she?

But then what? Would he be okay on his own when she continued on with her journey? Should she stay with him for an extra few days?

She'd booked for three nights, but had no idea how long he planned to stay or where he was headed next. For all she knew he could be headed straight for the airport.

She wanted to ask what his plans were, but something

held her back. She'd already infringed so much upon his privacy, it felt wrong to ask any more of him.

Besides, given the way he'd stared at her in the wee small hours of Sunday morning—the arc of awareness *that he remembered*—it was probably a very good thing the two of them part company. They were both trapped under heavy emotional loads at the moment and seeking relief.

That kind of relief, though, would be—

She shied away from even contemplating the consequences. It had the potential to ruin their friendship, destroy his relationship with her brothers and parents. His and Ryder's business would be affected...

She closed her eyes. She'd sworn to never let her family down again. Just for a moment she flashed to that cold impersonal courtroom and the grim white faces of her family.

Her eyes flew open. *No.* Sleeping with Noah would solve nothing, would ruin everything, and it would be letting everyone down. She couldn't bear it.

She couldn't use him like that. She *wouldn't* use him and sex as an escape from her panic for what her future held—panic that she wouldn't cope, that she wouldn't be enough. The step she was about to take meant sacrificing so many of the goals she'd spent the last seven years working towards.

She pulled in a breath, tried to temper the pounding of her heart. *But you'll be gaining so much as well.* She did all she could to hold fast to that thought. Because she would be. She'd be gaining the world.

But it didn't stop the dread, the nerves, the questions from circling through her mind on an endless loop. She craved a safety net...or a crystal ball that would let her see into the future and assure her all would be well.

She sensed Noah's quick glance in her direction and forced her mind back to the present moment. 'Would you like to do something fun while we're in Sydney?' she asked.

'What did you have in mind?'

She let out a slow breath at the interest that momentarily flickered in the backs of his eyes. She searched for something he might like to do. 'I've always wanted to do the bridge climb.'

He didn't look entirely thrilled at the prospect and disappointment pooled in her stomach. Still, he hadn't immediately discounted it either so she pressed what little advantage she had. Getting him out in the fresh air and moving would do him the world of good.

'You make the most amazing fitness machines.' Noah provided the engineering genius behind Fitness Ark while Ryder was the business brain. Noah incorporated the latest fitness innovations and married them to virtual reality technology. People didn't go to Fitness Ark just to get fit—they went there for an experience. 'I wonder if you could make a machine that would recreate the bridge climb experience? You need to have a certain fitness level to do the climb. If you could recreate it with both surround video and sound…' She shrugged. 'It'd be pretty special.'

Everything about him went onto instant high alert.

'Eyes on the road,' she said when he swung to stare at her. She didn't speak again until he'd turned back to the front. 'It'd probably cost a lot of money to make that kind of machine. It could be prohibitively expensive. But it might be worth exploring.'

He didn't answer, but an entirely different mood settled in the car.

She fake pouted. 'I bet I've left it too late, though. It's probably one of those things you need to book weeks in advance.'

'I'm sure I could organise something.'

Noah *knew* people. She pressed her hands together, her delight no longer feigned. 'Really?'

'Leave it to me, kiddo.'

His *kiddo* grated. She wasn't a kid any more and he knew it.

Maybe he was trying to set the same boundaries she'd been so desperate to find.

An unexpected thrill shook through her at the thought that Noah might find her attractive…even sexy. She did her best to suppress it, doing all she could to channel Bree-the-Serious-and-Sensible, rather than Bree-the-Wild-and-Reckless.

Something that became increasingly difficult to do when Noah turned towards the harbour rather than away from it when they reached the centre of Sydney. 'Noah, our hotel is that way.'

He shook his head, a faint smile curving his lips.

She dragged her gaze from that tempting mouth and pushed her phone under his nose. 'My navigation app says—'

'I made us other arrangements.'

Other arrangements? 'But—'

'Don't worry, I cancelled the reservation you'd made. You chose where we stayed in Coffs and paid for it. I figured it was only fair I did the same in Sydney.'

'But we're heading for the Rocks and a harbour view.'

'We are.'

Her mouth opened and closed when he pulled into one of the best hotels in the city. She'd have never stayed here in a month of Sundays. She'd have never been able to justify the expense.

He sent her a mock-stern glare. 'Don't rain on my parade here, Bree. You deserve a bit of pampering and so do I.'

He'd booked them a two-bedroom, harbour-view suite. When they walked in, she stared at the unbelievably luxurious furnishings and then the glorious view. 'This is amazing! Have you stayed here before?'

'A couple of times.'

She walked across to the window. 'I keep forgetting that you and Ryder could live like this if you wanted.'

His phone rang. He answered, listened and then nodded. 'Perfect. Thank you.'

What was perfect? And who was he thanking?

'That was the concierge. We're booked in for a sunset bridge climb tomorrow.'

She clapped her hands, bouncing from one foot to the other. 'That *is* perfect.'

'So?' He stared at her expectantly. 'What would you like to do this evening?'

It wasn't five p.m. yet. She stretched her neck to the right and then the left. 'We have a spa bath.' And the most glorious range of toiletries.

He laughed. 'After your spa, then, what would you like to do? If you're tired we can kick back here in the suite and order room service.'

She was tired. She'd forgotten how exhausting travelling could be, but while this room—suite—was about four times as big as both their rooms combined back in Coffs Harbour, it somehow seemed much more intimate.

Instinct warned her not to spend the evening in.

'Or I could see if I can get a reservation to Carlo's. I did promise you fine dining while we were here.'

Carlo's was considered one of the best restaurants in the country, and the mention of its name had Bree's mouth watering. But the photos she'd seen of the place had all screamed romance. The less romance she and Noah channelled at the moment, the better.

He was nursing a broken heart—or if it wasn't broken it was seriously bruised—and the last thing he needed was to be reminded of romance and all he'd lost.

As for her? She needed to get all the crazy, wild thoughts she'd been having back under wraps. Fast. They were nothing more than a panicked reaction to the changes she was about to make in her life. If she wanted to prove to herself that she was worthy of the trust being placed in her, then she *had* to be sensible. If she couldn't do that, if she couldn't make good decisions now...

Then she didn't deserve anyone's trust.

Dragging in a breath, she made herself smile. 'You know what I'd really like to do? I'd like to go for a water-front walk around to the Opera House. There are lots of eateries along the way. I'm sure we'd be able to find one that could fit us in without a booking. It's a Monday night so not exactly the busiest night of the week.'

He clapped his hands. 'Right, let's do that, then.'

The Sydney Harbour Bridge climb was amazing. Bree had known she'd enjoy it, but when they stood at the highest point and stared at the magnificence that was Sydney Harbour—surely one of the most beautiful sights in the world—exhilaration and adrenaline flooded her. A glance at Noah confirmed he felt the same.

'Best idea ever, Bree,' he breathed, awe and elation in every word.

'Make a machine that'll recreate this and I'll be there every single day,' she murmured back, making him laugh.

After the bridge climb they returned to the hotel to get ready for dinner at Carlo's. She didn't know what strings Noah had pulled to get a table, but the thought of dining there was too tempting to resist.

And it lived up to expectation. While the atmosphere

was intimate and warm, with candlelight and the sparkling lights of the harbour surrounding them, they were still too caught up in the exhilaration of the bridge climb to feel awkward. They simply talked non-stop the way they used to… BC—before Courtney. It made her realise how much she'd missed him. He was one of the few people she could let her guard down around and truly be herself.

She finally pushed her plate away and dabbed at her mouth with her pristine linen napkin. 'I can't eat another bite but that was the most spectacular meal I've ever eaten. It's been the best day.' She wiggled in her seat. 'I can't remember the last time I had this much fun.'

His gaze roved over her face and he nodded as if in approval. 'The night is yet young. What would else you like to do?'

'Heavens, I don't need anything else! Today has been such a treat and—'

'When was the last time you went dancing?'

Dancing? She couldn't remember. Ages and ages. She'd been so focussed on work and The Plan that dancing and going out hadn't been high on her list of priorities. 'I had a girls' night…um…a while back.'

Wow, it would be nearly a year ago.

His grin hooked up one side of his mouth. 'We don't have to be up early. We can laze around in the morning.'

She wasn't leaving Sydney till Thursday, and they hadn't made plans for tomorrow yet. A lie-in was definitely on the cards.

One broad shoulder lifted. 'I, for one, am still too revved to go back to our suite.'

A pulse thrummed to life inside her. She hadn't asked him yet what he planned to do once she set back off on her road trip.

The golden flecks in his eyes flashed. 'There's a club

in a rather exclusive hotel not too far away. A mock-up of an old speakeasy. Are you up for it?'

She didn't hesitate. 'Yes, please.' Maybe she'd find the courage to ask him his plans over another glass of wine… find a way to ask without sounding too bossy or smothery.

As he promised, the place was full of character and old-world charm with a long wooden bar that dominated one wall. Round wooden tables and chairs surrounded a dance floor while beyond them banquettes lined the walls, creating dimly lit corners that looked as if they'd been de-signed for sealing shady bootlegging deals.

Nineteen-twenties music pulsed through the speakers and, even though it was a Tuesday night, dancers crowded the dance floor. When Noah grabbed her hand and hauled her out into the middle of all those bodies, she didn't resist.

Grinning at each other, they moved to the music in uni-son. As the beat pulsed through her and took up residence in the thrumming of her blood, she lifted her arms above her head, turned on the spot and shimmied, feeling young and free and more alive than she could remember feeling.

Noah's grin was full of the same wicked delight. He slipped an arm about her waist, his eyes gleaming with a mixture of mischief and appreciation. *Masculine* appre-ciation.

The breath stuttered in her throat as her arms lowered to his shoulders. He held her close as he whirled them around the dance floor and she did what she could to stifle the sensations flooding her body. Dear God, this couldn't be right. It—

All thought stopped when he dipped her over his arm and leaned down over her, so close she could see the fine pores of his face and the way the stubble darkened his jaw. Their gazes locked. Everything seemed to still and slow.

Very slowly he righted her, the fingers at her spine moving back and forth in an unconscious caress. Or maybe it was deliberate. All around them bodies moved, but they stood in the midst of it frozen, an island unto themselves. Bree couldn't look away, couldn't break the spell. Didn't *want* to break the spell.

A white flare made them both blink and start, but it took her several valuable seconds before she realised it was the flash of a camera going off in their faces rather than her hormones playing havoc.

A camera?

Noah moved in front of her, his body shielding hers— immediately protective.

Damn! The tabloid press had found them.

Outrage made her chest swell. Why couldn't the vultures leave Noah be and give him a chance to collect himself after the public humiliation of the cancelled wedding? They were like hyenas—going after a person when they were wounded. Well, she for one wasn't going to put up with it. Seizing his hand, she towed him towards an exit on the other side of the dance floor.

Outside in the corridor, she searched for a sign to the elevators. Damn it! They were only six floors up. Keeping a tight grip of his hand, she raced towards the fire escape.

'Not down there,' Noah said, taking the lead and racing them around the corner instead. 'They're bound to have someone posted at the bottom.'

Devils. 'What are you looking for?'

'Staff service elevator.'

'Which way did they go?' a voice said not too far behind them. Footsteps approached.

It wasn't a service elevator, but... Pulling open the door of a storage cupboard, she dragged Noah inside and closed the door behind them, placing a finger against her lips. They heard whoever was following pass by and she let out a breath. While they might've given that particular photographer the slip, that didn't solve their problem of those who might be waiting downstairs.

Her heart plummeted when she glanced up at the stern set of Noah's mouth. This was so unfair. He deserved some peace.

She searched her mind for a solution when her gaze landed on a pile of neatly folded uniforms for the hotel's housekeeping staff. She tapped him on the shoulder and pointed. 'Nobody notices the staff.'

'Look, Bree, if I give them what they want you'll be able to slip into a taxi unnoticed and get back to our hotel unmolested.'

No way!

She picked up the nearest uniform and slapped it to his chest. 'Put this on.'

'And what do you suggest we do with our clothes?'

'There's a pile of laundry bags there. We'll put them in one of those. You can carry the laundry bag and we'll both carry room service trays with assorted bits and bobs on them. Nobody will be any the wiser.'

He hesitated.

'Do you want to talk to the press?' she demanded.

'Of course not.'

'Hurry, then. Change. And keep your back to mine. You don't need to know what colour my underwear is.'

This was foolhardy on so many levels, but Noah couldn't resist the fire in Bree's big brown eyes. There was a spirit, a vehemence, in their depths that he hadn't seen since…

Since Otis, he suddenly realised. It had been too long returning and he wasn't going to be the one to dim it.

He *loved* seeing it back there. It made her entire being

come alive. An answering fire flashed through him. She was right. He didn't have to let the press walk all over him.

An entirely different spark flashed through him when her arm—her *naked* arm—brushed against his. And then her hip. This room might be generous in terms of storage space, but it was far too small for two people to be undressing in simultaneously.

Don't think about the undressing!

Gritting his teeth, he pulled his shirt from his waistband and undid the buttons. He had it halfway down his arms, doing his best not to bump up against Bree too much, when the door to the storage room was wrenched open and a series of bright flashes half blinded him.

Hell!

He moved in front of Bree in an effort to shield her, but he was too late. A glance over his shoulder showed him shocked wide eyes. She clasped her blouse to her chest. The hot pink straps of her bra gleamed bright against the honey of her skin, and the sight of her had him biting back a groan of pure unadulterated desire. With a swift oath, he shoved the camera back outside and slammed the door, before locking it.

'I didn't lock it,' she whispered. 'How could I have been so stupid as to not lock the door?'

The sparkle had well and truly disappeared and his gut dropped to the soles of his feet. How could he have let this happen? He'd let her down. He'd let the entire Allenby family down.

'Plan B,' he ground out.

'Which is?'

He hated how small her voice had gone. She didn't rail at him for getting her into this mess, but her silence was a hundred times worse. 'I ring Security and they escort us out a back way unseen.'

'Okay.'

They were back in their own suite forty minutes later. She turned to him the moment the door shut behind them. 'What now?'

He had to do everything he could to protect her from further media attention. 'We leave at the crack of dawn and disappear—find some out-of-the-way place between here and Melbourne and go to ground for a few days.'

Her face fell. 'You're coming to Melbourne?'

His temples throbbed. 'I know I'm messing with your plans, Bree, and I'll try to get out of your hair as soon as I can, but—'

'I'm not worried about that!'

She wasn't?

'I'm just sorry the press are hassling you and not giving you a chance to…' She shrugged. 'You know?'

Yeah, he knew, but she always put everyone before herself. Regardless of what she said, he was screwing with her plans and her desire for a leisurely, relaxing holiday.

His hands clenched. He'd do everything in his power to mitigate the damage he'd caused. 'I'm going to talk to the hotel manager—just in case the press finds out where we're staying, and no doubt they will. I might need to organise a decoy for the morning.'

'A decoy?'

'An official-looking car—maybe a limo—with blacked-out windows and a driver who might happen to whisper in an ear or two that he's been hired to drive me and a friend to the airport.'

'Wow. Okay.'

'Can you be ready to leave at six in the morning?'

She nodded. 'Is there anything else I can do?'

He glanced at the clock. She'd be lucky to get three or four hours' sleep. 'Nah, I've got it covered.' He did what he could to keep his tone light, jolly even, but it didn't chase the shadows from her eyes. 'I'll see you in the morning, Bree.'

He strode away, wanting to swear and swear and swear.

The shadows hadn't disappeared from her eyes the next day, not even after they'd left Sydney far behind. The sparkle had gone, leaving them dull and flat.

For the first hour and a half she'd sat hunched in the passenger seat, staring dully out of the window. She hadn't put up an argument when he'd said he'd like to take the first driving shift, had just handed the car keys over without a murmur.

He gripped the steering wheel so tight his fingers started to ache, before setting the cruise control to stop inadvertently speeding. 'You okay over there?'

She forced herself to un-hunch—at least, that was how it seemed to him. As if rousing herself took a giant effort. 'Sure I am.' She sent him a weak smile that didn't reach her eyes. 'What about you?'

He deserved to burn in hell for dragging her into this mess. 'I'm fine.'

He could tell she didn't believe him, so he rushed on. 'You want to know the plan?'

She straightened some more. 'Yes, please.'

'I've booked accommodation for a few nights at a farmstay place on the other side of Albury Wodonga. It does mean driving for six hours again today, but if it gets the press off our tails...'

'It'll be well worth it,' she finished for him.

'It's called the Colonial Cheese Factory. Check it out on your phone. It's kind of quaint.' The moment he'd seen the pictures he'd known she'd love it.

He'd hoped it would bring a smile to her lips, so was

disappointed when she merely read out the website information. She nodded. 'It looks pretty private, except...'

His gut clenched. 'Except?'

'It says they cater for couples and family groups as well as larger gatherings. If they have other people staying there at the moment then our cover could be blown.'

'Nobody else is staying there or booked to stay there. I checked. We're halfway between Easter and the next lot of school holidays, and they said they're ridiculously quiet.' He'd made sure it would stay that way by booking out the entire venue.

She closed her phone. 'Sounds perfect, then.'

She'd made no mention of getting a chance to milk a cow or collect fresh eggs or...anything. 'They have baby chicks.'

She glanced at him, the tiniest hint of interest brightening her eyes. 'Cute, fluffy yellow chicks?'

He nodded, suppressing a smile. 'And piglets.'

Her eyes widened. 'Piglets? Oh, that sounds fun. I wonder if we'd be allowed to pet them...play with them.'

'We can. I checked. Because you're right.' He laughed. 'How could piglets not be fun?'

To his relief she laughed too. 'What's more,' he added, 'they'll also provide us with canoes to go bobbing about on the river if we want. Far away from prying eyes,' he said with relish in his voice when she looked less convinced by that plan. 'Silently gliding on the water... I can't remember the last time I went canoeing.'

She stared at him. 'You sound like you miss it?'

Her words made him blink. 'I guess I have. I didn't realise how much until our hosts mentioned it was one of the activities available. Their property backs onto the river.'

'You make it sound nice. We should definitely do that while we're there.'

He felt the weight of her stare and turned to meet it briefly. He opened his mouth, but she continued. 'You know, Noah, we can spend an extra night or two here if we want. There's plenty of time before I have to board the overnight ferry for Tassie.'

For the moment he was just happy to see a little colour in her cheeks. 'Let's just play it by ear, shall we?' Neither of them had checked the newspaper headlines yet. The moment she saw those she might want to kick his sorry butt to the kerb.

It made no sense, but the thought of that drilled into his soul, making him ache in a way not even Courtney's rejection at the altar had.

He clenched his jaw. Oh, it made sense all right. All the sense in the world. He hadn't loved Courtney while the Allenbys meant everything to him. The thought of them turning their backs on him made him sick to the stomach. He glanced across at Bree. Her shoulders had started to hunch again.

'Okay...' he tapped his fingers against the steering wheel '...game time.'

She shifted towards him. 'Game?'

'I'm sorry, Bree, but if I have to listen to any more ABBA I'm going to go mad. I'm driving so I get to make up the rules.'

She huffed out a laugh at that and he refused to question the spark of energy it sent racing through him.

'We're going to play the alphabet band game,' he announced. 'We go through the alphabet—A through to Z—and name a band starting with the letter. We can't name the same band.'

She straightened. 'I up your "band" game to the "band and song" game. The song doesn't have to come from the same band, but you get extra points if it does.'

'Game on!'

'I get to go first,' she said, too quickly for him to counter. 'A for ABBA and "Arrival".'

'"Arrival" isn't a song, it's—'

'Of course it is. It's the name of an album *and* a song. That means I should get triple quadruple points.'

'It's not a song. It's an instrumental piece.'

'You really want to be that picky?'

'I'm driving. My rules.'

He kept his gaze on the road ahead, but sensed her bristling beside him—all fired up and competitive. He grinned.

'Fine! A for ABBA and "Andante Andante". Ha! Bonus points are mine.'

'Air Supply and "Air That I Breathe",' he shot back immediately. 'And I get extra bonus points for getting the word Air in both the band and the song.'

A laugh gurgled out of her. 'You great big fat cheat! Anyway it's "*The* Air That I Breathe!"' Which made him laugh too.

It should've been a bad day—a really bad day. But he'd enjoy this bubble of fun while it lasted.

Noah blew out a breath. 'Are you ready?'

They sat beneath the large pergola behind the factory part of the Colonial Cheese Factory, which housed a huge dining room on the ground floor and dormitory-style accommodation above. Their quarters were in a surprisingly large two-bedroom unit. Two of these formed a wing that extended behind the factory, with the pergola filling the space between.

The owners had a separate house at the front of the property while an additional six cabins marched down towards the river. It was private, secluded and very beautiful.

They'd nursed cute baby chicks, made friends with the milking cow, petted a huge Shire horse and hugged squirming piglets delighted to find in them new playmates.

Bree tossed a handful of seed, from the supply they'd been given, and two magnificent peacocks swooped in to gobble it up.

He shook his head. 'I can't believe they have peacocks.'

'They do seem a bit of an anomaly,' she agreed. 'But a nice one.' She dragged in a breath. 'Okay, I suppose I have to see it some time, and I guess I'm as ready as I'm ever going to be.'

He wished he could spare her this. He wished he could spare them both.

With fingers that weren't quite steady, he loaded the article, complete with those scandalous photos, onto his tablet and then held it out for her to see. He'd read it earlier—had tried to prepare her for it.

Even though she'd steeled herself, she still flinched. He wanted to hurl the tablet into the hydrangea bushes on the other side of the drive. Instead, he let her pluck it from his hands to read the article. He shooed away one of the peacocks when it started pecking a little too close to her sneaker.

'They... I knew... But—'

Her pallor made him wince.

'I knew they'd make it seem like we were having a torrid affair,' she finally choked out. 'But...oh, God. They make it sound like I broke you and Courtney up!'

'I know, Bree. But we know the truth and so do the people who matter—your family. And any of our friends worth their salt will too.'

She nodded, misery etched in the lines of her mouth. 'I'm so sorry, Noah. This is all my fault!'

His head rocked back. 'What are you talking about?'

'If I hadn't talked you into trying to disguise ourselves that awful photo would never have been taken. And I don't know how to make things right. I rang Mum and Dad, Ryder and Blake the night it happened so they'd all know this wasn't your fault. And if I'd had Courtney's number I'd have done the same. I can still—'

'Why on earth would you want to ring Courtney?'

'To tell her the truth!' She gestured at the photo. 'You're never going to be able to make things right with her if she believes this garbage.'

'Why would I want to make things right with her?'

'Because you love her!'

What the hell…?

He stared at Bree and shook his head. 'I don't love Courtney, Bree.' He enunciated the words clearly. 'I don't think I ever did.'

CHAPTER FIVE

'ARE YOU SERIOUS?'

Was Noah telling her the truth? He really wasn't in love with Courtney? Some of the awful weight that had been pressing down on Bree's chest lifted.

He frowned. 'Of course I'm serious.'

That weight lifted even further.

'I'm *not* in love with Courtney.'

Reaching over, he reclaimed his tablet and switched it off before setting it on the table. She had a feeling he only did it to give himself something to do, an excuse to not meet her eyes.

The weight pressed back down. Was he lying?

Eventually he lifted his head, his gaze direct even as his eyes swirled with myriad different emotions. 'I'm not in love with Courtney.' His shoulders slumped. 'I realised that the moment I woke up with the hangover I deserved in Coffs Harbour.'

The weight disappeared for good. She wanted to jump up and cheer. *Entirely inappropriate, Bree.* She dragged in a breath. *Stay in your seat; keep your expression calm.*

'I thought you knew that.' His frown deepened. 'I thought…' One broad shoulder lifted. 'Once I had the time to consider it all in a halfway logical manner, I thought what happened in the vestry—with you refusing to tell

Courtney we were well suited—proved you'd recognised the truth long before I did.'

'What made you realise you weren't in love with her?'

He hesitated for a fraction of a second. 'You telling me about how you'd felt when things exploded between you and Otis.'

Oddly, Otis's name didn't make her flinch as it usually did.

'Courtney dumping me at the altar shocked me, and the rejection stung me right down to my bone marrow, but I'm ashamed to admit I was more concerned with what everyone would think than I was with why Courtney had decided to run.' He rubbed a hand over his face. 'I owe her an apology of epic proportions.'

He pulled his hand away. 'But you knew then, right, at the wedding?'

She half nodded, half shrugged. 'At the time I was convinced. I knew you *thought* yourself in love with her. But if you'd truly loved her nothing would've stopped you from going after her and trying to make things right.'

He glanced down at his hands. 'I should've told her I loved her when we were in the vestry, and then she'd have stayed and married me. That's what you meant, wasn't it, when you said earlier that I could still make things right?'

She nodded. 'Do you wish you had?'

He shook his head. 'It would've been a lie, a terrible lie, but I have an awful feeling I'd have said it anyway to save us from the embarrassment of cancelling the wedding—to save face. How shallow is that?' He glanced up, his eyes dark and shadowed. 'It makes me sick to the stomach just thinking about it. Who the hell have I become that I'd hurt someone so badly just to save myself from feeling humiliated?'

She gripped his hand. 'It makes you human like the

rest of us. At the time you wouldn't have thought you were lying. You would've thought you were fixing things and making them right.'

The smile he sent her pierced her heart. 'I thought marrying Courtney would prove that I'd finally made it—that I was a success, not just in my business life, but in my private life as well. But it turns out I'm no better than my parents after all.'

She shot to her feet and the peacocks started like maidens in a gothic horror movie, picking up their skirts and racing away. She clenched her hands so hard she started to shake. 'Don't you ever say that again! It's not true and hearing you say it makes me want to slap you harder than I've ever wanted to slap anyone in my whole entire life.'

To her horror, her eyes filled and a sob gathered in the back of her throat. She swallowed it down. 'Not that I ever would, of course. I'd never hit anyone, but I'd definitely never lift a hand against *you*.'

'Bree.' He rose too, his face gentling. 'Don't do this. Don't you think I know that?'

And then she found herself pulled into his arms and she was breathing in his warm, comforting scent so familiar to her. Except the breadth of his chest and the strength of his arms and the lean power she felt coursing through him as she wrapped her arms around him was far from familiar. And it had awareness flooding through her.

She revelled in it for a couple of delicious breaths and then eased away because she couldn't stay there, no matter how much she might want to. His arms tightened briefly before releasing her.

Taking her hand, he made her sit again and sat back down beside her. Did she imagine it or had he shifted closer? 'Bree, I know you didn't mean it literally.'

Given how fast and ready his parents had been with their fists, though, her comment had been far from sensitive.

'You've been my champion since you were a feisty eight-year-old.'

When she was eight and Noah eleven, his family had moved into a house one street over from the Allenbys. Bree had been riding her bike on the footpath one summer afternoon when Noah, with his father in hot pursuit, had come bolting out of the house. Mr Fitzgerald had grabbed Noah by the arm and had started laying into him with the nearest thing to hand—a fence paling.

She'd been so outraged she'd leapt off her bike and run at Mr Fitzgerald yelling she was going to call the police. Mr Fitzgerald had been so surprised he'd let Noah go.

Noah had immediately leapt in front of her as if to protect her from his father's wrath, but she'd had no intention of sticking around. She'd grabbed Noah's hand and they'd run all the way back to her place. She'd thrown herself into her mother's arms and had sobbed out the whole story.

Her mother had fed them cookies and milk, had taken care of Noah's bruises and grazes, and had talked to them in her usual even tones until Bree's fright had eased.

She never knew what her mother and father said to Noah's parents later that afternoon, but Noah said it had made them stop hitting him.

Instead they'd vacillated between verbal abuse and ignoring him completely. As far as Bree was concerned, they were scum of the earth. The moment Noah had finished Year Twelve they'd turned him out of the house, claiming they'd done their duty. She didn't think he'd ever spoken to them again. They'd moved six years ago.

And good riddance! The Allenbys were Noah's family now. That first evening, her mother had made up a bed for Noah in the twins' room and he'd stayed with them for three whole nights. At the end of which he'd been firmly established as an honorary member of the Allenby clan. It had been understood by all parties from that time on that Noah would attend Sunday night family dinners. Or else.

Her parents had also taken Bree aside and told her she was to never step foot inside the Fitzgerald yard again. They'd made her promise. Considering the incident now from the ripe old age of twenty-six, she could appreciate how many grey hairs she must've given her parents over that incident.

'I'm glad I was riding past your house that day,' she said.

His hand tightened about hers. 'Me too.'

She turned to face him more fully, swallowing when she realised how close his face was to hers. 'You're nothing like your parents, Noah. *Nothing*. And—'

'They were selfish.' His face hardened. 'What they wanted mattered far more than anything else. And in this instance I've been just as selfish. I wanted this idealistic life with the perfect woman, and I went after it with a single-minded focus that didn't take her needs or wants into account.'

'What are you talking about? You didn't compel Courtney to accept your proposal. You gave her every damn thing that she wanted.'

'Except my heart.'

Her stomach dropped to her toes. 'Oh, Noah. You'd have given her that too if you could've.'

'What I did…now feels heartless. I didn't mean to hurt anyone, but that doesn't change the fact that I did. I'm ashamed of myself, sickened at what I've done.'

She pulled in a breath. 'You made a mistake. It doesn't mean you're a bad person.'

She hesitated. He leaned towards her. 'Go on.'

'I just think…rather than being ashamed of where you've come from—your background—you should be proud of where you are now and all you've achieved. You've been hell-bent on creating some mythically perfect life for yourself, but have you actually asked yourself if it'd truly make you happy?'

He stared at her but remained silent, so she forged on. 'It seems to me that you've been living in the future in an attempt to vanquish the past.' She spread her hands. 'But what about the here and now? Shouldn't you be relishing it?'

He sat back with a shake of his head, the faintest of smiles touching his lips. 'When did you get so wise and deep? But…' His lips pursed. 'Maybe you're onto something. I've been so focussed on trying to prove something to myself—'

He broke off, hauled in a breath. 'It's going to take some thinking through. One thing is for certain, I sure as hell haven't been living in the moment.'

Maybe that was something she *could* help with. 'What *are* your plans now, Noah? Short-term, I mean. I know Ryder wanted you to keep a low profile until he could clinch the Fullerton deal, which I figured meant you staying out of Brisbane for the next few weeks. What were you planning to do in Sydney?'

'I didn't have a plan. I just didn't want to cramp your style for too long and Sydney was the biggest place on your itinerary. Seemed a good place to lose myself in for a while.'

She moistened suddenly dry lips. 'Why don't you come to Tassie, then, and do something you love while you're there?' She searched her mind. 'Like white-water rafting or… Tasmania has wildlife treks that sound amazing. You know the spiel—treks through the world's most southernmost temperate rainforest or pristine marine reserves. We're talking truly remote World Heritage locations. That would be right up your alley.'

The amber flecks in his eyes flashed. She'd never thought the word hazel captured their beauty. They deserved a better description…like forest gold.

'Or,' she improvised, 'maybe you could crew on a yacht heading back up the coast. Bass Strait is notoriously tricky and might provide you with one of those adrenaline rushes you seem to enjoy. Besides, it'd be hard for the press to find you if you're deep in virgin forest or out at sea.'

That made him laugh. 'I like both of those ideas. A lot. I'll do some research tonight.' He stared at her for a long moment. 'Are you sure you don't mind me tagging along?'

'Not at all.' In fact, she'd enjoyed having him along. She fought back a frown. Perhaps she'd been enjoying it a little too much. She *was* supposed to be focussing on the future, after all.

'You know I'm going to ask you again, why you're heading to Hobart?'

Who knew, maybe she'd even tell him? 'But not tonight.'

His mouth opened as if he meant to argue, but their host chose that moment to step outside from the quirky factory behind them. 'Your dinner is ready. Just let me know when you'd like to eat it and—'

Bree leapt up. 'Normally we eat much later, but now will be fabulous.' It was an hour and a half earlier than her usual dinnertime, but… She glanced at Noah. 'I'm starving, aren't you?' They'd barely eaten anything all day. 'We set off so early this morning.'

'Famished.' He rose too.

'I'll make you up a cheese and fruit platter to take back to your apartment to nibble on later?'

'Better and better,' Bree said with a smile that felt oddly

light and free. 'I have a feeling we're going to enjoy our stay here very much, Mrs Wilks.'

They were served huge bowls of the most delicious cassoulet she'd ever eaten, along with generous chunks of warm crusty bread. When the worst of their hunger had been sated, and Bree was wiping a piece of the bread through the gravy left in her bowl, because she couldn't bear to waste any of it even though she was now full, she glanced up to find Noah watching her. 'What?' Did she have food smeared across her face? She hastily wiped her mouth with a napkin.

'You figured out early on that I wasn't in love with Courtney. What made you change your mind?'

She pushed her plate away. 'You seemed so gutted on Saturday night, and when we talked about heartbreak and Otis, I realised I had absolutely no right to leap to conclusions about you and your situation.'

He shook his head, pushing his plate away too. 'You do, you know? We're friends, Bree. We've known each other a long time. Leap to all the conclusions you want. I don't mind.'

She couldn't smile, even though she knew he wanted her to. 'That thing that happened with the tabloids, despite what you say, Noah, it was my fault. Dragging us into that storage cupboard and donning disguises... It was a stupid thing to do.'

'It didn't feel stupid. It felt like we were taking back power. It felt like an adventure.'

She'd given him no say in the matter—had just ordered him about. 'And look what happened. I made things worse for you. And Ryder is now having to do double-duty damage control in Brisbane.'

Her stomach churned and she wished she hadn't eaten so much. 'It threw me back to my crazy wild days with

Otis and we all know how well that turned out. I let everyone down back then and I felt like I'd let you down again last night. And if you'd still been in love with Courtney I'd have ruined things utterly.'

'Bree—'

'I felt like I'd screwed everything up for everyone. And I've been trying so hard not to be that person.'

It was of paramount importance that she not ever be that person again. Her very reason for going to Hobart… the discussions she and Tina were about to have…the outcome of those discussions…it all relied on her no longer being rash and irresponsible. She couldn't let Tina and her daughter Tilly down, or Tina's parents. The very thought had acid burning her throat.

Noah's hand on hers brought her back to the present. 'Bree, you're no longer the same person you were then. You've grown up, matured, and you've learned from your mistakes. You need to be proud of all you've achieved too.'

She wanted to believe him, but she didn't believe in fairy tales. Not any more.

Noah dipped the paddle in the water and slid the canoe over the surface of the river, letting the natural beauty filter into his soul. Gum trees—mostly grey and ghost gums—lined the opposite bank while native undergrowth provided thick cover for the wildlife. He picked out the chatter of parrots, the distinctive call of a butcherbird and a warbling magpie.

As he closed his eyes calm flooded his soul. The raucous laughter of three kookaburras had him opening them again a little while later with a smile.

He glanced across at Bree, who rested her paddle crossways on her canoe and just let it drift, a dreamy expression on her face. He let out a slow breath, noting her shoulders had lost some of their tension.

He'd barely been able to believe what he'd heard last night. Bree wasn't a screw-up. He couldn't believe she saw herself as one. Nobody in her family saw her as anything but smart, driven...and kind. He'd said as much. The twist of her lips, though, had told him his words had made little impact.

What had happened with Otis had changed her. It had made her more careful, less carefree, more focussed on her work. It had hurt him, seeing those changes, but he'd understood them, understood her need to feel safe again. He just hadn't realised she'd blamed herself so completely for being taken in by Otis.

For heaven's sake, she'd only been nineteen and in her second year of university when she'd met and tumbled head over heels in love with Otis Collins. She'd had crushes before, but they'd all sensed that Otis was different. None of them had realised that beneath his 'good guy' persona Otis had been dealing drugs to fund his growing cocaine habit.

Hell! He'd attended every single Sunday night family dinner that Bree had invited him to, unlike some other persons who would remain nameless.

Even when Bree had started partying too hard and her grades had started to suffer, they'd all put it down to youthful high spirits. Her horror when she'd flunked one of her subjects had reassured them all that she'd get some balance back in her life and knuckle down to her studies.

They'd all been blind. Not to Bree—they'd read her perfectly. But blind to Otis. The police, thankfully, hadn't been so naïve or so trusting. They'd been keeping tabs on Otis for months and it was during a surprise raid on his house that Otis had slipped a significant amount of cocaine into Bree's handbag. When it was discovered, Otis had claimed Bree was the dealer and he was her patsy.

Of course, Bree's fingerprints were nowhere to be found

on the drugs and her drug tests came back negative, unlike Otis's. But she'd spent a night in a jail cell. She'd had to testify in court. Even now Noah could recall her pinched white face and the dark circles beneath her eyes, blue as bruises. For as long as Noah lived, he never wanted to see that expression again on her face. He'd do anything in his power to prevent it.

Otis, though, was to blame for all of that. Not her.

She'd admitted later that she'd known Otis occasionally took drugs and he had laughed at her concern, but he'd promised to stop and she'd believed him. She'd had no idea that his drug use had escalated or that he'd become a dealer.

She'd made a mistake in trusting Otis and that was hardly a crime.

The ringtone of her phone sounded from the riverbank—ABBA's 'Mamma Mia', of course—weirdly cheerful amid all of this bucolic serenity.

She glanced at him as he paddled up beside her. 'If this was a normal day in a normal week,' she said with a sigh, 'I'd ignore it.'

But it wasn't. Every time one of their phones rang, they tensed.

'I'll check it quickly and be right back.' She gestured around at the view. 'This is too glorious to be away from for too long.'

He watched her paddle back to the sandy shore and pull her canoe up beneath the trailing fronds of a pepper tree. She checked her phone and frowned. 'It's work,' she called out. 'I better call them back.' She punched in a number and then held it to her ear. She strode the length of the small beach to the weeping willow that marked its other end.

He couldn't hear what she said. She seemed to be doing more listening than speaking. The call was brief. When it was over she stowed her phone back with their picnic basket and other bits and pieces they'd brought down to the bank with them and pushed back out towards him.

He tensed at the angry glitter in her eyes. 'Everything okay? They haven't cancelled your leave, have they?' She'd not taken a proper holiday in an age. She deserved a break.

'I've been fired.'

'What?'

He stiffened so suddenly his canoe rocked and she reached across to steady it. 'Careful. You don't want to take a dip. The water's cold.'

He reached out to grab the side of her canoe to prevent her from paddling away. 'Why?'

She blew out a breath and glanced skyward. It was a perfect blue—he'd already checked.

'It was that damn tabloid article, wasn't it?'

'In a way.' She huffed out a mirthless laugh. 'Court-ney's father bought the practice this morning.'

Bree worked for a large physiotherapy practice that spe-cialised in sporting injuries and post-op recuperation.

'His first action as the new owner was to fire me.'

Courtney's father had bought the physiotherapy prac-tice with the sole purpose of...

'If you overturn my canoe, Noah, I'm going to be seri-ously unimpressed.'

He loosened his grip, but his heart thundered in his chest. 'That is—' he started through gritted teeth. 'I—'

'It doesn't matter. I actually qualify for a rather attrac-tive redundancy package.'

He sucked air into his lungs and forced himself to let it out slowly. 'You can bring your plan to open your own practice forward.' They all knew The Plan off by heart, they'd heard it so many times. Graduate with a double de-gree by the ripe old age of twenty-two. Work for several years gaining valuable experience while saving hard. Open her own practice by the time she was thirty, but ideally by age twenty-eight. She was twenty-six now. It was only twenty months early.

Her gaze slid away. 'The time's not right for that.'

He didn't ask why. She'd have a sound reason. 'Good.'

Her eyebrows flew up and she glanced back at him.

'It means I can table an offer Ryder and I have been wanting to extend to you.'

'Offer?'

'We've held off because we knew The Plan and your dream of opening your own clinic, being your own boss.' He shrugged. 'We get it. We both wanted to be our own bosses too, and we haven't wanted to pressure you to give up that dream.'

'Offer?' she said again.

'You know that Ryder and I plan to expand our gyms?'

She nodded. 'You've plans to open franchises in Sydney, Melbourne and Adelaide.'

'We don't just want to expand into new locations. We want to increase the services we offer.'

She stared at him expectantly.

He spread his hands wide. 'Like a physiotherapy clinic and the opportunity for appointments with a dietician. Your double degree plus the business training you've done on the side makes you the perfect candidate to head up that side of operations.'

Her jaw dropped. She leaned towards him. 'Are you making that up on the fly or have you and Ryder really talked about this?'

'Hand on heart.' He clapped a hand to his chest. 'We're still in discussions. He thinks we should table you an offer.'

'And you?'

Her voice had gone husky and it brushed against the

nerve endings of his skin, firing things to life inside him. 'I don't want you to give up your dreams to help us achieve ours. But one of Ryder's arguments is beginning to hold weight with me. He says just because we make you an offer doesn't mean you have to accept it, that having options is always a positive thing.'

Her lips lifted. 'That sounds like Ryder.' Her eyes started to sparkle. 'It sounds really exciting! I'd be building it from the ground up and—'

She broke off, her eyes losing that sparkle.

'What?' he barked, wanting the sparkle back.

'The timing's not right.'

'Why not? If you're between jobs and it's not the right time to open your own clinic…?'

She rubbed both hands over her face. 'The thing is, Noah, The Plan has changed.'

She'd changed The Plan? He blinked, frowned. Why was this the first he'd heard of it? *Why* had she changed it? It was *seriously* out of character. 'Is this because you've been fired?'

'No, not because of that.'

She smiled but it was full of a sadness he didn't understand.

'C'mon.' She hitched her chin in the direction of the bank. I don't want you capsizing our canoes. This is a conversation for dry land…and chocolate.'

He followed her back to the shore, skimming past her to heave both canoes up onto the bank and then offering his hand to help her out. She gripped his hand and stood, and then glanced up into his face and stilled at whatever she saw there. She pressed a hand to his cheek. 'Don't look so worried, Noah.'

She pulled her hand away and his skin burned from where she'd touched it. He wanted to grab her hand and put it back. He wanted her to keep staring into his eyes with that same soft warmth. He wanted—

Stop it.

Choking down the inconvenient attraction, he followed her to the picnic blanket. 'How can I not worry? It sounds serious.'

'It is serious.' She knelt on the blanket and rifled through the picnic hamper their hostess had provided for them. 'It's serious, sad…exciting…terrifying.'

She settled back with a chocolate bar and pulled off the wrapper. Breaking off a piece, she tossed it to him before popping a second piece into her mouth and gesturing for him to take a seat.

'So, you know Tina,' she started.

He suppressed the instinct to pace and forced himself down to the blanket, popping the piece of chocolate into his mouth with an equanimity he was far from feeling. 'Tina who you're visiting in Hobart? Best friends forever and all that. What about her?'

Bree and Tina had been inseparable until the end of Year Ten when Tina's parents had relocated to Hobart. The girls had kept in constant contact. They'd holidayed together at different times—while they were still at school, with each other's families. When they were at university they'd catch up whenever they could. With the recent concerns about Tina's health, Bree had made multiple trips to Hobart in the last couple of years.

'Blake has a theory you've met some guy in Tassie and that's why you've been visiting so often.'

'I wish that were the case. I really do.'

But her sigh said otherwise and his every sense went on high alert.

'Tina's brain tumour has returned.'

He sucked in a breath. Tina had undergone major surgery two years ago.

'There's nothing they can do. Initially they were hopeful that radiation treatment would keep it under control, but...'

She trailed off and his throat burned at the sadness in her eyes. 'How long has she got?'

'Best-case scenario is eighteen months.'

Hell. Life could be so unfair. 'I'm sorry, Bree.'

She nodded. 'It sucks.'

'You've been trying to spend as much time with her as you can?'

'Absolutely.' She glanced up, even more downcast if that were possible. 'And Tilly is only three.'

Tilly was Tina's daughter. 'And as Tilly's godmother you want to be there for her.'

Some little kid was now going to grow up without her mother. His hand's clenched. 'Tilly's father...?'

'He shot through when Tina was pregnant. He wanted nothing to do with either of them.'

He swore.

'Tina's parents are in their sixties. They had Tina when they were in their early forties.'

She stared at him half expectantly, but he didn't know what she was waiting for. 'They must be beside themselves,' he murmured.

'Gutted.' She glanced down at her hands. 'She's an only child—no brothers or sisters.'

No wonder Bree had been visiting so regularly. No doubt she was helping out wherever and however she could; offering all the emotional support Tina, Tilly and Tina's parents needed. 'Why haven't you told any of us about this before now, Bree?' They could've at least given her whatever emotional support *she* needed.

She moistened her lips. He refused to notice their shine

in the warm autumn sunshine. Or how they beckoned and sent a summer heat curling through him.

'Tina and Tilly don't really have anyone, Noah. I mean, Tina has friends—plenty of them—but none like me. We're practically sisters…and with her parents getting on…'

What on earth was she trying to tell him?

'Tina wants Tilly raised by a young woman like herself. She doesn't want her parents running themselves ragged in their later years when they should be enjoying their retirement.'

He stared. He couldn't utter a single word.

'She's asked if I'll be Tilly's guardian.'

He should've seen this coming. How could he have been so slow-witted?

'And I've said yes.'

CHAPTER SIX

BREE HELD HER breath after she delivered her life-changing piece of news. Maybe she imagined it, but for three beats of her heart everything went still—even the birds stopped singing—but then it all seemed to rush back at her with ten times the force.

Breathe, Bree, breathe.

'You're going to raise Tilly?'

She shoved more chocolate in her mouth and nodded.

She watched his every expression with an eagle-eyed concentration, waiting for concern, consternation…opposition. Opposition that she didn't have the ability to do it, that she wouldn't be able to provide Tilly with a stable home—that she was too ill equipped, selfish, and irresponsible to be trusted with such a role. That she was too much of a screw-up to ever be a maternal role model for anyone.

Instead, those extraordinary amber flecks in his eyes blazed gold and she blinked, momentarily dazzled. 'You are your mother's daughter.'

Her eyes filled. It was the biggest compliment he could give anyone.

'You're brave and true and so committed to the people you love. You have such a big heart, Bree, and I'm beyond awed that you've chosen to share all of that with Tilly—to provide her with all the love and security that she's going to need.'

He was?

'It's tragic that she's losing her mother at such a young age. But she has you and that makes her lucky.'

She did what she could to dislodge the lump in her throat. 'You don't think it's a crazy idea?'

'Not for a moment.' He leaned towards her. 'I'll do everything in my power to support you. Your whole family will.'

His words made her heart clench. 'I know. It's just… I'm terrified.'

It was liberating to admit it out loud.

He reached across to snap a piece of chocolate from the bar she held and nodded. 'It's a big step—an entire lifestyle change. But I don't doubt that you're up for the challenge. You'll do a wonderful job. You'll be a wonderful mother.'

She bit her lip. 'It wasn't part of The Plan.' She'd created The Plan after her experience with Otis, to keep her on track and make everyone proud of her—so she didn't let them down again.

'This isn't exactly the kind of thing one can plan for.'

'The thing is…' she popped another piece of chocolate into her mouth, her heart thumping '…in some ways it's *better* than The Plan.'

She stiffened. 'Not losing Tina, that's—'

She broke off, fighting the burn in her eyes and the ache in her heart. She still couldn't believe her dearest friend in the world had such a limited time left on earth. It was monumentally unfair. It made her want to yell and throw things…and cry until there weren't any tears left.

She pushed the gathering darkness away. She couldn't allow her grief for what would happen in the future to harm what time she had left with Tina. Her friend had a live-in-the-moment mantra and she'd begged Bree to follow it for the time being too.

She tried to find a smile. 'What I mean is having the opportunity to raise Tilly is an unbelievable honour.' It felt like a gift. 'I've been smitten with that kid from the day she was born.' She'd been Tina's birth partner, had taken annual leave to coincide with Tilly's birth to support Tina. 'I feel…incredibly lucky.'

Two lines appeared between Noah's eyes. 'You make it sound like a negative, but it's a positive, isn't it?'

She tried to appear casual when everything inside her clamoured and panicked—the exact opposite of the calm control she'd been trying to cultivate since she was nineteen years old. 'It's just…if having the opportunity to raise Tilly is so much better than anything on The Plan, what else on it is…lacking?'

'So change The Plan.'

He said it as if it were the simplest thing in the world, and for the first time it occurred to her that maybe it was.

'Obviously,' she started slowly, 'I've already had to change it.'

'To include Tilly.'

In that moment it occurred to her what a great uncle he'd make. With his patience, good heart and easy humour. One day he'd make a great dad too.

The thought made her mouth dry, though she couldn't explain why.

She tried to get her mind back on track and focus on the here and now. She cleared her throat. 'So I'm now thinking maybe I don't want to open my own clinic either.'

The words felt odd to say after she'd been saying them for the best part of seven years, but they also felt freeing. As long as she could create a new plan—and stick to it—

changing the old plan wouldn't send her careening off the rails or turn her into a reckless ninny.

Not if she was careful.

Noah had started to bite into an apple, but he halted—mouth open, teeth touching the skin, but yet to break it. He lowered the apple still intact. 'What…never?'

'Never say never, I guess,' she said, testing the freedom of a more flexible approach to plan making…and liking it. 'But not in the foreseeable future. I saw all the hours you and Ryder worked in the early days to get Fitness Ark up and running, the commitment it demanded of you.'

'Ask either one of us and we'd tell you it was worth every second.'

She nodded. They deserved their success and she was happy for them. 'For the next few years, though, I want to focus on creating a stable home for Tilly. And to be brutally honest, Noah,' she added quickly to forestall him from telling her that was an admirable goal, 'I'm not feeling the tiniest bit disappointed or wistful about not being my own boss.'

He finally bit into the apple, took his time chewing and swallowing, as if he was considering the things she'd just confided to him with that same slow deliberation. One of the things she'd always loved about Noah was the way he thought before he spoke.

She blinked. Loved? Loved in a completely platonic 'he's been my friend forever' kind of way. That was what she meant. *Of course.*

'If you want to run your own business, you have to want it really badly.'

She nodded.

'If you don't want it with a passion…'

'Then I shouldn't do it,' she finished for him. 'Which is why I have to come up with another plan.'

His face suddenly cleared. 'That's the reason for the road trip! To give you time to sort through all of this stuff—the wide open road as a metaphor for all of the possibilities at your feet.'

'Ha! Mrs Miller's English classes weren't lost on you after all.'

He grinned. 'Everyone loves a good metaphor.'

'I knew a road trip would force me to slow down.'

The smile slid from his face. 'I've messed that up for you.'

She shook her head. 'Having you along, our conversations, has made me realise something important. I don't have to replace the original plan with one equally rigid. I've been so focussed on the absolute right way to move forward that I'd developed a kind of blinkered vision.'

He didn't look as if he believed her.

'In the same way your plan to marry Courtney was blinkered.' She hoped it didn't upset him, her mentioning it. 'You can see now what a mistake it would've been—that it wouldn't have made either of you happy in the long term. And I'm starting to see the same with me and The Plan.'

His gaze abruptly turned from hers to stare out over the river. *Damn.* She had upset him.

She tried for levity. 'I'm breaking up with The Plan.'

He didn't crack so much as a smile.

'Noah, our conversations have made me realise that it's crazy to try and map out our entire futures. There are always going to be things we can't plan for.' If she could focus on just doing two things right—being a good parent to Tilly, and finding work that would satisfy her... oh, and keeping all reckless impulses under wraps—then maybe that would be enough. Maybe she could define that as success?

The rigid line of his jaw lost the worst of its hardness. 'That's true.'

'There are some non-negotiables, obviously. I'll need a home for Tilly and I to live. That means swapping apartment living for a place in the suburbs with a yard and that's close to good schools. I'll need a job so I can support us. Given my qualifications, though, finding a job I'll hopefully enjoy shouldn't be too difficult.'

For the first time it suddenly felt as if she could do all of this, and do it well. Without screwing any of it up.

'Bree!'

Noah seemed to light up from the inside out and it made her pulse hammer. 'What?'

'Then this is the perfect time for you to join Ryder and me at Fitness Ark. You'd be able to lay the groundwork for both the physio and dietician side of things before Tilly comes to live with you. When she does, we have a crèche at the gym, which would give you inbuilt childcare.' His lips thinned. 'Plus your job would be secure. The Frasers can't touch us.'

It sounded perfect. Utterly perfect. She'd love to be the person to expand that side of Fitness Ark's operations. Not only would she love the work and the variety it promised, but she'd never find a comparable job that would suit her half so well in a practical sense. But it was impossible.

A big black cloud loomed over her future and, no matter how hard she tried to shift it, it refused to budge. She needed to find a way to embrace it.

It won't be so bad, she told herself for the hundredth time. She forced a smile to suddenly uncooperative lips. 'Except for one small tiny thing,' she made herself say.

'What's that?'

'I'm planning to move to Hobart.' She shrugged, forced a laugh. 'So the commute would be a killer.'

He stared at her as if he hadn't heard her properly, as if her words made no sense. 'Moving to Hobart?'

'Relocating,' she said, leaving no room for misinterpretation.

He tossed his apple core into the river. 'Your entire family is in Brisbane, Bree. Your family is going to be your support network. Your parents will want to be grandparents to Tilly, while your brothers will want to be hands-on uncles.'

'And you?' she found herself asking.

He nodded. 'And me too.'

She knew exactly everything she was leaving behind, and she mourned it already. A weight pressed down on her, but she kept her chin high and refused to let her shoulders sag. 'But…you can all come to visit.' She hated how small her voice sounded. 'You will, won't you?'

'Of course we will. But why leave at all? In all likelihood Tilly won't be at school yet and—'

He broke off and she saw the exact moment he realised.

'Tina's parents,' he murmured.

'They're losing their daughter, Noah. I can't take Tilly away from them as well.'

Two days later they arrived in Melbourne, and were settled in a neat and tidy serviced apartment on the South Bank that enjoyed comprehensive views of the Yarra River.

Bree returned to the apartment after a day of browsing the shops, and wondered how Noah had filled his day. Closing the door with her hip, she set her various parcels to the floor—most of them gifts for Tina and Tilly—and pulled an envelope from her handbag.

She frowned, tapping it against her fingers as she waited for the kettle to boil. What on earth had she been thinking? It was totally inappropriate and—

'What you got there?'

Noah emerged from his bedroom, making her jump.

Worn jeans were slung low on lean hips and a navy T-shirt plastered itself to his chest. With his hair tousled and a faint shadow darkening his jaw he looked like every woman's vision of the ultimate dreamboat. Yearning rose through her hot and hard, her tongue snaking out to moisten arid lips. He followed the action, his gaze darkening.

They both looked away at the same moment.

Dear God. 'Oh, nothing.' She slid the envelope into the back pocket of her jeans before grabbing coffee mugs from the cupboard, but her assumed nonchalance failed when she realised she'd missed her pocket and the envelope fell to the floor instead, landing at Noah's feet.

Pouncing on it would be too revealing. All she could hope was that he'd hand it back without reading the logo stamped on the front.

His brows shot up the moment he leaned down to pick it up.

No such luck, then.

He pointed to the logo. 'Doesn't look like nothing to me.'

She blew out a breath when he handed it back to her. 'On the spur of the moment I got us tickets to tomorrow's game.'

Two of the Australian Football League's most iconic clubs were meeting for what was expected to be one of the clashes of the season at the MCG.

Noah's entire face lit up.

She'd so wanted to give him a treat to thank him for being so supportive about Tina and Tilly. She'd wanted to find something that would help chase away the shadows that lingered in his eyes.

So he'd made a mistake where Courtney was concerned. She knew what it felt like to make a mistake. He needed to stop beating himself up about it.

She bit back a sigh. 'But, of course, it was a stupid thing to do and a waste of money.' She'd bought the tickets on impulse, without considering the wider implications— but she didn't have to compound her mistake as she had in Sydney.

'What do you mean? We're not setting off on the *Spirit of Tasmania*—' the overnight ferry that would take them from Port Melbourne to Devonport in Tasmania '—until Monday night. There'll be plenty of time to watch tomorrow's game. We'll have all of Monday to pack and do any last-minute shopping.'

'Time isn't the problem, Noah. This is going to be one of the biggest games of the year. There's going to be a lot of media interest in the game. Which means the likelihood of you being recognised is disproportionately high.' Especially after what had happened in Sydney.

But… 'You can go!' She shoved the tickets at him. 'It won't matter if you get photographed alone.' He could still enjoy the treat.

His stance widened. 'We can both go.'

'I'm sorry, Noah, but I really couldn't bear any more speculation about our relationship in the papers. Tina and her parents must be having kittens already and—'

'Are you worried about their reactions to the Sydney fiasco?'

'Yes. No.' She pushed her hair off her face. 'Not really. I know they'll understand, but—'

'The timing has been less than ideal.'

She stabbed a finger at him. 'Don't even start thinking this is your fault. I just…' She pressed her hands together.

'I just don't want to give them anything else to worry about. They have enough to deal with already.'

He turned thoughtful, moved her gently aside. 'Tea or coffee?'

'Tea, please.'

He made the tea and they sat on the sofas that rested at right angles to each other. They'd each claimed a sofa of their own when they'd first walked into the apartment. He eyed her over the rim of his mug. 'What if I could guarantee that we wouldn't be recognised?'

'If you could guarantee that then I'd be there like a shot, but you can't.'

'Oh, ye of little faith, Bree. I can and I will.'

Noah spun on the chair and spread his arms wide. 'What do you think?'

Bree's jaw dropped, making him laugh.

'I'd have walked past you on the street and not even recognised you. And I've known you forever. Ahmed, you're a genius!'

Noah had met Ahmed at university, and, although Ahmed had switched from computer engineering to cinematography in their second year, they'd remained friends.

Ahmed was now working for a TV production company in Melbourne doing everything from make-up and special effects to film editing. All it had taken was a phone call from Noah explaining what he needed, and Ahmed had been immediately on board with creating believable disguises for Bree and Noah.

'Given everything that's happened over the last week, I figured it was time you copped a break, Noah.'

Had it only been a week ago that Courtney had left him standing at the altar like a fool?

One week and one day.

It felt as if his entire worldview had changed in the course of those eight days.

He snapped back when Bree moved across and bent down to peer into his face. She wore a dark wig in a shaggy Suzi Quatro style, and the make-up Ahmed's assistant had chosen completely changed her skin tone. Rather than her usual tropical tan she now had a pale nearly white, slightly pasty complexion. But he'd have still recognised her. Those melt-in-your-mouth milk-chocolate eyes were exactly the same.

Ahmed surveyed her and nodded his satisfaction. 'You are still pretty, but no longer so glamorously beautiful.'

She blinked and straightened, and Noah could breathe again.

'Glamorous? Me?' She laughed. 'You didn't tell me your friend was such a charmer, Noah.'

Something inside him stilled. Glamorous wasn't the word he'd have used to describe Bree, but maybe that was just because he'd known her for so long.

It was an undeniable fact, though, that Bree Allenby was a very beautiful woman. And he wanted her. With the kind of fierce desire that pumped an urgent heat through his blood and had his every sense drinking in the sight, sound and scent of her.

He wanted to add taste and touch to that profusion of sense sensation too—craved them.

Which meant he was going to hell.

He clenched his hands. He'd never *act* on those impulses. It was out of the question. He needed to exorcise all such thoughts from his mind.

He could've groaned out loud when she bent down to peer into his face once more. 'Even the colour of your eyes has changed.'

'Brown contact lenses,' Ahmed said.

'And you've given him a full bushranger beard. It's amazing how that one thing changes everything else.'

It had taken a long time to apply—a lot of hair and glue had been involved. He'd been ordered to not scratch his face. Which meant he now itched all over.

'It hides the shape of his jaw and chin...makes him look less clean-cut.'

He'd been careful to cultivate a clean-cut wholesomeness as a teenager in an effort to distance himself from his parents. They'd never taken any real interest in their appearance—other than to look like the kind of people you didn't want to mess with.

His gut tightened. Did he look like his father?

He reached up and stroked his beard. Bree's smile nearly slayed him.

'You look great. Talk about fun!'

In that moment he didn't care what he looked like. All he cared about was making sure she enjoyed herself at today's game.

'At least the shape of your mouth is the same.'

He ground his back molars together. *Don't think about mouths or lips or what the hell mouths and lips can do or—*

'Right.' Ahmed clapped his hands. 'Time for your new outfits. At the moment you both look far too put-together.'

'This man is so good for my ego.' Bree winked at Noah before striding off with Ahmed's assistant.

He watched her go, things inside him clenching and softening. How could a woman create such conflicting sensations in him? It was just...her ego shouldn't need boosting.

Why had he never realised how deeply her experience with Otis had affected her or how widespread those effects had been? Or that she continued to punish herself for that one youthful mistake? She was starting to forgive herself, though, was learning to trust herself again. No longer being so rigid about The Plan was proof of that.

Otis was losing his hold on her. Noah would do all he could to speed up the process. And he also planned to try and change his own focus as she'd urged him to—to concentrate on the positives and the future, rather than on the negatives and the past.

'C'mon, Noah, let's make you thoroughly unrecognisable.'

Twenty minutes later, Noah couldn't hold back a bark of laughter when he and Bree stood side by side and stared at their reflections in the floor-length mirror. They both wore football jerseys, and Bree had a beanie pulled down low over her ears. Her jersey and beanie clashed with the sparkly purple high-top sneakers she wore. It was an outfit she'd normally never be caught dead in.

Speaking of not being caught dead in an outfit, though... The tail of his flannelette shirt hung out beneath his jersey and over the top of his baggy jeans. He looked scruffy and unkempt. No one who knew him would *ever* recognise him.

She grinned at him like a little kid playing dress-ups. 'This was an inspired idea, Noah. I so have to take a photo of us.' Bree fished out her phone. 'They'll never believe this back home.'

Home. A weight pressed down on him. It wouldn't feel like home if Bree weren't there. Did she really have to relocate to Hobart?

Instinct told him that while her heart was wholly committed to Tilly and providing the very best life she could for the little girl—and he admired her more than he could say for that—she was less overjoyed at the prospect of relocating to the country's southernmost state.

Or was he simply projecting his own feelings onto her?

'Okay, we need pseudonyms to complete the charade.' Bree's voice broke into his thoughts.

'Something starting with an N for you. If I start to say "Noah" I'll be able to turn it into...' she reached up and tapped his beard '... Ned!'

He laughed at her overt reference to one of Australia's most notorious bushrangers. 'Fine, if I'm Ned then you're Bonnie.'

'Oh! Now I want to call you Clyde.'

'No, no,' Ahmed remonstrated. 'Don't forget the name of the game is to blend in and be as invisible as possible. Not to draw attention to yourselves. You are Ned and Bonnie, die-hard football fans from the western suburbs— Lilydale, if anyone should ask. You drink beer or soda, not wine, and you eat pies and hotdogs, not caviar.'

Bree nodded once. 'Got it.'

Her eyes sparkled and Noah couldn't help but be infected by her enthusiasm. He glanced at his watch. They'd have to make a move. 'I can't thank you enough for this, Ahmed.'

'I was glad to help. Now go and enjoy yourselves.'

The ground was crowded when they got there even though there was still an hour to go till game time. And not a single soul gave them so much as a second look.

No, that wasn't entirely true. There'd been a tense moment when they'd lined up to buy their lunch—pies and sodas as instructed by Ahmed—when the guy in front had turned and halted for a moment, his brow furrowing as he stared at Noah.

'Jacko? From Gallagher's Autos?'

Noah had been careful to keep his answer short and on point. 'Ned. Lilydale. Plumber.'

'Sorry, mate, wrong bloke.'

With a clap to Noah's shoulder he'd sauntered off with his beer. Bree—Bonnie—had buried her face in the back of Ned's shoulder to suppress her laughter. He'd had to suppress an urge to swing around and high-five her.

They found their seats and ate their food, and as the stadium filled up around them the air of expectation and excitement filled them both.

'There has to be at least fifty thousand people here,' she said.

He glanced around. 'Probably closer to sixty.' And not a soul recognised them. They could relax their guard and focus on the moment, and have fun. 'This was the best idea, Br—Bonnie. Thanks for getting tickets.'

She shrugged. 'I wanted to thank you for being so supportive. Besides, you deserve to let your hair down and have some fun.'

Those eyes could slay a guy when they looked at him like that. The thing was, he'd had fun—road-tripping with her. When he should've been cast down in the doldrums, he'd instead been rediscovering his love for life and adventure.

While Bree had used The Plan to keep herself on too tight a leash, he'd been holding himself back in a similar fashion in an attempt to mould and shape his life into something it wasn't. Or would ever be. He was starting to realise that what he'd thought would make him happy was nothing more than an empty promise.

His past didn't belong in the here and now; he had nothing to prove to anyone, least of all himself. The fact he could never attain that imagined level of perfection didn't leave him feeling like a failure any more either.

That was why he'd been determined to make today happen for Bree. The expression on her face when she'd realised the likelihood of them being recognised would prevent them from attending the game had speared through the centre of him. He'd wanted to make things right for her.

'N-Ned?'

He thumped back to the present. 'You couldn't have come up with a better treat.'

Her smile widened and it occurred to him that a large portion of her enjoyment was due to his enjoyment. It had all the hard places inside him softening.

When the game started, though, she couldn't hide either her enjoyment or her enthusiasm. She yelled and cheered as loud as anybody. The game was end-to-end stuff and everything it had been hyped up to be.

At half-time their team was up by only two points after having lost some ground in the second quarter. 'I'm not going to be able to put up with that tension for another half!' But her grin belied her words.

'I'm going to be hoarse by the time we're done,' he agreed.

They launched into a blow-by-blow discussion of the half. As the little sister of two sports-mad brothers, Bree could hold her own in any sporting match post-mortem. They were concentrating so hard on their conversation it wasn't until nearby cheers and friendly jostling from the crowd roused them. A neighbouring fan pointed at the big screen and Noah wanted to groan out loud. Kiss cam! How the hell had a bloody camera picked them out of a crowd this size for the ridiculous pastime of—?

His thoughts screamed to a halt when Bree seized his face in her hands and slammed her lips to his. He was too shocked to move, though his hands did go to her shoulders to steady her.

Dear God. His eyes fluttered closed. Her lips were warm and soft and eminently kissable.

Don't move.

Don't kiss her back.

Don't do anything.

Did he imagine it or did her lips cling for a moment longer than necessary?

And then she was back in her seat and cheers sounded all around them and the camera moved on to some other poor victims.

Not that he felt like a victim. He felt *electrified*.

'Sorry,' she murmured so only he could hear. 'I thought the less time the cameras were on us, the better.'

'Good thinking. It was a smart move... Bonnie.'

His use of her pseudonym made her smile, lightening things between them again, but underneath ran a new raw thread of tension and nothing he did could shift it.

The second half of the game was just as exciting as the first, but he couldn't shake his awareness of the woman beside him. Still, when the game went to the wire and their team won it with a goal in the dying seconds, they went as mad as everyone in the stands around them.

She threw her arms around his neck with a whoop of elation.

He lifted her off her feet, even though there was no room to swing her around.

She eased back. Their eyes met. She stilled, her smile slipping. He released her, letting the full length of her body slide down his. It sent a hot hungry surge of desire Mexican-waving through his blood. When her feet finally touched the ground she stepped away, instantly ducking her head to tuck the hair of her wig back behind her ears and readjusting her beanie.

Get a grip!

'Best game ever!' he said, putting on his finest game face.

Her answering grin was his reward. 'At the end I wanted

to win so bad I don't know how I'd have coped with los-ing. Seeing a game live is so different from watching it on the telly.'

They exited the stadium and the crowd thinned as he and Bree walked through the park, back towards their apartment. Their chatter petered out as if neither could maintain the pretence once they were away from the sta-dium full of people. They found themselves alone in the still night with the city lights shining like a promise in front of them.

Was he imagining her tension? Maybe she sensed the growing tension in him. Maybe he was infecting her with tension!

He searched his mind for a topic of conversation that would keep things light, keep things bearable until they reached the apartment and he could imprison himself in the sanctuary of his bedroom. *Alone.*

'Noah, about that kiss.' She swung to him as they strode across a little bridge that arced over a tiny tributary of the river, the water in it reflecting the city lights. 'I know I took you off guard and probably shocked you and weirded you out and stuff. In hindsight I shouldn't have done it. I should've done what you were doing and just faced them down, but I panicked and—'

'I wasn't weirded out, Bree.'

Her eyes looked huge in the moonlight. 'You weren't?'

Her voice sounded small and a little forlorn and it caught at him. 'The thing is, Bree, what I really wanted to do was kiss you back.'

Her eyes grew even bigger and rounder. But the expres-sion in them was neither shocked nor appalled.

His hand went either side of her on the railing, and he couldn't find it in him to regret his honesty. 'What I really want to do is kiss you now.'

CHAPTER SEVEN

NOAH WANTED TO kiss her!

Bree's heart leapt into her throat and pounded so hard and fast she could barely catch her breath.

In the half dark, wearing that full beard and those unfamiliar clothes, he looked both familiar and unfamiliar. With her own long dark locks and high-top sneakers, she felt like someone different, someone who…

She tossed her hair and lifted her chin. 'Kiss cam replay…' She pulled in a breath and assumed a sports commentator's voice. 'We've been treated to an extraordinary half of football here today, folks. The crowd needs halftime and a chance to catch their breath as much as the players do. And what a magnificent crowd we have in here today. Let's take a look and see who we can find in the crowd…'

She mimed a camera panning around the crowd.

'Now, there's a fine-looking couple—Ned and Bonnie—completely decked out in their team's colours. They have to be happy with the way their team has handled themselves so far. Come on, guys, pucker up for the camera…'

Noah's eyes burned like bright points in the darkness. Her heart pounded harder and faster as a crazy freedom pumped through her blood, making her want to laugh and dance and sing.

She cocked an eyebrow. 'They might need some encouragement, folks…'

She was playing with fire, but she couldn't help it. She'd kept all her impulses on such a tight leash for the last seven years and it felt as if all of them had suddenly burst free. Just for today she was Bonnie—a girl with no past and no hang-ups.

Noah-Ned stared at her, the expression in his eyes growing fiercer and more intense. She'd never seen that expression on his face before and it made him seem even more of a stranger.

'Are you daring me to kiss you?'

Her lips lifted—flirty, taunting…daring. 'C'mon, Ned…' she kept up the sports commentator's voice '…what are you…man or mouse?'

He moved in so close his warmth and his scent crowded her. Her pulse went wild.

'I'm not the kind of guy to back down from a dare like that.'

'That's what I'm counting on.' She reached up and touched a hand to his cheek. 'I've never been kissed by a guy with a beard before.'

'Then I think it's time to rectify that oversight.'

His lips lowered to hers—not with the speed of a man intent on proving he was man rather than mouse…or with the predatory hunger of a wolf—but a man intent on enjoying every tantalising moment of the kiss in all its build-up and execution.

The realisation made things inside her clench and soften, both at the same time. As if she were toffee and he were heat and the moment their lips touched there'd be melting and melding and even more melting.

His lips hovered over hers, mere millimetres away, and

she knew he was giving her the chance to change her mind and step back, but she wasn't going anywhere.

Every single part of her craved this kiss. And whatever price she might have to pay later, she'd pay it gladly.

And then the gap closed and his lips were on hers.

His lips were far gentler than she'd expected, softer and more...patient, more giving, more...*delicious*! Noah's kiss was utterly and captivatingly delicious as if it was purely designed to slowly seduce her every sense and have her clamouring for more.

And it was a lullaby of a kiss, which sounded wrong because that suggested it was sleep-inducing and that was as far from the truth as one could get. But if felt safe to let down every barrier she'd ever had and let herself be swept away by the excitement of the kiss because beneath it all it was like coming home after the longest day of your life and being welcomed with all your favourite things.

Bree wrapped her arms around Noah and held him close, opening herself up and welcoming this gift of a kiss with gratitude and something deeper—some part of herself she had yet to name—revelling in every delicious moment.

As if he'd been waiting for her full surrender, the pressure of Noah's lips increased. Not all at once, but the pressure, the depth of kiss, increased by increments until wrapping her arms around him wasn't enough. His kiss built a storm inside her, a storm that threatened to rage out of control. She pressed as close to him as she could, her hands tunnelling into his hair to drag him even nearer and she was cursing the barrier of their clothes.

Their kiss unfolded...expanded...transformed into a storm-tossed sea of need and heat and the only thing that would calm it was more...

More Noah.

His hand tunnelled beneath her shirt and the skin-on-skin contact—his hand exploring the small of her back—had her drawing back to suck in a breath, before her mouth collided with his again. Tongues tangoed and teeth grazed kiss-plumped lips in an ever deeper dance.

It wasn't until a series of catcalls and whistles broke into the desire-hazed fog of her mind and someone shouted, 'Get a room,' that she and Noah sprang apart.

Noah not Ned. That kiss had been pure unadulterated essence of Noah.

She touched her lips. They pulsed full and sensitive beneath her fingertips, burning with a new hunger and knowledge. Like Eve and the apple, Bree should never have flirted with temptation. She shouldn't have plucked the apple or sampled the fruit. Because that fruit—Noah—was forbidden to her.

Now she knew what he tasted like. And now she would always want.

Noah stepped in front of her as a group of men—all a little drunk and wearing football scarves and beanies—thunked across the bridge, good-naturedly razzing the couple and exchanging 'Great game' comments with Noah.

Bree's cheeks burned while everything inside her continued to jostle and clash as if the hurricane of need Noah's kiss had created inside her would never be stilled again.

'Bree?'

He'd given up the pretence too. He knew it wasn't Bonnie who'd kissed him but Bree.

She'd kissed Noah!

Noah, her friend forever.

Noah, her brothers' best friend, and Ryder's business partner.

Noah, her parents' *other* son.

Bree had never considered Noah in a brotherly light.

Never. But he'd always been one of her most important friends. And his importance to her family couldn't be overstated.

'Bree, are you all right?'

He bent down to peer into her face and she flinched.

He stiffened and stepped back, and absurdly then she wanted to cry.

She forced her chin up. 'I'm fine.' She couldn't do anything to damage his relationships with her family. A mistake like that would hurt everyone.

It would hurt him most of all.

She couldn't do it. She just couldn't. It would be a thousand times worse than the mistake she'd made with Otis.

This attraction was nothing more than a temporary aberration—them letting off steam because they were both under a lot of pressure. If it were anyone else, she'd see it through to its natural conclusion, but it wasn't just anyone.

She had to make sure nothing like this happened between them again. Gesturing that they should start walking, she said, 'Let's go somewhere a little more public before we talk about what just happened.'

He didn't say anything—his face had shuttered closed. Shoving his hands in his pockets, he led them towards the bright lights of the Southbank's restaurants and bars.

They found a vacant bench that looked out over the Yarra River. She sat. He remained standing until she asked him to sit too. She'd decided during the silence of their short walk that laying it out swiftly and without room for misinterpretation would be the best strategy. 'I don't want that to ever happen again, Noah.'

He gave a mirthless laugh. 'That's become pretty obvious, Bree.'

Had she hurt his feelings? She didn't want to hurt his

feelings. 'We're friends, not friends with benefits. That would never work for us.'

His expression didn't change. She opened her mouth to try and temper her words. With a superhuman effort she closed it again. It was better she hurt his feelings briefly now than to cause an estrangement between him and her family.

'Noah, my life is in flux at the moment.' She stared at the light reflected on the river rather than at him. 'And I'd be lying if I said I wasn't finding that confronting.'

He angled towards her. She glanced at him briefly and shrugged. 'Tina's illness guts me. I'm honoured to be entrusted with Tilly's welfare, though, and a part of me is excited at the prospect, but that doesn't stop it feeling overwhelming and frightening. I know a part of me has been searching for distraction and comfort.'

She wished he'd say something. Agree with her. 'I don't want to use you in that way,' she whispered. 'It'd be unforgivable.'

'Not unforgivable,' he finally said. 'Understandable... human.' He glanced up at the sky and then back at her. 'But if you think a kiss like that is a common thing, you're wrong.'

She knew then she only had to say the word and he'd take her back to the apartment and they'd make love all night. Everything inside her clenched with hunger and need. He *wanted* that to happen.

She did all she could to channel common sense. 'It would change things between us, and you matter too much for me to risk that. You matter too much to my family. And we all matter too much to you.'

His glare drilled through her and she could see he thought her a coward. It stung. 'It would be a bigger mistake than the one I made with Otis.' She thumped a hand to her chest. 'And I would hate myself for it.'

His head rocked back as if she'd slapped him.

'How on earth am I supposed to raise a child if I can't conquer such self-destructive impulses in myself? I never want to screw up on that Otis scale again.'

'What happened with Otis doesn't make you a screw-up. You were taken in by the guy—played. Hell, Bree, you were just a kid. It wasn't your fault. And in case it's escaped your notice—' his eyes flashed '—I'm not Otis.'

He wasn't, but she'd completely lost her head over Otis, and she'd let that override her judgement, had let it silence the warnings sounding through her. She'd turned a blind eye when she shouldn't have. She wasn't making those same mistakes with Noah.

Her every hormone clamoured to make love with him, but her every instinct warned her not to. She'd listen to her voice of reason rather than her bad angel, thank you very much.

'Nobody blames you for what happened back then.'

'I know.' And she did. She knew that none of her family held her responsible.

'But you blame yourself enough for everyone, right?'

His scorn made her stiffen.

'By your estimate, your judgement is far superior to everyone else's, right?'

Her mouth opened and closed but she couldn't push a single sound out.

'You can't accept that you made a mistake and move on. You have to keep punishing yourself instead.'

She thrust out her jaw. 'I'm moving on!'

'Sticking to a rigid, sterile plan isn't—' he made air quotes that infuriated her '—"moving on".'

'The Plan,' she bit out through gritted teeth, 'has become far more flexible, as you're well aware. And what's your definition of moving on anyway? Me sleeping with you will prove I've moved on? Hell, Noah, why on earth would I do that? Why would I—' it was her turn to make air quotes '—"move on" with *you*?'

He went so still it almost frightened her. She did what she could to get her voice back under control. 'You—'

He shot to his feet. 'You've said enough.'

She wanted to cry because he'd taken her words the wrong way—not just the wrong way, but the worst possible way. Maybe it was for the best. She needed to kybosh any chance of anything ever happening between them.

The expression in his eyes, though, cut her to the marrow. She couldn't do it. 'Eight days ago you were going to marry Courtney Fraser. Right at this very moment you should be on your darn honeymoon! I don't think you're in any better frame of mind at the moment than I am.'

She rose too. '*That's* what I meant, Noah. So you needn't go all dark and Heathcliff on me. I didn't mean that I think I'm too good for you and I sure as hell don't think you're beneath me.'

She started to turn away, but swung back. 'And the fact you thought for a moment that I'd think such a thing tells me exactly how screwed up you currently are.'

He dragged both hands back through his hair and then nodded. 'Point taken.'

'I'm going back to the apartment.'

'I'm not.'

Good. The less time they spent together at the moment, the better. She didn't ask him what he planned to do or where he was going.

'Tomorrow?' she forced herself to ask.

'I'm busy all day.'

Again, good. But her stomach gave a sick roll all the same.

'If I decide that I'm going to Tasmania, I'll meet you on the ferry tomorrow evening.'

So…he was jumping ship?

It was for the best, she told herself. Going their separate ways was the smart thing to do. If only she could make herself feel it.

Bree boarded the *Spirit of Tasmania* and told herself it was ludicrous to feel lonely. She'd never planned to have company on the trip. *This* was how it was supposed to be.

Dumping her suitcase in her cabin, which was tiny, nothing more than two shelves holding a single mattress each, a bench masquerading as a desk, and a tiny en suite bathroom.

'They never promised five stars,' she reminded herself, and then went out to explore the upper decks.

There was a variety of cafés, restaurants and bars, lounge areas to watch the big-screen TVs. She ventured outside when they cast off, but it was ridiculously windy so she hastened back inside.

She had a whole evening ahead of her—nothing scheduled, no pressure…nothing. She should be glad of it, should be enjoying the downtime. Instead of a blank canvas of possibility, though, it just felt blank and boring and as dull as the dark night outside the ferry's windows.

Treating herself to a glass of Shiraz, she retreated to a table for two by a window. Not that there was anything to see. The window merely reflected the room inside back at her. When she met the eyes of a bearded man in them it took her a moment to realise who she was looking at.

Noah.

She schooled herself to turn slowly to face him. His lips

lifted and so did his eyebrows. He gestured to the other chair at her table. He was a good eight feet away, but relief made her shoulders sag. She smiled and nodded back.

He sat with alacrity…and purpose. 'I owe you an apology. I acted like a jackass last night. I don't know what came over me.'

Relief flooded her, unbending her whole body. 'Yesterday was a crazy day. The Ned and Bonnie disguises, the euphoria of the game—' *that kiss* '—it's been a crazy week, Noah.'

The craziest damn week of his life, that was for sure.

Noah worked at making things right between him and Bree again, worked at making her feel good about herself and not blame herself for *anything*. That was why he was here, why he'd shown up.

Last night he'd gone to the casino, had played a few games of Blackjack before wandering the streets of inner-city Melbourne, trying to dampen the flame that kissing Bree had ignited inside him.

She was right—just over a week ago he'd been about to marry Courtney. He had no business kissing anyone.

He found himself resenting Courtney. Not for making a laughing stock of him when she'd walked out of their wedding ceremony—he'd deserved that. Not for hiding her fears from him and refusing to discuss them with him until it was too late.

He found himself resenting her for having distracted him from what had been right under his nose these last two years—*Bree*! And that made no sense at all. He'd never considered Bree in those terms, and he didn't want to start now.

Bree was off limits.

He'd never thought of her as a sister or anything like

that, but he owed the Allenbys everything. If Janice and Colin hadn't taken him under their wings he shuddered to think what would've become of him. He'd rather cut his own arm off than hurt them. Which meant a temporary hook-up with Bree was out of the question.

If he could only get the thought of it out of his mind.

If only that kiss hadn't blown his world apart.

He'd kissed a few women in his time, but no kiss had touched him the way Bree's kiss had. Maybe she was right. Maybe that kiss had been nothing more than a pressure valve helping them to release all of their pent-up tension.

But it had felt like more.

'You're on the hard stuff, I see?' Bree gestured to his can of soda.

He dragged himself back to the present. 'I figure my liver needs a rest after Coffs Harbour.'

She grinned, but an element of wariness remained in the depths of her brown eyes and at the edges of her smile. He needed to dispel that unease…and mistrust?

The thought she might no longer trust him was a physical pain. 'Bree, I promise what happened last night won't happen again. You're right, emotions have been running high this trip and I had no right to…'

Those brown eyes widened. He swallowed. He *wouldn't* kiss her. 'No right to try and find that kind of solace with you. You mean a lot to me. If I were to lose your friendship—'

'Not going to happen!'

The sharpness of her tone and the way she straightened eased some of the burning in his gut.

'And I'm sorry too. I shouldn't have…' she waved her hands between them '…either.'

Did she want to talk about it further? He sure as hell didn't, but he'd do whatever she wanted and needed.

'Let's draw a veil over last night. I think it'd be best if we never mentioned it again.'

'A line in the sand?' he said.

'A cone of silence.'

And then they were both laughing and her wariness slipped away, just leaving behind his buddy Bree. She gestured to his beard. 'How long are you going to keep it?'

'Ahmed said I'd get a few days out of it if I were careful, but I think I'll lose it tomorrow.'

She sipped her wine. He ran a hand down his beard. Did she like it? Was that why she'd kissed him—because he'd looked like a stranger rather than himself? Should he grow a beard for real?

'What's your plan when we hit Tassie, Noah?'

'I have a couple of days in Hobart before I head off on a week-long wilderness trek.'

Her eyes brightened. 'Really?'

'It was a great idea. Thank you.'

He went on to describe the ancient forests, mountain ranges, and river courses he hoped to see on the South West National Park trek he'd booked and that culminated in Port Davey, one of the most unique marine reserves on the planet. He was careful to keep things light and easy. Normal. Comradely.

Half an hour later he let out a long breath. For the time being he'd mended things between them. Bree wasn't staring at him as if he were a monster or someone she couldn't trust. If only he could make himself feel that same way— relaxed and at ease. But he still wanted to kiss her.

If he was brutally honest, he ached to do *much* more than kiss her and he didn't know how to rid himself of that all-consuming need.

He ground his back molars together. This whole attraction thing would fade. A week hiking up mountains and through virgin forest would help rid him of the wash of hormones that had built inside him.

Focus on making things right with her. That was what he needed to do. It was what he *would* do, regardless of how much the craving and heat buffeted him. He'd have a cold shower when he returned to his cabin. That'd help him put it all on ice.

Bree glanced past him and her gaze sharpened. 'Just give me a second.'

She made her way across to a woman huddled in a nearby armchair. Who…? Was she crying?

He was on his feet the second his suspicion was confirmed and at Bree's side.

The woman sent him a watery smile, before turning back to Bree. 'So the mix-up means there are four of us in a two-berth cabin. The kids are tired and grumpy…they both get motion sickness. And I already feel like I've not slept for a week.' She pushed her hair off her face. 'The ferry is full so they can't provide us with either a four-person cabin or an additional room.'

She waved a hand at them and shook her head. 'It was kind of you to come over, but I'll be fine. I just needed half an hour to myself. I'll need to go back soon. My husband is as worn out as I am, though he's trying to hide it…' She trailed off with a tired smile and a shrug.

Two adults and two children in one of those two-berth cabins? What a nightmare. 'I don't have a four-berth cabin to swap with you, but I can give you my two-berth cabin. Maybe you and your husband can divide and conquer and take a cabin and a kid each?'

The woman sagged as if such unexpected kindness had robbed her of speech, but it was the expression in Bree's eyes—their warmth and admiration—and the softness of her smile that made him feel like a million bucks.

'I couldn't possibly impose like that and—'

''Course you can,' Bree said. 'Noah can bunk in with me.'

'You're friends?'

'Have been for ever,' she continued in that breezy nonchalant fashion she had. 'It'll be like the old days when we used to pitch a tent in the backyard.'

Except Ryder and Blake had always been there too.

'It makes absolutely no difference to us,' Bree continued.

Bunk in with Bree? Bad idea. Super bad idea.

'Oh, I can't thank you enough! If you're sure…?'

He couldn't refuse. Her look of relief, as if a major weight had just been lifted off her, skewered him. 'Positive.' He injected every ounce of enthusiasm into that single word that he could.

In no time at all, his suitcase was in Bree's cabin—her tiny, tiny cabin—and he'd handed his room key to a very grateful Mrs Baker.

'That was a lovely thing to do,' Bree said when they sat down in the restaurant a short time later. 'The poor woman has been worn to a frazzle. They've travelled down from Newcastle with a five-year-old son and three-year-old daughter to attend a cousin's wedding in Launceston. They're obviously trying to do it as cheaply as they can, but somewhere along the way there's been a mix-up with their booking.'

'Happy to help.' In truth he'd made the offer before Bree could offer the Bakers her own cabin instead. 'With my suitcase stowed safely in your room, I'm just as happy to sleep in an armchair in one of the lounges.'

'You can't do that!'

He couldn't?

He stared into wide outraged eyes and swallowed. Evidently not.

'Noah, there's a perfectly good spare bunk going begging in my cabin. Like I said, it'll be like when we were kids and we camped out in the backyard.'

Except they were no longer kids. And her brothers wouldn't be there. And when they were kids the thought of kissing her had never entered his head.

But he knew what she was doing—she was trying to get things back to normal between them. She was trying to re-establish old boundaries. Boundaries that had been kicked to smithereens when they'd kissed.

If he wanted to prove to her that things between them were okay, he'd have to go along with this plan of hers without making a big deal out of it. 'Well, if you're sure, that'd be great,' he found himself saying.

Did he imagine the way she swallowed then as if to bolster her nerves? Was her smile a touch too bright? Did she forgo another glass of wine because she wanted to maintain her guard? Or because she didn't trust herself?

Don't!

His hand tightened around his glass of soda. *Don't even go there.* Because even if the answer to any or all of those questions was in the affirmative, it didn't change anything. He'd give her absolutely no cause for concern about anything tonight. He'd refuse to think of Bree in any way other than as a good buddy who he'd known for most of his life.

He most certainly wouldn't think about kissing her, remember how she'd felt in his arms, or recall the soft breathy sounds that had escaped the back of her throat when she'd kissed him as if her entire world had depended on it.

His fingers started to ache. With a concerted effort, he relaxed them. 'It'll be an early start in the morning. Apparently we're due to arrive in Devonport at six a.m.' If he played things right he'd spend no more than a few hours in her cabin. If he didn't go in until midnight or a bit later… and then got up at five…

That was five hours.

Five hours was nothing.

She'd be asleep.

He gritted his teeth. He could do this.

Noah glanced at the clock embedded in the shelf between the two bunks. *Two a.m.* Who knew two hours could crawl by so slowly?

The shallowness of Bree's breathing told him she was awake as well. He was tempted to ask her if his being here was bothering her, but that felt as if it would be breaking some unspoken pact and prove that things were different between them now.

He clenched his hands in the sheets. If it was the last thing he did, he'd make things right between them again. 'You awake?'

The briefest of hesitations and then, 'Uh-huh.'

'I was thinking about the Bakers and their two vomiting children,' he said. 'I expect they're having a rough night of it even though our passage has been pretty smooth so far.' Bass Strait could get notoriously rough and choppy.

'But their night will still be so much easier thanks to you.'

Her voice sounded soft in the darkness, and he couldn't explain why but it melted some of the tension that had him wound up tight. 'Bree, you said you were excited but also terrified about raising Tilly. What scares you?'

He heard her roll to her side to face him. 'Lots of things. Her heart is going to be broken when Tina dies. How do

I explain it to her? How do I help her through it? How do I make it up to her?'

His stomach clenched. She was taking on so much.

She released a long breath. 'The short answer is I can't make it up to her. I just hold her when she cries, tell her it's okay to be sad, and try to make sure we do some fun things too. I guess I just surround her in as much love as I can and do all I can to make her feel secure.'

'You're going to be a brilliant mother to her, Bree.'

'I hope so, but… What do I do if she gets sick? I know nothing about childhood ailments. And crazy things plague me. What if she hates her first day of school? When she's a bit older I'd like her to play a team sport, but what if she doesn't want to? Do I force her or do I back down? What if she doesn't want to go to university? I know Tina would want her to and—'

'Bree.' He pushed upright. 'You're looking for trouble before it has a chance to find you.'

'I know! It's crazy.' She paused, then, 'I'm afraid of the temper tantrums that will inevitably happen when she's a hormone-ridden teenager and I won't let her do something she has her heart set on and she shouts, "You're not my real mother!" at me.'

He slid back down, staring up at the darkness, his heart burning. 'You can't take that stuff personally.'

'I know. But I dread it all the same.'

'Your mum will be a huge source of help, not to mention information.'

'I'll be relying on her a lot. I wish—'

She broke off and his heart clenched. She wished she'd have her mother near. She wished she weren't leaving her support network behind. She didn't say it out loud, but he knew her too well.

'I know it'll all work out, Noah. I know I'll get the hang

of it. Plus everyone will visit and that'll help a lot too. There'll be lots of visits.'

'So many you'll get sick of them,' he promised.

'Never.' She laughed. 'Now, this is crazy o'clock in the morning. I'm going to take us through a guided meditation. Close your eyes.'

He did as she ordered, following her softly spoken instructions—tightening and then loosening different muscle groups, concentrating on his breathing until he felt himself floating away on a warm sea of well-being.

CHAPTER EIGHT

She was doing a brilliant job, Bree congratulated herself the next morning. At this rate she and Noah would be back to normal and firmly in the friends' zone again in no time at all. And they'd have forgotten all about Sunday night's kiss.

Except she'd never had to work so hard before to keep things *normal* between her and Noah. Or to think of him as a friend rather than a very adult, very hot male… To not notice the broad strength of his shoulders or the depth of his chest or the lean strength of hips she recalled pressed hard against her own and…

Stop it!

Try harder.

Noah was trying his absolute best too. She couldn't fault him or blame him for not cooperating. Since driving off the ferry at a ridiculously early hour, they'd grabbed take-away coffees from a fast-food chain's drive-through, they'd played along to a trivia quiz on morning radio, which between them they'd managed to get every question right. Actually, that had been fun.

But of a three-hour, twenty-minute trip, they still had an hour forty to go.

She launched into a description of the chocolaterie she'd had lunch at the previous day. With an entire day to kill, she'd driven out to the Yarra Valley where she'd stared at vineyards and tried to stop thinking about Noah. It hadn't worked. Nor had sampling the chocolate at the chocolaterie. But at least it gave her something to talk about now.

Eventually, though, her story petered out. She moistened her lips. 'What did you get up to yesterday? Anything fun?'

'I had lunch with Ahmed—took back the gear we borrowed—and met his new girlfriend, Susie.'

'Nice.'

A silence stretched. And stretched. Right. Let's abandon further conversation for the foreseeable future.

She was about to ask him to choose a playlist from the assortment on her phone when he said, 'I rang Courtney.'

Whoa, what? *Why?*

She glanced at him, very briefly. 'How did that go?' And then she frowned. 'She actually answered? She took your call?'

He laughed, but it lacked any real humour. 'Yeah, I wondered if she would too.'

Why had he rung her?

Before this road trip, before she'd noticed how damn hot he was and had discovered that his kiss could set her on fire and make her forget *everything*, she'd have simply asked him. But now it felt impossibly intrusive.

From the corner of her eye she saw him glance across at her. He gave a low chuckle that raised all the fine hairs on her arms. 'I can see you wrestling over there with yourself, Busy Bree.'

The old nickname had her blowing out a breath. 'I don't want to ask anything that'll make you feel awkward.' She flexed her fingers on the steering wheel. 'But I'm guessing if you didn't want to talk about it you'd have not raised the topic.'

'You can ask me anything you want.'

That sounded *too* inviting. It had things inside her burning and clamouring. It had questions like *Do you want to kiss me again?* hovering on the tip of her tongue.

She bit her tongue. Hard.

'Let me guess.' She made herself laugh, rather credibly, she thought. 'I can ask you anything, but you reserve the right not to answer?' She'd expected him to laugh too. She *wanted* him to laugh.

But he didn't. He'd gone serious.

Her fingers clenched the steering wheel. 'Why did you ring Courtney?'

He took his time answering. 'A few reasons. I wanted to make sure she was okay.'

Because he was a good guy. 'And is she?'

'She wasn't sounding particularly chipper, but she said she was fine. I wanted to apologise to her.'

She schooled her features. 'For?'

'For not being more understanding when she called the wedding off. And for...'

Her mouth went dry.

'She accused me of seeing her as a trophy, and in some respects she was right. Courtney's family come from old money so I knew she didn't want me for *my* money.'

Both Ryder and Noah had experienced money-hungry girlfriends in the past few years, since they'd become successful. It had made both of them gun-shy.

'I'd had this idea in my head of what my life would look like when I'd finally made it. For me success translated into making my life the exact opposite of my parents'.'

His parents had given him no love, no support. They'd never wanted children, and his mother had acted as if Noah were to blame for the upheaval a young child had created in her life. Rather than casting the blame where it belonged—with her and her husband's irresponsibility.

They'd seemed to blame him, not only for his very existence, but their own shortcomings. She'd never understood why they'd not given him up for adoption or surrendered him into foster care.

She'd once asked him and the answer had sickened her. He'd said they only kept him for the welfare money they received. They were truly awful people and he'd deserved so much better.

'Courtney's family is the polar opposite of mine.'

She could see how his vision of the Fraser family had seduced him. For a start they actually treated each other with respect. And they'd treated Noah with respect too.

'Courtney is smart, beautiful and accomplished.'

And cold, she wanted to say but didn't.

'She knows all of the right people, moves in all the best circles. It's shallow, but it all went to my head.'

'Not shallow,' she countered. 'Understandable.' The Frasers lived an unbelievably privileged and aspirational lifestyle.

His lips tightened. 'I realise now that my wanting to marry her was an attempt to erase the past. That wasn't fair of me. I needed to apologise.'

She couldn't imagine Courtney being overjoyed to hear such a confession, though.

She glanced at him again. 'Do you still want that kind of perfect life?'

One achingly broad shoulder lifted. 'We all have a vision of a perfect future, don't we?'

'I guess.' Her perfect future involved not letting her family down again.

'But I now know that it's less to do with externals and more to do with principles…like honesty, honour, integrity. I'll never use a person again like I did Courtney, to try and make me feel good about myself. You were right,

Bree. I should be proud of what I've achieved rather than ashamed of something I had absolutely no control over—like my childhood.'

His now clean-shaven jaw was thrust out. 'I've given my parents and their attitudes far too much weight in my life, but no more. I'm through with that.'

She wanted to hug him. A *friendly* hug. 'I'm glad you're finally moving on. You deserve better than to let it hold you back.' She flashed him a smile. 'You deserve your perfect future.'

'So do you, Bree.'

She was going to work hard to earn all the trust that had been placed in her—Tina's belief that she could provide Tilly with a loving home, and her family's belief that she was a good person. She wouldn't let them down.

'I also told Courtney what her father had done—having you fired—and suggested she might want to ask him to reverse that decision.'

Her eyes started from her head. 'You did *what*?'

He shrugged.

Dear God, what on earth had possessed him to bring her up in that conversation? 'Please tell me you explained that awful tabloid photograph of us.'

He folded his arms, his lips twisting. 'If she claims to know me so well—and she claims she knows me better than I know myself—then when I tell her that there's absolutely nothing going on between us, she should believe me.'

There *wasn't* anything going on between them. There was absolutely no reason why hearing him say it out loud should feel like a knife to the heart. 'But she didn't believe you?'

'She told me to go to hell, that she wouldn't be asking her father to reverse any such decision, and said she never wanted to hear from me again.'

She made a face. 'So it ended well, then.'

He laughed. 'Perhaps not as well as I'd hoped.'

'Oh, Noah, it wasn't wise to bring me up in that conversation. You'd just told the poor woman you'd fallen for what she'd represented rather than who she was. And while she might've known that, hearing it would still have stung.'

'She said she'd had a lucky escape!'

'She did. You both did!'

'And you being fired isn't right, Bree. I thought Courtney had more integrity than that.'

His lips tightened. She forced herself to focus on the road. Not on his lips and certainly not on the pounding of her heart. She refused to remember how his mouth had moved on hers or how their tongues had tangled and—

Stop it!

She rattled into speech. 'The whole getting fired thing might've happened at the perfect time anyway. It might be a sign that I should relocate to Hobart now. Get settled, find a job and start becoming a more permanent fixture in Tilly's life.'

'The only thing it's a sign of is the Frasers' spite. Courtney told me she was glad to be able to hurt me through you.'

Nice.

'And then told me she'd be glad to do me any future disservice that she could think of.'

She shrugged. 'I knew there was a reason I never liked her.'

'She also told me that all the publicity from the cancelled wedding has had business booming.'

Bree went cold all over, but after a few moments she shook it off. 'She wanted to hurt you in the same way she felt hurt. You know that, don't you?'

'Maybe. One thing's for certain—I'm glad I didn't marry her.'

'Are you done with feeling guilty about her?'

He raked both hands back through his hair. 'I'm still ashamed of the way I used her...'

He hadn't meant to use her, though. It hadn't been a conscious decision.

He blew out a breath. 'But I feel as if I can now draw a line under the whole incident and move on.'

She blew out a breath too. 'Good.'

He reached across as if to squeeze her knee and everything inside her froze. He reefed his hand back. 'I, uh... I have you to thank for that.'

'Me?' she squeaked. Dear God, don't let him say anything about their kiss setting him free or making him realise all the possibilities open to him now, or...anything like that.

'For inviting me on your trip. For discussing the hard stuff with me. It's given me a chance to come to terms with everything. I'm grateful, Bree.'

Was that why he'd kissed her—because he'd been *grateful*? It took a superhuman effort to not screw up her face.

He kissed you because you dared him to, idiot.

Forget about the kiss already, Bree!

The kiss didn't matter.

Except it felt as if it were one of the most momentous things to have ever happened to her.

She shook herself. She was just getting things muddled in her mind. The things she and Tina had to discuss, *those* were the momentous things.

'Cat got your tongue?' he teased. 'You have plenty to say when it involves me and Courtney, but nothing when I say something nice to you or pay you a compliment?'

She shook her head and smiled despite herself. 'I'm honestly glad the road trip has helped you deal with this stuff, Noah. You're a great friend and I know if our situations were reversed you'd do the same for me. Your friendship is important to me.'

'To you or to your family?' he asked quietly.

She glanced over at him in surprise, before focussing on the road again.

'And are we ever going to stop for breakfast?' he added as they drove into Campbell Town—one of the small towns en route to Hobart.

'If you see a likely café, point it out.'

'There.'

She pulled over and parked the car.

They were soon ensconced inside a warm and cosy café enjoying waffles with maple syrup and bacon. But the entire time his question burned through her. Was his friendship important to her family or to her personally?

Of course it was important to her family, that wasn't in dispute, but...

She thought about how much she'd loathed the idea of him marrying Courtney because she'd never thought the other woman would make him happy. She thought back to how freeing it had felt to talk to him about Otis. She recalled how easily she'd confided her decision to become Tilly's guardian to him—how natural that had been and how much his admiration and support had meant.

She realised then that Noah had always been the one she'd confided her secrets to first—not Ryder or Blake or her parents...and on some occasions not even Tina. Noah had always made time for her, had never trivialised her confidences or belittled them. He'd never made her feel...less.

Her phone pinged. She read the text message and then

held her phone out so he could read it too. 'You're invited to lunch at Tina's today.'

'I wasn't expecting that. I don't want to intrude.'

'You won't be intruding. She'd love to see you.' Another text hit her inbox. 'And her parents have offered you their spare room for the duration of your stay.'

'They don't have to do that!'

He opened his mouth and then straightened, his lips pursing. 'Are you sure they wouldn't mind?'

'Of course they won't mind. They'd not have made the offer if they did.'

She texted back, reciting her message out loud. '"Noah would love to come to lunch. Would also love to accept the offer of the room."'

At his nod, she sent it.

She set the phone back to the table. 'Your friendship matters to me, Noah. Not just to my family. You're one of the best friends I've ever had. I'm not sure what I would do if I were to ever lose your friendship.'

The thought made the day go dark.

He reached out and covered her hand. 'Not ever going to happen, Bree.'

'They adore each other.' Noah couldn't drag his gaze from where Bree and Tilly painted 'abstract' art on a huge piece of butcher's paper in Tina's backyard. Bree had pulled a huge packet of the stuff from the back of her car when they'd first arrived.

Once lunch was over, Bree and Tilly had raced outside with their paper and paints, as excited as if it were Christmas morning.

Tina laughed. 'I know! It's a joy to watch, though, right?'

'Right,' he echoed, because it was. But... 'How have

they become such good friends? I know Bree has spent a bit of time with you over the last couple of years, but it's just the odd three-day weekend here and there. I wouldn't have thought it'd be enough to foster this sort of connection.'

'They've always had a special bond. It's as if they just get each other. But all of that has been strengthened by our twice-weekly video conferencing chats. And believe me, we can have marathon sessions.'

'Twice a week?'

'Wednesday night is Bree's bedtime-story night where she reads a book to Tilly. Tilly always looks forward to it. And we have a longer session at some point over the weekend. Of course, with you guys travelling this week we've only had a couple of quick phone chats. Tilly has been on tenterhooks waiting for Bree to arrive.'

The little girl—a precocious dark-haired three-year-old—had been glued to Bree's side from the moment they'd arrived. She'd been less than impressed with Noah, though. She continued to glare at him with dark-eyed suspicion as if afraid he might try and monopolise Bree's time and attention.

'About what happened while we were travelling, Tina...' He glanced at the other woman, who currently looked healthy and well. There was no indication whatsoever of the ticking time bomb inside her. 'That damn picture splashed in the newspapers... It wasn't what it was made out to be.'

He glanced up when Tina's parents, Don and Corinne, joined them on the back deck. They'd insisted on cleaning up after lunch and had shooed everyone outside to enjoy the sun. 'I'd hate for you or your parents to think less of Bree or think you'd made a mistake in asking her to become Tilly's guardian.'

Tina laughed. 'Relax, Noah. Bree explained what happened and then chided me because I found it funny. But, c'mon, it is kind of funny.'

He fought a reluctant grin. 'You weren't the one who had to explain it to Ryder and Blake.'

That only made her laugh harder. Corinne joined in. 'It reminded me of when the girls were little.' She winked at Noah. 'They used to get up to so much mischief—not naughty, just high spirits—and would create the most elaborate justifications for why they'd had to do whatever it was.'

Bree and Tina had been in and out of each other's homes on a daily basis when they'd been growing up, and the memory of their laughter and antics made him smile.

Tina's mother glanced down the backyard at Bree and Tilly. 'Do you think, if we asked nicely, the girls would let us have a paintbrush and join in?'

'I'm sure of it,' Don said, lumbering to his feet and helping his wife to hers.

'Thank you again,' Noah said, 'for putting me up for a few nights. I really appreciate it.'

'We're glad you could stay, Noah,' Corinne said. 'We're looking forward to it.'

'It is nice to see you again, Noah,' Tina said as her parents made their way down to Tilly and Bree.

'It's nice to see you too.'

'So don't take this the wrong way…'

Everything inside him clenched. He *had* caused trouble for Bree—for all of them—hadn't he? Squaring his shoulders, he met Tina's gaze directly. He'd fix whatever needed fixing. It was why he was here. 'But?'

'I was surprised you accepted my parents' offer of their spare room.'

He let out a slow breath when he realised Tina had

meant it—that the tabloid articles and pictures hadn't bothered her. The relief was like a cold beer on a hot day. 'It
was really kind of them to offer and initially I was going
to refuse, but…' He sat up a little higher. 'The thing is,
Tina, Tilly is going to become a part of Bree's family.'

She nodded.

'Bree is a part of my family—not blood, I know, but
the family of my heart. Which means Tilly is going to become a part of my family too. Tilly is going to become
an honorary Allenby and Tilly's grandparents are going
to become a part of that circle too. I want to get to know
them. That's why I accepted the offer of their spare room.
I want to get to know them because we're all going to become important in each other's lives.'

Tina's eyes filled. 'That,' she whispered, 'is the most
perfect answer ever. You have no idea how much it means
to me…what a comfort it is.'

He swallowed the lump that lodged in his throat. 'I'm
really sorry things can't be different. I'm sorry that—'

'I know.' She reached out to squeeze his hand, fore-
stalling the rest of his words. 'But I've told everyone that
we're only allowed to focus on the here and now—no sad
faces. I just want to focus on the time I have left and make
the most of it.'

He nodded. They stared at the tableau in front of them,
chuckling when they realised Tilly had refused to allow
her grandparents to paint on her and Bree's painting, but
had set them up with paintbrushes and a piece of butcher's
paper of their own.

'Bree is so honoured that you've asked her to become
Tilly's guardian.'

'And I feel blessed that I have a friend who loves Tilly
almost as much as I do.'

They were quiet for a while, simply enjoying the gentle sunshine. Noah scrolled through his phone. 'I'm determined to win your daughter's approval before I leave on my trek.' He left the day after tomorrow.

'And how do you propose to do that?' Tina's eyes danced. 'Bree is Tilly's BFF and she won't let anyone else get in the way of that.'

'I'm going to win her over with bribery.'

He held out his phone to show her what he meant and Tina clapped her hands in delight.

'We could all make a day of it tomorrow,' he suggested.

'To tell you the truth, I'd welcome a day on my own with my parents.' She glanced at him. 'I'd be awfully grateful if you, Bree and Tilly made a day of it, though.'

He nodded. Sounded great to him.

'Go on,' Tina urged, her eyes dancing again. 'Go and win my daughter over.'

Noah couldn't remember feeling this nervous about anything in a long time. But forging a relationship with Tilly had become one of his highest priorities. Some time in the next eighteen months, that little girl would lose her mother. It would help her to have as many friends as possible.

And it would be important to Bree.

Tilly frowned as he drew closer. 'You can help Nanna and Poppy with their picture. You can't paint on ours.'

'Now, Tilly,' her grandmother remonstrated, 'what did we say about being bossy?'

Tilly stuck her bottom lip out in mutiny, before whirling to Bree. 'But it's our picture!'

'It is,' Bree agreed. 'But we have to be polite, remember? We have to be nice to everyone.'

'Please you can't paint on our picture thank you,' Tilly said, her eyes narrowed as she glared at Noah.

Bree's lips twitched and Noah didn't know how he managed to keep a straight face, except he knew that laughing would disgrace him in the little girl's eyes.

'But maybe Noah would like to paint a picture all his own,' Bree suggested.

Tilly's face cleared and she even deigned to select a paintbrush for him while Bree organised the paper. He thanked them both gravely. 'I want to draw a wombat and a kangaroo. What are you painting?'

'You're not allowed to look until we're finished.'

'Okay, cross my heart. I'll just concentrate on my wombat and kangaroo.'

Tilly stared at him for a moment, fiddled with the charm bracelet at her wrist…and then hustled back to Bree's side.

He hummed as he painted. When he reached the end of his song, he cleared his throat. 'Maybe I'll paint a Tasmanian devil too. And an emu.'

Tilly looked up from her painting. 'And a koala?'

He pretended to consider her suggestion. 'I don't think I'd be very good at painting a koala.'

'Why not?' the little girl demanded.

'I haven't seen one for a very long time.'

'But everyone knows what a koala looks like. Don't they, Auntie Bree?' She didn't give Bree time to answer. She swung back to Noah. 'Can I see your kangaroo?'

'Only if you promise not to laugh at it. I'm a bit rusty at this painting gig and I need lots more practice.'

Tilly promised and he held his painting up for inspection. She stared. She didn't laugh. 'Your kangaroo would be better if it was pink.'

'Pink?'

'We have lots of paper so you can practise lots and lots.'

Talk about a harsh critic! Behind Tilly's back Bree clapped a hand over her mouth to stifle a laugh.

'You know what I need before I draw a koala? I need a research trip.'

Tilly turned to Bree. 'What's that?' she whispered.

Understanding dawned in Bree's eyes. 'I think Noah is saying he needs to go and see a real live koala.'

Tilly swung back to him, her eyes wide. Noah pulled out his phone and showed them the picture of the wildlife park he'd shared with Tina earlier. 'What do you ladies think? Would you like to go and visit koalas and kangaroos and wombats and Tasmanian devils tomorrow?'

Tilly's whole face lit up. She grabbed hold of Bree's hand and swung on it. 'Can we go, Auntie Bree? Can we?'

Bree nodded. 'I couldn't think of anything I'd rather do.'

Tilly jumped up and down and cheered. The grin Bree sent Noah slayed him where he stood. 'Do you want me to show you how to draw a koala?' Tilly said.

'Yes, please.'

That frown lowered back over her eyes. 'We can still go tomorrow…even if you learn to draw a koala today?'

'We sure can.'

She held her wrist up, displaying her bracelet. 'I get a charm every birthday. I'll get another one soon when I turn—' She broke off to glance at Bree.

Bree held up four fingers. 'Four.'

'Four,' Tilly said, swinging back to him. 'Do you like it?'

'Prettiest bracelet I've ever seen,' he agreed. 'What charm are you hoping to get when you turn four?'

'A rainbow.'

'Nice!'

'Can you draw rainbows?'

He nodded. 'I'm very good at rainbows.'

'Would you like to draw a rainbow on our painting?'

He took the offer as it was meant—an official seal of approval—and it made his chest expand to the size of a beach ball. 'I'd love to.'

'You were amazing with her today,' Bree said to Noah the next afternoon after glancing around to check on Tilly, who had fallen asleep in her car seat in the back of the car. 'Thank you. It means a lot to me.'

'She's a funny little character.'

'And bossy.'

That made him chuckle. 'She's going to keep you on your toes.'

It was her turn to laugh. 'Absolutely.'

'But you're going to love every minute of it, and so are the rest of us. I'm really looking forward to getting to know her better.'

Her mouth fell open as if his words had taken her by surprise, and then her gaze softened. He forced his gaze back to the road, determined to ignore the hunger snaking through him. 'You're always going to be a part of my life, Bree, which means Tilly is too. I want to form a good relationship with her. We're all going to be there for you, but for her too. None of us will want either of you feeling alone or isolated.'

'Thank you.' She cleared her throat as if his words were in danger of making her cry. 'And I'll tell you something for nothing. I saw today what a wonderful father you're going to make one day. You have the knack.'

His shoulders went back. He had *the knack*?

He glanced into the rear-view mirror at the sleeping child and then at the woman beside him.

He hoped to have a family at some point in the future. A family that loved and looked after each other, supported, nurtured, and on occasion challenged one another. A family that loved and laughed together, and who clung to each other in the tough times.

He glanced at Bree and Tilly again and swallowed, his heart suddenly thumping. He couldn't be thinking…

Not with Bree and Tilly…?

He shook himself, pressed his lips into a tight line. It was just as well he was heading out into the wilderness tomorrow. He needed a timeout to get both hormones and emotions back under control.

Because he couldn't be thinking what he thought he was thinking. Right? It would ruin everything.

CHAPTER NINE

NOAH TRUDGED ALONG the harbour front, hands shoved deep in the pockets of his coat, shoulders hunched, as he stared out at water the colour of mercury—all silver-grey and mauve in the early morning light.

After seven days of trekking through some of the most awe-inspiring scenery he'd ever seen, he should be sick of walking. He should want a rest.

Too much nervous energy flicked through him, though, for that, and it was too early to return to Tina's parents' house. He refused to rock up on their doorstep before nine o'clock. And it was too soon to call on Bree.

He halted and frowned. *Was* it too early to see Bree?

Shaking his head, he forced his feet forward again. He'd been determined to take advantage of the time out the trek had offered him. After the fiasco that had been his wedding, and would've been his marriage if he and Courtney had gone ahead with it, it had become clear that his priorities had needed a major overhaul. The trek had provided the perfect opportunity for him to do that—he'd been off the grid and out of contact.

And yet instead of reassessing his priorities all he'd been able to do was think of Bree.

The fact she was going to become Tilly's guardian.

The fact she planned to relocate to Tasmania.

The fact he knew she'd rather stay in Brisbane than move to Hobart.

All those thoughts had circled around and around in his mind on a continuous loop.

Instead of focussing on fixing all that was wrong with his life, he found himself wanting to fix things for Bree, to make them perfect.

He raked both hands back through his hair. What on earth made him think he could fix Bree's life when he couldn't fix his own?

It was just…he'd always wanted to be her hero. Ever since they were kids.

Making her smile after some childish frustration or playground aggravation had been one of the few things that had made him feel he wasn't completely worthless. They were adults now, though, not children. And yet the impulse remained.

It hadn't just remained. It had *grown*.

Blowing out a breath, he shoved his hands back in his pockets and watched as a yacht threw off its mooring and adjusted its sails to begin its glide downriver to the mouth of the harbour and the open sea.

That was how he should've felt when Courtney had called a halt to their wedding—cast adrift on a cold, lonely ocean. But he hadn't.

Because he hadn't really loved her?

Or because Bree had dragged him along on her road trip and had kept him anchored?

For no reason at all, his heart started thumping—hard—as if it were trying to pound some sense and self-awareness into him. His mouth dried and he couldn't move. Between heartbeats he finally saw what it all meant—his ponderings and the yearning…his vigilance. He finally understood.

He saw how orbiting Bree, as if he were a planet and

she his sun, had given his entire life meaning—from the time he was eleven years old until now. It was Bree who'd always been his anchor.

With that realisation came the crystal-clear insight into the real reason he didn't want Bree relocating to Hobart. Not only would he miss her. Not only did the idea leave him feeling cast adrift. But…

No.

He shook his head, panic rising in his throat. *Don't be an idiot.* It didn't mean he was in love with her.

His hands clenched and unclenched, but he couldn't hide from the truth. The thought of losing Bree was a hundred times worse than the thought of losing anyone else in his life.

He'd been so intent on trying to create the picture-perfect life—to prove he was a success and therefore worthy of love and family—that he'd almost missed the fact that his perfect woman had been under his nose all this time.

He'd made a lot of mistakes this past year, but turning his back on his true destiny would be a mistake too far. If there was the slightest possibility that he could be her perfect man too…?

'Hell!'

He braced his hands on his knees and dragged in a breath. If he messed this up… There was so much to lose.

And yet so much to gain.

He straightened and stared at the yacht, which had grown smaller and smaller. Setting his jaw, he turned and headed back the way he'd come.

'I need a research trip,' Tilly shouted the moment she saw Noah later that day. Flying out through the front door and down the path to meet him, she took his hand and squeezed it tight in both her own much smaller ones. Something in his chest squeezed tight too.

He glanced up as Bree tripped down the front path, those milk-chocolate eyes dancing and her scent dredging him as she reached up to kiss his cheek. He wanted to close his eyes and breathe her in.

Correction. He wanted to gather her close and kiss her until neither one of them could think straight.

But one couldn't do that in front of a three-year-old.

He inhaled deeply, but he didn't close his eyes and he didn't gather her close. He needed to take care, move cautiously. He didn't want to do or say anything that would freak Bree out.

She nodded towards Tilly and laughed. 'You've created a monster.'

Tilly frowned. 'I'm not a monster, Auntie Bree!'

'Figure of speech, sweet cheeks,' Bree teased, tickling the little girl, who squealed and raced back to the house where her mother and grandparents waited.

'How was your trek?' Bree asked as they made their way inside.

'Fantastic. Spectacular scenery. Some days it was hard going, but the quiet, the solitude…the grandeur made it all worthwhile. It was a great idea, Bree. Thank you.'

She swung to look at him, eyes wide.

'Fresh air, strenuous exercise, no Internet connection— it was the perfect way to blow away the cobwebs and clear my head.'

Her eyes roved over him and things inside him clenched and burned at the approval he saw in their depths. 'It looks as if it's done you the world of good. You look…'

Her gaze heated and his heart thundered in his chest. 'I look?'

She swallowed. 'Really good.'

She continued to stare at him with wide eyes and a grin started up inside him. He wasn't imagining the hunger in her eyes. Bree still wanted him. She wanted him every bit as much as he wanted her.

It might not be love, but it was something—a start. He could build on it. 'Really good?' he teased, sending her a grin filled with flirtation and devilry.

Hot pink flooded her cheeks and she snapped away. 'Your week away has certainly agreed with you.'

And yet he hadn't felt this alive in the seven days he'd been away. *She* agreed with him.

Tilly tugged on his hand. 'C'mon, Uncle Noah. Come and see my picture.'

He allowed himself to be towed away. Tilly's picture would no doubt clue him in on this research trip she wanted to take. Would it be a kangaroo or a koala? Would he find himself spending tomorrow at the wildlife park again?

He shrugged. He wouldn't mind that one little bit.

'See!'

Tilly held up a picture for him to see. He had no idea what it was, but… 'That's not a kangaroo or a koala,' he hazarded.

'No, silly.' She set the painting down onto the sofa and pointed. 'That's sand and that's a big wave and that's a starfish.'

'Ah, I see.' He sat on the sofa and traced the starfish. 'So let me guess. This research trip you want to take is to the beach?'

She leaned in against his legs, staring up into his face so earnestly it was all he could do not to melt. 'I really, *really* want to go to a big beach with big waves.'

He nodded, pretending to think about it, but he was sold. Glancing at Bree over the top of Tilly's head, he raised an eyebrow and Bree grinned and nodded. 'You know what, kiddo, I think that's a great idea.'

With a cheer, Tilly threw her arms around him.

'Putty,' Bree said with an exaggerated eye roll.

'Wrapped around her little finger,' Tina agreed, wriggling her little finger in a good-natured taunt.

'Why don't we all take a trip to the beach tomorrow?' he suggested. 'One of the guides told me about a beach he loves about an hour north of here. We could take a picnic and make a day of it.'

Tina's face lit up. 'What a great idea.'

Behind her friend's shoulder, Bree smiled at him and mouthed, 'Thank you.'

Any time, he told her silently. Any time he could put that smile on her face, he would.

'We'd like to discuss something with you, Bree,' Corinne started after lunch.

So far their day at the beach had been a roaring success. They had the entire beach, with its long stretch of silvery gold sand and aqua surf, wholly to themselves. They'd paddled—it was too cold to swim—and played beach cricket and built sandcastles to their hearts' content.

The crisp sea air and exercise had put colour in Bree's cheeks and a sparkle in her eyes. Tilly had thrown her whole self into it with so much gusto she'd worn herself out and had fallen asleep on the blanket beside her mother as soon as lunch had been cleared away.

Bree, who had been distributing bottles of water and soft drink among the group, zipped up the cooler bag and turned back to glance at Corinne. 'What would you like to talk about?' She folded back down to the blanket with an easy grace that had his blood chugging.

'You already know how grateful and happy we are that you're going to be Tilly's guardian.'

'I'm the one who's grateful and happy,' she returned with her trademark big-heartedness.

'And we know that you're fully prepared to move to Hobart and make your life here.'

'Of course.' But some of the sparkle in her eyes dimmed and he wondered if the others saw it too. She sipped her soda before gesturing around. 'Look at everything you have on your doorstep down here. It's not going to be a big sacrifice.'

'But that's just it, honey. We think it is a big sacrifice. And we don't feel right about asking you to make it,' Corinne continued.

Corinne had been nominated as their spokesperson for her tact and her kindness...and because what she was about to propose directly impacted on her and her husband.

'We've come to see over these last ten days or so how much your family means to you.' Corinne smiled. 'We understand that and we know how vital the support of family can be.'

She shared a smile with her husband and daughter. Tina reached out to briefly clasp her mother's hand, and Corinne's eyes filled. 'It's not fair of us to ask you to leave all of that behind.'

Bree, who'd been watching intently, stiffened. 'What are you saying?' she whispered. 'I love Tilly. I'd make any sacrifice necessary for her. Are you telling me you no longer want me to take on the role of Tilly's guardian because you feel bad about asking me to move to Hobart?'

'Heavens, no, honey,' Corinne said, shaking her head.

'Absolutely not,' Tina said.

At the same time as her father said, 'No, no, lass.'

'If there were no other choice, then we would let you make that sacrifice and be even more grateful to you. But what if you could be Tilly's guardian *and* remain in Brisbane?'

Bree's eyes widened. 'Are you considering relocating to Brisbane instead?'

They all nodded.

Bree swung to Noah. 'Did you know about this?'

He shrugged. 'Yes, they told me when I got back from my trek, but—'

'And you didn't think to warn me?'

'Bree—' he reached over to clasp her clenched hands '—everyone needs to make the decision that is best for them. Just listen to what they have to say, okay?'

She searched his face before swinging back to face the others. 'Okay.'

'Well, honey, the thing is… Don and I have been finding the winters here a little too hard in recent years. I know we're not as young as we used to be, but we like to get out and about and be active. For a good four months of the year, though, we're finding ourselves reluctant to brave the weather and not wanting to leave the house. That's no way for us to live.' She sat back, shaking her head. 'These winters are making us feel old.'

'Of course,' Tina took over, 'they haven't wanted to confess any of this to me because they haven't wanted to cause any further upheaval in my life. But the truth is I don't care whether I live in Hobart or Brisbane. Both feel like home to me. I still have friends up north. So if Mum and Dad are going to be happier in Brisbane than here, then I want us to have made the move, like…*yesterday.*'

'Wow,' Bree breathed.

'We've been worried about taking Tina away from her

medical team down here. But we've checked and there's a team in Brisbane who come highly recommended and they've agreed to take over Tina's care.'

'That's no biggie.' Tina shrugged. 'We all know, though none of you want to say it out loud, that as my tumour progresses there won't be a lot that can be done for me medically anyway.'

Bree leaned towards her friend. 'Are you a hundred per cent sure about this, Tina? If we're going to be frank then I'll be equally frank. What's really most important here, for all of us, is to make whatever time you have left the best it can be.'

Tears filled Tina's eyes and the tears pouring down Bree's cheeks speared straight into Noah's chest as the women shared a fierce hug.

Tina eventually eased away. She stared down at her sleeping daughter, across to her parents, who were drying their own eyes, and then back at Bree. 'I'm sure. I'm so sure—' she suddenly laughed '—I want to sing and dance.'

Tilly's eyes flew open at her mother's words. She sat up and started to bounce. Noah hadn't known little kids could wake up so fast. 'Can we sing and dance, Mummy? Can we?'

On cue, Bree started to sing 'Dancing Queen' and everyone joined in, Tina and Tilly leaping up to dance.

When Bree held her hand out to Noah in an invitation to dance with her, he didn't hesitate. She starting doing a version of the sixties dance the Swim, so he did his own version of the Chicken dance to make her laugh.

The question that had been hovering in the back of his brain demanding confirmation had been answered.

He wanted Bree. Seeing her, being with her, made him feel alive. She gave him purpose. He wanted to be her hero—he lived to see her smile. It was official—he was in love with Bree Allenby.

The only question that remained now was what was he going to do about it?

'Are you feeling okay with everything? With all the changes Tina and her parents are planning to make?'

It was Saturday and Noah had taken Bree out for drinks in the city centre. They sat on tall stools in a converted warehouse just off Salamanca Place where the iconic weekend markets took place. The bar, with its vaulted ceilings and industrial brickwork, was full of character.

Bree had been hesitant to accept his invitation at first, thinking the less time they spent alone with each other, the better for the time being, but she was glad now that she had. He was just so darn easy to be with.

Buried deep inside her that inconvenient and insistent attraction continued to burn. But when they returned to Brisbane and normality she was confident it would dissolve, and it would be as if it had never existed in the first place. This was just a blip.

Besides, she had a feeling he'd asked her here to reveal his plans for the rest of his…well, vacation, if you could call it that. She had no idea if he planned to share the road trip home or not.

She had no idea if she wanted him to or not.

'Bree?'

She started. 'Sorry, miles away.' She gestured around. 'I love this place.'

'I thought it was about time you had a bit of downtime too.' He stared at her in a way that made her pulse jump. 'It's been an eventful trip, that's for sure.'

That made her laugh. 'In more ways than one.' She met his gaze. 'But in answer to your question, I am feeling more optimistic, more hopeful, more…blessed than I think I have any right to feel.'

'You deserve all of that and more.'

The warmth of his gaze sent a corresponding warmth zipping through her, but it wasn't the kind of heat that made her uneasy. It was just Noah being his usual generous and protective self.

During the course of her teenage years—and later as well—her brothers' protectiveness had often irked her. But Noah's never had. He'd always been careful not to impinge on her freedom or to let her think he thought her incompetent or incapable of making a wise decision.

He'd only ever wanted the best for her as she did for him.

'Do you truly think Tina and her parents want to move to Brisbane? Or do you think they're making a sacrifice for me? Or maybe Tilly?'

She'd move heaven and earth to provide Tina with everything she wanted and needed to make whatever time she had left happy and content. Sure, relocating to Hobart would've been a wrench, but she considered it a sacrifice worth making if it would make Tina and her parents happy.

'All of them are prepared to make sacrifices for Tilly's welfare, Bree, just like you. Don't discount that. It's at the heart of everything. It's the issue that everyone sees as the most important one. As they should.'

He glanced at her over the rim of his glass as he sipped his beer. A boutique craft beer he'd pronounced, 'Wickedly good.'

She sipped the glass of Shiraz he'd bought for her, relishing its deep, peppery plumminess. 'Are you saying they think Tilly will be happier in Brisbane?'

'Of course she will. That's a no-brainer. Tilly will be happiest where she's surrounded by people who love her.

Beyond her current circle, in Brisbane she'll also have your parents, your brothers and me. That means five extra people, beyond her mother, grandparents and you, who are going to embrace her and form part of her family. How can she not benefit from all that love?'

He made it sound idyllic.

'And then there's your wider circle of friends who'll be a support to you too. You have girlfriends with children— I'm seeing play dates, the comparing of notes on child development, and discussions about the pros and cons of various schools.'

That made her laugh. Her life was going to change in the most dramatic fashion, but… It didn't frighten her as much as it had at the start of this trip. Noah made it sound as if she could really, truly do this. His belief in her filled her with confidence and a newly found sense of self-assurance.

He covered her hand with his. 'What are you really worried about?'

She squeezed his hand before dragging hers from his hold. His touch sent an unsettling surge of desire through her, making all the fine hairs on her arms lift—as if they were all reaching out towards him.

She would *not* do anything foolish. She would *not* do anything impulsive. She would *not* act on this attraction and ruin everything.

She was starting to feel that she could finally become the kind of daughter her parents deserved, the sister her brothers deserved, not to mention the kind of friend Noah deserved.

Most importantly, though, she felt as if she could become the kind of mother that Tilly deserved—someone steady and reliable, unselfish and responsible, someone level-headed and balanced.

Oh, and the chance to do that on her home turf…

She closed her eyes. She was unbelievably blessed. She didn't need any more. She'd be content with what she had.

'Bree?'

And she had to keep her mind on track!

She ran a finger around the rim of her glass. 'I guess I don't want them to be sad at all they're leaving behind. I don't want them to regret this decision.' She met his gaze. 'I don't want them to be…less happy.'

The fact that the time Tina had left was so finite was hard enough for them all to deal with. She didn't want to add to that stress or sadness.

'What if I told you that I've spoken to each and every one of them on the subject?'

Her gaze speared back to his. She searched his face but saw nothing other than a frank openness. 'Have you?'

He nodded.

'And?'

He looked as if he wanted to take her hand again and her heart crashed about in her chest, but at the last moment he wrapped his hands around his beer, and she pulled her hands into her lap.

'Of course, they're going to miss the friends they've made here. And they have favourite places here that they love.'

Her heart clenched. She couldn't—wouldn't—ask them to give that up.

'But there's so much excitement too about returning to Brisbane that more than makes up for it.'

She searched his face again.

'Tina calls it going home.'

That smile of his flashed out and she couldn't help smiling back. 'Really?'

He nodded. 'Corinne and Don are looking forward to seeing old friends.'

He stared down into his beer, but the gold in his eyes flashed when he glanced back up at her, and it made it hard to catch her breath.

'They've not said much but apparently the winters here have become hell on Corinne's eczema and Don's bad knee. They both have arthritis. They truly long for a warmer climate. I can assure you, hand on heart, this move is bringing far more positives for them than negatives.'

She sagged, the last of her doubts disappearing. She reached across to grip his hand. 'Thank you. Thank you for checking all of that with them.' She didn't doubt for a moment that he'd done it because he'd sensed her concerns.

He shrugged. 'I just want everyone to be happy.'

He had the biggest heart of any man she'd ever met. 'I'm so glad you were with me on this trip, Noah. It's been a life-changing time and you've helped so much. Without your support...' She shook her head, unable to conceive what her world would be without it.

'You mean that?'

'Of course I do.' But something in his tone made her mouth go dry.

'I realised something startling when I returned from my trek, and yet, in hindsight, I guess it shouldn't have been all that surprising.'

Prickles of awareness raced from his palm to hers, and then to every far-flung corner of her body. Her breasts grew heavy, her stomach softened, and her lips parted in an attempt to drag air into cramped lungs. She wanted to wrench her hand away, but it seemed rude...unsupportive. So she gritted her teeth and left it where it was.

Noah had helped her so much over the last three weeks. She couldn't be so ungracious as to cut him short when he wanted to discuss something of personal importance with her.

She had no idea what his epiphany had been, but she could tell it meant a lot to him. She swallowed. She couldn't smile, that was beyond her, but she could listen. 'What did you realise after your week in the wilderness?'

He stared at her with dark eyes and her heart thudded harder and faster when he didn't immediately answer. She leaned towards him. 'Noah, you're starting to worry me.'

He leaned in closer too until his warm male scent, so familiar to her, dredged her senses. Those hazel eyes with their flashes of gold should've been familiar too, but she'd never seen that expression in them before. She battled the temptation to reach for him.

Don't ruin everything.

'I realised, Bree—' those eyes bored into hers '—that I'm in love with you.'

She froze.

'I think I've always been in love with you, I was just too blind to see it.'

She flinched away. 'No!'

'*Yes.*'

'Noah, this is crazy. Three weeks ago you were getting married to another woman! This trip has been an emotional roller coaster of a ride and—'

'I'm not on the rebound, Bree.' His lips twisted. 'Except, perhaps from my own stupidity. Courtney didn't break my heart. And I didn't break hers. We never had that kind of power over each other.'

She couldn't be hearing this. It couldn't be happening.

'You made me realise how hung up I still was about my past, and forced me to face the real reason I wanted to marry Courtney…and what a mistake it would've been if we'd gone through with it.' He shook his head. 'I won't blame her if she never forgives me.'

Bree would, but that was not what she had to focus on at the moment.

'The fact remains—I wasn't in love with her.'

But that didn't mean he was in love with Bree instead. She had to *fix* this.

'I couldn't love any other woman when my heart so wholly and totally belongs to you. I want to build a life with you. I want—'

'*No.*'

He paled. Her single word seemed to echo in the sudden silence that stretched between them. Noah's pallor speared into her heart, but she shook her head and did all she could to harden it.

'How can you dismiss it so quickly? How can you treat my declaration as if it means nothing?' His eyes throbbed with darkness. 'Why won't you take a moment to search your own heart? To take a look deep inside yourself and consider—'

'There's nothing to consider. Hell, Noah, you've been so set on creating this wonderful idyllic vision of a family with Courtney and now you've transferred all of that onto Tilly and me. I know you admire what I'm doing, and I know Tilly has squirmed her way into your heart, but as soon as you return to Brisbane and the real world you're going to see how mistaken you are.'

His mouth became a thin white line. 'Do you remember talking to me about heartbreak on the first night of the road trip? Do you remember how you described it to me?'

She remembered every damn word.

'What you didn't say was how there's absolutely no light or joy in the world when the person you love isn't near or when you discover they don't want you. That it's an effort to put one foot in front of the other. And that some hurts go too deep even for tears.'

He dragged a hand back through his hair. 'I know I've been blind, and I know I've been an idiot, but I've finally worked it out. Don't discount it simply because you're afraid or because you have so much going on in your life or because you think you can't trust me. I would *never* do anything to hurt you. You have to know that.'

Not intentionally, he wouldn't.

'After the conversation we had the first afternoon of our farm stay, Bree… Do you honestly think I'd try and manipulate you in an attempt to gain my mythic idyllic marriage? Do you think I've learned nothing these last few weeks?' He stared. 'You have to know you can trust me.'

She dragged in a breath, refusing to let his words seduce her. She forced her mind to her family, forced herself to remember the shocked expressions on her parents' faces when they'd bailed her from jail—the devastation her mother hadn't been able to keep from her eyes when she'd learned Bree had been arrested for drug possession. The fury and outrage in not only her father's eyes but her brothers' as well when they'd sat through Otis's court hearing when she'd had to give evidence. She'd known it hadn't been directed at her, but if it hadn't been for her they wouldn't have had to suffer through all of that. She couldn't bear to see any of them ever look at her like that again.

She would *not* mess up again.

Lifting her chin, she wrapped determination about her like a barricade. 'Hasn't it occurred to you that in becoming involved with me you'd be risking your relationship with my entire family?' She struggled to get her head around it. 'For heaven's sake, you're in business with Ryder. And I know how much my parents mean to you.'

On the table, his hands clenched to fists. He leaned towards her. 'All of it is worth risking for you. Can't you see? Without you, none of it matters.'

Everything inside her yearned and strained towards him. He looked so true and sincere…and so damn tempting. She beat it back down. 'It's not worth it to me!'

His head rocked back. His face turned grey. With a muttered oath he lifted his beer to his lips and drained it. He set it back down with a snap, his eyes flashing. 'So you're going to be a coward?'

What on earth…?

'I'm not Otis, Bree.' He gave a harsh laugh. 'It seems I've been an idiot *again*. While I might've moved out of my old way of looking at things, and doing what you urged me to do—looking towards the future rather than remaining stuck in the past—you're refusing to take your own advice.'

'I don't know what you're talking about.' She wanted to scoff, but her throat had grown too tight and her voice emerged small and choked.

'You're too frightened of making another mistake to risk your heart again in case you screw up.'

'So what if I am? I owe it to my family to not be that screw-up.'

'But what do you owe yourself? You're simply hiding behind your family as an excuse. Because you're afraid.' He leaned in close. 'But I've seen the way you look at me, Bree. I *know* you want me.'

Heat flooded her cheeks. She'd thought she'd hidden it, kept it from him. 'Lust isn't love, Noah. You know that.'

'Ever since we kissed in Melbourne, it's taken all of my control not to haul you into my arms and repeat the experience.'

Her heart hammered up into her throat. 'Don't you dare kiss me again.'

'And at least I'm honest enough to admit it.' He sat back, his nostrils flaring. 'I want all of you, Bree—your heart, not just your body. I'm honest enough to admit that as well. Even if you're intent on sticking your head in the sand.'

'What I want,' she said through gritted teeth, 'is for things to go back to the way they were before. I just want us to be friends.' Her heart thumped all the way up into her throat. She swallowed it down. 'Please tell me that's possible.' She couldn't keep the pleading note out of her voice.

He rose, nodding at their empty glasses. 'Ready to go?'

Panic fluttered through her. 'You're saying we can't be friends?'

'I want more than friendship from you. It was you who made me believe I deserved more than what I'd been willing to settle for. You can't quibble now when I refuse to settle for less.'

What did that mean in practical terms?

He stared at her, his eyes dark with pain—pain she'd caused. Everything inside her protested. Her eyes burned and her throat ached. But surely this was better than risking his relationship with her entire family? When he returned to Brisbane, he'd see that she'd been right.

'I think it'll be best if we don't see each other for a while.'

He couldn't mean that. 'How long is a while?'

'How long did it take for you to get over Otis?'

No!

He couldn't stay away that long. She had to find a way to make things right. She made herself breathe through the panic. When he returned to Brisbane, he'd see that she was right.

And then things would return to normal.

But no matter how much she told herself that, the fear continued to pound at her. The fear that she might've lost Noah forever.

CHAPTER TEN

'I HEARD YOU come in last night.' Tina glanced up from the breakfast table where she sipped a coffee. Tilly was glued to the TV where she watched cartoons in the allotted half an hour TV time Tina gave her each morning. 'It wasn't exactly a late night.'

Bree helped herself to coffee from the pot. 'I hate to disappoint, but my days of painting the town red are long past.' She stifled a yawn. 'Besides, I had a headache.' A headache that went by the name of Noah. And she didn't want to talk about it. She slid into the seat opposite. 'Hence the early night.'

Not that she'd managed much sleep. She'd tossed and turned until the wee small hours, searching her mind to try and make things right with Noah. The thought of not seeing him for however long it took him to get over this crazy notion that he was in love with her tormented her.

Whenever she'd closed her eyes, the pain that had raked his face when she'd told him—

She swallowed and stared down into her coffee. His darkness and despair when she'd told him she didn't love him... Even now it tore her to shreds from the inside out. She'd ached to find relief in tears, but they'd refused to come.

'You do look a bit pale.' Tina surveyed her critically. 'It's been a bit of an emotional roller coaster for all of us these last few days, Bree. If you're having second thoughts—'

'No!' She straightened so swiftly coffee sloshed over the sides of her cup. She grabbed a wad of tissues from her pocket and soaked up the spill, before reaching across and grabbing her friend's hand. 'No second thoughts, I swear. I just…'

Tina's gaze raked her face and Bree sensed she had her friend's full attention. 'You just…?'

Bree pulled in a breath. 'Are you really, truly one hundred per cent sure you want to move back to Brisbane?'

Tina laughed, her relief evident in her sudden smile. 'So *that's* what's been bothering you.'

That and Noah. But she didn't say that out loud.

'Oh, Bree, please stop worrying. There was a part of me that always knew you'd eventually move back to Brisbane.'

There was?

'It's your home. And now I'm getting the chance to have a peek at what Tilly's future life is going to look like.' She pressed both hands to her chest. 'I feel so fortunate to be able to do that. I know this is going to sound crazy, but—'

She broke off to pull in a deep breath. 'If I'm there at the beginning of Tilly's life in Brisbane, maybe she'll always feel that I'm close and a part of things, even when I'm no longer there. In the meantime, I get to see your family forging relationships with my little girl and growing to love her. Oh, Bree, don't doubt for a moment that this is what I want.'

The two women hugged—a hug of solidarity and sisterhood.

'Okay.' Bree drew back and made herself grin, reminding herself of Tina's 'Only happy thoughts' motto. 'I can stop worrying about that, then. Now we just have to work out the logistics.'

'Noah's already on it.'

She tried not to flinch at the mention of his name. 'What do you mean?'

'Did he not mention it last night? He's flown out to Brisbane this morning.'

Her mouth dried. He'd gone already?

Tina rolled her eyes. 'He made some transparent excuse about how he's been wanting to invest in real estate for some time now—grilled me and my parents about our ideal homes—and has gone off to, quote, *scope them out.*'

He was buying houses for Tina and her parents?

'He plans to buy them and then wants us to use them for as long as we want, rent-free.'

Bree huffed out a laugh. That sounded like Noah—generous to a fault.

'I'm more than happy to let him do the legwork and take the stress out of the move, but we'll be paying our way.'

Tina looked carefree and happy, and Bree blessed Noah a hundred times over. But...

He'd left without saying goodbye. And she didn't know when she'd see him again.

Staring out of Tina's big glass sliding doors, she could see that the sun shone, but in her mind storm clouds had turned the world dark.

'Of course, we have you to thank for all of that.'

That snapped her back. 'Me?'

'That guy has always done whatever he could to make your life easier, Bree. And we're reaping the benefits.'

'What are you talking about?'

Tina rolled her eyes. '*Puhlease!* Noah has always been your white knight. Ever since Dougie Green called you a prissy princess cry-baby when we were nine and Noah sat on him so you could draw glitter hearts all over Dougie's face before he had to go to football training.'

The memory had a laugh shooting from her. It had taken Dougie a long time to live that one down and he'd never called her names again.

'Noah has always had your back, Bree.'

And just like that, everything fell into place. Noah did have her back, just as she always had his. When he'd said he loved her, he'd meant it. He'd never play those kinds of games with her, she meant too much to him. And falling in love with him didn't make her a screw-up. It made her the smartest damn person on the planet!

She grabbed Tina's shoulders. 'I've made the biggest mistake! Last night Noah told me he loved me, but I told him it was impossible and that I didn't love him.'

'You did *what*? But you do!'

'I know! I mean I didn't realise it last night, but I do now.' Bree dragged both hands back through her hair. 'But he laid it on me without warning. I thought he was going on his trek to sort his head out and…and—'

She stared at her friend, appalled at how much she'd misunderstood *everything*. 'I had no idea that him and me, as a couple, was on the radar or…even a possibility.'

'He finally saw what has been plain to the rest of us.' Tina shook her head, 'Since, like, for *ever*.'

'Then why am I the last to work it out?' Bree demanded.

'Because you've been working so hard at being Little Miss Perfect.'

There was love in Tina's smile, not judgement. Bree sank back down into her chair. 'I was a coward.'

'You're not a coward, Bree. He took you by surprise and scared the bejesus out of you.'

'I was a coward,' she repeated, before glancing over at Tilly. 'That's not the kind of role model I want to be.' She wanted to teach Tilly to fight for the things she wanted, to have courage.

She swung back to Tina. She loved Noah with every fibre of her being. 'I need to make this right. *Now*. I have to see him as soon as I possibly can.'

'Go and pack an overnight bag. Quick! I'm getting you on the next flight out of Hobart.'

Bree leapt to her feet and started towards her bedroom. She swung back, massaging her temples. 'What day is it?'

'Sunday.'

She and Tina stared at each other. 'Sunday night family dinner,' they both said at the same time.

Every instinct she had told her he'd be there tonight. He'd want the solace of family. And she'd move heaven and earth to make sure she was there too.

Bree shoved a handful of notes at the taxi driver, with a hurried, 'Keep the change,' before grabbing her bag and racing to the front door of her family home. On Sunday evenings the door was never locked.

Dropping her bag in the entry foyer, she hurtled into the dining room.

Every head swung around at her abrupt entrance.

Including Noah's.

She pressed a hand to her chest and sent up a prayer of thanks that he was there, before she registered that he'd been in the process of rising to his feet with an, 'I'm sorry, but I have to go.'

She took a step towards him. 'Please don't go,' she whispered, her heart hammering.

He fell down into his chair as if the shock of seeing her had robbed his legs of strength.

'Honey, we weren't expecting you for another week at least,' her mother said, 'and—'

'Something came up,' Bree inserted quickly to forestall the volley of questions. She then pointed around the table at her family and then pressed a finger to her lips. 'I know this is going to be really hard for you all,' she said, 'but not a word.'

Dragging a breath into lungs that didn't want to work, she met Noah's burning gaze, the love gathering beneath her breastbone making her ache.

She wanted to race across and throw herself into his arms, press her lips to his and just touch him. She forced herself to remain where she was. He might not want her to touch him and how could she blame him after her coldness last night?

'What are you doing here, Bree?' he finally said.

He looked pale and the strain about his eyes made her want to cry. She couldn't stop from walking around the table to him and touching a hand to his cheek.

He'd pushed his chair back and she dropped to her knees beside him and took his hands in hers. 'I'm so sorry, Noah,' she choked out. 'Last night I panicked and—'

'It's okay, Bree.' His words emerged stiff but resolute. 'You can't help the way you feel.'

She saw then exactly how much he did love her, because even now, while in the depths of his own pain and despair, he was trying to make things easy for her. She shook her head. 'It's not okay, because last night I lied—to you *and* to myself.'

His gaze speared to hers. Hope burned to life in the hazel of his eyes, but he quickly annihilated it.

She couldn't be too late. *She couldn't.* Her life would be dust and ashes without this man. She wasn't letting him go without a fight.

She lifted her chin. 'I love you, Noah. I probably always have. It's probably the real reason I loathed Courtney…and why I gave every girlfriend you've ever had the derogatory moniker of Noah's Nymphette.' She grimaced. 'Not exactly progressive of me, huh?'

His eyes narrowed and he searched her face as if he suspected her of lying.

'I love you, Noah,' she repeated, because she'd never get sick of saying it.

He shook his head. 'This isn't the way to make things right, Bree.' He spoke gently, but his words were laced in steel. 'Sacrificing yourself to keep the peace and make sure everyone is happy is not the answer.'

Her chin hitched up even higher. 'I'm not sacrificing myself! I'm trying to win my happy ever after. Last night when you told me you loved me, I panicked. All I could see were the million and one ways I could screw us up… and not just us.' She gestured around the table to encompass her family.

She tightened her grip on his hands. 'But I was focussing on the wrong things. What I should've been focussing on were the million and one ways we make sense. I'm your champion and you're my hero. Us being together is right…and perfect.'

He blinked.

'This morning I realised that being with you was worth taking any and every risk necessary. So…' She swallowed, starting to run out of steam, achingly aware that her entire family was staring at her with the kind of expressions that screamed *train wreck*. 'So I came here as soon as I could. To tell you I love you; to try and fix things.'

Had she missed her chance with him? Had he closed himself off so completely from her because of the stupid things she'd said last night?

She met his gaze, not sure she'd ever felt more vulnerable in her life. 'Please tell me I'm not too late. Because there's something else I forgot to tell you about heartbreak—when you hurt the person you love it's as if you've stabbed a knife into your own chest. When I think of last night and the way I turned away from you—the things I said—it's a hundred times worse than when Otis betrayed me.'

She swallowed back the sob that pressed against her throat. 'I'll understand if you want nothing to do with me now. I only wish I could take away all the pain that I caused you, and take it onto myself. You're the best man I know, Noah, and you don't deserve anything but love and happiness.'

His gaze searched hers, those eyes dark and penetrating. His nostrils flared. 'You mean it.'

He uttered the words so quietly she had to strain to hear them. She nodded.

His lips swooped down then and captured hers in a fierce kiss that stole her breath.

He eased away, his eyes just as fierce as his kiss. 'You know I'm going to demand everything from you, Bree? I'm going to ask for it all.'

'Which is just as well, because I don't want anything less from you either. This is forever,' she added when he stood and drew her to her feet.

'It's forever,' he agreed, a light flashing in his eyes making the gold flecks in their depths sparkle, his mouth curving into the widest of smiles that sent her pulse dancing.

With a whoop, he picked her up and swung her around, and it felt as if they were both flying. She wrapped her arms about his neck and threw her head back. 'I love you, Noah!'

He set her on her feet again, his love shining from his eyes. 'I love you, Bree.'

She kissed him, a kiss full of jubilation, and when she eased back a moment later she became aware of the dining room, and her family...and Sunday night family dinner.

Everyone stared at her and Noah with a mixture of astonishment, confusion and a strange blend of denial and approval. 'Not a word,' she told them. 'I don't care what any of you think. This is the smartest decision I have ever made. You'll see. And while we're on the subject I don't want you bailing Noah up or giving him any grief about this.' She glared at her brothers. 'If he ever changes his mind about me—'

'Not going to happen,' Noah said, shaking his head.

'Whatever happens,' Bree stressed over the top of him, 'Noah is a member of this family, and he'll always be a member of this family. I want everyone here to remember that.'

Her mother dabbed at her eyes and smiled at them mistily. Her father cleared his throat—once, twice, and merely nodded. Blake and Ryder glanced at each other and broke into grins. 'About time,' they said in tandem.

'My champion indeed,' Noah murmured, staring down at her with a compelling mixture of tenderness and heat. 'And I plan to always be your hero, Bree. What do you want right now?' He smiled. 'What feat can I perform for you?'

It was spoken in jest, but Bree knew exactly what she wanted. 'I want you to take me into the garden where we can have a little privacy so you can kiss me senseless.'

So he did.

A long while later she was sprawled on his lap on a garden bench. She reached up to touch his face. 'I'm so sorry about last night. I'm sorry I panicked and couldn't see what seems so obvious to me now.'

He pressed a finger to her lips. 'I'm the one who should be apologising. I gave you no warning whatsoever what was in my heart prior to Saturday night. I just blurted it out and expected you to be on the same page. I should've realised sooner how much it would frighten you. I should've known how worried you'd be that if things didn't work out between us I'd lose your family. Because you know how important your family is to me.'

He touched her face. 'Dearest Bree, I should've taken the time to woo you and win you over—to listen to your fears and then work through them with you to show you they were groundless. I should've given you time to adjust rather than storming off. I should've proved to you that you're more important than anybody or anything in the world by sticking around and fighting for you.'

'I should've been braver.'

'You couldn't be braver if you tried,' he said, seizing her lips in a kiss of pure exaltation that made her blood dip and swoop as if she were on a fairground ride—filling her with excitement and exhilaration. And joy.

He lifted his head, his fingers caressing her face. 'My beautiful, brave Bree.' And then he kissed her with such tenderness she melted.

When he lifted his head some time later, she had to blink the tears from her eyes. 'I can't wait until we're *alone* alone,' she whispered.

The gold sparks in his eyes flared.

'Oh!' She sat up a little straighter. 'You were leaving. When I first arrived, you were about to go. Am I keeping you from something?' He'd been away from work for a good three weeks. There were probably a million things he had to do, hundreds of matters demanding his attention.

His low laugh had her very centre softening. She wanted to beg him to laugh like that again.

'I was about to head to the airport to catch the next flight back to Hobart. I was going to find you and tell you that I loved you but respected your feelings on the subject…and then I was going to do anything and everything to win your heart.'

She pressed a hand to his chest, awed that this amazing man loved her. Beneath her palm his heart beat hard and strong. 'You were coming back for me?'

He nodded.

She wondered if it was possible to feel happier than she felt right at this very moment.

'You know I want to marry you, Bree?'

'Of course.' She feigned nonchalance, as if that fact were self-evident, but a thousand fireworks went off inside her.

'I think you'd love to have Tina as your maid of honour and Tilly as flower girl.'

He was right, but that meant… 'You want to get married sooner rather than later, huh?'

'I'll understand if you want to wait. The press will have a field day, and the speculation will be…trying.'

'Only if they can drag themselves away from speculating about Courtney partying on that Greek billionaire's yacht.'

He grinned. 'You saw that?'

'Read it on the plane.' She shrugged. 'I hope she's having fun.' She found herself wishing Courtney the same kind of happiness she'd found. 'Noah, I don't care what the press says. I love you.'

'And I love you.'

'Then I propose we get married when we want, live our lives on our own terms, and be happy. What do you say?'

'I say that's an excellent plan.'

And then he kissed her with an enthusiasm that left her in no doubt how much he approved of her plan.

EPILOGUE

Two years later

'WE NEED TO go on a research trip,' Tilly announced.

Noah glanced up from the picture he was drawing. Tilly's voice had taken on that too-innocent edge and he had to suppress a grin. 'Why? What do you need to study in more detail?'

She turned her picture around. 'Do you know what that is?'

He'd got much getter at this game during the fourteen months Tilly had been living with him and Bree. He and Tilly spent a lot of time drawing together. It was their thing. Especially in that awkward hour after dinner and before bedtime, like now.

He pursed his lips. 'It looks like a dog.'

Tilly frowned. 'But it's not very good. It's supposed to be a baby dog—a puppy.'

'So...we need to find some puppies, is that what you're telling me? So you can learn to draw them better?'

Tilly nodded so hard he was afraid she'd make herself dizzy. Over the top of her head, he and Bree shared a secret smile.

'I guess I better see what I can manage,' he agreed. 'I'll put my thinking cap on.'

He and Bree had bought Tilly a puppy and were planning to give it to her at the end of her birthday party tomorrow. Tomorrow when she turned six! The last couple of years had flown by.

Tilly launched herself into his arms. 'I love you, Daddy.'

'I love you too, Princess.'

Eight months ago Tilly had announced to him and Bree that she wanted to call them Mummy and Daddy, like all the kids in her class called their parents Mummy and Daddy. 'Because you are,' she'd said. 'You are my mummy and my daddy.'

The memory could still make his chest swell and bring a lump to his throat.

She raced over to Bree and pressed a kiss to Bree's baby bump. 'It's my birthday party tomorrow, Baby. If you were here you could have some of my unicorn cake and play games and wear a princess dress too.'

She climbed up into Bree's lap and Bree snuggled her close. His heart gave a giant thump. His wife was the most amazing mother. She and Tilly adored one another, and he knew that Bree would adore whoever else came along in the future with that same ferocity.

He glanced at that baby bump and his heart expanded. He'd never known it was possible for a man to be this happy.

Tilly bit her lip. 'My party is going to be fun, isn't it?'

Their daughter was a worrier. 'You bet,' Bree said with so much confidence, Noah couldn't help but smile. 'Just you wait and see. It's going to be a huge success. How can it be otherwise when Nanna and Grandma are in charge of the food, Poppy and Granddad are in charge of the party decorations, and Uncle Ryder and Uncle Blake are in charge of the party games?'

Tilly's face cleared.

'What's more,' Bree added, 'you have the best princess dress in the world to wear and there's going to be a unicorn cake.'

'And I have Mummy's fairy charm.' Tilly held up her wrist, the dangling charms on her charm bracelet twinkling.

'And that definitely has to be a good luck sign. Your party is going to be sprinkled with fairy dust.'

Tilly nodded, happy again.

Tina, before she'd become too sick, had purchased a charm for Tilly's every birthday until she'd turned eighteen. It was Tilly's most treasured possession, and it had become a tradition to give the charm to her the night before her birthday.

When Tilly was in bed, Noah made Bree a chamomile tea, grabbed a soda for himself and they headed out to their back deck with its view of the Brisbane River. It flowed by steady and calm, reflecting back the night sky with its three-quarter moon and myriad stars.

Setting her mug to the table, Bree walked over to lean against the railing. She'd been a little quieter tonight than usual.

'Tired?' he asked, walking over to slide his arms around her waist and pull her back against him.

'A little.'

'You should be worn to a frazzle with all of this party organisation.'

That made her laugh. 'I've hardly had to lift a finger. Everyone else has insisted on doing the heavy lifting.'

'They love it,' he told her. And they wanted her to take it easy at the moment, to take care of herself.

She laughed again. 'They do.'

As Noah had always suspected, Bree's entire family had embraced Tilly and her family as their own. The whole clan was looking forward to tomorrow's party with the kind of glee generally reserved for grand final day and family weddings.

Which immediately had him flashing back to his and Bree's wedding nineteen months ago. It had been small and unassuming, and it couldn't have been more perfect.

'How's the training going with your new second in command?' With her upcoming maternity leave looming in four months' time, Bree was training up her assistant to take over while she was away.

Bree had grown the entire physio and dietetics side of operations at Fitness Ark from the ground up and it had proved successful beyond all of their wildest expectations. The franchise continued to go from strength to strength.

'She's an absolute wonder. We want to keep her, Noah. She's too valuable an asset to the company to let someone else poach her.'

Which was what had happened with her previous assistant. He made a mental note to discuss a pay rise for her with Ryder and the accountant next week.

She rested her head against his shoulder. 'The doctor called me in for an appointment today.'

He immediately stiffened.

'Relax.' She chuckled. 'Everything is absolutely perfect.'

She placed her hands over the ones he'd spread possessively across her expanding belly.

'Then why did the doc want to see you?'

She turned, her arms going around his neck. 'There was something in my previous scan that puzzled her. She wanted to do another ultrasound just to make sure.'

He frowned, but her eyes were shining and not a trace of worry lined her face. She was so beautiful she stole his breath. 'Make sure of what?' he murmured, resisting the urge to kiss her.

'To make sure she was counting the right number of arms and legs.'

He stared, not understanding.

'Today's scan confirmed it.' Her eyes danced and her smile was as wide as the sky. 'Noah, we're having twins!'

He could feel his jaw drop and his eyes widen. 'Twins?' he parroted.

She nodded, excitement radiating from every pore. She cupped his face. 'Tell me you're happy rather than freaked out.'

With a whoop, he picked her up and swung her around. Setting her on her feet again, he bent and kissed her with all the feeling in his overflowing heart.

'Oh!' She clutched his arms when he finally lifted his head, her eyes dazed. 'Perfect response.'

The pulse at the base of her throat fluttered and that familiar heat coursed through him. 'I'm married to you, we have a daughter, and now we're going to have twins… life can't get any more perfect.'

She reached up to cup his face, her eyes soft and full of love. 'You deserve every ounce of happiness and every good thing this world has to offer you.'

'You really think so?' some devil made him ask.

Her eyes widened. 'Of course.'

He swung her up in his arms. 'Does that mean I can talk you into an early night? That would *definitely* add to my current happiness.'

She pressed her lips to his cheek. 'I thought you'd never ask. An early night sounds perfect.'

He strode inside with the woman he loved in his arms, determined to show her exactly how perfect he thought her.

* * * * *

FALLING FOR THE
SARDINIAN BARON

ROSANNA BATTIGELLI

MILLS & BOON

For Sarah, Jordan, and Nathan,
with love always. xoxoxo

CHAPTER ONE

DESPITE THE AIR-CONDITIONING in the baggage claim area of Cagliari Airport, Ella could feel the prickling sensation of perspiration beading along her temples. She took off her jean jacket and stuffed it into her carry-on luggage before rifling through her handbag for an elastic band to put up her hair in a ponytail.

Watching the last of the passengers retrieve their luggage from the conveyor belt and head for the exits, she wondered at the cause of her driver's delay. Gregoriu Pinna was to have been at the airport early, waiting for her.

Flinging her handbag over one shoulder, Ella propped her small carry-on on top of her larger suitcase and turned around swiftly, her luggage ramming hard into a body.

She gasped at the same time that her victim expelled a loud grunt, the force of the impact making him lose his footing momentarily, but he managed not to fall. Ella let her hand drop from covering her mouth. *"Mi scusi,"* she apologized, squinting up at him as she retrieved her carry-on. "I didn't see you…" And then she realized she had slipped into English. *"Non—"*

"I understand English" came the man's clipped reply.

Ella's mouth snapped shut, and she waited, expecting him to respond with a gracious "No worries." But he just stood there, his sunglasses and thick beard most likely concealing an irritated expression that mirrored the edge in his voice. He wore a navy T-shirt that revealed tanned, muscled arms, and faded jeans, from what she could make out in the two-second shift of her gaze.

"You are Ella Ross." His tone was dry, and his lips had twisted slightly.

"Um, yes," she said, frowning. "But you're not—"

"—Gregoriu Pinna."

She arched an eyebrow. "So you're taking his place? Is he okay? I was worried that he might have been in an accident…"

"He was not."

Ella let out a sigh of relief. She waited for the man to say more. Explain what had happened to make *him* take Gregoriu's place. But he just stood there, appraising her coolly. She felt her cheeks tingling with what she knew would immediately be a telltale flush.

Did she have to pull every word out of this guy's mouth? And why was he dressed in such casual clothes? Where were his navy jacket and trousers? The gold D embroidered on the jacket's lapel, she had been informed, would be the way to identify a DiLuca employee.

Ella's boss at *Living the Life* magazine had been contacted by an agent of reclusive Sardinian billionaire Massimo DiLuca to have the DiLuca family interviewed for the lead story in August. Publisher and editor-in-chief, Paul Ramsay, had offered *her* the assignment.

She shifted as a wave of fatigue hit her. Was he intending to stand there indefinitely? She was starting to get a kink in her neck, looking up at this skyscraper of a man.

And then the thought occurred to her that maybe this emissary's English was limited. She felt a twinge of remorse for being so judgmental.

"And *you* are…?" she said in as polite a tone as she could muster.

"Gregoriu's replacement." He reached for her luggage. "Follow me, please. I will take you to the hotel." He turned and started walking toward the exit.

Ella hesitated. He had a strong Italian accent but seemed able to communicate well enough. Could this guy be an imposter? Perhaps he had done something terrible to Gregoriu after squeezing some information out of the poor guy, and now he was pretending to be someone he was not. Maybe he was looking to rob her after driving to some secluded spot. She glanced around worriedly, trying to spot a security officer.

The man swiveled around suddenly, and Ella remained where she was, blinking up at him for a few seconds before finally blurting, "*Scusi*, but I think you should show me your ID."

Is that a flash of a smile? Ella wondered. *Or just a shadow?*

He released his hold on the luggage, reached into the back pocket of his jeans and pulled out his wallet. He strode over to her and flipped it open.

Ella peered at the photo. No sunglasses, no cap. Dark hair and a groomed scruff, not a thick beard. Noticeably long eyelashes that framed dark, almond-shaped eyes that looked rimmed with eyeliner. Her pulse quickened. She recognized the face on the photo. She had seen it during her research, and it had always appeared above a designer suit. She hadn't found anything more recent than three years earlier. Ella's gaze flew to the information identifying him, but she didn't have to. She just needed a few moments to collect herself and try to stop the flush on her cheeks from becoming an intense flame.

As calmly as she could, Ella gazed up at Baron Massimo DiLuca.

"Grazie, signor barone DiLuca," she said, nodding, her voice as clipped as the stiletto heels walking past them. Massimo almost chuckled at the formality of her tone. He might be a baron and one of the richest men in Sardinia, if not Italy, but he certainly did not need to be addressed in such a stiff and formal manner.

"My title is not necessary, *signorina* Ross," he told her drily. "I'm fine with just *signor.* Actually, given the fact that we're about to spend a week under the same roof, *Massimo* is even better."

Her brows arched but she didn't reply.

"And I suppose I should apologize, not introducing myself right away." He looked around. "I just didn't want anyone to hear me… People make a big fuss when they find out I'm around. And then the cell phones come out to snap a thousand pictures, and the inevitable reporter appears and starts hounding me." He gestured toward the exit. *"Andiamo.* Let's go." He shoved his leather wallet back into his jeans pocket and wheeled Ella's luggage ahead of him. When he came to the revolving doors, he stopped and gestured for her to precede him.

Moments later, Massimo had placed her suitcase and carry-on in the trunk of his silver-gray SUV and Ella was sitting in the passenger seat next to him, her handbag in her lap. While she was absorbed in putting on her seat belt, his gaze took in her travel-tousled hair in its ponytail—light brown with what looked like natural gold highlights—her slender neck and arms, and a loose-fitting coral cotton dress that had bunched up when she sat down, revealing smooth, shapely legs. She had applied coral nail polish on her fingernails and the same to her toenails, which peeked out of low-heeled wedge sandals.

Massimo looked away before she could catch him staring. The last thing he wanted was to make her uncomfortable and to give her the wrong impression of him.

It was just that this Ella Ross was younger than he'd expected. In his early communication with her boss, Massimo had requested someone who was proficient in Italian and good—no, *excellent*—at his or her job. That was one of his expected criteria of anyone in his employ. If they valued their job, they would strive for and achieve excellence, he reasoned. This belief extended from those who worked at his luxury resorts to his housekeepers and personal chef.

Massimo had conveyed to him that he wanted an experienced journalist who would demonstrate cultural sensitivity toward his family, especially since his mother's English was limited.

The woman now sitting next to Massimo was the right person for the assignment, her boss had claimed, and had proceeded to sing her praises. Massimo had followed up with his own online search. The first article he found was from the *New York Times* and included a photo of Ella Ross accepting an award. It was a side shot, so he had been able to see only her profile, partially obscured by her shoulder-length brown hair and dark-framed glasses. She was wearing a navy business suit and low-heeled shoes. The article had mentioned that Ella Ross had won some prestigious newspaper-and-magazine award for excellence in journalism.

That had satisfied him that her boss had made the

right choice. And it had pleased his mother when he had told her.

But seeing her up close at the airport, in a ponytail and casual cotton dress, Ella had looked barely older than twenty-one, if that. And it had taken him aback, although he had no intention of showing it.

Massimo realized he was tapping the side of the steering wheel. He glanced back at Ella, nodded and started the ignition. Once he had left the airport parking lot and had merged into the Cagliari traffic, he said, "I suppose you are hungry, no? Before we head to the hotel, I will stop at a *pasticceria.* You can have a snack…perhaps a brioche or one of our traditional Sardinian pastries. I could use an espresso, too…"

"It's not necessary, but if you need to stop for a caffeine fix—" she gave a soft laugh "—I'm game." And then, as if embarrassed by the familiarity of her tone, her smile dissipated and she shifted her gaze to the rows of pastel-colored buildings and clusters of tourists and locals ready for post-siesta shopping.

He frowned. His English was quite good, but there were phrases now and then that were baffling. What *game* was she wanting or expecting to play? He pursed his lips. Perhaps he should test *her* proficiency of Italian. He certainly didn't expect her to know or understand any of the Sardinian dialect, which was very different from the official Italian language.

"Che tipo di caffè prende? O preferisce una bevanda fresca?"

She turned to him with raised brows. *"Un espresso va benissimo. Oppure una limonata."* She shrugged and gave a small laugh, a sound that reminded Massimo of one of the delicate chimes in his island garden. "I suppose it all depends on how hot I am when we enter the pastry shop."

Hearing her speak Italian perfectly sent an unexpected tingle through Massimo's veins. There was no awkward pausing or butchering of the pronunciation. Her words had flowed out quickly and smoothly, without hesitation. If he didn't know any better, he'd think Ella Ross was Italian.

Massimo nodded, and concentrating on the winding road ahead, he thought about the word *hot*. She had used it innocently, of course, but he couldn't help thinking about its other meaning, a meaning that he was perfectly aware of…and how it applied to his guest.

He shook his head. He shouldn't even be having such thoughts. It didn't matter to him whether Ella Ross was *hot* or not. She wasn't here to bewitch him with her fawn-like eyes, perfect coral lips and curvy body. She was here to do one thing and one thing only: interview him and his mother for next month's lead story in *Living the Life*.

"Oh, look, a wedding!"

His passenger's enthused tone jolted him out of his thoughts. Massimo slowed down to a stop behind a line of cars that had done the same to catch a glimpse of the activity in front of the medieval high-domed Cathedral of Santa Maria. The bride and groom were holding hands and posing for the photographer while the group around them watched. Elaborate flower arrangements in huge ceramic planters were positioned on either side of the massive, engraved double wooden doors and down the stairs to the road, their fuchsia blooms matching the gowns of the bridesmaids' dresses and the bride's bouquet.

"Aw…" Ella said as the groom kissed his bride and

suddenly swept her off her feet to twirl her around. The crowd erupted in cheers, and moments later, the photographer gave the signal for the tossing of the confetti.

Massimo felt a tightening in his chest. The scene had ignited memories that still felt like arrows piercing his heart. He and his wife had gotten married at this cathedral, and watching the young couple in front of the ornate facade now was like having his past flash in front of him.

He felt another jolt at the applause and cries of *"Bravo, bravo"* as the groom gave his bride a second and more thorough kiss.

Ella turned to him sheepishly, her cheeks flushed. "I'm a sucker for rom—um—I mean happy events…" Her words trailed off, and her smile disappeared as she met his gaze.

He caught his own expression in the rearview mirror. His brows were furrowed, his lips compressed in a hard line. No wonder she was looking at him strangely.

The car in front of him started moving and Massimo focused his attention on driving, aware of the Vespa riders that were zooming in and out of traffic, taking every opportunity to get ahead.

He turned into a side road, and a couple of minutes later, pulled into a parking lot that was almost full. *"Ecco. Siamo arrivati!"* He leaped out of the SUV and opened the door for his guest. *"Prego."* He nodded, gesturing for her to step out. "We are here at the *Pasticceria della Mamma*. Now you can get your espresso or lemonade."

He couldn't help glimpsing the length of her legs as she swung around and got out. A sudden seaside breeze made her dress billow up, and a couple of young men across the street gave a low whistle. He scowled at them, and they laughed and walked away.

"Not all tourists show good manners," he said curtly as they entered the pastry shop. "Or control." He led her to an empty table in the back corner of the room, one of a dozen that were painted the same colors as the macarons in the glass display that ran the length of the counter.

He removed his sunglasses and smiled at the approaching waitress before looking expectantly at Ella.

"Un espresso, grazie." She smiled at the waitress and glanced at the display of pastries. "Oh, my goodness, I can't resist," she said with a laugh. *"Una sebada, per favore."*

Massimo's brows arched. She had obviously done some research, requesting a traditional Sardinian dessert—a sweet pastry that was fried and filled with lemon-scented pecorino and topped with warm honey.

"Lo stesso per me, Maria," he said, flashing a smile at the waitress.

"You didn't have to tell me, *signor* DiLuca," she replied cheerfully with a heavy Italian accent. "You order that nine times out of ten!"

He laughed and caught Ella's gaze on him. She really did have fawn eyes, dark and wide—like the expanse of sea he'd often look out at from his bedroom balcony at midnight—

Whoa! Why was his mind even formulating such thoughts? She was here on business, and he had no business conjuring up thoughts like that about her. Thoughts that sounded like they were part of a romantic sonnet…

He was not interested in romance.

Been there, done that.

And it had left him with a broken heart.

CHAPTER TWO

ELLA'S GAZE WENT from the baron's eyes to the dimple in his cheek. He was so distractingly good-looking… And although she generally wasn't a huge fan of beards, his was rather attractive. Thick but tapered in all the right spots, his sideburns descending evenly to his jaw, his moustache perfectly symmetrical. And below his lips—completely visible and perfectly shaped—the inverted triangle of hair above his beard made him look like what she imagined a baron would look like, even though his baseball cap, T-shirt and jeans made him appear an ordinary guy…if you could call strong, tanned biceps, broad shoulders and a muscled chest ordinary.

God, she was *staring*! Ella averted her gaze as the waitress arrived with their espressos and *sebadas.* As she sipped her espresso, her thoughts flew to her previous boyfriends. There were two guys she had dated at university for a while—a short while—but she had been too focused on her studies to even consider letting things develop beyond a certain point. Both had wanted more than she was willing to give, and Ella had been the one each time to end the relationship.

Her last boyfriend had been a writer named Dustin whom she had met a couple of years after starting her current job.

As a freelancer, he had contributed to *Living the Life* magazine. Since he lived in Toronto, Ella's boss had shared the connection. Dustin had been the one to contact her, first by email and then by phone. Ella had liked his easy manner and sense of humor, and after a few phone conversations, he had asked her out. They had done dinner, the movies, a basketball game, and he had even taken her for dinner at his parents' home.

He was good-looking, with dirty-blond hair and blue eyes. They had spent about a month getting together for dinners, shows and the occasional stroll in scenic High Park. They had kissed after about a week of dating, but his kisses hadn't stirred her. Hadn't activated her pulse.

Ella had been comfortable with him, but she had never felt the desire, the electricity—not even a spark—that the heroines in the novels she read seemed to experience.

She had wondered at her lack of desire, let alone passion, and the thought occurred to her that maybe she was putting all her ardor into her career. She loved traveling, interviewing people around the world and working on her pieces for her magazine in her upscale Toronto condo overlooking High Park. Maybe she just didn't want to give up her independence... As the weeks had gone by, Ella had realized she liked Dustin more as a friend and colleague than as a date, and she had decided it wasn't fair to let him think there was a future for them together.

After the dinner at his parents' place, it became clear to Ella that Dustin thought things were just fine between them and introducing her to his family indicated his more serious intentions. It had jolted her, and she knew she had to make him aware that they were not on the same page and they should stop dating. He had been hurt—and she had felt bad about it—but ultimately, it had been the kindest thing to do.

He had sent her an email a couple of months later, saying he had connected with someone he was certain was his soulmate and he hoped he and Ella could remain on friendly terms.

And they had, occasionally emailing or chatting on the phone.

Ella thought about what her adoptive mother had told her when she had confided in her about Dustin and guys in general. "If he doesn't put stars in your eyes, then he's not the right one for *you*."

This memory made Ella's heart ache. She missed her mom, and the tight relationship they had shared, which some of her friends had envied. She had been able to talk to her about anything, and Cassandra had listened, encouraged, advised, comforted and cheered Ella on. Every daughter should be so lucky...

She remembered how one of her classmates had once blurted, "And she's not even your real mom," after overhearing Ella say in a conversation she was adopted, and Ella had turned to her, her eyes glinting ice. "She is my real mom," she had replied in staccato tones, and the girl had smirked and walked off. Later, Ella had shared her hurt feelings with her mother, who had drawn her into her arms and murmured, "If I'm not real, then who was it that made your favorite Sardinian dessert for you tonight?"

Ella couldn't help smiling, her memories of her mother now bringing her more smiles than tears, unlike the first year after her mom had passed. As Ella bit into the pastry she had loved since childhood, she closed her eyes and nodded. "Heavenly," she said with a contented sigh. "I'll have to start making them again..."

Her last word trailed off, and she groaned inwardly. She really had to think before blabbing away. She wasn't here to tell the baron anything about herself or her connection to Sardinia.

"You've made these before?" Massimo's eyes narrowed as they peered at her over his espresso cup.

"Um, yeah, I went through a 'let's cook something from around the world' phase," she fibbed. "I was intrigued by what I read about Sardinia, cooking or otherwise…although I didn't have fresh pecorino, so I used ricotta instead." She bit into her *sebada* again, savoring the lemon-scented pecorino mingling with the honey. "Man, this is really good. Do you cook? Or bake? Oh, how silly," she said with a chuckle. "Of course a baron wouldn't be doing his own cooking. Or his wi—"

She stopped in horror. She had been making a general statement but realized how inappropriate it was— especially the last part—since the baron had lost his wife three years earlier. She had read about it online while doing her research. It had saddened her, and the accompanying photo of the two of them on their wedding day had jolted her, left her wondering if she would ever look at a man adoringly the way the baron's wife was gazing at him.

Now she bit her lip hard, mortified at her insensitivity and impulsiveness. The baron's mouth had compressed into a thin line, and his forehead had creased momentarily. Ella's heart sank. He had caught her gaffe. Her mind scrambled for the right words to apologize…

Massimo drank his espresso and set down his demitasse. When his gaze returned to her, his mouth had curved into a smile. And there was a glint of amusement in his dark eyes. And no sign of a frown. Per-

haps he hadn't caught the near *wife* reference after all…
Thank God.

"Actually, being a *human*, I enjoy cooking. Mind
you, I do have a chef, also, but there are days when I'm
in the mood to be alone and, how do you say, whip up
my own dinner. Try something new…"

Ella nodded. "I like to try new dishes, too," she said,
breathing an inward sigh of relief.

"Another espresso?" he asked, as the waitress
brought him a second cup.

"No, *grazie.* I'm good. And good to go." She un-
clasped her handbag and reached inside for her wallet.

"*Per carità*… You are my guest. The bill is taken
care of." Massimo's voice brooked no argument, and
she looked up and met his enigmatic gaze.

He downed his espresso before rising to stand behind her, a hand on her chair.

She stood up, and he tucked her chair in as she
moved aside, his arm brushing against hers for a moment. She caught her breath involuntarily and, hoping
that the tingle in her cheeks wouldn't change to a trai-
torous flush, she strode brusquely to the door.

"*Signor* DiLuca, if I may ask," she ventured as they
buckled up moments later, "you didn't seem to be worried about people coming up to you in the pastry shop."

"Please… Massimo." His eyes pierced hers. "That's
because the *Pasticceria della Mamma* is where the tourists go. And they don't know who I am. The locals
go elsewhere." He put on his sunglasses, engaged the
clutch, and seconds later, he was pressing the accelerator. He shot her a glance. "And now to the hotel…"

"Is it very far?"

"About twenty-five minutes from here… But don't

worry. You don't need to make conversation. You'll be too busy looking at the view."

"I'm not worried," she replied lightly. "And I don't generally have a problem making conversation."

"Of course not. That's your job."

After leaving the congested street of the cathedral, Massimo stepped on the accelerator, and in a few moments, they were on the highway heading south.

The Baron was right; who wanted to talk with a view like this? The bewitching sun-sparkled sea with its varying shades of turquoise, blue green, cerulean, blending into and over each other, and far off in the distance, deepening to royal blue and even indigo. Sailboats bobbing on gentle waves. A cloudless baby-blue sky that looked like a perfectly pressed bedsheet…

There were bursts of color at every turn. Magenta bougainvillea trailing over terraces and balconies, poppies gently waving their brilliant red-orange faces at them as Massimo drove by, plush-looking hills and mountain sides streaked with golden broom.

The coastal route was breathtaking with its adjacent sandy beach that looked like a long strip of sifted white flour. Limestone crags and unusual rocky formations leaned into the sea, and Ella was sure that she spotted ancient granite caves like the ones she had read about in her travel guides about Sardinia, opened by the Romans who had conquered the island. As they passed a secluded cove, Ella exclaimed at the sight of a colony of pink flamingos.

Massimo slowed down and veered off to the shoulder of the road so she could take some photos. "Our beautiful island is on the route of many migrating birds," he told her. "You will see many other wonders while you are here…"

Massimo opened the sunroof window and a salt-tinged breeze wafted through the vehicle, diffusing the musky scent of Massimo's cologne, mingling it with hers. Ella breathed in and out slowly. This was her first visit to Sardinia since she was four, and now she could kick herself for not having booked a trip earlier, like after she had graduated.

But then again, she really hadn't had the time. She had won a national writing contest in one of the leading Canadian newspapers, subsequently getting a part-time job there doing lifestyle pieces, and then worked her way up to doing court reporting and city-beat articles. Eventually she had applied for a position at *Living the Life* magazine. Her pieces in the national paper had impressed the owner of *Living the Life*, and he had hired her. Paul Ramsay's magazine was distributed all over the world and featured extravagant and sometimes elusive celebrities and VIPs. The magazine would cover all her travel expenses when Ella needed to interview someone face-to-face.

"Some celebrities and personalities are demanding that way," Paul had said with a smile in a follow-up meeting online. "I'm sure you won't mind…"

And she hadn't. She had traveled to California, Vancouver, Paris, Rome, Ireland, the Caribbean, and of course, New York. How could she have turned down the assignment and the opportunity to spend the first week in July at Massimo DiLuca's exclusive private island off Sardinia?

And now here she was, on the island where she was born…and had been given up for adoption…

A wave of emotion swept through her and she felt a prickle at the corners of her eyes. Where would she be now if her biological mother hadn't given her up? What would she be doing? She turned her head to dab at her eyes before any tears could emerge. Since Paul had offered her this assignment two weeks ago, her mind had been a whirlwind, thinking not only about the interview but also about the emotional impact going back to Sardinia would have on her.

Ella had thought about her family history, which her boss knew nothing about, and how returning to the place of her birth was something she had considered, especially in the last couple of years...

The universe was providing her with the chance to reconnect with her adoptive father's family and perhaps discover what she could about the mother who had given her up twenty-eight years ago...and maybe find her...

She blinked.

"Are you okay? Did something get in your eye?" Massimo pressed the panel to close the sunroof and checked the air-conditioning.

"I'm fine," she said. "My eyes must be sensitive from lack of sleep. Usually I have no problem falling asleep on overnight flights... The wine helps," she added, forcing a light chuckle. "But for some reason, I was a little restless this time."

"Well, soon enough, you'll be at the hotel, and you can catch up on your sleep." Massimo gestured with one hand toward the glimmering expanse of sea. "The sound of the waves outside your window will be like a—a *ninna nanna*."

"A lullaby." She nodded. "I wish! I'll have to imagine it. My hotel isn't near the sea. My boss gave all the details to your employee in charge of the arrangements..."

Ella saw the corner of his mouth twitch slightly, puzzling her. He obviously knew where he was going— Paul had sent him the details of the hotel—so how did he not know it wasn't by the sea? There was something else that perplexed her about him, and that was why *he* had replaced Gregoriu instead of one of his other employees, given his reluctance to engage with the public. Surely a baron had more important things to do? Seeing to the running of his own ancestral estate? Perhaps meeting with a high-ranking politician to discuss initiatives for the tourist industry? Making a sizeable donation to a children's charity? Ella had noticed earlier that he wasn't wearing his wedding band. Perhaps it was a painful reminder of his loss...

She couldn't help wondering if there was anyone new in his life. Nothing in her research had indicated that he was seeing anyone; perhaps there was a Sardinian custom about dating after a period of bereavement.

Ella checked her watch. She had planned to spend the day doing more research at her hotel before the Di-Luca employee picked her up to bring her to the baron's private island. It would be a couple of days before the interview actually started, which was plenty of time to search out more details about this elusive tycoon. Doing the DiLuca piece was important—a publishing coup for the magazine, actually—and she wanted to make sure she hadn't missed anything that might enhance the story.

The interview and subsequent piece were her first priority. Maybe, if she wrapped up early, she'd attempt to call her uncle. But now was not the time to think about that...

She wondered if Massimo DiLuca would think she was nosy if she inquired about Gregoriu. She might as well; if it was a private matter, he would tell her. "*Scusi, signor* Massimo, I was just wondering...about Gregoriu, I just hope he's okay?"

Massimo slowed down and stopped at a traffic intersection. He turned to Ella. "I'm sure Gregoriu would be happy to know that you were concerned about him. Let me reassure you, so you don't lose sleep over it... Gregoriu had to rush his wife to the hospital."

"Oh, my goodness! Is she okay?" She frowned. "I'm so sorry to hear that."

"Don't be sorry. Gregoriu and Lia are now the proud parents of an eight-pound, two-ounce baby girl." He flashed her a smile before putting his foot back on the accelerator.

Massimo concentrated on the road as he drove along the coastline, glancing occasionally at the *americana* in the seat next to him. He should actually refer to her as *canadese,* since the former was a general term for anyone living in North America and the latter applied specifically to Canadians. She had exclaimed and clapped in pleasure at the baby news and then had fallen strangely silent, her brow knitting as she gazed out the window.

The next time he glanced her way, her eyes were closed and her head had drooped slightly in his direction. At any moment, he expected her to land against his shoulder or upper arm. The thought caused his muscles to tense.

He looked over again after concentrating on a sharp curve in the road, and Ella's head was now aiming for his chest. Her soft hair brushed against his upper arm, and he drew in his breath involuntarily. Her perfume had a fresh, zesty scent, like that of winter mandarins, and her thick eyelashes rested above cheeks that were peach pink. He swerved slightly, causing a rush of adrenalin, and he cursed under his breath over his momentary distraction. Thank goodness he had been on an isolated stretch of road, having switched off the coastal highway minutes before. And the movement, followed by the jerking of the gears caused her to move away from him and continue to nap, to his relief.

He took a few deep breaths to slow down his pulse and concentrated on driving but was unable to keep his passenger from entering his thoughts.

Like the way her eyes had widened in genuine dismay when she had almost mentioned his wife. He could tell that she hadn't meant to specifically refer to Rita. So he had pretended to be unaware...

He sighed, recalling how the moments, weeks and months after Rita's passing had been a blur. He'd lost her suddenly, the cause being a heart defect that no one in her family had been aware of. She had collapsed during a garden party at his parents' villa, where he and Rita had lived in one wing, and although the ambulance had arrived quickly, she was gone by the time it had passed through the ornate, automated enclosure to the villa.

He hadn't been able to carry on in his position as President and CEO of the family business. His mother, who had shared the helm with his father before *his* passing two years earlier, had taken over again for a couple of months, allowing Massimo time to grieve away from the public eye. Massimo had been devastated over losing his father, with whom he had shared a tight bond, and the shock of his wife's unexpected death had siphoned his will to continue working.

DiLuca Luxury Resorts was a billion-dollar industry that attracted clients with deep pockets to the many dozens of incomparable resorts nestled in Sardinia's most enchanting and picturesque bays. People came for the breathtaking views of the sea, unspoiled beaches and the unique culture of an island which had been coveted and dominated by, among others, the Phoenician, Roman, Spanish, Piedmont, and ultimately, Italian populations.

Massimo had eventually returned but had chosen to continue a large part of his responsibilities from his home office, instead of DiLuca headquarters in the capital city of Cagliari.

Massimo glanced at Ella. She had to be exhausted after her delayed flight. They'd be at the hotel in a few minutes, and she could go to bed right away if she wished. Or if she preferred, she could rest, take a refreshing shower and then dine with him in the hotel's two-Michelin-starred restaurant.

When he finally stopped at the hotel doors, Ella started, her eyelids struggling to stay open. She blinked, straightened and peered out the window at the gold lettering on the entrance doors. *Villa Paradiso*. She swiveled in her seat to face him. "This isn't my hotel, *signor* DiLuca. There must be some mistake… I had booked a night's stay at *L'Albergo al Sole.*"

Massimo raised an eyebrow. "I am aware of that. But I cannot have my guest stay at anything but a five-star resort."

"My hotel was four stars," she countered, "and I know your family is generously footing the bill, but I can't expect you to pay for something like *this*. It's much too much."

"You will like it here, you will see. I've already notified *L'Albergo al Sole.*" Massimo promptly climbed from the car and greeted the concierge.

A moment later, Ella stepped out and went around to his side. Her eyes widened at the sight of the luxury cars in the parking area, two of them his. She held up a hand in protest. "I can't expect you to—"

"*Signorina* Ross, it is only for one night. Please accept our Sardinian hospitality… My mother would be very upset at me if she found out you had stayed elsewhere. And it's very embarrassing to be scolded by your Sardinian *mamma* when you're thirty-six," he added with a smirk.

"Fine," she conceded with a sigh. "I wouldn't want to start on the wrong foot with your mother. *Grazie*. And if I can call you Massimo, you can call me Ella."

"*Prego*. Okay. Now let's go in. I'm sure you're anxious to relax in your room. As I am."

"You're…?" She frowned, cocking her head slightly.

"Staying overnight as well, and tomorrow I will take you myself to my villa. *Andiamo*. The concierge will bring up your luggage."

"I—I'll just need my carry-on, thanks."

"*Va bene*." He walked over to say a few words to the security guard at the door before gesturing to Ella to step ahead of him. When she got to the door, her gaze froze on the door handles, two large gold Ds.

"Is this—?"

"Yes, one of my resorts." He nodded and flashed her a smile. "Welcome to *Villa Paradiso*."

Massimo was pleased with Ella's reaction as they strode through the marble foyer, past the intricately carved wooden table with its massive pedestal vase filled with a flamboyant arrangement of red roses and a variety of lilies.

He greeted the employees at the check-in desk, introduced Ella and shared the news about Gregoriu. After their clapping and exclamations subsided, Massimo informed them that he looked forward to dining at the restaurant in an hour or so.

Moments later, they handed him a room key, which he

glanced at before passing it to Ella. "If there is anything you require, please do not hesitate to call the front desk," he told her. He gestured toward the gleaming gold elevator doors. "After you. I will show you to your room."

When the doors opened up to the seventh floor, Ella gasped at the view from the large floor-to-ceiling windows opposite them. She rushed over and placed her palms directly on the glass as she peered out at the endless stretch of sea.

"Oh, my God," she breathed. "This *is* paradise. I couldn't tell this place was built on the side of a hill. This view is…breathtaking."

"I'm glad you like it. Hopefully, you will like your room, as well."

"Are you kidding me?" Ella murmured moments later as she stepped into her suite. Massimo watched as she did a 360-degree visual sweep of it, her eyes widening as she took in the spaciousness and luxury of the appliances and furnishings. And the king-size bed, with its two-tone turquoise duvet and fluffy assorted pillows. She gave another gasp at the sight of the doors opening to a room-length balcony overlooking the sea. "I must have a peek," she told him and was gone before he could respond.

He watched as she surveyed the expanse of water, her hands gripping the balcony railing. He could hear the soft gush of the waves and knew it wouldn't be long before they would be lulling her to sleep. His gaze shifted to the king-size bed. Ella was small; she would be lost in it…

Why were his thoughts veering in that direction? In the three years he'd been living without Rita, he had never entertained the idea of dating another woman, let alone imagining one in bed. Not that he was imagining

Ella and *himself* in the same bed; he had just pictured her there alone, nestled under the huge duvet…a two-second blip that meant nothing.

So why was he suddenly feeling so disloyal to Rita's memory?

He frowned. He should go. He'd like nothing more than to take a relaxing shower to ease some of the tension he had in his shoulders, have a glass of wine on *his* balcony while the sea breeze dried his hair and then go to dinner.

His suite was a floor above hers and twice the size. It was his haven when he had business to take care of in Cagliari, and when he did not, the suite was never used for other people. And although for the last year, he had spent a portion of his day communicating online instead of in person, it was always a pleasure when he was here to take in the spectacular sunrises and sunsets at the first resort built by his family.

Ella came back in, shaking her head. "I can't believe this. A terraced hillside resembling the Garden of Eden, a massive infinity pool and that gorgeous sea. Right outside my window. Am I dreaming?"

Massimo gave her a terse smile. "No, but you will be soon." He turned to leave and then stopped at the door. "Please take all the time you need tomorrow. You'll probably still have jet lag." He reached into his back pocket and pulled out a card. "Call me when you're ready to leave… Oh, here is your carry-on." He thanked the employee, and when the latter had gone, Massimo turned to face Ella again. "If you're not too tired, you are welcome to join me in the restaurant in an hour. If you are, I will wish you good-night now, Ella," he said with a curt nod. "And *sogni d'oro.*"

CHAPTER THREE

ELLA WATCHED AS the baron strode out of her room, glad he couldn't see her eyes prickling at his last words. Words only one man—her father Micheli—had ever said to her.

Ella had loved her adoptive parents Cassandra and Micheli, and she could still remember the sadness in their lives when Micheli died. She had been only four years old, but she occasionally had a cloudy memory of crying in the home they were sharing with Micheli's parents.

Most of what she knew about him was from stories her mother had told her, although Ella did have vague memories of sitting on her father's lap while he read to her and of him singing her a song at bedtime with funny-sounding words before kissing her good-night and murmuring *"Sogni d'oro."*

Of course she eventually discovered from her mother that the song was a traditional Sardinian lullaby. Ella hoped she would certainly have *sweet dreams* as her father, and now Massimo, had wished her before leaving. *Dreams of gold* was the literal translation, and it seemed so apt, especially with the sun beginning to set right now, a saffron ball in a gold-streaked sky.

Just watching the horizon change, like an artist's

palette, before her eyes made her heart twinge. She had missed twenty-four years of skies like this, having been only four when her mother had moved them back to Canada. Not that she didn't love Canada; it boasted spectacular beauty from coast-to-coast, with its stunning oceans, majestic Rocky Mountains, lush valleys with world-class vineyards, and diverse landscapes and varying climates in each province.

Living in Ontario, dotted with over two hundred and fifty thousand lakes, Ella had loved exploring the rugged northern shores of Lake Superior and the picturesque places around the other Great Lakes. Her apartment was just north of Toronto, so she was close to Lake Ontario, an hour away from Lake Simcoe, and close enough to the magnificent Muskokas, with their pretty towns and smaller lakes with such fanciful names as Fairy Lake, Butterfly Lake, and Honey Harbour.

But being in the country where she was born, stepping on Sardinian soil and breathing the sea air outside just moments ago, a bevy of emotions were now swirling within her, causing a bittersweet ache in her chest.

This was still her country. She had dual citizenship, and over the years, she had wondered when she would be able to return. Her mother hadn't had the same desire, too heartbroken over the loss of Ella's father and the memories they had shared there.

When Micheli's father had died, Ella's mother had called to give her condolences and arranged for flowers to be delivered to Micheli's mother. And then when *she* had died eight months later, Ella's mother had sent the floral bouquet to Micheli's only brother, Domenicu. Ella had been nine when her *nonno* and *nonna* had passed, but she still had memories of her mother telling her about them.

Cassandra had occasionally called Domenicu after that, but over the years, the communications had dwindled. As well as the reasons to return to Sardinia. Cassandra had been working two jobs to support herself and Ella, and traveling out of country had not been possible, for reasons of time and money.

And Ella had been focused on her studies, and later, her job.

Cassandra had kept phone numbers and addresses of the relatives in a small notebook that Ella had found in her mother's kitchen drawer weeks after the funeral. Ella had tucked it away in her handbag, overwhelmed with grief, but when Paul had offered her the assignment in Sardinia, she had pulled it out, added the number to her cell phone contacts and had gone online to try to find information about her uncle.

Her heart had skipped a beat when she'd found that his number and address were the same, but Ella had had no intention of actually contacting him before her trip. She had a job to do with relatively short notice and she hadn't wanted any emotion dealing with her past to interfere with her task.

Now, finally back in Sardinia, reconnecting with her uncle was a real possibility if she still had the nerve. Ella had extended her stay by one week after her assignment, but she had begun to question if she could deal with such an emotional reunion in such a short amount of time. And the even greater emotional ramifications of finding her birth mother. Maybe she could plan a longer trip in the future and deal with everything then…

Ella forced herself to switch her thoughts to the man she would be interviewing in the coming week. Intrigued by the brief information her boss had given her, Ella had begun doing some preliminary research on the

DiLuca family, and surprisingly, there wasn't as much information as she had expected to find. It seemed that the DiLuca family of the current century had preferred to be more low-key than the past generations of barons and baronesses. Except until now, with the upcoming official opening of a state-of-the-art cardiac research center in Cagliari, which they had funded.

Massimo DiLuca and his mother had conceived of the project to honor their respective spouses, with the hope that continuing research would save future lives. They had enlisted an international team of architects and medical experts, and the complex would soon open its doors to accommodate some of the top cardiac researchers in the world. The upcoming ribbon-cutting ceremony would be followed by a seven-course dinner with musical entertainment and dancing in one of the building's international symposium halls.

In the latest media releases about the project, there had been speculation as to whether Massimo DiLuca would preside at the ceremony with his mother, since he had avoided the public spotlight for three years. Was the reclusive billionaire ready to face the world again?

Ella had found a few photos and articles about Massimo's parents and their investment into the resort business and how it had taken off. And then she had come across the shocking news that Massimo had lost his wife suddenly, three years earlier. Ella had stared at the online obituary of Rita Floris—she had kept her maiden name, like most Italian women—and the photo of Rita, smiling indirectly at someone. She had felt deep sadness for the loss of such a young life, and for her widowed husband.

She could understand why the baron would want to stay out of the limelight while dealing with his grief.

And she doubted even now, after three years, he would bring up anything personal about himself or his late wife during the interview.

A shiver ran through her at the recollection of her first glimpse of the baron, with his strong chest and arms in a muscle-revealing T-shirt and jeans, and his abrupt, elusive manner that had made her imagination go wild. Ella shook her head, wanting to erase the memory of her initial impression. What she couldn't erase was the image of Massimo DiLuca's dark chocolate-brown eyes, revealed once he had removed his sunglasses in the pastry shop. And the sheen on his lips from the honey-drizzled *sebada*…

She had expected to have a day to herself before meeting him, to prepare herself emotionally. The term *reclusive* could have so many different connotations, she had thought when her boss had first told her about the assignment. Yes, the baron had agreed to be interviewed about the DiLucas' thriving resort business, the *baronessa* Silvia's upcoming birthday and the official opening of the DiLuca Cardiac Research Center. But perhaps he was doing so reluctantly and would be difficult to work with. She could very well be going to fairy-tale surroundings but dealing with an absolute ogre.

After seeing a rare photo of him online, Ella's pulse had quickened. The photo was from a black-tie event the baron and his wife had attended, and only her back had been visible, but he'd been captured fully by the photographer. The look of him—beardless, black tux and wine glass in hand—had caused a reaction in her that was probably typical of most women when they saw him or came into his sphere… And there was nothing ogre-like about him. At least not physically.

Well, she was in his sphere now. And his manner

wasn't ogre-like, either. Granted, her initial impression of him hadn't been the most positive one but was understandable, given his abrupt manner and the way his cap and beard had concealed his identity.

Taking a deep breath, Ella opened up her carry-on and retrieved a short nightie and took it with her to the spacious gold-and-crystal-accented washroom, where she was relieved to be able to finally take a shower. As she lathered with the lilac-scented soap, Ella's thoughts replayed moments from the time the baron had appeared at the airport up to the time he had shown her to her room.

Massimo's manner and tone had seemed different when she had returned from the balcony. Somewhat cooler… Perhaps he had been a little annoyed by her exuberance over her view and room. Could it be Sardinian women were more reserved with their emotions? She shook her head. What did she know? The sole Sardinian she had ever come in contact with had been her father, and that had been for only the first four years of her life.

Well, soon enough, she'd be on the baron's private island, staying in his guesthouse, and interviewing him up close and personal. And her instinct was telling her that she'd be learning much more about him. Maybe more than he wanted her to know…

Ella stepped out of the shower and quickly towel dried her hair and body. She slipped on her nightie and wrapped the provided bathrobe around her. It didn't take long for her hair to air dry on the balcony while she enjoyed the view. Moments later, she was lying between the luxurious cotton sheets, sighing with pleasure before feeling her eyelids get heavier.

"This is living the life," she murmured, smiling.

She felt so pampered, and as she began to drift contentedly toward sleep, Ella wondered if this was how a *baronessa* felt…

The ringtone on his phone told Massimo he was getting a text. He stretched to get his phone on his night table and read Ella's message.

I'm almost ready. I'm just on my way to the breakfast room for a quick cappuccino.

He texted back.

Va bene. I will meet you there in a few minutes.

He thought about his dinner the night before. He had wondered if Ella would be joining him and trying her first traditional Sardinian dish, a seafood *fregula* with saffron broth. He had also ordered a local wine, but the *signorina* had not shown up. She must have been exhausted. It had been over thirty degrees Celsius yesterday. Perhaps that was why her cheeks had been flushed so often.

Massimo's thoughts shifted to the baby photo Gregoriu had texted him last night, followed by the same feeling of sadness he always seemed to get recalling how, since his wife had not been able to conceive, they had just agreed to explore adoption possibilities a week before she passed.

He leaped out of bed, willing himself to suppress any further thoughts in that direction. He showered quickly and changed into a pair of white pants and a salmon-colored shirt. He chose a wide-brimmed hat from his selection on the top shelves of his walk-in closet, and putting his sunglasses in his shirt pocket, he took the stairs instead of the elevator to the terrace floor.

Now that he was in his own resort, Massimo didn't have to be concerned about anonymity. The tourists wouldn't know who he was and his employees all knew not to address him by his last name in front of the guests. Entering the room, he scanned the tables and spotted Ella by the far railing, gazing out at the sea, her cappuccino in hand. He strode toward her, thinking what a perfect picture she made wearing a white eyelet blouse over a long, flowered skirt with a matching red belt, her hair held back by a red band.

The warm morning breeze was ruffling her hair and skirt, and she turned moments before Massimo reached her table. It gave him an unexpected jolt. She looked so…refreshed, her glossy red lips parting slightly before smiling a greeting.

"*Buongiorno, signorina* Ross," he said, nodding. "*Prego*, please." He gestured toward her chair. She sat down and took a sip of her cappuccino, leaving a red imprint on her cup and a bit of froth on her lip. She casually licked it off, and at that moment, she looked across at him. He shifted slightly and said a few words to the passing waitress, who nodded with a smile.

He turned back to Ella. She was looking at him with raised brows.

"I was speaking to her in my Sardinian dialect," he explained. "By the way, *signorina*, there is no such thing as a 'quick cappuccino' here. We like to take things nice and slow. I suggest you let go of your North American ways while you're in Sardinia."

He paused as the waitress returned, accompanied by a waiter. She set down an espresso for Massimo and another cappuccino for Ella and a dish for each of them. The waiter placed an oval platter in the middle of the table with divided sections of assorted breakfast pastries—including *sebadas* and *amaretti*—and various cheeses, cold cuts and fruit.

"Mamma mia!" Ella said. "I didn't expect—"

"—to eat?" Massimo lifted an eyebrow. "I hope you are not on a diet. There are so many Sardinian dishes you need to try while you're here."

"I don't diet," she said. "I'm actually a very healthy eater. I wasn't hungry a little while ago, but now, seeing this feast before my eyes—" she picked up her fork "—my mouth is watering!"

Massimo nodded curtly. "It's unfortunate you weren't able to enjoy your first Sardinian dinner last night. I guess you were very jet-lagged."

Ella gave him a sheepish smile and then let out a chuckle. He raised an eyebrow.

"Yes, I was very jet-lagged," she said, as she fixed her plate. "But I had a good sleep and I'll feel even more energized after this lovely breakfast."

He watched her cut up her cantaloupe and prosciutto and then spear it with a fork. *"Buon appetito,"* he nodded. "Enjoy."

Massimo fixed himself a generous plate before asking the waiter to bring some bottled water and a pitcher of freshly squeezed orange juice. Ella didn't seem to be aware of his fleeting glances at her as they ate.

"I think this is a good time to be frank with you, Ella." *Now was as good a time as ever to get something off his mind.*

CHAPTER FOUR

ELLA FINISHED HER cappuccino and set it down. She met his stare, her hands clasped together under her chin. Had she committed a faux pas? Breached some kind of Sardinian breakfast protocol?

Her breath caught in her throat. He was damned good-looking, with his perfect set of teeth and lips, mesmerizing eyes with their rim of thick lashes and dark hair with wavy tips that she could tell were still damp from his shower... *Full stop!*

Mortified where her thoughts were heading, Ella diverted her attention to the platter and chose a couple of *amaretti* before facing him again. *What did he have to be frank with her about?*

"It's nothing personal," he said gruffly. "But I wasn't too happy about doing this set of interviews."

"Um, well, my boss *had* mentioned you weren't pleased about the original plans," she said with a slight shrug.

"*That* would have been a circus," he said curtly. "I didn't want my home to be invaded by an army of reporters and photographers."

"And it won't be," Ella said lightly. "The army is down to one soldier. *Me.*"

"Which I agreed to—" he nodded with a twist of his lips "—because I want to make my mother happy."

"But *you're* not happy."

"It's…complicated," he said, his eyes piercing into her as if he were trying to decide if he should explain further.

"Look, *signor* DiLuca, I plan to follow the conditions you specified in the contract with my boss. I interview you in the morning, the afternoon is my own to work on the piece, and later on, I interview your mother at her villa after the renovations are done. Any photos I take will be viewed and approved by you before I send them to my boss." She raised her eyebrows. "Oh, and I stay in your guesthouse to avoid having you go back and forth from your island every day." She held out her hands. "Did I miss anything?"

"No." He leaned back, crossing his arms.

"So?" Ella cocked her head. "What exactly is…the problem?" She had almost said "your problem," which would have sounded rude and inappropriate. But she was starting to feel the heat and just wanted Massimo to get to the point.

"I am aware of your achievements," he said, "and your ability to communicate in Italian, which is what I wanted, as my mother isn't proficient in English." His eyes narrowed. "My mother has gone through a long period of—*lutto*—you know, when my father died."

"Mourning." Ella nodded, her voice softening. He wasn't mentioning his own situation, but she imagined he was inferring the same.

"Yes. And just in these past few months, she has started to allow herself to enjoy living again. I just want to make sure that you understand and can be sensitive to my mother, who may have moments of sadness, even now. She needs someone who understands loss."

Something twisted in Ella's chest, an unexpected hurt that the man sitting across from her would assume she had limited life experience and would question her sensitivity and understanding about loss. *How judgmental!* She felt the hurt give way to mingled disappointment and a flash of anger. Feeling a sizzle in her chest, she leaned toward him on the table, her arms crossed in front of her.

"Please allow me to clarify something, *signor* Di-Luca," she said succinctly. "I understand loss and grief quite well." She paused, struck by a wave of emotion but determined to maintain her composure. "But in any case, I haven't gotten to where I am today without being professional above all else. And that includes being sensitive."

What a colossal fool he was. He had seen her eyelids shuttering as if she had been suddenly struck with temple pain, flutter briefly, then open, the vulnerability replaced by an assertive steeliness. He had touched a nerve, but there was no way she was going to display her emotions. His gut feeling told him that he needed to do some damage control.

"I'm sorry if I have offended you, Ella. I was wrong to have judged you because of your age." He cleared his throat. "And I'm sorry for…for the loss you have experienced. It seems I dislike it when others presume to know me and my life without having the full facts, yet I have just done the same to you."

He inhaled deeply. Losing Rita had aged him, aged his heart. And although Ella hadn't shared any details about her loss, he should have known better than to make assumptions about her past experience.

"I hope you can forgive me for *my* insensitivity," he said. His gaze locked with hers, and he hoped she could see the sincerity in his eyes.

Ella drew in a deep breath and let it out slowly. "I suppose I can try to do that," she murmured.

He raised his eyebrows.

"Okay, I can do that," she said more decisively with a toss of her head.

"Thank you," he said, one corner of his mouth lifting. He glanced at his watch. "I'm ready to leave anytime you are."

Massimo felt some of the tension in his shoulders dissipating as his speedboat glided away from the dock, and when the way was clear, he cruised toward one of the distant small islands scattered like a rosary chain in the sea. He couldn't wait to get there and relax with a long, cool drink. The morning had been somewhat intense. And maybe he'd go for an afternoon swim. But first, he'd show Ella to his guesthouse. He imagined she would probably like to settle in and maybe organize her work area. The guesthouse was on a lower slope and situated a hundred and fifty feet from the villa. It overlooked a cove with a small beach of its own.

Since his stay in the guesthouse while the villa was being constructed, no one else had occupied it, not even his mother when she visited. She found the trek to the villa difficult with her arthritic knees and chose to stay in one of the villa's spare rooms.

Massimo had been reluctant to go along with his mother's original plans for the series of interviews, cringing at the thought of being at her place with a team of photographers and reporters from *Living the Life* magazine, not to mention the many friends she wanted to invite along with their eligible daughters. She hadn't been that subtle about getting him out in public again, and he had adamantly refused, only leading her to assume a hurt demeanor.

It was enough, he had told her, that he would be present at the official opening of the DiLuca Cardiac Research Center the day after her birthday and would not be leaving it to her alone.

Much as Massimo was tempted to stay out of the media spotlight, his conscience wouldn't allow him to shirk his responsibility as a baron. His family had engaged in philanthropic projects contributing to the public good for as long as he could remember, and it would not be right for him, as the current baron and one of the Cardiac Center's benefactors, to be absent at the official opening. He had been the one to conceive of the endeavor and to put together an international team to see to every aspect of its development.

His mother had been on board from the start, and she had been touched by the fact that through Massimo's initiative, and the DiLucas' massive financial commitment to the project, the Center would be a world leader in cardiac research, benefitting millions of people. A charitable venture to honor her husband and Massimo's father, and Massimo's wife.

It would be the first public appearance Massimo would be making since Rita's passing. And the Center would be one of the main interview topics *Living the Life* magazine wanted to highlight in their August issue.

Finally, Massimo and his mother had reached a compromise: he would consent to participating in an interview with only one journalist, who would spend the week in his guesthouse, and his mother's birthday event would be at her villa with her close friends minus their eligible daughters.

So, to prepare for Ella's visit, Massimo had the place professionally cleaned, the spacious pantry and restaurant-sized refrigerator fully stocked, and the bedroom and washroom refreshed with new linens and towels. Along with a few scented soaps and bath items, made with local products like juniper, saffron and olive oil.

The house was a two-story structure with a bedroom loft and en suite bathroom and a separate office. The main floor consisted of an open-concept kitchen, dining and living area, with floor-to-ceiling windows facing the cove and endless stretch of turquoise sea. Massimo had wanted to distract himself from his constant grief during the year that he'd be in the guesthouse, and he had spared no expense in indulging himself. The floors were of Orosei marble from Sardinia's east coast, and the modern furnishings were also locally made from the most sought-after craftsmen.

Massimo had also enjoyed perusing a number of antiquarian shops, their owners often showing him unique pieces in private rooms. One item was a decorative sword said to have belonged to a Moorish prince, and a pair of ornate wine goblets had been identified as originating from somewhere in fifteenth-century Iberia, most likely Spain. Sardinia had been part of the Kingdom of Aragon, which was modern-day Spain.

The walls of the kitchen were painted the lightest shade of lemon. The high-end appliances gleamed against a backsplash of hand-painted tiles, which Massimo had commissioned based on those he had seen in paintings of his ancestors. And the curved peninsula, topped by a nine-foot slab of pink granite from the Gallura countryside, was a chef's dream. And it included a chef—if Ella wanted—or she could cook up something herself. The kitchen had double doors that led out to a courtyard with huge terra-cotta planters overflowing with herbs, tomatoes and other vegetables. One section had a decorative pergola with clusters of grapes growing all around it.

Massimo stole a glance at his guest. She was sitting forward in her seat, totally absorbed in the views around her. The breeze made her hair flick around her face and her dress flare up around her legs. With those sunglasses she was wearing, coral-red lipstick, and long skirt with a red belt and headband, she looked like a classic film star. Innocent and *hot* at the same time.

He groaned. Why were his thoughts veering in that direction?

Because you're normal? his inner voice said mockingly.

"Really?" he said aloud.

"I didn't say anything," Ella replied. "It must have been a mermaid whispering in your ear." And then she *giggled*.

Massimo flashed her a look of concern. Where had that comment come from? She wasn't wearing a hat. Could the midday sun have given her sunstroke?

"Have some bottled water, *signorina*. It's in the cooler bag behind my seat."

"I thought I mentioned you can call me Ella."

"Like *Cinderella*?" he said with a chuckle.

"No, actually, it's, um, it's just Ella." She glanced away. "Oh, look at the beach! Is that pink sand?!"

"It is. It's produced by coral when it's broken down, and the currents nudge the grains onto the shore instead of pushing them out to sea."

"Wow. This is such an enchanting place. There's so much I'd like to explore once I've done the interview"

"Oh?" Massimo glanced quickly at her. "You're not going back home right away?"

Ella smiled enigmatically. "I have my holidays after the interview, so I decided to extend my stay for a week."

"I see." For a few moments Massimo concentrated on navigating through the deep blue waters around a series of tiny uninhabited islands and limestone crags. "So where are you staying?"

Ella shrugged and almost looked uncomfortable at his question. "I haven't booked a spot yet. I didn't have time to do a lot of research before I arrived, so I figured I'd decide while I was here. I might stay in the Cagliari area or head north to the Maddalena Islands." She gazed wistfully into the distance. "And then there's the Emerald Coast. It sounds so enchanting when you say it in Italian… *La Costa Smeralda*. And I'll probably visit the island of Caprera…"

"Ah, the island of Garibaldi, the much loved—or resented—icon of Italy's 1861 unification."

"I'm fascinated by Italy. I lucked out getting this assignment."

"From what I understand, it wasn't luck at all," he said. "It was your talent. *And* your ability to speak Italian." His mouth twitched. "*Allora, parliamo italiano?* As they say, 'When in Sardinia…'"

CHAPTER FIVE

ELLA NODDED AT Massimo's request for them to speak in Italian. His accented English was rather pleasant, but when he spoke in his native Italian or regional Sardinian dialect, it seemed to ignite some kind of visceral reaction in her. Like now.

His voice was deep, sonorous, and evoked his island heritage. A heritage they shared...

So why hadn't she revealed that to him when he had asked her about her name? Told him her full name was actually Marinella Rossi? And she had changed it to Ella Ross during a period of angst and rebellion in her late teens, conflicted as to why her birth mother had given her up for adoption and wanting to reject anything that had originated from her Sardinian past, even though it was her adoptive parents who had named her.

Reflecting on it as an adult, Ella had realized she had been struggling with her identity at that time and had attempted to create a new one, starting with a name change. And then one day, finding some old photographs taken when Ella was a child, which her mother had put away in a drawer, Ella's curiosity about her heritage had been aroused. She had started to ask questions, and she knew her mother was pleased, finally able to share details that Ella had previously shown no interest in.

Ella had been devastated when her adoptive mother passed away suddenly from a heart attack a year ago. There were so many things she would have liked to ask, so much she had wanted to say to the woman who had been a loving mother from the start, even during Ella's challenging years. As she mourned her loss, Ella vowed that one day she would return to Sardinia, the place where her parents had met, fallen in love, married and adopted her. And maybe even find her birth mother...

"Ecco! Stiamo arrivando!"

Massimo's words shook her out of her reverie. She had been gazing at the passing scenery for a while without really seeing it. And now they were approaching his island, a sphere of lush green, ringed with white. Ella couldn't make out the actual villa, but a couple of minutes later, she caught glimpses of its light apricot exterior between the feathery boughs of mixed pines and cypresses. The beach, which had seemed like a thin strip as they approached, was in fact a wide band of the whitest sand Ella had ever seen, and the water lapping up against it was a heady mix of turquoise and sea green, sparkling under the rays of the midafternoon sun.

She glanced at Massimo as he idled the boat up to the dock. She hadn't been unaware of the way he looked—and fit—in those white pants and salmon-colored shirt; her pulse had leaped as soon as she had seen him approach her table on the terrace. She had immediately downplayed her involuntary reaction in her mind, telling herself that when she had turned around from gazing at the stunning view, she hadn't expected to see him right there, only a few feet away.

Ella suddenly realized that the speedboat's rumble

had subsided. And that Massimo had turned and caught her staring at him. She was relieved she had her sunglasses on...

"Benvenuta a Villa Serena," he said, a brief smile accompanying his welcome. He held out his hand to help her step out of the boat. "You have lovely shoes, Ella," he said, switching back to English, "but I hope you also brought a practical pair for the beach and for the path between the guesthouse and the villa. It's uneven in places, and I wouldn't want you to twist your ankle."

Ella felt the strength of his clasp as he helped her. "Thanks," she murmured. "And yes, I brought several pairs of shoes." She watched as he retrieved her suitcase and carry-on. She went to grab the carry-on, but he put up his hand. "I'll take them up. You can concentrate on walking."

Ella followed Massimo to the path beyond the dock, which was parallel to the beach before curving its way between rows of oleander bushes, the sweet scent of their pink blossoms mingling with the sea breeze. What a beautiful backdrop to where she would be conducting her morning interviews with Massimo. She felt a shiver of excitement run through her at the thought of the time she would have after working on her piece to walk barefoot in the sand that resembled icing sugar and then take a dip in those pristine waters.

She stumbled suddenly on a tree root, and Massimo turned at her exclamation, dropped her luggage and leaped to her side, grasping her before she fell. Ella found herself face-planted against his chest instead of the ground, his beard brushing her forehead. Her heart was clanging...or was that *his*?

She closed her eyes momentarily and breathed in his scent. And then her eyes jerked open. What was she doing? She pulled away awkwardly. "Sorry about that," she blurted. "I should watch where I'm stepping. Especially with these shoes," she added ruefully.

"Tutto bene?" he said, glancing down. "No twisted ankle?"

"All good," she said. "Thank goodness. That would have been horrible. For me *and* for you."

"I think you're still tired and not over your jet lag." His brow furrowed. "The guesthouse is just ahead. I suggest you settle in and relax, have a nap if you wish, and in a few hours, I will come back and show you around. And then after dinner this evening, we can go over the interview schedule. *Va bene, Ella?"*

"Va bene, barone," she said lightly. *"Grazie."*

His eyes narrowed. "The feudal system in Sardinia ended almost two centuries ago. So it is not necessary to address me with this formal title. Besides," he added, his lips curving into a smile, "when you call me *barone* it makes me feel like *I'm* a century old."

"Well, I look forward to finding out about your centuries-old heritage—and maybe some colorful Di-Luca ancestors—during our interview tomorrow morning," she said, returning his smile.

"Welcome to the guesthouse." Massimo looked back and saw Ella's eyes widening as they approached.

"I thought this was Villa Serena," she blurted. "I was expecting a little guesthouse."

He gestured toward a canopy of trees above which they could now glimpse his villa. "I—what's the word—*indulged* myself. I had this guesthouse built first, so I could oversee the day-to-day progress of the villa. I preferred this to a tent." He smiled crookedly, setting down Ella's luggage by the entrance door. "Something that wolves and wild boars couldn't get into."

"What? There are wild animals on this island?" She glanced furtively around her.

He laughed. "I haven't actually seen—or heard— any. My mother insists that I'm the only wild creature here, choosing to live in isolation…" He saw Ella's lips tilt upward tentatively, and he repressed his urge to laugh.

"I can see that you're not sure what you have gotten yourself into," he said wryly, opening the door for her. "But I promise you, Ella, you will be safe." His gaze swept over her. "Especially if you change your shoes."

Massimo waited for her to enter, then he followed with a piece of luggage in each hand. "Where would you like these?"

"Oh, you can leave them right there. I'll bring them later to the bedroom."

"Why don't I just take them now, so that I don't have to worry about you falling on the spiral stairway to the loft?" Without waiting for her to answer, he strode across the foyer to the living area, and looking back over his shoulder, said, "I might as well take you on a quick tour before I disappear into my own cave."

"Um, okay." She glanced around.

"And the fridge is stocked if you would like a beverage or a snack."

"Thank you. That's very thoughtful."

Massimo nodded and headed up the stairway to the second level. He had designed the loft with floor-to-ceiling windows so that it had views of the sea on every side. From the king-size bed, the facade of the villa could be seen over the crowns of the trees. And patio doors on one wall opened to a roomy balcony, flanked on its side by a fig tree that his gardener had planted, along with other fruit trees and flowering bushes.

"Oh, my goodness," Ella said, gazing around her. "I can see why you wanted to stay here. This is about as close as heaven as I can imagine."

Massimo felt a tightening in his stomach at the mention of heaven. It had been more of a *haven* than heaven at the beginning, a place where he could lose himself in the house plans instead of feeling constantly overwhelmed by grief. But when those dark moments came, when the recurring feelings of shock and disbelief resurfaced, not only during the day but in his dreams, he would seek respite in the perennial rhythms of the island: the ebb and flow of the sea at dawn, gushing at his feet; the silky feel of the white sand as he walked the entire stretch of the beach before it butted up against a granite outcropping, and then he would turn around and do the long trek back to his guesthouse, distract himself with computer work, before embarking on the task of cooking.

During that year of construction, Massimo had turned down his mother's offer of sending one of her chefs over to at least take cooking off his mind. He had wanted nobody around him while he tried to make sense of what had happened in his life and to figure out how he would move forward.

Seeing that Ella had gone to survey the view from the balcony, Massimo turned to look at the bed. The new linens suited the room. He was actually glad to have had the original ones removed, washed and donated to charity. In a way, it was symbolic, starting something new and fresh.

He had spent a long, lonely year in that bed, sometimes tossing all night. But on some nights, he'd sit out on the balcony and gaze up at the star-filled sky or the moon; he'd feel the sheer immensity and mystery of the galaxy, and somehow, it would give him a speck of hope, that Rita was where she was destined to be and so was he. And he realized more and more that the sooner he accepted reality, the sooner he would have peace...

It hadn't hurt, either, that he had consulted a bereavement counselor for a few months. As the head of DiLuca Luxury Resorts, he had always felt confident, in charge when it came to his business. And it wasn't just because it made him billions. He had a genuine love of his island, and he wanted people from all over the world to experience it, to go home with the jeweled sea and enchanting Sardinian landscapes forever in their memory.

But when he'd lost his wife, he had felt as if he had been cast out to sea in a tiny boat with no rudder. During a vicious storm...

The counselor had helped him maneuver slowly but surely toward a sheltered cove, using his sheer will, somehow giving him the strength to battle the angry waves that threatened to crush him.

Now, looking at his bed, the memories of that time resurfaced but without the sharp pang of grief. It was more like a moment of resigned sadness. And it felt strange to imagine someone else sleeping in his bed and sharing dinner with him later...

Now that he was living in the villa, he had hired a personal chef—who also happened to be a close friend—to come over three times a week. His mother had insisted that Massimo dine with Ella every Sunday "to engage with humankind," and the remaining three days, Massimo cooked for himself. Today would have been Angelo's day, but he had another commitment and would be coming the following day instead. So today, Massimo would be cooking...*for two*.

His thoughts were interrupted by the return of Ella, beaming.

"I am very grateful for your generosity in allowing me to stay here," she said, her eyes crinkling at the corners.

Massimo shrugged. "To be honest, I was thinking more about myself and how to get through these interviews with the least disruption to my routine."

Ella's smile diminished. "Well, I appreciate your candor, *signor*—I mean Massimo. I'll make every effort not to be a fly in your ointment. And now, if you don't mind, I'll unpack and leave you to your routine—" she glanced at her watch "—until our meeting later this evening to go over the week's agenda."

CHAPTER SIX

ELLA'S FACE HAD begun to tingle at Massimo's surprising bluntness. And she had responded with a little bluntness of her own.

His forehead creased, but she turned away to avoid any further conversation and walked over to where Massimo had set down her luggage.

She heard his husky *"arrivederci"* and footsteps as he left, and she busied herself emptying the contents of her carry-on on top of the bed. When she glanced out the balcony doors, which she had left open, she caught a glimpse of Massimo's back as he ambled up the incline leading to his villa.

Yes, he had made it clear more than once that he considered the prospective interviews disruptive...

Ultimately he had agreed to them to please or appease his mother, so like it or not, he'd have to put up with a few changes to his routine. And *her.* It wasn't as if she were staying a month; the week would fly by.

Ella transferred the clothes on the bed into the large dresser. After emptying some of the items of her big suitcase into the deep drawers and hanging others in the walk-in closet, she placed the two pieces of luggage into one corner of the closet and made her way to the en suite bathroom.

After a refreshing shower, Ella slipped on her flip-flops and sauntered over to the walk-in closet. She rifled through the dresses she had hung up and decided on a lemon yellow sundress with decorative faux pockets, a lemon-shaped button on each flap.

Feeling reenergized, Ella plugged in her adapter and set up her laptop on the desk in the loft. She attached her earphones and reviewed her list of questions for the next morning's interview while listening to classical music. She tweaked a few queries and added some new ones before going over her notes for the remaining days, including those for the interview with the *baronessa*.

When Ella finished reviewing and amending her comments for the last interview, she turned off the music, shut down her laptop and removed her earphones. She checked the time and gasped. She had been so absorbed with her notes that she hadn't realized that almost three hours had gone by. She started at the sudden knocking at the front door.

The entrance door had been left open, and Massimo's *"Buona sera"* carried easily from the screen door to the loft.

"I came by an hour ago and called out to see if you cared to join me for a tour around the villa and a bite to eat, but I guess you didn't hear me," he said loudly.

"Come in. I'll be right there." Ella ran her fingers through her hair and quickly descended the spiral staircase.

"Don't rush. We're on island time," he said, his mouth quirking.

Ella grabbed the railing. "Oh, my," she said, closing her eyes. "I just felt dizzy." She let her head lean against the post.

She stiffened slightly at the feel of his arm around her shoulder seconds later.

"Let me help you to the couch," he said brusquely. "You should have some water. And something to eat." His brow furrowing, he added, "I have a feeling you haven't acquainted yourself yet with the refrigerator."

When Massimo started to guide Ella into the living area, she was overcome by another wave of dizziness. She felt herself starting to swirl and slide as if in slow motion, and ended up in a swing of some sort. When she opened her eyes, she saw that the swing was actually Massimo's arms carrying her to the couch.

"Don't move," he ordered, setting her down gently. He watched her for a few moments, his eyes pinned on her. Then he nodded. "I'll be back with some water."

Ella had no intention of moving. She would see how she felt once she had a drink. So much for their meeting in his office to discuss the interview schedule, which he had drawn up and emailed to her a few days before her flight. Well, she couldn't see *that* happening tonight. It would soon be dusk, and lovely though the island might be, Ella wasn't thrilled with the idea of walking back to the guesthouse alone after the interview. She hadn't been able to tell if he was actually joking about the wild boars and the wolves...

Ella sat up slowly as Massimo came back holding a tray with a tall glass of water and a platter of cold meats, cheeses and fruit. She couldn't help looking at the muscled arms that had swept her up and carried her across the room moments ago. Imagining herself flopped against his chest ignited a thrumming in her own chest.

"Ecco l'acqua," he said as he set down the tray on

the circular coffee table. "Have a drink. It will help clear your head."

Ella nodded and took the glass. She had a few sips and was about to put it down, when Massimo urged her to keep drinking. "You could be dehydrated," he said. "It was hot and you didn't have a hat on the way here. And if it's not that, it could be that you've gone hours without eating. No wonder you're dizzy."

He gestured toward the platter as he sat in the accent chair opposite her. *"Prego."*

"Oh, my goodness, this can't be all for me."

"It could be, but if you'd rather share…"

"Of course." She looked at the selection of cheeses and slices of salami and prosciutto. "Are these home—?"

"Made by my mother," he said with a crooked smile.

"Your *mother*?" Ella had to stop her jaw from dropping. His mother was co-owner of a billion-dollar resort business. Why would *she* be doing this kind of work?

"It is hard to believe, I know. *Prego*," he said, indicating for her to help herself, and then he prepared his own panino. "Mamma loves to cook. She does have a personal chef or two, but she likes to prepare a lot of food that her parents and grandparents made themselves. 'Someone has to keep our family traditions going' she tells me all the time." He gave a deep laugh. "So she will return home from a long board meeting, and a little while later, she will be in the kitchen, preparing *sebadas*, or *spinaci al pecorino*, or *purpugia*—"

"What is it? The last thing you said."

Massimo's eyebrows shot up. "It's a pork dish that's marinated and—how do you say—*saltata in padella*?"

"Sautéed. What kind of marinade?"

"Is this part of an interview, or are you actually interested?" he said, leaning forward.

Ella bit her lip. Noticing the slight rolling of his eyes, she suspected that he didn't want to waste his time with someone who was faking an interest in what he was saying.

"I'm *very* interested," she said quickly. "I would like to know more about Sardinian cooking. My father—" She froze and stared back at Massimo, her mind scrambling to think of a way to answer. *Another near slip.*

"Your father…?"

"Um, yes, my late father…liked to cook. And I…like to cook, too," she finished weakly.

His jaw relaxed and she caught a flash of empathy in his eyes. "*Va bene,* I'll tell you. You chop some herbs and crush some spices into a bowl with garlic, white wine and vinegar. We use sage, rosemary, mint, bay leaves, fennel seeds and black peppercorns. You put the sliced meat in the marinade for one or two days, turning the meat over. And then you remove the slices, pat them dry and cook the meat in a skillet with olive oil."

He looked directly at Ella as he kissed the fingers of his right hand in the way that Italians expressed their pleasure at food or anything else. The gesture made her nerve endings tingle. For a couple of seconds, she allowed herself to be stuck in his gaze, realizing how sensual his eyes really were, with that dark rim around them. She wondered if the trait came from the Spanish or Moorish influence in the island's history.

Ella forced herself to break away from her trance-like state. "That sounds so aromatic, with all those herbs," she said, reaching for her glass. She drank the rest of her water and checked the time on her watch. "Thank you for the food," she said. "Everything was so good. I will thank your mother personally when I meet her."

"Which will be on Sunday," he drawled, before popping a piece of fontina cheese in his mouth.

Ella frowned. "But I thought I read in the email that Sunday was your day off?"

"It is. And it's tradition for me to go over to my mother's villa for dinner."

"Well… I don't want to intrude on your family traditions."

Massimo's lips curved slightly. "You are the guest of the DiLucas for one week, and so for one week you will join us in our traditions, big and small. And knowing my mother, she will be sure to—" he stroked his beard "—how do you say it? Oh yes, cook up a…a storm."

Ella flashed him a smile. Her face had a flush to it now, unlike earlier, when she had felt dizzy. Her pallor had been noticeable when she had first come down the stairs, but when she had slumped against the post, his adrenalin had jackknifed and he had leaped to her side, his heart clanging against his ribs. And when she had another spell moments later, he had scooped her up immediately to prevent her from falling.

In the kitchen, he had grabbed a pitcher of water from the refrigerator and poured some into two glasses. He drank his first, trying to steady his heart from the shock of seeing a replay of his wife passing out. And then he had wasted no time in getting the tray that he had had prepared for Ella. She needed water and nourishment. *Immediately.*

The *panino* and water had helped. Her color had returned and apparently her spirit, as well.

He stood up and checked his watch. "There's really no point in going over the interview schedule tonight. Why don't you just relax for the rest of the evening? There's actually a guest bedroom on this floor. I'd feel much better if you slept down here." He glanced up at the staircase leading to the loft. "I wouldn't want you to have another dizzy spell, Ella."

"I feel fine, now that I've had something to drink and eat," she said with a shrug. "You don't have to worry about me."

"That's where you're wrong," Massimo said crisply. "You're a guest on my island. Therefore, I'm responsible for *you*. And for your safety."

He saw Ella's eyebrows arch and caught a flicker of indecision when she followed his gaze back to the stairwell.

"Maybe you should just stay in a guest room at my villa for tonight," he said, stroking his chin. "Or, you can stay *here* but *I* will sleep in the guest room on this floor. Either way, I'll be close by, in case you need me."

He saw Ella's eyes flicker with…surprise? Suspicion? Good heavens, was she thinking…? Of course she might think it. She was alone on an island with a billionaire whose reputation she knew little or nothing about. For all she knew, he was a rake who was using her dizziness as an excuse to manipulate the situation by pretending to be concerned for her health and safety.

"Look, *signorina*," he said, feeling he needed to address her with some formality. "You don't have to worry. There's a Moorish sword displayed on one wall in your room. You can easily remove it to defend yourself if you feel the need." His mouth twitched, but he could see that she wasn't amused. Or convinced.

"I'm sorry. I don't want you to be uncomfortable. I think it's better if you just stay here, and I will stretch out on the chaise lounge on the beach. If you are not feeling well, you just need to call me from your balcony overlooking the cove. I just want to make sure you will be okay tonight," he added in what he hoped was a gentle tone, but it came out sounding gruff.

Ella gaped at him. "But…what if a wolf or wild boar—?"

He burst out laughing. "Let me reassure you, Ella, there are no wolves on my island. As for wild boars—" he shrugged "—my ancestors sometimes had to fight them with bare hands." His eyes narrowed. *And I've had to fight worse demons.* He felt a tightening in his chest. "But those ancestors all survived."

He stood up brusquely. "The only wild boar we will encounter on this island is the one from the market, served for dinner in a *ragù*. I will accompany you up the stairs, Ella, and then I will leave you to enjoy my night under the stars."

CHAPTER SEVEN

DECIDING THAT HIS dark eyes were sincere, Ella made her way carefully up the spiral stairway and walked slowly into her room, her gaze landing on the Moorish sword. A shiver ran through her, not because of fear, but because of the sense of mystery around Massimo DiLuca.

Changing into a nightgown, she thought about the man in whose company she had been for less than two days. Yet in that short time, she had glimpsed different sides to him. He was a good son, had shown Ella his generosity and sense of humor, concern and empathy, but there was also an intensity about him that she suspected he kept in check.

Perhaps it was a trait he had inherited from his wild boar-wrestling Sardinian ancestors. She had a sudden image of him in a torn linen shirt, his muscled chest and forearms glistening with perspiration, his eyes blazing with passion as he confronted a charging boar.

Oh. My. God. What was she doing? This was not good. *No, no, no.* She had to get these kinds of thoughts out of her mind. Get this Sardinian out of her mind. At least in that way…

Good luck with that, an inner voice chuckled. *He's hardly like your last boyfriend. This one is a man who's willing to sleep outside to make sure you're okay during the night.*

Ella's pulse quickened. She turned off the light and walked to the open balcony doors. The sky looked like a blue-black quilt speckled with clusters of stars. Ella caught her breath. They looked so close… The half-moon, suspended jauntily at an angle, was reflected in the waters of the cove, undulating ripples, their gentle swoosh on the shore sounding like a meditation app she had sometimes listened to.

Her gaze shifted to the outdoor furniture set farther back from the beach on a large landscaped area with a diagonally tiled section. Massimo was lying back on a cushioned chaise lounge with his hands joined behind his neck, staring out at the water. He must have grabbed a throw on his way out; it was bunched up against his leg.

He was actually going to sleep outside.

Either he was crazy or just a hell of a nice guy.

Watching Massimo in the dark gave her a strange feeling. What if he looked up and saw her? Ella turned away and went over to lie down on the bed. The breeze was strong enough to reach her, but it was pleasant. She would probably not need the bed covers tonight.

But how could she possibly fall asleep when the man—the billionaire—she would be interviewing tomorrow had decided to camp out on a chaise lounge outside his guesthouse, just because he was concerned about her?

Ella shifted to one side of the bed. At times she had wondered what it would be like to have a partner, someone you trusted with your secrets and your life. But those thoughts hadn't lingered. Her goal was to be the best that she could at her chosen career, and unless her future forever man was able to put stars in her eyes, she had reasoned to herself, then her work would continue to be her focus.

Ella flipped her pillow over and, after a few restless minutes, felt her eyelids starting to droop. The mattress was perfect...

Her eyes flew open. How could she allow herself to sleep when Massimo was sacrificing his comfort for her? She turned to view the sky. And the stars, which seemed even brighter now. Sighing, she rolled out of bed and padded to the balcony.

Peering down, she saw that he had turned to one side, his arms crossed at his chest. He had fallen asleep.

A warm feeling of tenderness washed over her, followed by a hint of guilt. She couldn't let him stay there the whole night.

"Massimo," she called out.

He leaped out of the chaise and looked up. "Are you all right? Are you dizzy again?"

"No, I'm fine. It's just... I can't let you sleep all night out there." She paused. "So if you intend on staying, then...you might as well stay in the guest room. That way, at least we'll both get some rest."

For a few moments Massimo didn't respond, and Ella wished she could see his face out of the shadows.

"Va bene," he said huskily. "I am glad you are okay. *Buona notte."*

Ella watched as he grabbed the throw and disappeared into the shadows.

She glanced up at the sky and felt a knot form in her throat. When she was young and missing her father, her mother would gently tell her that he was in a place called heaven, where there were many beautiful angels and that when she looked up at a sky full of stars, it was their wings sparkling, and he was close by...

She got back into bed and realized that she had left her bedroom door partially open. She thought about closing it and then decided against it. Massimo DiLuca would not be intruding on her privacy. He had already shown a selflessness that had stunned her, reinforcing her gut feeling he was a man of integrity and honor.

Ella pulled the light bedsheet over her, leaving her arms uncovered. It was strange to think of sleeping under the same roof as this enigmatic baron, and just as strange to think about being in the same bed that he had slept in.

She heard some movements and felt her pulse quicken. And then she heard his footsteps receding and a door opening and shutting. Closing her eyes, she willed herself to fall asleep. They would be meeting tomorrow morning, and she wanted to appear alert and articulate. And in the afternoon when she was on her own, she'd go online and book a place to stay once her interview sessions were over. She had decided that it made sense to find a place in Posada, where her uncle still lived and where her father came from.

It was a heady feeling, knowing that she was finally back in Sardinia and could soon be connecting with an uncle who had been part of her early life. Maybe he could shed some light—if he knew anything at all— about the mother—no, *woman*—who had given her up for adoption.

And maybe help Ella to find her.

In any case, Ella considered only one person her mother, and that was the one who had chosen her. *Cassandra*.

If she ever had children, she would name her little girl

Cassandra. And call her Cassie, too. And if she had a boy, she would give him her father's name. She wouldn't use the English version of Michael. No, she would keep it Micheli, to honor the Sardinian man who had adopted her and loved her for four years, before…

Ella's eyes welled up. The photos her mother had of those years were precious to her. She had gone over them so many times with Cassandra, who had shared them with Ella from the time she was able to understand, telling her how much her *papà* had loved her and how he had taken her everywhere: to the piazza for a jaunt, sitting on his shoulders; to his parents' farm to pick olives; to the sea for an early-morning swim; or to the countryside for a picnic. One of Ella's favorite photos was one a family member had taken of her parents, smiling as they both held her between them, as they celebrated her fourth birthday, her last with her father…

"Oh, *papà*, I've come home," she whispered, dabbing her eyes with the edge of the bedsheet.

Massimo took off his shirt and pants and tossed them on top of a chair. Now that he was in the guesthouse, he might as well be comfortable. He opened the shutters of the large window and stretched out on the bed, the half-moon lending the room some illumination.

His heartbeat had settled down after rocketing twice in the last few hours. Ella Ross had given him quite the scare. First with her dizzy spell, and just a few minutes ago when she had called him from the balcony. Thank goodness that she hadn't experienced another episode. Still, he wondered if he should arrange for her to see a doctor… He'd ask her tomorrow.

He breathed in and out deeply. The breeze was refreshing after the heat of the day, and he would have been comfortable enough outside, but he couldn't say that he was disappointed to be spending the night in this king-size bed. After the jolt of hearing Ella call his name, he had been genuinely surprised at her comment.

So, she trusted him...

The last thing he had expected today was to be spending the night in his guesthouse. With his Canadian guest. And although she had consented to having him sleep inside, he imagined that she might be feeling a little awkward, as he was.

She wasn't what he had expected.

He was intrigued by her, actually. He liked the fact she hadn't put on any airs or pretenses. She hadn't tried to impress him, and she had had no problem letting him know how she felt, like when she had shared the fact that she had suffered loss in her life. He had regretted being so judgmental.

When his lifestyle had been more public before the passing of his wife, Massimo had generally observed people found it hard to be themselves around him. Being a billionaire either made people stay away from him, mistakenly thinking themselves as inferior, or they blatantly tried to ingratiate themselves with him.

Ella hadn't shown either tendency. And that put him at ease about the upcoming interviews. He just hoped she wouldn't have any further episodes of dizziness.

He closed his eyes. The sheets felt cool on his bare chest and legs. He wondered if Ella was just as comfortable in his bed. An image flashed in his mind of her face on his pillow, just the way it had been resting against his chest earlier...

Something pulled in his chest. Something that caught Massimo by surprise.

He didn't want to go there.

He redirected his thoughts to a safer place: the next day's agenda. He was to have shown up at the guesthouse at 9:00 a.m., accompany Ella to his villa, offer her a cappuccino and biscotti and then proceed to his study for the first official interview.

But since he was already at the guesthouse, he would take the liberty of preparing espresso and cappuccino for them the next morning. And the refrigerator and pantry were fully stocked, so he would put together a breakfast tray. That was, if he was up before she was.

He paused. This all sounded so...so intimate, the way a man would act for his lady or vice versa. But, he reasoned to himself, there was no point leaving in the morning only to return a while later. And there was no reason that they couldn't deal with this situation in a professional way.

Since they hadn't gone over the entire week's agenda this evening, they would start with that first thing in the morning. He imagined the interview itself would focus on the history of the DiLuca family, its origins, noteworthy ancestors and the role of a baron throughout the centuries, for starters. That in itself could take the whole day, he mused wryly, let alone a couple of hours or so.

Massimo turned on one side to gaze at the star-dotted sky. A few seconds later, he caught the flash of a falling star. Had Ella seen it? It would have been something, seeing it while outside... He felt a surge of pride and gratitude, living in such a beautiful region. He hoped Ella would be able to enjoy some of it in the week she was here. She had the afternoons to herself, and he had already stated in the letter to her boss that he would arrange for her boat trip back and forth from *Villa Serena* to Sardinia whenever she wanted.

He remembered that Ella would be staying for an additional week. She should really think about booking a place as soon as possible. Sardinia was a prime holiday destination in the summer, and prices would be higher during this peak season, especially in the most popular resort region, the *Costa Smeralda*, if that's where she wanted to stay.

Leaving it this late could make finding a place challenging. He'd diplomatically pose the question of what kind of accommodation she was looking for in the morning. Not that he was interested in knowing her budget, but he could advise her as to some possibilities. He knew many resort owners, and not only ones with high-end establishments.

Massimo heard the sudden high-pitched call of a scops owl, its intermittent cry sounding like a timer going off, and a second, more distant call. He was used to these night sounds, and they generally didn't disturb his sleep. But he wondered if Ella was hearing them now or had already fallen into a deep slumber.

He closed his eyes. He needed to stop thinking about her if he wanted to get a half-decent sleep tonight...

CHAPTER EIGHT

ELLA WOKE UP when her alarm went off. She reached over to stop it and realized that the aroma of coffee had wafted into her room. She sat up and squinted at her surroundings, disoriented for a moment. And then she remembered she wasn't alone. The reclusive Baron DiLuca had spent the night in the guest bedroom. In his own guesthouse. Rubbing her eyes, she got out of bed and padded to the en suite bathroom for a quick shower, aware of the soft drumming in her chest. She still couldn't believe that he had been willing to sleep outside the entire night so he could be around if she felt dizzy again.

Well, she felt absolutely fine now. Refreshed and ready for a cappuccino before heading to Massimo's villa for the first interview. She headed over to the closet and looked for something professional but also light and comfortable.

She chose a pair of tropical-themed palazzo pants and a fuchsia silk top with short sleeves and slanted hemline. She put on a pair of cream wedge sandals and made her way out of the loft and down the spiral staircase.

"*Buongiorno*, Ella." Massimo nodded, his gaze sweeping over her. "Your cappuccino is ready."

"My goodness. I didn't expect to be treated like royalty." She crossed the living room and entered the adjoining kitchen.

Massimo laughed. "You would be an easy queen to please," he said. "Not like the queen bee, who expects to be royally served with honey."

"Well, I don't aspire to such extravagant tastes," she replied with a fluttering of her lashes as she sat at the curved island. "I come from humble beginnings."

"Oh?" Massimo's eyes narrowed as he set down her demitasse. "What exactly is your heritage?"

Ella had a sip of her cappuccino. Why was she always saying things that she regretted? "Um, I'm Canadian."

"Are you sure?" he said, his mouth quirking. "You seemed to hesitate."

Ella laughed uneasily. "Well, you know us Canadians. We have a variety of cultures in our heritage." She reached for a brioche from the plate he had prepared. "Thanks, by the way, for getting all this ready."

Massimo nodded. "*Prego.* I hoped you wouldn't mind."

"It's *your* guesthouse."

"*Sì,* but you're the guest. It's your space now." He raised his eyebrows. "I trust you had a good sleep? The bed was comfortable enough?"

The intensity of his dark eyes and the mention of his bed, where she had imagined him sleeping, caused spears of heat to swirl through her. "Yes, thank you. It was such a beautiful night. The sky was amazing. I've never seen so many stars up there. And I actually saw a shooting star." She stopped, realizing she was rambling.

"Did you make a wish?"

Ella's eyebrows lifted. "Oh, do Italians do that, too?"

"Yes, there is a feast day for a martyr on August

tenth, *La Festa di San Lorenzo*. It coincides with a meteor shower, and the falling stars, or *stelle cadenti*, are said to be San Lorenzo's tears." He gazed at her intently. "So did you make a wish, Ella?"

She liked the way her name sounded pronounced the Italian way: lighter and with a slightly longer drawing out of the double *l*. 'Of course," she said. "It's the first time I ever saw one. Maybe that's a good sign."

"Well, I hope you get your wish," he said.

"What about you?"

Massimo gave an enigmatic smile. "I leave the wishing to the kids…and the romantics," he added, eyeing her meaningfully. "I like to believe I create my own destiny."

Ella bit into her brioche. So that's where he was at… "Doesn't it take some of the magic out of life?" she said wonderingly. "I mean, not expecting any surprises to suddenly come your way?"

The crinkling around Massimo's eyes had smoothed out, and his smile had faded. "The surprises of the universe can be quite cruel," he said curtly.

Ella wasn't sure how to respond. Massimo had to be thinking about his late wife. And she wasn't about to venture anywhere near *that* territory. Not that she wasn't empathetic; she just didn't want it to seem like she was digging for information about a subject with sad or traumatic memories.

And she doubted that he wanted to discuss anything about his wife, if the thin line of his lips was any indication. "Well, I suppose we should get started on interview number one," she said lightly.

"If you're finished with your cappuccino, I'll take it, and then we can be on our way," he said, and when she nodded, he leaned forward to grab the cup, but his hand stopped in midair and went instead to her cheek, where he wiped off what she figured was a dollop of custard from her brioche.

Massimo's face was just inches away from hers, and as their eyes locked, Ella was sure that he could hear the accelerated thumping of her heart. She wanted to glance away but somehow couldn't, and seconds later, he was the one who backed off.

Ella stood up, grabbed her handbag, and strode to the door. He caught up to her and held it open, and soon they were walking up a slope made of pavers in the grass that was flanked on both sides by flowering pink and white oleander trees. The scent was sweet and heady, and Ella made a mental note to herself to look for a perfume with that flower essence.

At the ring of his cell phone, Massimo retrieved it from his back pocket and checked the message. He laughed softly. "Look at this," he said, and held out his phone. "Gregoriu and Lia's baby. And here's the one he sent me yesterday."

"Aww, she's so beautiful. And look at all her hair!"

He leaned in to look again, his arm brushing against hers. "She takes after her mother in that department," he said with a laugh, looking up.

Ella smiled, her breath suspended for a moment with his face only inches away from hers. The crinkling at the outer corners of his eyes and his grin were so...so distractingly attractive. When he looked down to reply to the text, without moving away, Ella felt a warmth spreading through her at the proximity of his neck, and the pulse at the base of his throat.

He put his phone away and gestured to Ella to continue walking.

The walkway curved through the last of the oleanders and opened to a view of *Villa Serena*. The path now changed from intermittent paver stones to one of huge granite slabs arranged in a curving design that led right up to the villa entrance.

The grounds were breathtaking. And huge. Ella hoped she could take a better look after the interview. She didn't imagine Massimo was up to giving her a tour now. There were landscaped areas with crescents of yellow, red and pink begonias, a separate rose garden, and a variety of flowering bushes, including giant rosy peonies. And beyond, the Olympic-sized infinity pool that gave the illusion it flowed seamlessly into the chameleon-like sea, shifting from turquoise to midnight blue.

It took her breath away.

This was a wonderland, and Ella was in complete awe of the fact that the man she was walking with had had this paradise created for him. Her gaze shifted to the sprawling stucco villa with arched doorways and windows, ceramic-tiled roof, and outdoor lounge area with thick sprays of violet cascading over a whitewashed wall. It had to be wisteria. So enchanting. And romantic... At least for *her*. Ella felt a wave of sadness, thinking of the baron living here by himself. It was his choosing, of course, but didn't the fact that his wife wasn't there to share it with him emphasize his loss? His grief? He hadn't made any mention of his personal life nor did she expect him to...

Her boss had advised her to avoid any reference to Massimo's wife and her passing, as per the baron's specifications. The latter expected the interview to focus on three things and three things only: the DiLuca Luxury Resort Company, the upcoming opening of the DiLuca Cardiac Research Center and his mother's birthday.

Ella gazed at the man who was walking ahead of her now and felt almost guilty, liking the way he looked in those perfectly fitting white trousers.

You're only human, an inner voice reassured her. *The fact that he's a widower has nothing to do with his appearance. You're allowed to find a man attractive.*

And then he suddenly turned around, causing her arms to instinctively fly up to stop herself from crashing into him. For a moment their eyes locked, and Ella realized her hands were planted flat against his chest.

"Sorry," they said simultaneously, and Ella took a step back, letting her arms fall to her sides.

"You must have been going over the interview questions in your mind," he drawled, the corners of his eyes creasing. "I was informed that you're very skilled at your job. And—how do you say—*focalizzata*."

Yes, she had been focused all right. *On his backside.*

Ella was sure her cheeks were blazing. *Good God, what a way to start the first day of interviews.*

Massimo led Ella through the marble foyer and then an arched doorway to his study. He gestured for her to sit in one of the armchairs and he sat opposite her. The arched windows looked out to a clear view of the sea, and he enjoyed spending his work hours here, with the salty breeze wafting in and nothing but blue sea and sky in his line of vision.

She was taking in the view now, and as he observed her profile, he realized with a jolt that she was the first woman, other than his mother, to have set foot on his island and in *Villa Serena*. When they had entered minutes ago, he had suggested to Ella that they get started with business, and then he would take her for a tour— if she liked—later.

Massimo knew quite well there were a few unattached socialites—mostly daughters of his mother's friends—who would like nothing better than for him to show an interest and invite them over. He couldn't help being a little cynical, wondering if it was their anticipation of winning his favor and ending up enjoying a lifestyle even more opulent than the one they already had or if they actually cared about knowing him as someone other than the billionaire resort magnate.

He wasn't in a hurry to get involved. In the three years since his wife passed, he had gone through all the heart- and mind-wrenching stages of grief, and this past year, could say to himself that he had accepted the reality of his loss and was ready to move forward. Even if it was at the pace of a snail…

He saw Ella turning away from the view. She pulled her recording device out of her handbag and set it on the accent table between them.

"Why don't we go over the schedule for the week before we begin?" he said, reaching for the papers on his desk nearby.

"Of course, since we didn't get that done yesterday," she said ruefully. "I have it on my laptop."

"Non c'è problema," he said. "It won't take long. And no need to open up your laptop. I printed off copies of the file."

Massimo handed her a page with the schedule. He hadn't been thrilled about doing the interviews, but now that Ella had arrived, he was anxious to get started. He went over the timetable for their morning sessions and the times for the ones she would be doing with his mother. When they were done, he placed the file on his desk and sat back in his office chair.

"Allora, cominciamo?" This morning's session

would be about the DiLuca family history and how his late father had started the resort business.

"Yes, let's begin," Ella said, nodding, and turned on the device. "First of all, thank you for allowing me to record these interviews." She smiled. "Tell me about your ancestors, *signor* DiLuca. How far back can you trace your lineage?"

He leaned back in his armchair. He explained that his earliest known ancestor had been an enterprising merchant who had amassed a fortune in two areas: silk and spices. It was passed on from generation to generation that this Federico DiLuca had begun with raising his own small collection of silkworms, keeping them munching happily on mulberry leaves. He had boldly traveled to China and had reputedly brought his fine silks to the court of Genghis Khan, who commissioned him to be a regular provider. Before too long, Federico was doing a brisk trade on the Silk Road.

"That's very intriguing," Ella said, jotting notes down on a pad, despite the fact she was recording. "Was Federico married?"

"Yes, he was. And a father of nine children."

Ella's brows arched. "Wow. And you mentioned spices?"

Massimo nodded and explained that Federico had brought many new spices from India and China to Italy and to his own region of Sardinia, along with other treasures, like the zizibus tree with its olive-sized brown berries. The Roman emperor had rewarded Federico for his trade initiatives by granting him the title of Baron.

Massimo could see Ella was genuinely interested, her eyes lighting up as he went through the most notable descendants of Federico in the subsequent centuries, including some Robin Hood–like brigands in the 1860s, who ended up becoming folk heroes. When he got to his great-grandfather Alberto, Massimo explained that Alberto's older brother Leonardo—just before the Allied invasion in 1943—had tricked him out of his rightful inheritance and destroyed his reputation, and Alberto ended up dying penniless, his family on the brink of starvation.

"And my grandfather Teodoro, who was twelve when World War II ended, swore he'd find a way to restore the family's good name and fortune.'"

"How did he do that?" Ella leaned forward. "He was just a kid."

"In his day, you were pretty much a young adult at that age. He worked eighteen hours a day for a wealthy landowner, who unlike others who exploited their laborers, rewarded Nonno Teodoro after a few years with a plot of land, some farm animals and a bonus. Teodoro became respected for his honesty and work ethic, and later on, actually became mayor of the village. He eventually discovered documents that revealed Leonardo's dishonesty and corruption, and the law officials restored his title and transferred most of Leonardo's land and holdings to Teodoro.

"My father was Nonno Teodoro's only child and heir. Like our ancestor Federico, he possessed a sharp business sense that eventually led to investments in the resort business. And he taught me everything I know…" He felt his voice unexpectedly cracking with emotion.

"That's really fascinating," Ella said. "You are fortunate to know so much about your family history." She clicked off the recorder and placed it back in her bag along with her notepad. "I wish—" She stopped short. "I'm sorry, it's nothing," she said, averting her gaze.

"Please, finish what you were about to say, Ella. I'm curious about your family history."

Was she actually squirming in her chair? Her cheeks were becoming almost as flushed as ripe persimmons, and she was biting her lower lip. Something was on her mind, something personal…

She eyed him hesitantly, almost as if she were wondering why he would be interested in anything about her. The vulnerability in the depths of her eyes caused his heart muscle to constrict involuntarily, and he realized what he was seeing was evidence of an emotion that he was all too familiar with…*loss*.

Ella set down her notepad and pursed her lips. She inched forward in her armchair, her hands on the armrests, and looked like she wanted more than anything to take flight.

"Ella, *cosa c'è?*" he prompted. "What is bothering you?" He leaned forward and hoped she could see the sincerity in his eyes.

She inhaled deeply and shook her head. "I don't want to bother you with my…personal issues. I'm not here to waste your time."

His eyes narrowed. "It's not a waste of time," he said. "Or a bother. *Prego*."

"I had told you I was adopted," she finally blurted. "But what I didn't tell you was that I was adopted. *Here*. In Sardinia."

CHAPTER NINE

THERE! SHE HAD done it, revealed something about her private life that she hadn't intended to share, least of all with Massimo DiLuca. But something in his eyes had unlocked her trust, and she heard the words spilling out of her mouth before her critical mind could stop her.

"You are… *Sardinian*?" he said huskily.

"Yes. My mother was Canadian, my father Sardinian. My adoptive parents, that is. My birth mother—and presumably my biological father—were Sardinian."

"Were?" His eyes narrowed, like an eagle zooming in on a movement in a field.

"I know nothing about them," she admitted slowly. "My adoptive mother went on a trip to Italy, met my dad in Sardinia. They married, and when she found out she couldn't have children, they decided to adopt. *Me*."

His brow furrowed. "But they didn't stay here? How did you end up in Canada?"

"My father died in a car accident when I was four," she said, swallowing. "My mother returned with me to Canada a few months later." She looked down, staring at her clasped hands. "She passed last year."

"I'm very sorry for your loss, Ella," he said softly. "What were your parents' names?"

"Cassandra and Micheli," she murmured. "Rossi."

"You anglicized your last name to Ross." His eyes bored into her.

His tone was not judgmental, but Ella sensed that he was curious as to why she had changed it.

"It's a long story," she said dismissively. "In a nutshell, I went through a troubled time, struggling with my identity. Struggling with the fact that my biological father took off, refusing to acknowledge his responsibilities, and my birth mother gave me up. I wanted to detach from everything Sardinian, everything Italian. Yes," she answered his unspoken question, "even though my Sardinian father had adopted me. I was so confused…"

He stared at her, his mouth pursed, his hand stroking his beard. "I don't blame you," he said quietly.

The empathy in his voice made her eyes begin to mist up. She squeezed them shut for a moment, determined to stem the tears. "I'm sorry," she said. "I didn't mean to get you involved in my drama." She straightened in her chair, and her handbag, which she had placed over the back of the chair, tipped over, spilling some of the contents.

With a groan of frustration, Ella bent to pick them up off the floor and shoved them back into her handbag. She stood up. The first interview was done, and she was anxious to get back to the guesthouse to review her notes and listen to the recording again.

Massimo stood up and glanced at his watch. "I think this would be a good time for a snack, yes? And something to drink." He frowned. "You look a little pale."

Ella blinked. "Um, sure." She would get to her work after that.

"Andiamo in cucina," he said. *"Cappuccino o bevanda fresca? Aranciata, limonata?"*

"Orange juice is fine," she said, and followed him as

he strode through the arched doorway. She could use something cool and fresh. Something that would revitalize her after the emotionally draining episode that had just occurred.

All she wanted to do was forget it. File it away in her mind until the week's interviews were done. Then she could focus on her personal life. Possibly reaching out to her uncle, to start.

As they walked to the kitchen, Ella couldn't help being distracted by the spaciousness and elegance of rooms that flowed into and around each other, connected by a series of incredibly high-arched doorways under vaulted ceilings enhanced by polished wood beams.

Massimo looked back at her as they were walking through the living area and said, "All the larger wood pieces are genuine chestnut and walnut, created by a master carver." Ella nodded, liking the look of the modern furniture: an extra long leather sectional and accent chairs with sleek, carved-wood embellishments, and the intricate, inlaid decorative pieces, like the chessboard on one side table and the main coffee table, which was, Massimo explained, constructed with the technique of geometric marquetry and featured a variety of woods, including cherry and maple.

The furniture's wood finishes contrasted well with the cool white palette of the walls. The main wall featured huge sliding doors leading to an outdoor living space that looked out onto the pool and the sea beyond. Another wall had two alcoves, one with several shelves filled with books, another with decanters and glasses and a concealed wine cooler below. Massimo pointed out the main wine cellar was in an underground room accessible from the butler's pantry.

Ella was glad that the conversation had shifted from

her family history to Massimo's home. She wanted to focus on the reason she was here this week, not the missing pieces of her life… That had to wait until she was finished with the DiLuca family.

She had done interviews in some pretty impressive homes in places like Vancouver and California, but Ella had never seen anything like this villa. If the living room was over the top, the kitchen was even more impressive. The long island, with its gleaming Sardinian stone, spanned the length of the cabinetry.

At Massimo's invitation, she sat on one of the high swivel chairs. She felt as if she were in a soda shop, watching as he took out a juicer and oranges and proceeded to make freshly squeezed juice. He handed her a tall glass and made one for himself, as well.

He remained standing on the other side of the island. When he was halfway through his drink, he set it down and leaned forward to look at her directly. "I'd like to continue our conversation," he said quietly.

"I left my recorder—"

"No, not that conversation." When she didn't reply, he added, "The one about your family."

She waved a hand dismissively. "My mom and dad were wonderful, loving parents. I am happy they chose me. Case closed," she said bluntly.

"Yes, perhaps that part is closed. But you have another part of your history that is not," he said. "Is that why you're staying in Sardinia for a week after our interview sessions are finished? To find some answers about—"

"Well, *maybe*. I'm not sure if my uncle knows anything more than I do." She shifted in the swivel chair. "Thanks for the orange juice. Now if you don't mind, I'd like to head back to start working on the piece."

Massimo said nothing for a moment and then glanced at his watch. "My friend and personal chef is arriving shortly and I will be discussing tonight's dinner menu with him. Is eight o'clock a good time for you?"

"Yes, that's fine. Thank you."

"Foods you dislike?"

"What Italian food could I possibly dislike?" she said, and gave a small chuckle.

He nodded. *"Bellissimo."*

His gaze was direct, his dark eyes gleaming like river stones. "I hope you don't think I was trying to pry, Ella, but I suppose it might have looked that way." He shrugged. "I'm sorry."

She raised a hand. "I'm fine," she said, but it came out sharper than she had intended. "It's just...a sensitive subject. And I don't expect you to understand my situation. Most people can't understand what it's like, either to be adopted or to have to adopt. How can they, unless it happens to them?" She glanced down, feeling a prickle behind her eyelids. "It's just not a topic I like to get into with people who have no idea..."

"...how it feels," he finished for her, his eyes narrowing. "Well, I had no intention of talking about this, Ella, but I do want to set the record straight."

She looked up. He stared over her shoulder for a few seconds. In the distance she heard the thrum of a motorboat. When Massimo gazed back at her, he rubbed at his beard for a moment. "I don't know what it's like to be adopted, Ella, but I know how it feels when your wife can't have children and you both decide that you want to adopt a baby and give her or him your love and the best in life."

She tensed as his words sank in, her heart starting to thump erratically.

As he ran the fingers of one hand through his hair, her gaze riveted to the muscles tensing along his jaw.

"And I know how it feels when a week later, your wife passes," he ground out the words, his voice a low rumble, "and your dreams of adopting a baby die with her. So even though I didn't actually adopt a child, Ella," he continued, his eyes narrowing, "I can truly imagine how lucky I would have felt—and my wife as well— to have been able to have chosen a baby as our own."

"I—I'm very sorry for your loss," she stammered. "I knew about your wife, but I—"

"You don't have to explain. I didn't want to focus on that in the interview. But we're not doing an interview. This is off the record."

"I'm sorry you weren't able to adopt. I—I know I was lucky to have been chosen and raised by two good people. People who wanted to be parents and who... who loved me," she said, choking on her last words.

"I'm sure they felt lucky too," he murmured, his voice husky. "I wish I had been able to have that opportunity." His gaze bore into hers. "It couldn't have always been easy for you, though."

Ella crossed her arms and sighed. "No, it wasn't always easy. I was teased by some of the kids in my class, who had found out I was adopted. They were mean, saying my birth parents must have been on drugs or that I must have been ugly when I was born and my parents couldn't stand to look at me so they gave me away." She bit her lip. "Kids can be so cruel. Because I was 'different,' I was often last to be picked when there were teams to be chosen. Or not invited to some birthday parties." She paused, frowning. It was amazing these past injuries still had the power to cause her pain.

"That must have felt hurtful."

"And lonely." She nodded. "I kept it from my parents, not wanting them to feel hurt, too."

"You were a sensitive little girl."

The empathy in his voice made her swallow. If she didn't leave soon, she'd be awash in tears.

Ella was blinking at him, her forehead creased, looking like she was on the verge of tears. He hadn't wanted to upset her; he had just wanted her to know that his earlier words weren't shallow. His stomach had twisted when she had first revealed her mother had given her up for adoption, and at that time, he couldn't bring himself to formulate the appropriate words to show his empathy.

What could he have possibly said? "I'm sorry your mother gave you up for adoption?" Especially since he and Rita had hoped for a mother to do just that...

He swallowed, feeling as if there was a wedge of grief blocking his esophagus. Those memories were still raw at times.

They had talked about the possibility of adopting after discovering that she couldn't conceive. Rita had looked at him with a twinkle in her eye, and said she'd be happy with either a boy or girl, but that there were so many adorable baby clothes out there for girls. And a week later, she was gone, along with all their dreams for the future.

Ella opened her mouth to say something, but the drone of the motorboat drowned out her words. They both turned and saw it approaching the dock, and a few moments later, the rumble subsided.

"That would be Chef Angelo," he said. "He has two Michelin stars to his credit, and he loves cooking so much he accepted my request for him to come to *Villa Serena* several times a week to prepare a feast. Afterward, he hurries off to his seaside restaurant in Cagliari, the *Mare e Cielo*, which is all you see when you're there, as it sits on top of a hill. Why don't I introduce you before you go back to the guesthouse?"

Ella shook her head quickly. "Thanks, but I have a slight headache. Please pass on my regrets."

"You will still join me for dinner?"

"If this headache doesn't linger, perhaps," she said. "And about what you said before." She pursed her lips. "I'm sorry if I—"

He put up a hand. "Please. Don't worry. I understand."

He accompanied Ella to his office to retrieve her handbag, and then they proceeded to the foyer and he opened the door for her. She nodded and said "ciao" before continuing on toward the guesthouse.

Massimo turned and waved to the man who was not only a celebrated chef in Sardinia, recognized also on the mainland and in Europe, but a good friend too. They had been each other's best man, and had often gone to social events together with their wives. Angelo had been there for him during the rockiest time of his life: the year after Rita had passed.

Massimo greeted Angelo with a hug. Angelo was like a brother to him.

"What would *signorina* Ross like tonight?" He raised an eyebrow at Massimo.

"She's not fussy. See what you can find and work your magic, Angelo."

Angelo went to gather fresh herbs from the courtyard garden outside the kitchen, and Massimo went up to his room. He wanted a few moments to himself to process everything that had just occurred between him and Ella.

He opened up the balcony doors and stood at the ornate railing, watching the foamy surf creep up to the beach and leave a scalloped design that reminded him of the lacy edge of a wedding gown. And then the design dissipated as the waves broke and receded back into the sea. Massimo filled his lungs with the fresh sea air and exhaled slowly.

The atmosphere on *Villa Serena* had changed, he realized. For better or worse, that was something he had yet to determine. He did know one thing: somehow, discovering that Ella was born in Sardinia brought a whole new dimension to the situation. What were the chances of a journalist from a New York City magazine actually being Sardinian? Sardinian-Canadian now...

Massimo hadn't planned on revealing any details about his personal life to her. He talked to very few people about his late wife; his circle of trust included predominantly a grief counselor, his mother and Angelo. But when Ella was implying that he didn't understand anything about being adopted or wanting to adopt, he had instinctively wanted to explain.

And surprisingly, his words had come out fairly easily compared to how difficult it had been in the first months and year to even say the word *died* or even *passed*. And he hadn't even shared the part about his wife's infertility and their decision to look into the adoption process to his mother or Angelo. He had discussed that aspect of his grief with only his counselor.

From his balcony, Massimo could also look across at the guest villa and the balcony of the room where Ella would be sleeping. He thought about where they had left off when Angelo arrived and wished that they had been able to continue the conversation.

Ella hadn't seemed too willing to talk about her plans to stay in Sardinia once their interview sessions were over. She had been very abrupt, changing the subject immediately. It was obviously a sensitive subject, and one she had been planning to deal with completely on her own.

Not that he had any notion of butting into her affairs when it came to exploring her family history.

But he *had* wanted to ask her where she would be staying for the week after the interviews.

He shook his head. Why was he trying to solve her problems? If she hadn't already booked a place, why should he even worry about it? Ella Ross… *Rossi*…was an adult, quite capable of looking after herself.

"Ella Rossi," he murmured, liking the way her Italian name sounded. He took one last glance at his guesthouse and went back downstairs. On the way to the kitchen, he passed his office, where a bright flash on the floor by his desk caught his eye. He walked in and reached for it, his eyebrows lifting when he saw that it was the gold lettering on the cover of a passport.

He would give it to Ella when she came for dinner. He strode over to the sideboard and deposited it into one of the drawers before heading to the kitchen to see where Angelo was at with the preparation of his courses.

CHAPTER TEN

As soon as she returned to the guesthouse, Ella set down her notepad and recorder by her laptop on the desk in the study and returned to the kitchen for water to take with a tablet. She would look over her notes and listen to the recording once her headache had subsided.

She plopped onto one of the recliners with a view of the cove. The adrenalin was still pumping through her since Massimo had dropped the bombshell about his and his wife's plans to adopt.

She hadn't been able to face meeting his chef after that, and she had made her way quickly to the guesthouse, her mind a jumble of thoughts and questions.

Whatever Ella had been expecting Massimo to say after her blunt comment about people not having any idea when it came to adoption issues, it hadn't been *that*. It added a new layer to her understanding of what he had gone through, as if losing his wife hadn't been enough.

Ella's mother had often shared with her how happy and excited she and Micheli had been, knowing that they would be able to adopt. And how they had been even more delighted the first time they saw her two days after she was born. She hadn't been given a name, and when Cassandra had taken her in her arms, she had looked out the window at the sea and then, misty-eyed, had said to Micheli, who had had his arms around her, that she wanted to call the baby Marinella, the diminutive form of *marina*, a name of Latin origin meaning "of the sea."

"She's our little Sardinian miracle," Micheli had replied, bending to kiss the baby gently on the forehead. *"Benedica."*

Ella blinked back tears. Every time her mother had recounted the story, Ella had become emotional. Especially at her father's whispered blessing.

And now, to know that Massimo had been robbed of the opportunity to know the joy of adopting, and to imagine how devastating it had been for him to lose his wife and their shared dreams, was overwhelming.

He had lost a partner, just as her mother had lost hers. Ella had been only four at the time, but she could still vaguely remember her mother's sadness, her crying. Her mother's tight hugs when Ella had asked, *"Quando ritorna a casa papà?"*

She had wanted to know when her father was coming back home even after they had moved to Canada. When Ella was older, her mother told her that she had been sad too, crying for her *papà*, especially at night, missing story time and his bedtime blessing. Her mother would reply with the same story about heaven, the stars and angel wings, and him being close by...

Ella had been comforted by her mother's words as she had tucked her in, her mother's whispered *"Buona notte, Marinella,"* the last thing she heard before falling asleep.

Ella swallowed. Her mother had continued to call her Marinella after she had decided to change her name. And Ella hadn't actually gone so far as to formally change it. Her mother had also continued to speak to her in Italian regularly so she wouldn't forget her first language, which Cassandra had studied in high school and university before taking a trip to Italy when she had graduated.

Ella's thoughts flew back to the man she would be in close contact with for the week ahead. She had made a mistaken judgment about him, and she hoped that the air had been cleared between them. She would get a feel for the situation at dinner tonight…

It would be hours before dinner, though. The headache tablet had started to kick in, and Ella decided to return to the study. She would work on the piece for a good stretch and then take some time later in the afternoon to walk along the beach, and maybe even go for a swim in the cove.

Satisfied with what she had accomplished, Ella shut down her laptop and strode to the kitchen.

She peered at the contents of the pantry and the fridge, and decided to make a fruit salad with a little honey and lemon juice. She left it on the island while she went to the bedroom to change into a bathing suit and a loose top and shorts. She applied some sunscreen to her face, arms and legs, stuffed a hat and towel into a beach bag, and put on a pair of canvas flats and sunglasses before returning to the kitchen for her fruit salad.

She took it out with her and walked down to the cove. Sitting on the chaise lounge where Massimo had almost spent the night, she enjoyed her sweet snack while watching the surf tumble onto the shore in a frothy explosion and recede with a gentle swoosh back into the translucent turquoise waters. The late afternoon sun felt wonderful on her face and she tilted it to the sky, breathing in the salt-tinged air contentedly.

Feeling like a pampered cat stretched out on a patch of soft grass, Ella breathed in and out slowly, thinking what a great place this would be to do an outdoor yoga routine in the morning. Or even later in the day. She set down her empty bowl on a side table and decided to walk along the beach and return when she was good and hot, ready to be refreshed in the sea. She put on her hat and set off, marveling at the fact that she had the island practically all to herself.

She pictured Massimo walking along the beach before diving into the crystal-clear waters and emerging moments later, his muscled shoulders and arms glistening with the jeweled drops of sunlit water.

And then she berated herself silently for having such wayward thoughts, only to have a rebounding one: she was human and Massimo was a gorgeous man that many woman would want to—

No. Stop thinking. Keep walking.

Ella scanned the beach for shells and collected ones with unique colors or shapes and put them into her shorts' pockets. It was a perfect summer day, the sun hot but not scorching, with the sea breeze fanning her cheeks.

The only sounds she heard were the cries of seagulls and other unfamiliar birds and the surf. She tried to imagine what it was like actually living on the island… Massimo must have found it to be healing, with the lush vegetation, and the sea with its soothing murmur always around him.

After about a half hour or so, Ella heard the thrum of a motor. Angelo must have finished whipping up dinner for the evening and was heading back to his restaurant. She checked the time on her watch and saw that she had time for a quick swim before getting ready to go to *Villa Serena* for the meal.

By the time she arrived at the cove, Ella was more than ready to cool off. She slipped out of her top and shorts, flung them on the chaise lounge along with her hat and watch, and after removing her canvas flats, she walked gingerly into the lapping waters. The surf met her with a foamy rush, making her catch her breath. She dove in and came up refreshed and exhilarated. She swam for a bit and then floated, letting her muscles relax completely as she looked up at the baby blue sky.

A sensation of pure delight filled her, and she wanted to simultaneously shout out her joy and cry. The last time she had splashed in Sardinian waters was with her parents when she was four. And now she was back, twenty-four years later. Ella made an instant decision to save her tears of nostalgia for another time. Her mother and *papà* would want her to be happy now, not sad.

With a sudden feeling of freedom, Ella let out a whoop and as she treaded water, she slapped at the waves playfully and eventually allowed the surf to push her toward the shore.

She emerged from the sea with a light heart, but when she squeezed her eyes to clear her vision, she froze.

She wasn't alone.

Massimo was striding through the oleander path toward her. Had he seen her splashing about in the water? He must have. She shivered as a slight breeze swept past and, eyeing the large towel she had left on the chaise lounge, realized in dismay that the baron would reach her before she could walk over and grab the towel. And it would look pretty foolish if she made a dash for it.

Sensing the sweep of his dark eyes over her even

from a distance, Ella self-consciously crossed her arms, certain her face was lobster red if the sizzle under her skin was any indication.

Massimo had texted Ella that Angelo had left and, if her headache had subsided, she could join him for a pre-dinner drink, but she hadn't responded. He had gone down to knock at the guesthouse door. When she hadn't answered, he'd figured she'd gone for a walk, and a quick check of the cove had confirmed this, as he could see the direction of her footprints.

He had gone back to the villa, but when she still hadn't returned after forty-five minutes, he had begun to worry. He had headed to the cove and caught sight of her in the sea, her arms flapping wildly. He had felt a jolt in his chest, and his adrenalin had kicked in, priming his body to leap in to save her. And then she had swiveled around and it had been clear that she was having fun. He had taken a few deep breaths to calm his pulsing heartbeat before continuing on toward her.

When Ella had emerged from the water, her tangerine one-piece swimsuit clinging to her and rivulets from her dark hair dripping over her, he had experienced another jolt.

It was just the surprise of seeing another person in the water, on his beach, nothing more.

A person by the enchanting name of Marinella.

Massimo had felt his pulse spike as the words of "Marina," an older but popular Italian song came to him, about a man falling in love with a brunette called Marina, but she didn't want to hear about it, and the man wondered what he should do to conquer her heart.

At that moment, Ella had caught sight of him and stopped in her tracks. Massimo could see his presence had jolted her, as well, and not wanting to make her uncomfortable, he had stayed where he was.

"*Ciao*, Ella." He waved. "I texted, but there was no answer. I had come to see if you were feeling better and if you wanted to join me for a pre-dinner drink."

"Yes, I'm feeling much better. I—I'll just need a few minutes to change and then I'll join you."

Massimo turned and made his way back to the villa, unable to make the image of Ella splashing about in the sparkling waters disappear from his mind.

In the dining room, Massimo poured himself a glass of Prosecco and surveyed the table he had set for the two of them. It had been so strange, laying out a second place-setting for someone other than his mother. And he had had to think about where exactly to position Ella. He couldn't possibly have her sitting at the opposite end of the table, which would have been ridiculously too far away. He finally decided that he would change his own place setting from the head of the table to the next seat, and Ella's would be directly opposite him.

Massimo sauntered into the living area and set down his glass on the coffee table before sitting on one of the reclining armchairs facing the opened retractable-glass walls. He felt a slight tension in his stomach muscles and wondered if it had been caused by his concern over Ella or if it was because he was about to have dinner with a guest. *A woman.* And the first visitor to stay on his island.

It was purely business. And practical, since she was here for the week. They would enjoy Angelo's four-course dinner and then she would return to the guest-house and he would…

What would he do?

Ordinarily, he was alone in the evening, which was

pretty well always unless Angelo had time to linger or stay for the meal. Which was rare, since he was running an acclaimed restaurant that his guests frequented not only for the Michelin-rated food but for Angelo's lively presence.

And if Massimo's mother came for a visit, it would usually be for an early-afternoon lunch. So Massimo spent evenings walking along the beach, swimming either in the sea or his pool, reading, writing down ideas and making rough sketches to enhance his resort business, watching a documentary or classic film, and occasionally trying out a new Sardinian recipe.

Tonight…he shrugged. He would see…

He reached for his glass and let a swirl of the Prosecco tingle his taste buds. Angelo had prepared a platter of *salati*, tasty appetizers that he would take out when Ella arrived.

After Angelo had gone, Massimo had changed into a teal shirt and light gray trousers. Belt but no tie. That would have been too formal. He had assessed his image in the full-length mirror in his dressing room and had thought *still too formal*. He had then folded the sleeves up to below his elbows. Satisfied, he had headed downstairs and had texted Ella, and then had made his way to the guesthouse to see if she was there.

At the sound of footsteps outside, he quickly rose and went around to the front entrance. Ella was approaching with a tentative smile on her face. Her short-sleeved turquoise peasant dress made her look so…young and carefree. She was carrying a gift bag, and when she was at the entrance, she handed it to him. "A little something from Canada," she said, "to thank you for your generosity in allowing me to stay in your guesthouse."

"That wasn't necessary…but thank you." He held the

door open for her. "*Prego.* Come and have some Prosecco and appetizers while I open this," he said, setting the bag on his armchair.

As she sipped her drink, he reached into the gift bag and extracted a bottle of Niagara ice wine, a maple-leaf-shaped bottle of Ontario maple syrup, and an official Toronto Maple Leafs cap. He nodded appreciatively. "*Grazie*, Ella. That was very kind."

"I also wanted to apologize for making assumptions about you earlier," she said. "That wasn't so kind."

His eyes narrowed. "So we're even, then."

"Wh-what do you mean?" she said, her brow creasing.

"I had made assumptions about you. About your age and experience…" He raised his eyebrows. "So are we good, then?" he asked with a chuckle. "No more fighting?"

Ella's eyes widened. "You haven't seen fighting, *signor* DiLuca." She had another drink of her *aperitivo.* "And remember, I hold the coveted Moorish sword in my castle. Woe to the foolish one who tests my patience."

Massimo laughed. "I'm making a new assumption… that I now hold the title of Foolish One and not Baron."

She tilted her chin up then nodded solemnly. "Correct."

He smiled, and picked up their empty Prosecco glasses. "I think we'd better get started with dinner."

"May I help?" she said, following him into the dining room.

"Yes," he said, "you can help by starting with some appetizers." He set the platter on the table and pulled her chair out. She sat down and he pointed to the selection that Ella was eyeing with interest. Chickpeas with fennel, olive-oil-and-lemon-drizzled octopus salad, spiced olives, and a variety of cheeses and crostini. She helped herself to a small portion of each.

"I want to find a good Sardinian cookbook while I'm here," Ella said, in between bites.

"Your mother—?"

"Was Canadian, as I had mentioned," Ella said. "She learned a few recipes from my father's mother— like *sebadas*—and once we moved back to Canada, she made them once in a while, knowing how much I loved them."

They ate the first course, an artichoke-heart soup, in companionable silence for a few minutes. Massimo hadn't been sure how he would feel, sharing a meal with a woman after the past few years… He stole several glances at Ella, pleased that she was enjoying it.

Angelo had timed things perfectly, Massimo thought, leaving to get the pork stew with fava beans that had been simmering for a couple of hours in the oven.

"So you want to reacquaint yourself with your Sardinian heritage?" he said, pouring a ladleful of the stew onto each of their plates. He passed her a bowl filled with thick slices of *civraxiu*, a hearty dipping bread.

"Yes, which is why I'm staying for a week after our interviews." Her eyes widened. "Oh, my gosh. I was supposed to look into booking a place." She set down her fork. "I must do that right after dinner."

"I can help you," he said. "I have contacts all over. But first, let's enjoy this and Angelo's homemade cookies with an espresso, and then we can find you a place."

He poured them each a glass of strong red wine, a *Cannonau di Sardegna* from one of his own vineyards. *"Salute,"* he said, raising his glass toward her in a toast.

"Salute," she replied. She inhaled the bouquet and

swirled it around before tasting it. "Very nice." She smiled. "It tastes like… Sardinia."

He laughed and gestured at her stew. "Enjoy this other taste of Sardinia."

He watched as she took her first bite.

"It's delicious. Please thank Angelo for me."

He took out his cell phone and sent Angelo a quick text.

Done!

At the end of the course, Ella sat back with a sigh. "Everything has been delicious. *Grazie*, Massimo." She gave him a warm smile, and the genuine appreciation in her eyes caused a quickening in his chest.

He had craved solitude after his wife passed, and except for the times when Angelo or his mother came by, he had spent the bulk of the last three years in solitude on his island. Now, having shared a pleasant hour dining with Ella, an inner voice suggested that perhaps he was ready to start making some changes in his life… and entertain the thought of letting more people…or maybe another woman…in his world.

Their gazes connected several times over the fruit course and later as they were drinking their espressos, and Massimo didn't know whether he should be happy about the effect she was having on him physically or if he should be heeding the alarm signal in his head.

Massimo swallowed his espresso and set down his cup.

"Scusami," he said. He reached over to open the drawer of the sideboard and withdrew her passport. "I'm sure you don't want to lose it. You had dropped it on the floor of my study, and it ended up under my desk."

Ella raised her eyebrows. "No, I don't want to lose that." She leaned across the table to take it from him. "Although I wouldn't mind losing the photo," she said with a chuckle, opening up the booklet. "I look pretty grim, since they want you to refrain from smiling."

"I can't imagine you looking grim," he said, his mouth quirking.

She smirked and held up the photo for him to see.

He smiled at her almost stern expression and then his gaze shifted to the information on the right-hand side of the photo.

Something clanged against his ribs when he read the name.

Not Ella Ross or Ella Rossi, but Marinella Rossi.

"Marinella," he murmured, and gazed at her in wonder.

She started, and setting the passport down on the table, she gazed at Massimo wordlessly for a moment.

"Would you like me to continue to call you Ella or should I address you as Marinella?"

"Um, well, I…either one works, although my mother and father's family were the only ones who called me Marinella. The other people who have called me that— like at the airport back home—always pronounced it like the first part of *marinate*. I do prefer Marinella pronounced the Italian way."

"I wouldn't be pronouncing it any other way," he said with a soft laugh. "Just as I like the fact that you pronounce my name the Italian way, and not 'Mass-im-o.'"

Her cheeks had blushed to a deep pink, and averting her gaze to check the time, she said, "How about I help you with these dishes, and then I can look for a place to stay…?"

"How about you don't and we head directly to my office computer? I'm sure you're anxious to find a place before they all get booked up, which is not unusual at this time of year."

"Va bene." She nodded. "If you're sure."

He stared at her wordlessly for a moment, distracted by the way her dark eyes looked like glistening chestnuts after a downpour. *"Sì, Marinella,"* he said finally. "I'm sure."

CHAPTER ELEVEN

"You never told me where your father was from," Massimo said as he sat down at his desk. He had pulled up a chair for Ella right next to him. "And if there are any relatives still there."

"He was from the medieval village of Posada. My *nonna* and *nonno* had only two sons, my father and his brother, Domenicu. They had a farm on the outskirts, not on the hillside itself, and they lived off the land. *Zio* Domenicu would be the sole living relative left, unless he married and had children." She inhaled and exhaled deeply. "And I know nothing about my birth parents, except that my mother was young when she had me, and my biological father apparently denied any responsibility. He took off, moving to the mainland, and my mother never revealed his identity." Ella fell silent as old emotions churned inside her.

As a child, she had created so many possible scenarios: her mother really wanted to keep her, but her parents forced her to give her up because they couldn't afford to feed one more person; her mother's rich parents had sent her away for nine months to keep it a secret from their rich friends and would have nothing to do with a child whose father's identity was unknown. And on and on.

Ella wanted to believe that her mother had wanted her, but being under age, she had no choice but to consent to the will of her parents. Her biological grandparents had become the villains in Ella's eyes when her adoptive mother had revealed to her about her birth mother being so young.

Massimo let out a heavy sigh. "I can't even imagine how difficult all this must have been for you. Wondering why your biological parents…"

Ella felt the back of her eyes start to prickle at his words. "It does something to you, you know, makes you question your identity, your worth, even." Her eyes blurred and she shut them tight, pressing against them with the heels of her hands. "Sorry," she said. "I don't want to ruin the evening."

Ella felt Massimo's hands over hers. She felt her body tense up. He brought her hands down and reached into his pocket. "New handkerchief," he said huskily. "Never used…and no, you're not ruining the evening." He dabbed gently at her eyes and when he was done, she opened them, and for a long moment, their gazes locked.

He moved back. Rubbing his temple, he said, "You're not used to the Sardinian sun, Ella, and you were out for quite a while today. You're probably more tired than you think…so why don't we look at this tomorrow morning? Don't worry, we'll find you a place."

Ella nodded. Yes, she was tired. Physically and emotionally. She did not decline his offer to walk her down to the guesthouse. It was dark with few stars tonight, and she didn't want to meet any night creatures, winged or otherwise.

When they got to the main doors, she thanked Massimo for the exceptional dinner and for accompanying her.

"Prego." He nodded, a corner of his mouth tilting upward. *"Buona notte, Marinella."* He opened the door for her. *"Sogni d'oro."*

Massimo sprinted back up to his villa, sure that the drumming he was hearing was originating in his chest and not the forested part of the island.

He'd wanted to kiss her.

Thank God he hadn't.

She would be here for four more days, and the last thing he desired was to complicate things.

Before that moment occurred, he had just wanted to hold Ella's hands, wipe her tears. But when she had opened her eyes, he had caught a glimpse of her Sardinian sensitivity and strength...and he had been overcome with a desire to immerse himself in those depths. The first time he had felt any such desire for so long...

Massimo tossed his shirt on a chair and strode to his balcony. Looking up through his telescope at the stars or moon always relaxed him. Tonight the moon was especially luminous, and he watched it for several minutes. The night breeze was cool, but he welcomed its feathery strokes over his heated body. Looking over the moonlit crowns of the oleander trees in the distance to the only room of the guesthouse that was lit, and where Ella would be getting ready for bed, Massimo's heart clanged with a sudden realization.

He was alive.

Massimo woke up during the night, and as he stared at the open doors of his balcony, the details of the previous evening came flooding back.

How Ella had enjoyed the Sardinian feast Angelo had prepared. The brief teasing exchange between them.

And how Ella had shared more of her personal feelings about being adopted… It had bothered him earlier to hear kids had been mean to her, and he thought now how sad he'd be if he knew that his adopted child was being teased or bullied.

He fell back into a troubled sleep, and when he woke up again, the east window revealed a sky streaked with bands of orange and gold as the sun emerged from the horizon. It was earlier than usual for his morning jog, but his brain was too busy for him to stay in bed.

In minutes he was dressed in his jogging clothes and was out the door and on the beach. One of the reasons he had fallen in love with this island, other than for the solitude, was because of its impossibly long beach and enchanting cove. His real estate agent had arranged for a few flights around Sardinia, and Massimo had spotted the diamond-shaped island with the pretty white rim that turned out to be a sparkling strip of pristine shore.

He never regretted the decision to build *Villa Serena* on this idyllic island. While he lived in the guesthouse, and even after he moved into the villa, he spent as much time outdoors as inside. He enjoyed his early morning jog, and he often ended the day with an evening stroll.

Massimo checked the time on his watch before starting his job. By the time he was done, he'd still have plenty of time for a shower and an espresso before Ella arrived. In fact, he'd have time to call his mother, also, and confirm the details for dinner at her villa.

What would his mother think of Ella? Massimo's instinct told him she would approve. There was no pretentiousness about Ella, unlike some of the daughters of his mother's friends. And he wasn't so naive as to believe that his mother had wanted to have this party for her sixty-fifth birthday for her benefit alone. No, his *mamma* was *furba*, a sly one, wanting to nudge him in the direction of eligible women.

He shook his head. He would indulge his mother with a birthday to remember, but as much as she wanted him to see him settled, it would happen on his own terms, and when he was ready.

Massimo slowed down and then jogged on the spot while reaching for his water bottle. The sun, looking like a shiny persimmon against a sky tinged with splashes of apricot and pink, was reflected in the sea. He stopped and took it all in, never tiring of the views. It had been a balm from the very beginning, when he was still reeling from the blow of his wife's passing, a reminder that beauty existed alongside the dark moments in life.

He recalled another such moment during his first night in the finished guesthouse. He had been walking around the exterior of the property, pleased with the landscaping, but he had suddenly experienced a stab of loneliness, knowing that it was for his eyes only. His gaze had riveted on the wildflower accent garden and a Corsican swallowtail butterfly that had fluttered into view and settled onto a plant. It had stunning yellow-and-black markings on wings that were intermittently opening and closing, and small blue spots edged the hind wings, along with two red spots. Massimo had watched, transfixed, struck by the ability to experience sadness and pleasure simultaneously.

And then it had fluttered away, making him think of how Rita had been in his life for a short period and was gone...

Every time he had seen a swallowtail butterfly after that, Massimo had felt, foolish or not, as if it were a sign Rita was at peace, and he had been comforted.

Massimo jogged back to his villa and had a refreshing shower. It was still early, but he could tell that it was going to be a scorcher of a day. The timed sprinkler system had begun to water the gardens, and as he prepared his espresso, he contemplated going for a swim in his pool once the interview with Ella was over.

After finishing his espresso, Massimo worked in his study, reviewing the weekly reports that his resort managers sent him. Afterward, he checked the progress of his latest resort, still in the construction stage and as yet unnamed. It was located in the Maddalena Archipelago, with an enchanting pink beach and mesmerizing views of translucent waters ranging from cerulean to turquoise. Perhaps he'd fly out there after his mother's birthday and the opening of the DiLuca Cardiac Research Center. Maybe it was time to start coming out of his self-imposed seclusion and go back to surveying the progress of his resorts in person.

Maybe he should loosen up in other ways, too.

He reached for his cell phone. There was no reason why he couldn't invite Ella to join him for a swim after the interview session. It wasn't as if he were breaching—or intended to breach—any professional protocols. He had a huge pool meant to be used, and perhaps Ella would appreciate the offer. Why shouldn't he demonstrate his hospitality in this way?

He sent a text before he could change his mind.

Her response came a minute later.

Sure.

And then another one a few seconds after that.

As long as I'm not in deep water, lol.

Massimo stared at the screen. A coil of electricity surged through his veins at the fact that Ella was comfortable enough to tease him…

If anyone was in deep water, it was *him*.

CHAPTER TWELVE

AFTER FINISHING HER cappuccino and hazelnut biscotti, Ella went up to the bedroom loft and slipped on a canary yellow swimsuit with white polka dots and straps that tied around her neck, retro-style. She chose a white short-sleeved shirt and a navy wrap-around skirt to wear over the top of the suit for the interview.

As she dressed, she was aware of a fluttering in her stomach. Inviting her for dinner was one thing. It was just being hospitable. But she had never expected the baron to invite her to spend any *personal* time with him. And swimming in his pool was definitely personal. But obviously it was something he did with people staying in his guesthouse.

And then she remembered that she was the first person to stay in his guesthouse.

She thought about what she had impulsively texted back to him. She had instantly regretted taking such a familiar tone with him, but a few moments later, he had responded with a laugh emoji, and she had sighed in relief.

And she also had to ignore the sensation she had felt last night when he had gently wiped her tears and when, seconds later, she couldn't look away from the startling intensity in his eyes.

She had gone to bed with a hundred contradictory thoughts in her head. Thoughts that told her she was living in a world of fantasy, thinking Baron Massimo DiLuca was actually attracted to her. That the Sardinian wine she had enjoyed with her dinner was causing her head to swirl with these ridiculous notions…like the one of him wanting to kiss her…

Shaking her head dismissively, Ella grabbed her bag with her recorder, notepad and personal items, and after slipping into a pair of flip-flops, headed to *Villa Serena*.

She breathed in the sultry morning air, heavy with humidity. By the time she reached Massimo's villa, she felt a sheen on her face and forehead, and she quickly pulled a tissue from her bag. A swim would be a welcome relief after the interview.

Instead of sitting in his office, Massimo suggested doing the interview in the living room, where they could be more relaxed. He carried in two tall glasses of lemonade and motioned for Ella to sit on an armchair by one accent table, and he moved to one edge of the sectional nearest her.

"Tell me about your father," she said, after turning on the recorder.

Massimo stared at Ella for a few seconds.

"You had mentioned your father was your *nonno* Teodoro's only child and heir and that he had a sharp business sense that eventually led him to make some good investments," she prompted, looking up from her notes. "And earlier, you had said *Villa Paradiso* was your family's first resort…"

He nodded. "*Papà* bought it when it was a small, run-down hotel called the *Albergo al Mare*, the Hotel by the Sea. He saw the potential in the vast property it came with. He had the building torn down, and he worked on new designs with an architect friend, then called in any and all of his friends in the construction business to help in his venture. *Papà* was savvy, even in the pre-computer era, and wasn't afraid to take risks."

Massimo shifted his gaze to the sea, where white-caps were popping up and down in the distance. His voice had softened, and Ella could hear in his tone the admiration and respect he had for his father. "*Papà* accessed all the advertising avenues he could find, and it wasn't long before tourists were flooding to *Villa Paradiso*," he continued, gazing back at Ella. "Of course it has been renovated over the years to reflect the times and the particular tastes of our clients."

"Luxurious tastes," Ella murmured. "And tell me more about how your father 'taught you everything you know.'"

Massimo talked about his father's work ethic and his devotion to his family. "He worked hard, but he always made sure to kick a soccer ball around with me when he came home…"

He swallowed, and Ella felt a twinge in her heart.

"And he often took me on site to show me the construction progress. I was always struck by the way he treated everyone who worked on the project, from the architect to the cleaning staff. He was a good man," he said, his lips pursing as he looked away.

Ella stopped herself from saying "and so are you…" She decided to divert her line of questioning to the matriarch of the family. "Has your mother influenced you in any way?"

Massimo looked at her and laughed. "*Mamma* influences everybody she is with. You will experience the phenomenon that is my mother tonight."

Ella listened to Massimo explaining what a doting

mother she had been throughout his childhood and adolescence, and what a dynamic business partner she had been with his father. And still was with him. He suddenly stopped when his phone buzzed. "Speak of the devil." He laughed, winking at Ella.

Ella turned off the recorder. She was glad he was distracted and couldn't see her cheeks. She had several sips of her lemonade and couldn't help listening to Massimo's side of the conversation. She liked the way he sounded when he spoke Italian…in his deep voice, with its husky notes. She closed her eyes and just listened to the melody of it and not the words themselves. Suddenly it changed, and she realized he had transitioned to Sardinian. And then back to Italian before saying *arrivederci*.

Massimo's obviously tight relationship with his mother made Ella's loss of her own feel even greater. Her chest felt weighted down with sudden grief. What the baron and *baronessa* shared was the closeness that she had had with her adoptive mother. God, she missed her…

Ella squeezed her eyes tightly. She had to get control of herself before—

"Stai bene, Ella?" Massimo said.

Her eyes flew open. He was leaning forward and staring directly at her.

"Yes, I'm fine," she blurted. How long had he watched her like that? She peered at her notes and continued with her questions about the early years and how the DiLuca resorts had become renowned as elite holiday destinations. And how they had chosen the particular locations for their resorts.

When the two-hour segment was done, Massimo rose from the sectional and said, "Snack or swim?"

"I'd rather have a swim first, thanks." Ella put away her recorder and notepad and looked at him. "Where shall I—?"

"There's an outdoor change area," he said. You'll see it as soon as you step out into the lounge. I'll be there shortly. I'll change upstairs."

Moments later Ella walked into the spacious room that included several changing cubicles and an open, turquoise-tiled section in one corner for pre-swim showers. She removed her blouse and skirt and hung them on the hooks inside her cubicle. After fixing her hair in a ponytail and showering quickly, she proceeded to the infinity pool.

The water temperature was perfect. Ella walked down the pool steps and waded farther in. She immersed herself up to her neck, and when she bobbed up again, she caught a glimpse of Massimo entering the change room. Her heartbeat quickened. She began to swim toward the infinity edge, her adrenalin surging at the thought that any minute, the billionaire baron would be in the pool with her.

It just seemed so unreal.

She was treading water just as Massimo emerged from the shower. Ella was relieved he was wearing swim shorts and not the briefs that many Italian men seemed to prefer when at the beach. It was hard enough not staring at his muscular torso and legs as he walked, without having to focus on anything more…more defined.

From the opposite end of the pool, Massimo waved and dove in. He emerged halfway across the pool, shook his head and then began to swim toward her. Ella's heart pounded. It was one thing to be sitting across from Massimo DiLuca during an interview; it was quite another to watch him do a powerful breaststroke toward her.

"Bello, no?" he said, now treading water only a few feet away.

Ella knew that he was referring to either the pool or the view or to the act of swimming in such a gorgeous location, and she quickly replied, *"Bellissimo."*

"You're welcome to use the pool anytime while you are here," he said. And then he grinned. *"Facciamo una gara, Marinella?"*

"Uh, assolutamente...no!" She laughed. "I'm not prepared to race someone who gets to practice in a place like this for much of the year."

"Dai, come on, it's just for fun."

Ella couldn't believe what she was hearing. Massimo DiLuca, the reclusive baron, trying to convince her to have a friendly race.

"Va bene," she capitulated. "But you're taller than me, which will give you the advantage."

He chuckled. "You can start a few seconds before me."

She nodded. "Game on!"

Massimo was surprised at himself for suggesting a race and even more surprised Ella had agreed. It had been a long time since he had felt the desire to be playful, and now that he had blurted the proposition to Ella, he couldn't very well change his mind.

"Freestyle?" he said.

"Freestyle." She nodded.

He got out of the pool and walked to the deep end. Ella followed and as she proceeded to join him, Massimo felt his pulse quicken. Ella looked so picture perfect in that yellow swimsuit. It had a simple style, like something out of a 1950s film, and its mix of innocence and charm really suited her. And what he liked about the way Ella moved was that she wasn't walking as if she were on a catwalk displaying the latest fashions. She wasn't trying to impress anyone.

Yes, he liked that. He liked *real*.

When they were both standing outside the edge of the pool, Massimo nodded. *"Sei pronta?"*

"Yes, I'm ready," she said, shifting from one foot to another.

"Allora… You can start!"

Massimo watched Ella dive in, waited five seconds, then dove in, also. He caught up easily to Ella and they swam side by side for several yards. Their hands brushed into each other, and as Massimo lifted and turned his head, he saw a fleeting glimpse of her focused expression.

It made him smile…and splutter as the pool water immediately found its way into his mouth and down his windpipe. It broke his stride, and he began to tread water as he coughed and cleared his throat.

He looked ahead and saw Ella raise her arm up triumphantly as she reached the other side. When she turned to see where he was at, she put her hand up to her mouth, her eyes crinkling. He smirked and gave a shrug before resuming the front crawl toward her.

"I didn't realize you were so competitive," he said, his mouth twitching as he reached the edge of the pool.

"I didn't know you liked to drink pool water," she retorted, laughing.

He chuckled, shaking his head. "Swim or snack?"

"Snack. My win has made me ravenous."

Massimo stroked his beard. "I think the winner should treat the second-place winner."

"To…?"

"Whatever you think is a treat," he said with a mischievous gleam in his eyes.

"Hmm. I'm not in the habit of treating men, and I'm not sure if what I consider a treat for myself would be appreciated by a man."

"And what exactly would you consider a treat for you—or women in general?"

"A bubble bath. A visit to a bookstore. A night out at a fancy restaurant. Curling up in my pajamas to watch a classic film with a bowl of popcorn. *Or ice cream.* A nice mass—" Ella stopped abruptly and just blinked at him.

Massimo smiled, almost positive—from the appearance of pink rosettes on her cheeks—that Ella had meant to say a massage.

"Well, except for the bubble bath," he continued, "I would be happy with any one of those treats. But no pressure. You have a few days yet to choose my treat. *Surprise me.*"

Massimo went into the villa to shower and get dressed while Ella used the change room. As he lifted his face up to the rain shower, he thought about how comfortable he had felt, talking with Ella. *Marinella.* Joking around with her. *Having fun.*

It sent shock waves through him, igniting a shot of adrenalin throughout his veins. He *liked* being with her. *A lot.*

And he had come so close to kissing her last night…

Ella had shown her vulnerability when it came to her identity, and he had been overcome with a feeling of protectiveness, wanting to enclose her within his arms and hold her tight.

With the water streaming over him, Massimo allowed the truth of the matter to sink in. The matter being feelings that he never thought he'd feel again. Happiness. *Desire. Wonder.*

She's leaving in less than a week, an inner voice reminded him. *So don't—*

Of course. He knew what the message was going to be.

Don't get any ideas. Don't start something that you know can't go anywhere. Don't put Ella in an awkward situation.

Massimo felt the momentary high he had known plummet. Like it or not, his inner voice was right. Ella would be gone in a few days. She had a personal mission to accomplish once the week was over, and then she'd be leaving Sardinia to return to Canada.

She did not seem like the kind of person who would be interested in a fling for a few days, and neither was he. Nor had he ever been while married to Rita. Whatever feelings Ella had ignited in him, he had to suppress them. Concentrate on the reason why Ella was here and get through the remainder of the week. And after his mother's birthday party and opening of the Cardiac Research Center, return to his normal routine.

Although maybe it isn't so normal...

He stepped out of the shower, toweled himself briskly and changed into jean shorts and a blue T-shirt before heading downstairs to the kitchen, determined to keep his distance from Ella, emotionally and physically...

But he had offered her a snack, so he decided to make a light frittata, since his mother would surely be orchestrating a feast for tonight's dinner. He prepared the ingredients, and when he was ready to start cooking, he glanced at the doorway, wondering what was taking Ella so long. And then he noticed a slip of paper on the granite counter.

He frowned as he read it.

*I'm sorry, Massimo. I can't believe how distracted
I've been. I was supposed to book a place today...*
  *I don't want to bother you with my responsi-
bilities, so I'm heading back to the guesthouse to
take care of things. I'll have a snack there.*
  Thanks for the use of your pool.

Massimo reread it. Feeling deflated, he put everything he had prepared in the fridge, his appetite gone.

CHAPTER THIRTEEN

ELLA RESISTED THE urge to look back at the villa as she hurried to the guesthouse. She flopped down on the couch and stared out at the turquoise waters in the cove. But what she saw was the crystalline depths of the baron's eyes as they had joked around in the pool. The magnetic pull of them that she had found so hard to draw away from. The occasional twinkle that had caused a skip in her heartbeat.

And she hadn't been immune to his body, either.

It was obvious that Massimo worked out. It had taken every ounce of her resolve not to stare at his sculpted shoulders, arms and chest. His strong, muscled legs. The sight of him approaching the pool had given her a jolt, and later, when he had been less than a few feet away from her in the water, her nerve endings had done a frenzied dance. She had bantered with him, not wanting to reveal how his proximity was affecting her, but all the while, she had been conscious of the whitecaps swirling in her chest...

She was treading on dangerous ground.

She had never felt this way with her previous dates. Not that Massimo was a date. And not that she had taken the time, except with Dustin, to move beyond the initial couple of encounters.

Ella brushed away all thoughts of Dustin and refocused on the way she was reacting to Massimo DiLuca. And they hadn't even kissed...

Which was why the alarm signals had gone off in her brain. She had no real personal experience that she could draw upon.

How could she encourage such feelings? This was unchartered territory, and if certain situations presented themselves that put her and Massimo in close proximity, she had no idea how she would react.

Or maybe she did.

And that would be unprofessional. She was here to interview Massimo DiLuca and his mother, not to allow herself to get weak-kneed over a man.

Besides, she was leaving in a few days. Why would she want to get herself in a position where something might happen? Something she would ultimately regret?

Which was why she had decided to leave.

She would enter *Villa Serena* only to conduct the interviews from now on. And she would swim in the cove instead of the baron's pool. She'd have plenty of time to enjoy a pool at the resort she'd be booking.

Letting out a long, drawn-out sigh, Ella headed to the study, where she had left her laptop on the desk. She sat down and, moments later, scanned the list of resorts in and around Posada. After an hour of checking both resorts and B and Bs, Ella decided to stay at an *agriturismo,* a farm run by a family with a view of the Tyrrhenian Sea and private access to the beach. It was a couple of miles from Posada, but she could either rent a car or a bike if she was adventurous. The price was reasonable and she'd have a private bathroom and free Wi-Fi. Meals were optional and there was a restaurant and a pool.

The place looked absolutely charming with its pristine white stucco exterior, rounded wooden doors and balcony planters bursting with color. It was like something out of a fairy tale, its cobbled path snaking its way to the front entrance between shamrock-green manicured lawns that resembled thick, luxurious quilts.

Ella checked the booking calendar and was elated to see the following week was available. She promptly booked and paid the reservation fee and indicated that she'd take the meal plan of breakfast and a later dinner.

Sighing in relief, Ella closed her laptop. She went back to the entrance, where she had left her swim bag, and proceeded to the laundry area to wash her swimsuit. She stifled a yawn as she made herself a *panino* with fresh *mozzarella di bufala* and mushroom antipasto that she found with other jars of preserves in the pantry, which she realized was climate controlled.

The snack only made her drowsier, and realizing she was still experiencing jet lag, Ella decided to relax on the chaise lounge in the shaded section of the outdoor patio.

She closed her eyes and listened to the soothing sounds of the surf as it unfurled on the beach and then bubbled back into the sea. The scents of roses, oleander blossoms and various potted herbs wafted over to her with the gentle sea breeze, and she couldn't help feeling that she was in an enchanted garden.

The screen behind her eyelids began to display scene after scene of her trip to Sardinia, from the time she encountered the baron by almost knocking him to the ground, to the bantering between them in his pool.

He was taking too much time in her head.

She squeezed her eyes tight. And he was infiltrating her senses. Maybe she'd better go back inside and go over her notes instead of letting her imagination wander in this direction…

At the sound of a cough, she quickly sat up.

He was standing there for real, in shorts and a T-shirt. And sunglasses. He looked a little different, though… and then her gaze fell on his beard. He had trimmed it.

He nodded curtly and started to turn away but stopped to face her again.

"Did you find a place to stay?" he said huskily.

"I did. It looks lovely, the price was right, it was just the kind of unpretentious place I was looking for—" She froze, realizing how that must sound. "I didn't mean—"

"Don't worry about it," he said with a dismissive wave. "I just came by to tell you dinner will be at eight tonight at my mother's. Can you be ready by six? I'll drive the boat across, and from there, it will take another half hour by car."

"Um, sure. Oh, what should I wear? Casual or more dressy?"

Massimo's lips quirked. "Whatever you're comfortable with. Unpretentious is always good."

Massimo caught the flash of uncertainty in Ella's eyes. He probably shouldn't have said that; it made him sound like he had taken offence at her earlier comment.

"Seriously, it's not a formal event, so no ball gowns." He smiled, but she didn't reciprocate. Didn't she realize he had been teasing?

"That's good, because I left all my ball gowns at home," she said nonchalantly. "And now if you'll excuse me, I have to go over my notes from this morning."

"Of course," he said, his smile fading. She had tried to soften her tone, but she hadn't completely succeeded. *"Arrivederci."* He waved, and moments later, before passing through Oleander Lane, or *Via degli Oleandri*, as he called the path leading to his villa, he turned his head to glance back, but Ella had already disappeared into the guesthouse.

He felt a hint of disappointment…and confusion. She had seemed relaxed earlier in the pool, and comfortable joking around with him. What had happened to change her mood?

With almost two hours wait time before they had to leave, Massimo decided to go over his work email and then check the updates on the Maddalena Island resort. There were cameras set up at different spots on the exterior and interior of the building so he could virtually view the daily progress that was being made.

He was happy to see what had been accomplished since his last physical visit to the site. The project should be completed by the end of the month. He liked to choose a new architectural firm for each new resort, selecting not only the best in Italy but around the world. One of the firms that had caught his interest a few years earlier was a Canadian company that had won a prestigious award for its ecological initiatives. He had subsequently enlisted one of their teams to be in charge of the landscaping and rooftop gardens at the Maddalena resort.

What Massimo hadn't decided upon yet was the name of the resort. He had fiddled around with a few possibilities, *Mare e Meraviglia* being one of them, liking the way Sea and Wonder evoked a place of enchantment. He reached for the notepad and doodled some sketches with the two Ms intertwined, adding waves and a beach. He wondered if he should add the usual D for DiLuca in the design and then decided against it. Maybe the two Ms but with a change of the second word. *Mare e Magia*. Sea and Magic.

And then he impulsively wrote down *Marinella* and sketched waves around her name. He felt his stomach muscles tensing as he thought about how close they had been in the pool. And how natural it had seemed for her to be there…

He shook his head as if doing so would brush away his thoughts about her. With a sigh of frustration, he pushed the notepad aside, shut down his laptop, and headed to his room.

CHAPTER FOURTEEN

ELLA SURVEYED THE two dresses she had laid out on the bed, one short, one long. The short one was a sleeveless jersey dress with a ruffle around the V-neck and a flared hem that came just above her knees. It was teal blue, one of her favorite colors. The second was a yellow floral-print wrap-around maxi, also sleeveless, with drawstring waistband.

She decided on the shorter one. It was loose and comfortable, and she had a pair of teal blue sapphire earrings that matched perfectly. Hanging up the floral maxi dress, Ella felt a current of anticipation run through her, thinking about her meeting with *baronessa* Silvia DiLuca. Would she be down to earth? Arrogant? Controlling? Massimo had called her *the phenomenon that is my mother.* That sounded positive. Hopefully the evening would go well...

Why wouldn't it?

Ella was curious to see and chat with the woman, who was obviously a powerhouse, having reached such a level of success with the resort business she had started with her late husband.

Ella checked the time on her phone. She had several hours to go over her notes and recordings, work on her piece, and review the questions she had for the *bar-*

onessa tonight, either before or after dinner. But first, she'd grab a cool drink…

Minutes later she was in the study, notes and recorder on one side of the massive desk and her laptop open and turned on. She began replaying the first recording with the intention of pausing regularly to transcribe the text, but as Massimo's voice came on, Ella found herself riveted by the sound of his voice. She leaned back in the burgundy leather office chair and just listened. At some point, she closed her eyes and as Massimo talked about his father, she picked up some inflections and nuances that she hadn't been aware of when they were actually doing the interview. When the first session came to an end, she started, feeling as if she had snapped back to consciousness after being hypnotized.

Massimo's voice had been hypnotizing…

It had lulled her with its deep timbre and occasional huskiness, and as she had listened, she had found herself visualizing his face: his flashing eyes, the curve of his smile, his brow furrowing, his fingers stroking his jaw as he thought about his response.

Ella felt a heaviness in the air and took a long sip of her iced lemonade. There was definitely an increase in humidity from the morning.

Or was it a spike in her body temperature from listening to Massimo's voice?

Ella shook her head in annoyance at her rogue thoughts. Thoughts she had vowed to suppress.

For the next three hours, she concentrated on her task of transcribing the recording and then continued working on the piece she had started the day before. Finally, she shut down her laptop and after reviewing her questions for the *baronessa* on her notepad, she stood up and stretched, contented with what she had accomplished. She checked the time and realized she should be getting ready. She set her recorder and notepad on the credenza near the entrance. Hurrying up the spiral staircase and in the shower moments later, Ella mused over the evening ahead with the *baronessa*, immediately redirecting her thoughts when they veered in the direction of the baron…

After drying her hair and styling it in loose curls, Ella slipped on the teal blue dress and surveyed herself in the mirror. She liked the way the flared hem moved with her. Smiling, she put on the drop earrings. *Perfect.* Not too casual nor too dressy.

Her pulse spiked at the sound of a doorbell. She had thought it funny Massimo would have had one installed, given the fact that he was the only one on the island… But then again, maybe he had planned to rent it out one day or let a friend visit. At the second ring, Ella quickly put on a pair of low-heeled pumps and headed downstairs to answer the door.

When she opened it, she was slightly breathless from rushing down, and she stood blinking at the baron, too close to him to give him the once-over.

"Hello." They said it at the same time.

"You look…very nice," he said, his dark eyes focused on her face.

"Thanks. You, too." The words slipped out. She had *not* meant to say "you, too." "I mean, you look…" Good God, why was she even trying to explain? "…fine," she finished limply.

Massimo chuckled. "I'll take *fine*, although it seems like I've been downgraded from *very nice*."

Ella felt her cheeks tingle. She shifted her attention to her notepad and recorder on the credenza. "I'll just be a minute to grab my bag." She had forgotten it in the loft. And she had a second bag containing a gift for the *baronessa*, a print by the late Canadian First Nations woodland-school artist Daphne Odjig, a pioneer in developing indigenous art in Canada. Ella had traveled to Manitoulin Island, Odjig's place of birth, and had wanted to choose a gift that represented the spirit of Canada's First Peoples... In fact, the name *Manitoulin* meant *spirit island* in the Ojibwe language.

As Ella turned away, the tingling in her cheeks intensified as she imagined Massimo's gaze following her up the spiral staircase. When she returned, she saw that he hadn't budged and was watching her intently as she descended.

He held the door open for her, and minutes later, they were in Massimo's speedboat, skimming across the calm sea. Ella couldn't help glancing at Massimo's profile, his eyes narrowed in concentration and his mouth occasionally tilting upward. She wondered what he was thinking...

Maybe she shouldn't have bristled earlier when he had made the comment about wearing something unpretentious. She had assumed that he was deliberately emphasizing her gaffe, and she had taken offence. Which was ridiculous, really, since if anyone should have taken offence, it should have been *him*.

Well, it seemed that he didn't have anything he wanted to say now...

And she couldn't bring herself to make small talk. Ella bit her lip at the awkwardness between them, feeling the tension radiate throughout her body.

He suddenly turned to glance at her. *"Tutto bene?"* he said, slowing down the engine.

"Uh, yes, *sì*, everything's fine," she blurted the white lie.

"I hope you're not preoccupied about meeting my mother. She's very easy...uh..."

"Easygoing?" Ella couldn't help smiling inwardly.

"Yes, that's it. Easygoing." He chuckled. "And very hospitable...just like her son." He flashed Ella a grin. "But she's the better cook."

Ella felt her tension dissipating and her pulse quickening simultaneously. It was the way his eyes crinkled along with his perfect smile.

Moments later, when they reached the dock at *Villa Paradiso*, Massimo moored the vessel and offered Ella his hand as she stepped out of the boat. He had put his sunglasses back on.

She took his hand, liking the feel of his strong grip.

When he let go and started walking toward the parked vehicles, she followed, looking for the SUV that he had picked her up in. She spotted it, but as they approached it, Massimo paused suddenly and then strode past it, stopping at the passenger side of a silver-gray Lamborghini. Its smooth, streamlined shape, with its distinctive angles and curves, took her breath away. It reminded her of a stealth jet. *Sleek and sexy,* she couldn't help thinking. *Just like its owner...*

"Prego," he said, opening the door for her, with another pulse-activating smile.

Massimo felt a surge in his chest as he let his Huracán release its potential on the Strada Statale 131, the state highway toward Cagliari. This latest vehicle purchase had been his treat to himself after moving into his villa. And it wasn't because he wanted to flaunt his wealth or be pretentious. He had simply loved the look and feel of it, unleashing its power on the long strip of highway like a predator in hot pursuit of its prey.

Letting it rip had been like giving vent to all his primal instincts, releasing the powder keg that had been building up inside him after the death of his wife. Its engine thrumming in his ears had reverberated throughout his body, just like now, making his heart race along with it.

Massimo sensed Ella's excitement, and her gasp at every acceleration made his heart pound harder. She was the first woman he had taken for a ride in his Huracán. The first woman he had *wanted* to take for a ride…

As he maneuvered through a curve, Ella's hand shot out and clasped his thigh. He had already reduced his speed, but he decreased it even further, knowing there was no vehicle imminently approaching from behind.

"Sorry," she squeaked, her voice several octaves higher. She pulled her hand away. "I thought we were going to spin out of control."

"Sorry, I didn't mean to scare you, Ella," he said, glancing quickly at her. "But let me reassure you I had complete control. We're approaching the city limits of Cagliari now, so I'll behave…and my mother's villa is another thirty-five kilometers away. We'll be there very soon."

As her eyes widened, Massimo gave her a mischievous grin. "Would *you* like to drive?"

Ella blinked at him as if he had lost all sanity. "Uh, no, thank you. I'll leave the navigation to you, since I don't have any experience in flying a jet."

He let out a deep laugh. "*Va bene.* But admit it, the flight was exciting." He merged into the city traffic and shortly stopped at a red light.

"It *was*," she said, and for several moments, their eyes locked.

The honking of a vehicle behind them made Massimo realize the traffic light had turned green. He turned his attention reluctantly back on the road.

What was it about this woman that drew him to her?

You know... an inner voice said pointedly.

He felt his abdomen muscles tensing. Yes, he *did* know. She made him remember that he was a man...

But what was the point of acknowledging it? Whatever feelings were beginning to germinate in his consciousness, Massimo knew he couldn't allow them to grow. *How could he?* She would be leaving in four days. Whatever emotions she had been able to resuscitate in him, whether she knew it or not, he'd have to ensure that they wouldn't see the light of day.

With his reduction of speed in the town limits, Ella had relaxed, and Massimo noticed her leaning back and taking in the sweeping views with a smile. When he pulled into his mother's serpentine driveway, she straightened and reached for her seat belt.

He clicked on a remote device that he kept in each vehicle and watched as the ornate gates to his mother's villa opened noiselessly. There were no parked vehicles except those of his mother's. Her chef had finished his part of the feast, Massimo thought, smiling. And his mother would have spent a good part of the day concocting all kinds of Sardinian delights with which to regale Ella.

The Huracán glided through, and moments later, Massimo parked it in one of the available spots next to his mother's Alfa Romeo Giulia and her Mercedes minivan. He smiled. His mother was a classy lady, with or without her fine cars and luxurious tastes. She had a kind heart and made a lot of substantial donations to charities, without fanfare. She was especially devoted to children's causes.

Massimo let his hands slide down from the wheel. "Are you ready to meet my *mamma*?"

Ella nodded and tilted her head to look out the window, but not before Massimo had caught a slight creasing of her brow. Was she thinking about *her* biological mother? He felt a twinge in his chest, imagining how difficult it had to be, knowing your mother gave you up for adoption but not knowing why.

Maybe one day Ella would return to Sardinia to try to find out.

He checked his watch. "Shall we go in?" he said. "My mouth's already watering, thinking about the feast she has prepared." He clicked open his door to climb out and, in several strides, was at Ella's door.

She reached for her work bag and the gift bag and moments later, they were walking side by side toward the arched carved-wood door of his mother's villa.

CHAPTER FIFTEEN

ELLA HAD TO struggle to keep her jaw from dropping as she stood in the baronessa's spacious foyer with its gleaming Murano chandelier fashioned like a bouquet of cascading blue irises.

Silvia DiLuca welcomed Ella in Italian, followed by a few words in English and a warm hug. She had striking features, dark hair arranged in a braided bun and the same almond-shaped eyes as her son, with long lashes. She wore a loose peach silk blouse with olive green palazzo pants.

She wanted to take Ella on a quick tour of the house, then get the interview done in the gardens. "And then I feed you," she laughed before hugging both Ella and Massimo, who was smiling indulgently at her.

"I'll be waiting for you ladies in the living room, enjoying the soccer game," Massimo said wryly. *"Divertitevi."*

"Of course we will have fun," his mother retorted, slapping him none too gently on his backside as he strode away.

He turned and gave a deep laugh. "You're lucky you're my mother," he teased, and then gave Ella a wink.

Ella followed the *baronessa* through the main floor

of the sprawling villa, her cheeks tingling. The way Massimo had looked at her had caused her heart to flutter. No, not flutter, *flip*.

Her brain and heart were clashing, and for a few moments she was listening to their arguments. Her common sense was telling her that she was foolishly falling for the baron. Her heart was urging her to feel whatever she was feeling, to be open to…

Don't even go there, her brain ordered. *You're leaving. There's no possibility of that happening. Besides, it's a one-way feeling, girl. He's not ready for lo—*

"Ella, this is my kitchen."

The *baronessa* entered the massive room, complete with a real wood-burning hearth and an island that was longer than Ella's apartment kitchen. "What a beautiful room!" Ella smiled. "And whatever you're cooking smells wonderful!"

"Please, you call me Silvia, *va bene*? Now I take you to my gardens."

Outside, Ella drew in her breath. "This is an absolute Garden of Eden," she said. "How enchanting."

Silvia led her through themed gardens that were meticulously designed and partitioned by boxwood hedges and featured marble statues and fountains, citrus trees and pergolas, and flower varieties Ella had never seen before. One area was exclusively for herbs and resembled a monastic garden with its terra-cotta planters and cobblestone paths. Everywhere she looked, Ella spotted a different variety of tree: palm, prickly pear, cypress, lemon, mandarin and persimmon.

They stopped at a serene park-like section with a pond shaded by giant palm trees, and Silvia motioned for Ella to sit opposite her on one of the ornate benches.

Ella took her recorder out of her bag, and after opening her notepad to the interview questions, clicked it on. She smiled at the *baronessa*, feeling relaxed, not only because of the peaceful ambiance of the gardens but because of the twinkle in those dark brown eyes, eyes that her son had inherited.

The hour flew by, and Ella was pleased with the responses Silvia had given her, clearly demonstrating not only her business savvy but her community-minded initiatives and her charitable acts. Her voice had wavered when she conveyed how important the DiLuca Cardiac Research Center was to her and Massimo, and Ella had felt her heart twinge, thinking of how mother and son were channeling their grief in ways that would ultimately help so many others. And then the *baronessa* had winked at Ella and enthusiastically brought up her upcoming birthday party.

Ella put away her recorder and notepad in her bag, and they started walking back to the villa.

"Who or what inspired you to create these lovely gardens?" She smiled across at Massimo's mother.

"It was my husband," Silvia said softly. Speaking in both Italian and halting English, she told Ella how he had supported her love of art and design and had encouraged her to plan the gardens at their first resort. She had ended up designing all of them. "He was a wonderful man who understood my passion," she said wistfully, her gaze shifting to her grounds. Suddenly she turned to Ella. "What is *your* passion, Ella? Do *you* have a wonderful man in your life?"

Massimo strode to the huge window overlooking the gardens. He had spotted Ella and his mother earlier sitting by the pond and had smiled at his mother's animated hand movements. She was no doubt talking about her two passions, her gardens and cooking. He couldn't see their faces clearly or hear their conversation, but Ella was leaning forward, and through the open shutters, he heard their occasional shared laughter.

Forty minutes later, Roberta, his mother's dining server, set out the appetizers, a variety of local cheeses and spiced olives, and a special Sardinian bread called *carta da musica*—thin, crispy rounds resembling sheets of music parchment. Afterward, they enjoyed the *culurgiones* his mother had made, ravioli with a filling of sweet potato and pecorino served with a butter-sage sauce. The main course was fennel-encrusted swordfish with asparagus spears drizzled with olive oil and sea salt.

After the dessert of *amarettus*—the Sardinian word for *amaretti* made with bitter almonds and lemon peel—and *sebadas*, Ella leaned back with a contented sigh, which made his mother chuckle. "Now you know why the interview came first, Ella."

They left shortly after coffee and liqueurs and the usual hugs from his mother. She and Ella had embraced, as well, with his mother murmuring *"Buona notte, cara"* to her.

The evening air was hot and humid, and when they were in his car, Massimo turned on the air conditioner. "I have a feeling we might get some rain tonight," he said. "Hopefully we'll be back home before then."

"Mmm…" she replied.

He glanced at Ella as he fastened his seat belt. She seemed much more relaxed than before. Mellow, actually. It could have been the shot of *mirto* she had tried, an amber Sardinian liqueur made from myrtle berries. He had declined it in favor of a second espresso, but he felt rather mellow himself. A combination of the great food. *And company.*

"I gather your interview with my mother went well."

Ella turned to him. "Very well," she said with a smile. "Your mother was a pleasure to interview." She chuckled. "Not at all a dragon."

He let out a deep laugh. "You must have made a positive impression on her. Correction… I know you made a great impression on her."

She looked at him curiously. "How do you know?"

He didn't answer right away as he made his way through the villa gates. Once they closed behind him, he said, "*Mamma* has always claimed to have a certain intuition about people. She sensed it with you right away."

Ella's brow creased. "How would you know that?"

"She only takes her best friends or people she feels she can trust into her gardens. That is her sacred space. Her private space. Ordinarily she would conduct an interview in her study." He came to a stop sign. "Trust me," he said, flashing her a smile before driving on. "I know my mother."

"Well… I'm flattered," Ella murmured.

"I'm not trying to flatter you, Ella."

She didn't reply, and his quick glance in her direction caught her puzzled—or maybe hurt—expression as she turned to look out her window.

"That didn't come out right," he said, wishing he could just park the car and talk to her face-to-face. But he couldn't risk wasting time if he wanted to get back to the villa before the downpour.

"What I meant to say was I'm not telling you this to boost your ego, Ella. I'm telling you this because it's the truth." Out of the corner of his eye, he saw her turn to look at him. "And one more thing…she said, '*Buona notte, cara,'* to you. She doesn't use that term lightly. There's only one other person she called a *dear.*"

"Your father?"

"No. She called him *amore.*" He swallowed. "She called my late wife Rita, *cara.*"

Massimo felt a surprising relief once he told Ella this, as if a buildup of pressure inside him had been released.

His mother liked Ella.

And so did he. He didn't see it as a betrayal to Rita for either one of them. Rita would always have a place in his mother's heart. And his.

But had his admission made Ella uncomfortable? Is that why she hadn't said anything? He ventured a quick glance at her.

She was smiling at him.

Feeling a surge inside his chest, he grinned back and merged onto the freeway, anxious to get back to *Villa Serena*. Ella gasped as the Huracán accelerated and her hand shot out and landed on his leg.

And it seemed to rest there for a while before she pulled it away...

When they arrived at the Paradiso, Massimo looked at the gathering clouds. "We should be able to make it back before the rain starts," he told her. They would be fine in the boat's cabin, but he didn't like the idea of driving the boat at night in a heavy rain.

A quarter of a mile away from his villa, they heard the first rumblings of thunder. Ella turned to him, her eyes wide. He increased his speed, and the rain began pelting the boat just as he was docking. He held out a hand to Ella and she clambered out. "How fast can you run?" he said.

"Faster than you can swim," she teased.

He clasped her hand tightly as they dashed toward

the villa, but halfway there, the rain turned into a downpour with the boom of thunder reverberating around them. They reached the villa entrance just as jagged spears of lightning branded the sky.

Inside the lit foyer, they stood dripping, and as they caught the reflection of their faces in the oval mirror, they both started to laugh. "I'll go grab some towels in a minute," he said, unbuttoning his shirt. After taking it off, he squeezed the excess water out and used it to wipe his face and head. He noticed that Ella was trying not to stare, but their gazes met several times.

She couldn't very well take her dress off, and because of the height of the mirror, she probably hadn't been aware of the fact her loose-fitting garment was now clinging to her provocatively, highlighting the curves and shadows that had been previously concealed.

The soft but quick beat of his heart seemed to suddenly match the boom of thunder that made Ella jump, seconds before the lights went out. His arms instinctively shot up to steady her. In the darkness, feeling her wet, shivering body against him, his arms wrapped around her as if they had a will of their own. Her breath fanned his Adam's apple, igniting a sizzle through him that coincided with the series of lightning flashes that illuminated them briefly through the villa windows.

Ella didn't move. Massimo closed his eyes, his chest heaving, allowing himself to just experience the moment. *The feeling.* The wonder of his whole being, body and soul, wanting to…to…

Her lips brushed against his jaw. With a groan that was muffled by the next clap of thunder, his hand slid up to cup the back of her head while his lips found hers. He froze for a moment as they made contact, and then he lingered, first over her lower and then her top lip. Ella's hands reached upward to trace a path on his back, and the way her fingers moved over him, giving a slight squeeze every few seconds, was threatening to undo him.

At her sudden intake of breath, he pressed her tightly against him and kissed her deeply, his heart clanging wildly when she reciprocated.

Massimo could taste the myrtle liqueur on her tongue. His pulse skyrocketed. His hands dropped to blindly find the hem of her dress, without breaking off the kiss. His fingers trembled as they closed over the drenched material...

And then the lights flickered back on.

It was like getting a bucket of cold water poured over his head. He released the hold on her dress, and as the kiss ended, they stood looking at each other, both dazed.

He didn't know whether he should apologize or kiss her again.

"Ella—"

"I—I have to go," she said, crossing her arms self-consciously in front of her.

They could both hear the rain pelting the villa's tiled roof and windows, followed by a menacing series of thunderclaps.

"You can't leave now, with this storm," he said huskily. "The path down to the guesthouse will be too dangerous. And there are too many trees that are a target for lightning." His eyes narrowed. "You'll have to spend the night."

CHAPTER SIXTEEN

ELLA WATCHED HIM disappear around the corner after telling her that he would return with some towels.

She loved storms…as long as she was inside. She'd watch a deluge from the window seat in her bedroom and wait for the lightning to sizzle across the night sky.

This storm would have been amazing to watch from the guesthouse, with the stupendous views of the cove, but she wasn't about to head there after Massimo's warning.

He was right. It *was* too dangerous to go out. But what was even more dangerous was the storm inside her. And she couldn't put the blame entirely on the baron. Or the weather, although running up to the villa with her hand in his had certainly started it. Followed by Massimo taking off his shirt, the ear-splitting boom of thunder that had caused her to practically jump in his arms and the lights switching off.

Pressed up against him in the dark and feeling the touch of Massimo's hands and lips had ignited a yearning within her that she hadn't been able to suppress. His kiss had been powerful…*seismic*. If it hadn't actually caused the floor to split and quake around her, it certainly had shaken her to the core.

But the return of the electricity had shocked her back

to reality…to the knowledge that allowing anything further to develop would be a big mistake. Just allowing herself to be kissed by the baron—*and kissing him back*—had not been the wisest thing to do. It had never happened in the past with a client, and she could not let it happen again.

No matter how physically attracted she was to him.

No matter that being in his sphere made her pulse spike in a way she had never experienced with Dustin or the other guys she had dated.

And despite her earlier feeling that Massimo wouldn't be interested in her, his lips and his body were telling her something different.

It didn't matter.

She had to choose reason over recklessness.

Simply because she would be leaving soon, and the last thing she wanted was to complicate matters by giving in to what her body seemed to be yearning for.

Ella shivered. If only they had arrived ten minutes earlier… She would be in the guesthouse, comfortably watching the storm in her robe, instead of standing here soaking wet in a dress that had become too revealing for comfort.

And now she had no choice but to spend the night under his roof.

The lights flickered as the baron returned with several extra-large towels. He had changed into a black T-shirt and jeans. He handed two towels to Ella and dropped one on the floor where he had been standing. She wrapped one around her body and used the other one for her hair.

"I'll take you to a guest room," he said brusquely, as if he were a resort employee speaking to a paying guest. "It has an en suite bathroom, if you'd like to take

a warm shower. And there's a bathrobe on the hook behind the sliding door. There are hangers for your wet
clothes in the walk-in closet." He handed her a bag.
"Slippers, since your shoes are soaked."

Ella followed him past his living room and up the
grand staircase to the second level.

"Buona notte," he said, giving her a curt nod. "I've
put a bottle of water on the night table. If you need
anything else, just let me know. My room is at the end
of the hall."

"Thank you," she murmured stiffly, avoiding his
gaze as she entered the room. "Good night."

She clicked the door shut without looking back. Realizing that she was still shivering, she hurried to the
washroom and ,moments later, felt the soothing jets of
warm water ease some of the tension from her body.

Much as Ella wanted to linger, she made it a quick
shower instead and, minutes later, after drying her hair,
climbed into the king-size bed. The shutters were open
and she could see and hear the downpour, feeling her
usual excitement at the continual rumblings of thunder
and the intermittent flashes of lightning.

The deluge had brought with it a refreshing breeze,
and Ella shivered, still feeling the electricity of Massimo's kiss.

She would have to forget that kiss while conducting
the remaining interviews.

And during the *baronessa*'s birthday and the grand
opening of the DiLuca Cardiac Research Center.

The pelting rain had changed to a soft and steady
flow, and her glance shifted to the balcony. Maybe she'd
be able to sleep if she closed the shutters. Maybe the
darkness would help erase the image of Massimo from
her mind.

As Ella strode to the balcony, lightning streaked the sky, followed by a deafening thunderclap. She let out a shriek. And then the rain intensified and she quickly closed the balcony doors and the shutters.

A shaft of light appeared, and Ella turned to her partially open door.

"Ella, are you okay?" Massimo wasn't visible, but she could hear the genuine alarm in his voice.

"I'm fine. It was the thunder—it scared me half to death." Ella grabbed her robe and put it on. "I think it's going to take me a while before I can—"

Another rumble drowned out her words.

"How about a cup of tea? *Una camomilla?* I guarantee that will make you fall asleep."

"Um, well… Okay, thank you."

He hadn't been able to sleep, either. But it hadn't been the rain or the thunder. It was the memory of Ella in his arms, his lips on hers…

As they walked downstairs, Massimo couldn't help thinking how natural it felt, the two of them heading to the kitchen in their bathrobes to make a pot of soothing chamomile tea.

"Make yourself comfortable in the living area," he told her. When he set down a tray on the coffee table a couple of minutes later, he found Ella sitting on the sectional looking through one of his books on the festivals of Sardinia. She looked up at him. "I know so little of my country of birth," she murmured. "The history, the traditions, the dialect…"

"That will start to change in a few days once you meet your uncle," Massimo said, pouring her chamomile tea.

"I'm not sure if I should disrupt his or his family's

lives with a sudden appearance," she said, stirring in some honey.

"But you are his family. Don't you think your uncle would want to see you, know that you're well after all these years?" he said, hearing the urgency in his voice.

Ella looked across at Massimo, her brow wrinkling. "I…imagine he would. But if I connect with him, it might lead to…other things."

Massimo knew he was nudging her into a sensitive area of her life, but he told himself he was doing it to help her.

"Like finding out about your biological mother and father?" Massimo said quietly.

"My mother, actually." She traced the rim of her cup with her finger. "She never revealed who the father— my father—was. The papers listed him as *straniero*."

"A foreigner." Massimo said curtly.

Ella set her cup down with a trembling hand. "In any case, I can't see that happening. If there was any way of finding out more about her, wouldn't my adoptive mother have told me?"

"She might not have wanted to explore that, especially after moving back to Canada after the trauma of losing her husband," Massimo said gently. "And maybe she was waiting for *you* to indicate your desire to find your birth mother. In any case, there are ways now…"

"That would be opening a Pandora's box," Ella said, shaking her head adamantly. "I don't think I'm ready to deal with that now, especially since I'll only be here for a week after this assignment." She bit her lip. "I just want to enjoy a week of sun and sand before heading back home. And if during my week, I decide to try to contact my uncle, then I will."

"Are you happy with your life back home?" he murmured.

Where was he going with this?

"As happy as I can be," she said curtly, not bothering to curb the defensiveness in her voice. "I've got a great job. I get to travel and enjoy perks most people would love to have." Her brows arched. "Are you happy with *your* life? I mean—"

Massimo's eyes narrowed. "To quote someone I know, 'As happy as I can be,' given the circumstances."

"I get the impression that you could be happier," she ventured.

"I get the same impression. About *you*," he said.

He saw Ella take a deep breath. "You can tell me to mind my own business, but…but maybe you might be ready to…to be with people again."

Did she really mean a woman?

A knot settled in his throat and he couldn't reply immediately. The reality of his life hit him. Hard.

He was alone.

He had everything he could possibly want that his money could buy.

But he didn't have a woman who would love him for himself, not his billions. And he didn't have a child… or children.

He glanced at Ella. Something in the depths of her eyes was inviting him to keep talking.

"Three years ago, I vowed to stay single, unable to bear the thought of…of being with another woman," he began haltingly. "I was certain that I would never be able to love again. All the emotions I had experienced with Rita vanished from my life along with her, leaving a dark, empty space." He paused, remembering how he had felt the vacuum in his chest every day, the only visitors being grief, shock and disbelief that happiness and love had been snatched away from him.

"I wanted to hide from the world, cringing at things I had enjoyed with Rita, like strolling by market stalls in a piazza, walking along a beach at night. Or holiday shopping." The sound of Christmas music months after she passed had sent pain spiraling through him. "I couldn't take the laughter of groups enjoying lunch on a restaurant patio. Their carefree chatter just emphasized what was lacking in my own life. So I did everything possible to stay away from people."

He told Ella how he had become increasingly reclusive and had grown a beard. And when he did go out, he'd deliberately dress in casual clothes with a cap and glasses to further disguise himself.

"I just wanted to hide from the world. Mourn my lost dreams." He felt the backs of his eyes prickling. "I realize now, Ella, that if I want to be happy again, I have to make new dreams. With new people."

Massimo swallowed the jagged lump in his throat. He set down his cup and leaned forward, his hands under his chin. "I know we haven't had exactly the same experience, Ella, but we've both suffered loss in our lives. *Great loss.* You took a big step in coming to Sardinia, and now you have a chance to gain something. *Someone.*"

He stood up and went around the coffee table to sit next to her.

"Now *you* can tell me to mind *my* own business… but I think it would be good to call your uncle while you're here. Make that connection. After tomorrow's interview, I'll be happy to drive you to where you'll be staying and take you around the area so you're familiar with the town."

He grasped her hand and gazed earnestly into her eyes. "And if you'd like, Marinella, I'll come with you to find your uncle and his family, if he has one. *Va bene?*" He squeezed her hand lightly. "I think you need to find *your* people, and you're right about *me* needing to be with people again, too."

CHAPTER SEVENTEEN

ELLA HAD FELT her heart begin to thump erratically when Massimo had sat next to her. Now she was trying to process her jumbled thoughts about what he had just told her. Was he inferring about being open to letting others into his life? Like her?

She blinked at him wordlessly for a few seconds. He was offering to accompany her in her personal business. That was something friends did.

Was he offering to be a friend? And after sharing that scorching kiss, *could* they be just friends?

Her gaze dropped to her hand that he still held. And then she looked up at him again to search the depths of his eyes for answers. He must have sensed her hesitation, for he gently withdrew his hand. "I don't want to stick my nose in your business…if you don't want me to, Ella."

"You…you must have more important matters to take care of with your own business," she replied hesitantly.

"I can take a day off from my business," he said with a smirk. "Anytime I choose. And the boss—you've heard of that elusive fellow, *barone* Massimo DiLuca— he's pretty reasonable, when I have a good excuse."

Ella felt the corners of her mouth lifting. "What

about the *baronessa*?" she said. "She might have something to say about her son shirking his duties…"

Massimo let out a deep laugh. "*Baronessa* Silvia *is* a dragon when it comes to business matters," he said, his eyes crinkling. "Or she wouldn't have got to where she is with DiLuca Resorts. But I happen to have heard that she has quite a soft spot for her wonderful—and extremely handsome—son."

Ella burst out laughing. "Maybe her wonderful son has a face only a mother would love."

As they laughed together, Ella felt warmth radiating throughout her nerve endings. And in Massimo's eyes.

This was exactly what friends did. Laugh and joke around. But there was something more. She couldn't pull her eyes away from him…and he was looking at her with a tenderness she had never seen in the eyes of any of her dates in the past. He didn't have to say anything. He was showing her that he cared.

Something leaped in her heart. She was home. In Sardinia. And soon, she could be—*would be*—connecting with a member or members of her own family. Massimo was right.

She suddenly realized how much she really wanted to do this…*had* to do this.

And she hoped her *zio* Domenicu and any or all other members would welcome her and accept her in their lives. Because if she was sure of one thing, now that she'd had a taste of her homeland, it was that she was ready to return. She had a history here, even though she still had to discover much of it. This was her *motherland*.

Suddenly Massimo put his arm around her, and she let her head rest against his chest. "We'd better get some sleep," he murmured, his breath fanning her cheek. "I think it would be better to head out early to Posada. We can have the interview on the drive there, otherwise there won't be enough time to do everything I want to do… with you."

Massimo embraced Ella at her bedroom door. He didn't want to meet her gaze. And weaken…

"Buona notte, Marinella," he said, and turned away, forcing himself to keep on walking until he was in his own room. He shut the door and strode to his balcony. The rain had subsided along with the humidity, leaving a light breeze in its place. The sea had calmed, and he listened to the gentle gush of the tide's ebb and flow. Gentle yet sensuous in the dark…

Massimo breathed in deeply, trying to process the emotions swirling in his head. He hadn't seen this coming. He hadn't expected to have the deepest recesses of his heart revived. By a foreigner who wasn't a foreigner. A woman who shared the same heritage.

Yet up to now, he hadn't felt the desire—or need— to be open to a friendship—*let alone relationship*— with another woman, Sardinian or otherwise. What was it about this Marinella Rossi that had managed to find an opening in the protective barricade around his heart?

Massimo glanced up at the sky. The clouds had mostly dispersed, allowing the stars to pierce through the blackness. He thought about Rita, and the star directly above him seemed to glow brighter. Something many of the older generations of southern Italians, Sardinians and Sicilians included, would believe a sign from heaven. He didn't consider himself to be superstitious in that way, but as he watched the star for a few moments, he sensed Rita would be happy for him.

"Grazie," he murmured and went inside. He set his phone alarm and tossed his robe on the ottoman at the foot of his bed before getting under the covers. Closing his eyes, he listened to the rush of the tide, savoring the peace in his heart.

CHAPTER EIGHTEEN

ELLA HADN'T BEEN able to sleep right away. She'd worked
on her developing story for the magazine, inserting
some of the points she had jotted into her notepad. And
then she had surveyed the series of questions for the
next interview, which would be conducted in Massimo's
Lamborghini instead of his villa.

Finally, she had put her work aside and had gone to
bed with a bubbly feeling. *Like champagne,* she had
thought with a wry smile, *ready to spill over with excitement.* Massimo had reached out to her, offering to
accompany her to a meeting with her uncle, and she had
been relieved she wouldn't have to go alone. Although
she didn't think that she had actually told him yes.

In bed, Ella had thought about connecting with her
uncle once she finished her assignment for the magazine. She had *zio* Domenicu's number and address—and
once she discovered if he would be open to having her
visit, she'd make arrangements to go there. But since
Massimo had offered to take her to Posada, she had
decided she might as well summon up her courage and
call her uncle the next morning.

Now, waking up to bands of sunlight streaming
through the open shutters of her balcony, Ella felt a flutter of mingled excitement and anxiety. She checked the

time and decided she'd attempt a call to her uncle before going down for breakfast. She dressed quickly, all while going over what she'd say in her head. She reached for her cell phone, and finding Zio Domenicu's number in the contacts, she called it with trembling fingers.

After a few rings, she was ready to hang up, losing her nerve. And then someone picked up. *"Pronto."*

The voice was younger than what she had expected to hear. So maybe her *zio* had married and had children. This "child" sounded like a young man. He would be her cousin. She swallowed hard. *"Buongiorno. C'è il signor Rossi? Domenicu Rossi?"*

There was a pause on the other line. Ella's heart thudded, filling her eardrums.

"Chi parla?" The voice had become a little sharper.

"Mi chiamo Ella," she said, the backs of her eyes beginning to sting. *"Marinella... Rossi. Siamo parenti..."*

Telling her cousin that she was a relative resulted in a longer pause. And then he called out excitedly to his father. *"Papà! Papà! Vieni subito!"*

And moments later, she was talking, her *zio* was crying, and after she told him that she would be in Posada for a week, there were more tears. By this time, he had her on speakerphone and the rest of the family—big or small—was chattering excitedly among themselves, especially when she said that she'd be visiting the area to check out the place she had booked.

Her uncle immediately insisted she stay with *them*. Ella didn't want to hurt his feelings, but she told him she didn't want to impose and that they could talk more later in the afternoon after her friend drove her to the farmhouse. She didn't have the heart to tell him that returning to the place she had spent the first four years of her life might be too much for her and she would have to take it step by step...

Ella blew out her breath slowly after she said good-bye and turned off her phone. She hadn't expected to be doing this before the *baronessa*'s birthday. But now that she had made the connection, her spirits were soaring. Her uncle had sounded thrilled at her call, as had the rest of his family. *Her family.*

Feeling as if she had won a lottery jackpot, Ella skipped lightly down the stairs, her nostrils taking in the smell of coffee. There was something about the way an Italian espresso filled a room with such an aromatic scent.

She couldn't wait to tell Massimo.

He turned when she entered the kitchen, his gaze sweeping over her. She halted in her tracks. He had shaved off his beard, leaving just a light scruff on his upper lip and face. If he had been handsome before, now he looked...*gorgeous.*

She couldn't help giving him a once-over, as well. Tan, belted Bermuda shorts and a tailored white short-sleeved shirt that he wore tucked in. Fitted and fabulous...

"Buongiorno, Marinella."

Her head snapped back up. *"Buongiorno*, Massimo."

"Cappuccino?"

"Sì, grazie." She took a place at the kitchen island, and when he set down her cappuccino, she thanked him again and told him about contacting her cousin and telling him she'd be visiting this afternoon.

He finished his espresso. "I'm happy for you," he said huskily. "I'm glad that you will be reuniting with your uncle and his—*your*—family."

Ella smiled. "I feel good about this," she admitted. "Now I have a reason to return to Sardinia…"

Massimo's smile froze. She didn't notice; she was enjoying her almond brioche. Her words revealed so much to him, mainly that Ella was focused on her family in Sardinia. Not him.

There was no reason for him to feel slighted. Or disappointed. Yet he couldn't help it. He thought they had shared something special last night. Not just an intoxicating kiss but moments of shared feelings and vulnerability.

He had obviously misunderstood. Not the kiss; he had sensed Ella's desire as much as his own, and that was normal and natural. She was a beauty, and his body hadn't been immune to that. Especially with her being in such close proximity. The lightning hadn't struck *him* during the storm, but *she* had.

And he had succumbed to more than just her physical beauty. Her intelligence, her sensitivity, and her honesty had reeled him in, as well.

But he was delusional to think—or expect—that anything could progress. After tomorrow, she would be gone. She'd still be in Sardinia, but she'd be reestablishing a connection with her *zio* Domenicu and his family, which was clearly what they both wanted.

And what do you want? an inner voice pressed.

Massimo poured himself another espresso. There was no point going there… No point at all.

It was probably a mistake to have offered to take Ella to Posada, but he couldn't very well retract his proposal now. He'd have to just get through the day and his mother's birthday tomorrow, and then they'd say their goodbyes.

"Do you have everything you need?" he said brusquely as she finished her brioche. "Or do you have to stop at the guesthouse?"

"I'd like to change before we head out, if that's okay."

He nodded. *"Non c'è problema.* I'll meet you at the dock." He stood up. "You can just text me your uncle's address."

Fifteen minutes later, Ella had changed into a pair of tangerine Capri pants and a white tank top under a floral cotton shirt. She had her hat and sunglasses on, and as she approached the speedboat, Massimo felt a tightening in his chest.

Ella held on to her sun hat as he sped away from the coast. He focused on steering, and although he sensed Ella's gaze on him several times, he deliberately avoided looking her way.

When they were in his Lamborghini and cruising on the freeway, Ella pulled out her recorder and notepad. "I doubt we'll get a good sound." She frowned. "But I'll still record you while I take notes."

"Prego." He nodded. "I'm ready when you are."

"What is it like, working with the *baronessa*?" she said. "Tell me about your work relationship…and has your mother mentioned retirement plans at all?"

Massimo flashed her a wry smile. "I'm a very lucky person, being able to work with her. She's smart, creative and generous with our employees. She listens to my ideas and vice versa. Although she's cut back on her work hours, she hasn't brought up retirement."

For the next few minutes, Massimo answered questions about his mother's birthday, after which Ella informed him she had made up a list of shots that she would like his photographer to take for the magazine.

"And as you requested," she added, "you can approve them and then have them emailed to me."

She then proceeded to ask about the genesis of the Cardiac Research Center that would bear the DiLuca name.

It was a project extremely important to him and his mother, he told her. It was a long-term personal and financial commitment that would honor the memory of their loved ones, and help countless people in the future.

When they were done, Ella put away her recorder and notepad and concentrated on enjoying the scenery. She looked intently out at the stretches of farmland, exclaiming at the sight of the Rio Posada, and near the left bank of the river, in the middle of a plain, Massimo pointed out a conical prehistoric monument built with large blocks of stone.

"We're in Torpè, and this is called Nuraghe San Pietro," he said, "named after the ancient Nuraghic tribe in the region. We could stop and have a look on the way back, as I'm sure you're anxious to get to Posada."

"I'd like that," she said. "I had read about the Nuraghe and also Mount Tepilora and Tepilora Park. It looks absolutely stunning."

"Ah, yes, the home of the golden eagle and excellent hiking trails."

"I'd love to check out the trails, too…but not today," she added quickly. "My priority is to reconnect with my family."

"Of course. And that will happen very soon." He gestured at the sign ahead.

A few minutes later as they approached Posada, Massimo pointed out the medieval village clinging to the side of a limestone cliff—its cluster of colorful homes cascading down the hillside toward the sea, like a flow-ing peasant skirt—and a thirteenth-century tower and ruins of the *Castello della Fava*.

"It's so beautiful," Ella said wistfully. "It looks like something out of a fairy tale."

"Which is why it has been named one of the most beautiful villages in Italy. Do you remember any of it?"

She shook her head. "I was only four when we moved to Canada. I don't have any specific memories, other than a blue door and—" her mouth curved into a smile briefly "—some chickens."

"What about people? Your relatives? Do you remember them?"

"Vaguely. But my memories might actually be getting confused with the photos my mother—Cassandra—showed me of the four years we spent in Posada."

Massimo heard the tremor in her voice. His hand reached out to clasp hers, but he withdrew it when she abruptly turned her head to look out her side window.

He felt a twist in his chest. She may not have seen his attempted gesture of empathy, but perhaps it was just as well. It was a reminder for him to stay neutral…

He began the ascent toward Posada's historic center, distracted by the groups of teenagers and people—both men and woman—who stopped and stared at his Huracán or whistled their approval. Having visited Posada before, Massimo knew where he could park privately, near a hidden scenic outlook on the mountain that he and Ella could walk to. It was worth stopping at, with its panoramic view of the countryside and endless Tyrrhenian Sea.

As they made their way up steep steps and through cobbled side streets lined by homes of ancient stone and charming stucco houses painted coral, cream, yellow or white, most having arched doorways and large glazed planters overflowing with blooms or featuring a flowering tree, Massimo felt conflicting emotions.

He was happy to be with Ella, showing her the land of her birth, but simultaneously unhappy, knowing that he had a very limited time in which to do it. There was simply too much to discover and enjoy in a day. In less than a day.

Ella gasped, as he had imagined she would when they arrived at the scenic outlook. Surprisingly, they were the only ones there. Checking the time, he realized it was after noon and tourists were probably flocking to the restaurants all vying for their patronage.

"This. Is. Magnificent." She looked downward and Massimo heard her draw in her breath again. "Oh, look, Massimo," she said, clasping his forearm, "the beach, with the ancient watchtower and the Church of San Giovanni. I can't get over this view. The beach sand looks like a strip of caramel—and, oh, my gosh, that turquoise water... I wish I had brought my bathing suit." She squeezed his arm. "Thank you for bringing me here." And before he could respond, she impulsively gave him a hug.

CHAPTER NINETEEN

ELLA REALIZED THAT Massimo wasn't reciprocating the hug. She let her arms drop stiffly and stepped away from him, feeling as awkward as a teenager at her first dance. She didn't intend to ask him why he had turned into one of the stone statues they had seen in a piazza on their way to the terrace lookout. It was obvious. Now that she was officially finished interviewing him and would be leaving the day after tomorrow, he was assuming his baron demeanor, just as he had when he'd been at the airport to pick her up.

And what exactly had she expected? That he would pull her tightly to him and kiss her the way he had before?

The altitude was to blame. She felt on top of the world standing on this terrace on Mount Tepilora, and she had been temporarily swept away with a rush of pleasure at seeing an eagle's-eye view of her village, the surrounding countryside and the enchanting blue waters of the Tyrrhenian, catching the sun with every wave and mirroring the cerulean blue of the sky. This was as close to heaven as she could possibly be. And she had been filled with gratitude that Massimo had thought to bring her here. So she had hugged him. Without thinking.

But Massimo's literally cold shoulder had brought her back to earth. *Hard.* She might as well have been hugging the trunk of one of the holm oaks on the hillside. She and Massimo were realms apart. And it was obvious that he thought so, too.

The best thing to do would be to get her business done here, and then return to his island, get a good night's sleep and brace herself for her final days with the DiLucas.

She suddenly felt exhausted. And hot.

"I think we should go to my uncle's farm now," she said, keeping her voice steady, "and then we can head back to *Villa Serena*."

She saw his brow furrow.

"You don't want to stroll around the village? What about checking out your *agriturismo*? I thought you wanted to see where you'd be staying for a week."

Ella shook her head. "It's not necessary. I'll call to let my uncle know we're on our way." She tossed her hair back and started to walk away. There would be plenty of time to stroll around during her holiday.

She couldn't let the baron ruin her day, she told herself. She had family to visit. Family who would hopefully show her warmth. And maybe even love…

Massimo had programmed the address of the farmhouse on his GPS and as they descended the hillside toward the farmland on the lower slopes, he wondered at Ella's sudden change of plans. And mood. He figured it was nerves, finally about to meet the family she was connected to by blood. He could understand wanting to make that her priority instead of sightseeing…

Her hug had caught him off guard. Before he could reciprocate—and he had wanted to, despite his intentions to stay neutral—she had backed away. Now she was staring out the side window, and he was reluctant to make conversation. She was probably going over what she wanted to say to her *zio* Domenicu. It would no doubt be a very emotional reunion.

Massimo turned into a rougher country lane and Ella suddenly swiveled around to look at the screen. "We're almost there," she murmured, and leaned forward, her eyes narrowing.

He drove slowly, passing enclosed fields of pasture where a herd of sheep and goats were grazing at the wild grasses around the gnarled trunks of olive trees, their silver-green foliage rustling in the warm breeze. Farther along were fenced-in rows and rows of crops, interspersed with fruit and fig trees, and a series of separate sheds with enclosed pens. They saw rabbits, a sow with its litter, and a cow. And as Massimo rounded a curve, they came to the last shed—a henhouse with a clutch of chicks squabbling over seed—and a view of the country house beyond. With a blue door.

A dog started barking from an enclosure, and the blue door opened. The man standing on the doorstep started waving to them, and as Massimo came to a stop, the man began striding toward the car, a welcoming smile on his weathered face. Ella glanced at Massimo for a moment, her eyes blinking as they filled with tears, and then she opened the side door and ran out to her uncle.

CHAPTER TWENTY

"Stavo aspettando per questo momento," zio Domenicu told her, wiping his own eyes.

"Anch'io," she replied. She had been waiting for this moment, too.

"Are you going to leave your friend sitting in the car?"

"Zio! You speak English?"

"Yes, *bella*. I wanted to be prepared for my little Canadian niece when she came back." He gave her another hug. "Your family is waiting inside. But first, introduce me to your *giovanotto*."

"He's not my young man," she wanted to reply, but her uncle was already walking toward Massimo, who had climbed out of the Huracán and was extending his hand. *"Barone* DiLuca, this is my *zio* Domenicu," she said.

"Piacere." He smiled at her uncle. "But please call me Massimo. And now that I've delivered your niece safely, I'll be on my way." He turned to Ella. "Just text me when you're ready."

"No, no!" Domenicu said. "You are a friend of Marinella and very welcome in our home." He put up his hand. "No arguments, *giovanotto*."

Massimo laughed. *"Grazie, signor* Domenicu, but I think Marinella might want some time alone with you and your family."

Her uncle looked pointedly at her. It was obvious that he expected her to invite Massimo in. "You're welcome to stay," she said, her cheeks flushed as she met Massimo's gaze, unwilling to breach what she knew was typical Sardinian courtesy.

"*Brava*," her uncle said, and he put one arm over Ella's shoulder and the other over Massimo's. "Let's go inside."

As they began walking toward the entrance, the blue door burst open again and a group ran out to meet them.

"Meet your *famiglia*," Domenicu laughed, squeezing Ella's shoulder.

In the next few minutes Ella met *zio* Domenicu's wife, Lina, their daughter Maria and son-in-law, Tomasso, and Maria and Tomasso's four-year-old little girl, Angelica. They greeted Massimo with the same enthusiasm, and Ella wondered if they, too, thought that she and Massimo were a couple...

They were ushered inside where *zia* Lina and cousin Maria had prepared a feast. They sat at the long harvest table that Ella's father had made, *zio* Domenicu told her, his eyes misting.

"He is with us in spirit today, along with your mother."

Ella's eyes misted, too, and when she dabbed at them, Angelica, who was seated beside her, gave her a hug. Ella returned Angelica's embrace, and when Ella straightened in her seat, she saw Massimo out of the corner of her eye reaching out to place his hand over hers. Confused by his caring gesture, after he had displayed indifference to her hug on Mount Tepilora, Ella slid her hand out from under his and avoided meeting Massimo's gaze, focusing instead on what her uncle was saying.

She bit her lip. There were so many emotions bouncing around in her chest right now, and she would need time to process them.

Zia Lina began passing around the serving dishes, joking in Italian *she* would start crying if they didn't eat before the food got cold. That lightened the atmosphere, and Ella laughed along with everyone. She praised her aunt and cousin for the amazing spread, starting with the platter of fried calamari, followed by baked eggplants and a tomato *ragù* of pork sausages served with *culurgiones*. For dessert, Maria brought out *pardulas*, small pies she had made filled with ricotta, saffron and lemon.

As Ella sipped her espresso, gazing at her relatives around the table, she felt that her heart was ready to burst with happiness. It was as if she had never left Sardinia, as if she'd had weekly dinners with her uncle, aunt and family, and this was one of those dinners.

It hadn't been awkward with Massimo, either, as she had initially feared. He had chatted easily with everyone in Italian and English and had even slipped into a lively Sardinian exchange with her uncle at one point. She had never seen Massimo smile or laugh so much, and every time her gaze returned to him, she had felt her pulse quickening.

Now *zio* Domenicu was saying that he was looking forward to getting to know Ella, and invited her again to stay at the farmhouse. "We have Maria's room empty," he said, before asking Ella where she had booked her accommodations.

She told them about the *agriturismo* and how she could visit often, once she rented a vehicle. As Ella described some of the features that had attracted her, she saw Maria and Tomasso exchange a surprised glance.

And then they burst out laughing, joined in by her *zio* and *zia*. She cocked her head at them, puzzled by their reaction.

Her cousin gave her a beaming smile. "The *agriturismo* belongs to me and Tomasso," she said. "So now we know that the 'Ella Ross' who booked it is in fact our Marinella Rossi!"

By the time they arrived at Villa Serena, Massimo knew Ella was ready to call it a night. The meal and congenial conversation with her family had extended into late afternoon. Ella had been quiet during the car ride back and in the boat. He could see by her dreamy expression she was processing everything that had happened.

He was happy for her. Her relatives were good, hard-working people, and it had been obvious they were thrilled not only with Ella's return to Sardinia but with her intentions to spend time with them for a week. They had made it clear that she was welcome to visit whenever she could travel to Italy.

They had all been delighted to hear Ella had unknowingly booked the family *agriturismo*. And he had noted Ella and Maria, who he'd learned was six years younger than Ella, had really clicked. What a relief it must be for Ella to reconnect with her *zio* after all these years and know that he'd married and now had a family.

Along with the happiness he had felt for Ella during the visit, Massimo had also been aware of something stronger tugging at his chest. It had felt so right to be at Ella's side, not only witnessing but understanding her feelings. He had felt a powerful emotional connection that he had doubted he'd ever feel again with a woman.

And he realized it was a connection that had begun the moment she had rammed into him at the airport and had grown steadily with each moment they had spent together.

When they came to the villa entrance, Massimo offered to walk her to the guesthouse.

"I'll be fine," she said, putting up a hand. "Thank you for driving me to Posada today. I hope you didn't mind the extended visit."

"Not at all. I enjoyed it." His eyes locked with Ella's. Her eyes were bright and her cheeks were flushed, the same color as the peonies in his gardens. Her lips, slightly open and free of lipstick, sparked a sizzle along his veins. Was he the only one feeling the magnetic pull, the aching desire to close the distance between them and…?

Massimo forced himself to look away. "I hope the good weather holds out for my mother's birthday tomorrow," he said, scanning the sky. "She deserves sunshine and blue skies…just like you," he added huskily.

"I hope so, too. *Buonasera.*"

"Buonasera… Marinella."

Massimo watched her until she disappeared from view, and then he waited until he saw the lights of the guesthouse come on. He could hear his heart beating along with the swishing of the surf and the chirping of cicadas.

The afternoon with her newfound family had been so enjoyable. They had been so loving with Ella, and they had treated *him* like a member of the family, as well.

That's what he wanted, he realized.

To share Ella's family with her. But what did *she* want? Was there a chance in his wildest dreams that her feelings were the same?

Minutes later, soaking in his whirlpool tub and gazing at the gold-and-saffron bands around the setting sun and reflected in the calm sea waters, Massimo wondered how and when he could tell Marinella that he was ready…

For a second chance at love.

CHAPTER TWENTY-ONE

ELLA REACHED FOR her cell phone to stop the alarm. She had gone to bed too late last night. After returning to the guesthouse, she had been too wired to sleep. Thoughts of her family had swirled in her mind, along with a never ending loop of images of Massimo and twinges of regret that she had acted ungraciously when he had been trying to show her empathy.

After changing into a teddy, Ella had decided to transfer her mental energy to the piece she had started putting together for the magazine's August feature. The last interviews would take place at the *baronessa*'s birthday party and at the opening of the research center, but Ella had enough material to do a rough first draft.

Close to one-thirty in the morning, she had realized she had drifted off at the computer. She had turned it off and climbed into bed, exhausted but content with what she had accomplished. Once she had the rest of the material, she'd finish the piece in the next day or two, send it off, and then she'd have most of her holiday left. She couldn't wait to stay at Maria and Tomasso's *agriturismo* and spend more time with her family.

Ella forced herself to get out of bed. She strode to the balcony and looked out. *Baronessa* Silvia was going to get her blue skies and sunshine today. An unexpected lump formed in Ella's throat. She wished she could have spent more time with Massimo's mother. She would have loved to have had a cooking lesson with her.

And Massimo? her inner voice murmured.

Ella looked over the trees at *Villa Serena*. "Wishful thinking," she replied aloud. And then she berated herself for even entertaining such thoughts. Massimo DiLuca was out of reach. He had demonstrated that by the way he had frozen when she had hugged him. She had wanted to slink away in embarrassment…

But he hadn't been totally devoid of feelings. Extending his hand to her had been his attempt to show his empathy for her loss. He had lost his father. And his wife. He could identify with how Ella must have felt, learning that she was sitting at a table her father had made.

And then he had shown his warm side with her family, chatting and laughing with each one of them. He had looked as if he were enjoying their company. Ella's heart had filled when she saw how he was with Angelica after lunch. She had brought out some toy figures, and he had played with her, assuming a different voice for each figure. Angelica had laughed each time and had given him a hug when he was done.

Ella had felt her heart twist. He would have made a great father, had he and his wife been able to adopt…

He could still be a father. If he allowed himself to date and eventually commit to a new relationship.

If he…

No! She needed to stop wasting her time in delusional thoughts. An espresso would help her clear her mind and focus on what she needed to do today. Without bothering to get dressed, she went downstairs, and a few minutes later, Ella had her espresso with one of the *pardulas* that Maria had made. Maria had run out of the farmhouse to hand Ella a container as she and Massimo were getting into his Lamborghini. "You can share them over breakfast," she had murmured in Italian, winking at Ella before running back inside.

Ella had immediately felt a hot tingling in her cheeks. Massimo might not have seen Maria's sly wink, but he must have heard her words. For the entire drive, Ella had avoided looking at him, focusing instead on the passing scenery.

Now, biting into her second pastry, she thought about the birthday party that would be starting in a few hours. She would meet Massimo at his dock. It would be her last ride in his speedboat, and at the end of the party, he would be driving her to *Villa Paradiso*, where she would spend the night. And the following day, after the grand opening of the Cardiac Center, Maria and Tomasso would be picking her up and proceeding to their *agriturismo*.

Ella put down her cup and went to stand by the retractable glass door overlooking the cove. Opening it, she felt a wave of mingled awe and sadness as she took in the view. Awe at its timeless beauty and the perpetual motion of the sea. Sadness that she would be leaving this special haven the baron had chosen to help him heal. Her eyes welled up. How many times he must have stood here, too, witnessing the beauty of nature while feeling the ache of loss… It had been his retreat from the not so beautiful side of reality.

With a sigh, Ella climbed the spiral staircase to the loft. She surveyed the clothes still hanging in the closet. She might as well start packing, but first she needed to pick out what she wanted to wear to the *baronessa*'s party.

An hour later, Ella had her suitcase and carry-on luggage packed. She brought them down one at a time and set them by the entrance door. Returning to the loft, she glanced at the coral dress she had chosen and placed on the bed, a sleeveless maxi wrap dress with a tulip hem. She had bought it days before her flight to Sardinia, along with a red-coral bracelet and coral-flower studs.

After a last glance in the mirror and a quick scan of the room to make sure she had everything, Ella headed downstairs just as the doorbell rang. Her pulse leaped as she caught sight of Massimo at the glass door. Descending the spiral staircase, she took in his appearance in stages. Sunglasses. White shirt. Black trousers. Gleaming brown leather shoes. And back to his face.

His handsome face. A face she…*loved. The man she loved.*

Ella froze on the last step of the staircase. She stood immobilized. She had never allowed herself to admit this…until *now.* Now, on her last day on Massimo's island.

She had come to Sardinia with two intentions: to do the interviews for *Living the Life* magazine, and then to decide whether or not to connect with her uncle and his family if he had one. She had realized her first objectives.

And now she was ready to consider a third possibility…of returning and searching for her birth mother. Of course Ella had to also consider that if she located her mother, she might not want to connect with the daughter she had given up…for whatever reason. And Ella would feel the sting of being rejected a second time. Or she would be willing to establish some kind of relationship. Either scenario would be emotionally overwhelming.

She would work on preparing herself for either outcome.

It wouldn't happen during this trip. But Ella was determined to return to Sardinia again and again until the final piece of the puzzle of her history was found.

What about Massimo? her inner voice pressed.

Ella *hadn't* planned to fall for a Sardinian... To fall in love with a man whose heart had suffered, a heart she wanted to have and to hold...

Ella snapped out of her reverie. The only thing that she'd be holding soon was her luggage as Massimo dropped her off at *Villa Paradiso* after the party.

Massimo's breath caught in his throat as he watched Ella come down the spiral staircase. She looked...stunning. Like one of the coral roses in his gardens. His heart began a drumbeat that simultaneously excited and pained him.

He didn't want her to go back to Canada. He could handle her being with her Sardinian family for a week, but the painful part was accepting that she would be crossing the ocean soon and he might never see her again.

He couldn't let that happen.

The universe had taken someone away from him, and if that could happen, then the reverse could, too. He had to trust Rita was in another spiritual realm and she would want him to *live*, not hide himself away forever.

The universe was giving him another opportunity to love. And he wasn't going to blow it.

He had to tell—and show—Ella how he felt. That he wanted her, body and soul. That he wanted to share everything he had with her. And since she had reunited with her family, he'd do everything in his power to help her find her biological mother...if and when she was ready.

She opened the door and he stepped inside. *"Sei bellissima, Marinella."*

"Grazie." She frowned, almost as if she couldn't believe he was saying such a thing. She leaned over to pick up her briefcase and the small carry-on.

"I—I have to tell you something," he said gruffly. "I should have told you yesterday…"

She set down the items and looked up at him.

"I don't want you to go."

Ella's brows furrowed. "Your mother's expecting me."

He laughed softly. "Not *there*, silly."

She shook her head. "I don't understand."

"I don't want you to leave Sardinia."

"You're joking."

"No, non scherzo, Marinella."

"Uh, w-why? I mean, why not?" Ella blinked.

"Because I have fallen with my head over my heels for you." He looked at her tenderly, hoping she would see that his words—whether he had gotten them right or wrong—were spoken with his heart.

"But…yesterday you acted as if I was poison when I hugged you."

"I wasn't expecting a hug. And you moved away too quickly, as if *I* was poison." He gently cupped her chin with one hand and bent his head to look deeply into her eyes. "I want you to be in my life, Marinella. Not just for this week but for always. *Per eternità.*"

She shook her head. "Someone pinch me," she murmured. "I must be dreaming."

Massimo gave a soft laugh. "I'm not going to pinch you. I never want to hurt you. And no, you are not dreaming." He leaned closer and kissed her coral lips. "I have so much I want to tell you," he murmured against her ear. "But I need to know something…"

"Yes."

"Do you…" He kissed her again, thoroughly.

"I said yes," she said, breathless.

"But you don't know what I'm about to ask…" He stroked her temple before tracing her lips with his fingers.

"I do."

"You can read my mind, *bella*?" His arms encircled her waist and he pulled her close.

She pressed her cheek against his chest. "I can read *this*," she said, tapping his heart with her finger. "And it's going faster than your Lamborghini Huracán."

Massimo chuckled softly and took her left hand in his. "Marinella, you brought laughter and happiness back into my life. I said I don't want you to leave Sardinia, but I can accept you traveling back to Canada when you want to. With *me*. I have yet to explore that magnificent country." He paused for a moment, conscious of the pounding in his chest.

"I don't want to hide from life anymore, Marinella." He rubbed along his chin. "See? That's why I shaved most of my beard off. I'm ready to show my face again. To live again. With *you*, my Sardinian beauty." He embraced her tightly, kissing her forehead. "*Ti amo, Marinella.* And I would be the happiest man in the world if you would accompany me to my mother's birthday and the opening of the Research Center tomorrow, *amore mio*. And be with me for the rest of my life… *Va bene?*" His lips brushed gentle kisses over her temple, cheek and ended with a hungry kiss that left them both breathless.

"*Va bellissimo,*" she replied with a sigh. She looked up to gaze lovingly into his dark eyes before flashing him a mischievous grin. "Now can we get going? I'm dying to taste your mother's food."

He laughed and pointed to her luggage. "How about we leave this at my—*our*—villa? We can sleep in tomorrow morning and enjoy Maria's *pardulas* for breakfast." He winked before scooping Ella up in his arms and twirling her around, his heart bursting as she wrapped her arms tightly around his neck and murmured, *"Ti amo, Massimo..."* in his ear.

EPILOGUE

ELLA BLINKED AS the sunlight caught on her vintage solitaire engagement ring, the two-carat stone absolutely stunning in an intricate floral setting and filigreed band. And next to it, her gold wedding band in its elegant simplicity. She never tired of looking at them, just like she never tired of looking at her husband.

Now she knew what her dear mother had meant about a man putting stars in her eyes…

From the moment Massimo had uttered *"Ti amo"* before his mother's birthday celebration, Ella's heart had overflowed with the love that had been developing since she set foot on his island. Her island, too.

Sardinia belonged to both of them. And they would continue to live at *Villa Serena*. See the glorious sun rise and set together.

She would enjoy learning how to prepare traditional Sardinian dishes with the *baronessa*, who had embraced her with tears in her eyes when Ella and Massimo had told her that they would be getting married and spending the rest of their lives together. They had waited until all her birthday guests had left and were enjoying a celebratory drink of *mirto* in her gardens when Massimo had shared the news. Silvia's eyes had widened as she glanced from Massimo to Ella, and then she had leaped up, and with clasped hands and eyes directed skyward, she thanked the heavens and declared that they had just given her the best birthday gift of all.

A few days later, Chef Angelo had brought over a vintage bottle of champagne and had prepared a special dinner in their honor...a new dish he'd named *Il Mare per Marinella*—The Sea for Marinella—a lobster bisque and sautéed scallops drizzled with Sardinian lemons and Canadian maple syrup.

Ella had attended the official opening of the DiLuca Cardiac Research Center with her uncle Domenicu and his family. She and Massimo had decided that they would wait to make a public announcement about their engagement, to keep the focus on the Center.

Ella had watched Massimo, standing tall and gorgeous at the black-tie event, as he shared what the Cardiac Research Center meant for him and his mother. His voice had wavered slightly as he announced that it was their gift to the community and the world in honor of his late wife and father. And the *baronessa* had spoken next, graciously thanking everyone who had had a hand in the development of the Center, and declaring her and Massimo's confidence and best wishes for the renowned team of researchers whose work the DiLucas were proud to support.

Everyone had fallen silent, and the room had erupted in applause while photographers and a television crew hovered around Massimo and his mother, visibly excited about the baron's reappearance in public.

Ella had worn an elegant black gown with satin accents and a silver shawl. As the cameras had flashed around him, he had looked toward the crowd and his gaze had connected with hers. His serious expression had given way to a smile, one that Ella knew without a doubt was meant for her, and her alone.

And then he and the *baronessa* had cut the ribbon, followed by the celebratory banquet. Although Massimo and Silvia were seated at the head table with local dignitaries and the leader of the research team, they both went around after the dinner to mingle and thank the guests at each table.

Ella had felt a rush of heat searing through her veins at the way Massimo's eyes had swept over her before meeting hers. And she had experienced the same feeling later at *Villa Serena*, when they were standing on his balcony. The indigo sky looked like a velvet dress sparkling with sequins, making Ella feel like she was in an enchanted world.

Massimo had gently removed her shawl and after looking deeply into her eyes, had bent to trace the length of her neck with soft kisses. Each one had sent her pulse racing, and by the time his lips had reached hers, Ella's heart was pounding. She had wrapped her arms around his neck and returned his kiss with a hunger that matched his.

And when she had thought she'd ignite from the passion between them, Massimo had swooped her up and carried her to his bed.

He had shown his love for her with his body and soul all night, the starlight from the open doors of the balcony mesmerizing on the curves of their bodies. Ella had lost herself in the stars Massimo had put in her eyes, and they both lost track of the times they had murmured *"Ti amo"* to each other.

Ella had thought her heart would burst from happiness and joy.

She had spent the following day finishing her piece

for *Living the Life*, and emailed it to her boss, satisfied and excited. An hour later, Paul had called her to congratulate her, impressed and enthused, as well. Ella had stunned him with the news about her and Massimo after that and promised to call him with the details after her holiday.

The week in Posada had been delightful. She had spent the days getting to know her *zio* Domenicu and his family, who had showered her with love and affection. And had included her in their farm and *agriturismo* routines. During quiet moments alone with her uncle, he had revealed a few details his brother Micheli had shared with him secretly about something he alone had known about Ella's young birth mother. He had discovered this information after accidentally overhearing part of a conversation at the adoption agency before a scheduled meeting…

Ella had felt a shift in her heart at the news. She had felt both anxious and excited. When she had told Massimo later, he'd promised to contact people who would investigate the proper social-services channels to possibly locate her.

During her week in Posada, Massimo had insisted that she enjoy this time without him, although he had always traveled back from *Villa Serena* to join them for a fabulous dinner.

And to join Ella later in her bed…

She smiled now, watching him approach with a breakfast tray. It was a glorious day in early September, warm and sunny, and she had wanted to sit out on the living room patio. They were still in their robes and had planned to spend the day relaxing and going over their plans for a five-day visit to the Maddalena Islands. They would be presiding at the official opening of their new DiLuca resort and staying in the penthouse suite reserved exclusively for them.

Massimo's eyes had twinkled like the diamond ring he'd held when he had proposed to Ella on his yacht during a weekend trip to check out the new resort back in August. After sliding the ring on her finger and giving her a kiss that was as scorching as the Sardinian sun, he had told her he had decided to call the resort *Il Mare di Marinella*—Marinella's Sea.

She had been moved to tears and declared that she would come up with a surprise for him.

Two weeks later, they had exchanged vows in a private church ceremony near the *baronessa*'s villa, followed by a small reception for their closest friends in her gardens. The wedding planners had decorated the tent canopy and tables with flowers that Silvia had wanted Ella and Massimo to choose from her own gardens, and Chef Angelo had picked a special team to prepare a sumptuous seven-course dinner. Ella had insisted on spending their wedding night at *Villa Serena*, where their love had begun.

The rest of August had passed with every moment spent together there, creating new memories…

And now, she was ready to give Massimo the surprise she had promised him.

His hair still tousled, he smiled crookedly as he placed the tray down and leaned over to kiss her. "I want to spend the rest of my life like this, Marinella, enjoying the peace and quiet of our island together."

He poured the espresso and set it down before sitting across from her.

She shook her head. "It won't be quiet for long, *amore*." She smiled and arched her eyebrows.

His brow furrowed and he set down the cup with a

clatter. And then his eyes widened. "Do you mean...? *Are you...are we—?*"

"Yes! I am, *amore*! We're going to have a ba—"

He leaped up and kissed her, cradling the back of her head. When he pulled back, he put a tentative hand on Ella's belly, his eyes misting.

"I told you I'd come up with a surprise for you..." Her voice wavered, and she tried to blink back her own tears, but they started trickling down her cheeks.

"You made me the happiest man in the world when you told me you loved me and would be my wife," he murmured, wiping her cheeks with the sash of her robe. "And now, you've given me the best gift I could ever hope for." He looked deeply into her eyes. "Do you know when...?"

"The night of the official opening of the Center. Remember the sky that night? I had never seen so many stars in the heavens."

"And I was in heaven that night, seeing the stars in your eyes," he said huskily, kissing her again.

Ella sighed contentedly. "Well, what do you think about naming our baby Stellina...our little star? I just have this feeling we're going to have a girl."

He gazed at her thoughtfully for a moment. "Do you know what a 'blue star' is?"

Ella frowned. "No. I've never heard the term. Why?"

"In astrological terms, a blue star has a mass greater than the sun, and is one of the brightest in the constellation, appearing blue to the human eye."

Ella cocked her head at him, wondering where he was going with this.

"And so, Marinella, why don't we call our baby Stellina Celeste? Our little blue star?"

"It's perfect," she murmured, wrapping her arms around his neck and kissing him.

"And if we have a boy?" His brow furrowed. "We should have a name in mind, just in case."

"How about Angelo? Our little angel?"

Massimo let out a deep laugh. "I know someone who would be absolutely thrilled. Either way, Chef Angelo can be the baby's godfather."

He waved a hand at the breakfast tray. "Now I get why you haven't been wanting your usual espresso… How about one of these *sebadas*? You need to keep up your strength, *amore*. Are you hungry?"

Ella cupped his chin and turned his face her way. "*Sì, barone.* Very." She grinned, and showed him with her kiss.

* * * * *

COMING SOON!

We really hope you enjoyed reading this book.
If you're looking for more romance, be sure to
head to the shops when new books are
available on

Thursday 5th August

MILLS & BOON

THE HEART OF ROMANCE

A ROMANCE FOR EVERY READER

MODERN

Prepare to be swept off your feet by sophisticated, sexy and seductive heroes, in some of the world's most glamourous and romantic locations, where power and passion collide.

HISTORICAL

Escape with historical heroes from time gone by. Whether your passion is for wicked Regency Rakes, muscled Vikings or rugged Highlanders, awaken the romance of the past.

MEDICAL

Set your pulse racing with dedicated, delectable doctors in the high-pressure world of medicine, where emotions run high and passion, comfort and love are the best medicine.

True Love

Celebrate true love with tender stories of heartfelt romance, from the rush of falling in love to the joy a new baby can bring, and a focus on the emotional heart of a relationship.

Desire

Indulge in secrets and scandal, intense drama and plenty of sizzling hot action with powerful and passionate heroes who have it all: wealth, status, good looks…everything but the right woman.

HEROES

Experience all the excitement of a gripping thriller, with an intense romance at its heart. Resourceful, true-to-life women and strong, fearless men face danger and desire - a killer combination!

To see which titles are coming soon, please visit

millsandboon.co.uk/nextmonth

MILLS & BOON

Coming next month

SECOND CHANCE TO WEAR HIS RING
Hana Sheik

She laughed lightly then, her eyes sparkling, the hint of gloominess from earlier gone. He wished he didn't have to ruin the peaceful moment. But time was pressing, and they couldn't stand around reminiscing all day. Soon she'd want to return to her office, and he still had his piece to say.

"Amal, what was your doctor's prognosis for the amnesia?" he asked. Saying her name was tripping him up. It sounded too familiar on his tongue. Like coming home. But he was undeserving of the happy relief that welled up in him.

As for this amnesia business—he couldn't shake the absurdity of it.

Her memory loss was perfect for him, and yet terribly painful, too. Perfect in that it saved him from explanations and reliving heartbreak, and painful because he was going through it alone.

She had no recollection of their long-distance conversations about building a future together, let alone his marriage proposal and her hasty rejection.

In her mind, it seemed their long-distance romance had never existed. While he recalled—and replayed, clip by clip—how their friendship had blossomed into...more. Something he'd had no name for until she herself had shyly confessed to liking him romantically.

No, she said she loved me.

And he had asked for time to process it.

Process it he had—and that was when he'd come to her, closing the seven-thousand-mile gap between them with a diamond in one hand and his heart in the other. He'd planned to offer her both—and he had. But she had shocked him with her refusal.

How could she not remember?

Did it matter, though? He knew it didn't alter the situation they were in now, standing and facing off like strangers. He'd do better to focus his energy on what he could change. Like having her consider the options of medical treatment elsewhere.

"The doctor said I could regain my full memory."

She folded her arms over her chest.

"There's also a possibility that I could stay like this forever. The timeline for my recovery is uncertain," she said softly, defeat beating at her words.

"And yet you could seek better medical care and technology elsewhere," he said.

She snapped her bemused gaze to him.

"I know you heard my mother and I speaking," he said.

Amal opened her mouth, closed it, and frowned. Smart of her. No point in wasting time and breath arguing about her eavesdropping. Actually, right then he appreciated it. It saved him from explaining what he'd already told his mother. That he had business in Ethiopia.

"Why not join me? You could visit with a doctor in Addis Ababa, and we could try for a second opinion."

Continue reading
SECOND CHANCE TO WEAR HIS RING
Hana Sheik

Available next month
www.millsandboon.co.uk

LET'S TALK
Romance

For exclusive extracts, competitions
and special offers, find us online:

f facebook.com/millsandboon

🐦 @MillsandBoon

📷 @MillsandBoonUK

Get in touch on 01413 063232

For all the latest titles coming soon, visit
millsandboon.co.uk/nextmonth

JOIN US ON SOCIAL MEDIA!

Stay up to date with our latest releases, author news and gossip, special offers and discounts, and all the behind-the-scenes action from Mills & Boon...

 millsandboon

 millsandboonuk

 millsandboon

It might just be true love...

MILLS & BOON
MEDICAL
Pulse-Racing Passion

Set your pulse racing with dedicated, delectable doctors in the high-pressure world of medicine, where emotions run high and passion, comfort and love are the best medicine.